WILD WOMEN

Simon Leigh

SIX EVENTS IN THIS BOOK ARE MADE UP

If you figure out
which, you'll be invited into
the sequel to this novel as a character,
if you're up for it – send your list to
the author, and
the nearest
guess wins.

Write to Simon Leigh (aka Steven Butts) at
his email address, which is niftily situated at the back of the book.

Most UKA Press Books are available at special quantity discounts for bulk purchase for sales promotions, premiums, fund-raising, or educational use. Special books, or book excerpts, can also be created to fit specific needs.

For details, write: Special Markets, UKA Press, 55 Elmsdale Road, Walthamstow, London, E17 6PN, or email: andrealowne@ukauthors.com

Published by the UKA Press
55 Elmsdale Road, Walthamstow, London, E17 6PN, England
Olympiaweg 102-hs, 1076 XG, Amsterdam, Holland
St. A, 108, 2-5-22 Shida, Fujieda, Shizuoka, 426-0071, Japan

Copyright © Simon Leigh 2005

Simon Leigh has asserted his right under the Copyright, Designs and Patents Act 1988 to be identified as the author of this work.

This book is sold subject to the condition that it shall not, by way of trade or otherwise, be lent, resold, hired out, or otherwise circulated without the publisher's prior consent in any form of binding or cover other than that in which it is published and without a similar condition including this condition being imposed on the subsequent purchaser.

First published in Great Britain by the imprint UKA Press: 2005
This Edition published by the independent UKA Press: 2007

The UKA Press World Wide Web site is
http://www.UKAPress.com

A CIP catalogue record for this book is available from the British Library
ISBN   978-1-905796-09-0 / 1-905796-09-9

Edited by Don Masters, St. A; and Filipa Komuro, Ox.

Cover Design by Peter J. Merrigan

Printed in the United Kingdom of Great Britain, and in the USA

2 4 6 8 10 9 7 5 3 1

Six of the events in this book are lies. No, this isn't one of them. One's just a date – check the record – and one is his/my meeting with a pair of brilliant creatures (whom I met, but not there) which leaves four events that couldn't possibly have happened to me/Steven (but maybe just did).

I am grateful to family, friends, colleagues, teachers, enemies, and strangers. Without you, there would be no story.

Without my editor, the so-called Don Masters of UKA Press, there would be no book either. The Man Who Never Sleeps is a hard man to argue with when you're wrong. 'Don,' I thank you for not demanding more tiresome sex.

*'If you're going to tell people the truth,
make them laugh. Otherwise they'll kill you.'*
– Mae West, quoting GBS

Contents

1. Getting There 9
2. Snow 18
3. A Snowy New Year 32
4. More Snow 39
5. Another Trip 48
6. Hockey on Ice 54
7. British Racing Green 59
8. The Three Stone Trick 64
9. Long Flight 74
10. 2B Denbigh Place 84
11. An Awkward Moment 97
12. A Special Day 102
13. A Day on the Hill 115
14. That Jill 124
15. A Long Night 132
16. Linda Comes Home 142
17. O Lucky Day 153
18. The End 167
19. Spring in the Air 168
20. Wedding Party 175
21. Class Act 180
22. Another Wedding 189

23.	Spring	196
24.	Party Time	199
25.	Canadian Tyre	203
26.	The Moncton Experience	211
27.	Race Day	215
28.	Gravity	223
29.	Who Knows?	230
30.	Neck Problems	239
31.	La Danse Moderne	242
32.	Ol' Man River	246
33.	Eddie takes Over	260
34.	Off to the Races	267
35.	Show Time	278
36.	A Tough Business	286
37.	Out and About	299
38.	And?	302
39.	A New Soul Mate	320
40.	Landing in Toronto	324

WILD WOMEN

UKA PRESS, LONDON

Getting There

The whole flight from Australia she hogged the window seat. The whole twenty-four hours in the air she blocked his view.

Squinting between her long auburn hair and the window, he'd managed to glimpse red-tile rooftops, the old grey coat hanger of the Bridge, the complex blue amoeba shape of Sydney Harbour, then, banking, The Heads, a golden boomerang curve of sand – then the dark green smear of pollution from the Bondi sewer outfall and prime fishing spot, 'The Murk,' spreading into the ocean and down the coast – the Sydney-Hobart yacht racers complained about it fouling their white hulls...

Then the last surfers insanely far out, a lone yacht, perhaps in trouble, sails half-down, then nothing but endless blue Pacific.

North-easterly forever, with 'Spanish roasted' peanuts, dinky drinks and shrunken meals served at odd intervals as if the laws of time travel insist everyone eat a second breakfast, followed almost at once by lunch. Steven Butts was glad to eat his, and hers, too.

In her ominous silence, his ex-live-in girlfriend Eddie willed him to take it. Just take it. But don't speak the word 'chicken' or 'steak,' or it'll be all over.

And that was the point. Eddie wasn't eating. Not a peanut.

She wasn't enjoying the view. Her eyes were clamped shut. She wasn't even being sick. Her chunder bag, held firmly under the chin, remained empty. She was concentrating on not being airsick. That's why he wasn't allowed to talk to her.

This was maddeningly typical, and typically maddening. He wanted to talk. He'd noticed once or twice, ever since he moved in to live with her, six months ago, that night she had him for dinner in her new little rented house on Bent Street, then he had her and stayed on – and that was another thing! It was supposed to be his place. Typical! At work he'd heard about the Bent Street place coming vacant, mentioned it to Eddie and drove her past it.

He'd resolved to quit his own sordid room at the end of the month, lease Bent Street and move in – but she beat him to it! She braved her parents, left their beach-side home, and moved in, a total misunderstanding – anyway, he'd noticed that often of late she would fall disturbingly silent. A headache of some sort.

'Please – if I move my head I'll be...'

That's why, although her ticket – paid for with money borrowed from him, by the way – didn't say 'window seat,' she'd taken it anyway. Something about needing to press her forehead against cold glass. As he craned around the back of her hairy head, he saw she still had her eyes shut under the sunglasses.

Her eyes never opened. Not for the exposed film-strip of sunset, not for the final glimpse of the Southern Cross, last call for the thick slice of Milky Way that lights the southern sky, not for the presumably dazzling night landing at Honolulu to refuel, or the takeoff.

Not for the coastline of America (or was that Canada?), the Rockies, the endless more miles of trays and comedy on the headphones and free alcohol and the same meal and the same comedy loop again, waking suddenly with his head falling off his sore neck, some once-in-a-lifetime sight surely passing outside.

Steven had missed it all, seeing only the too-familiar back of Eddie's head. But she brightened with the landing in Toronto (or was it Montreal?), and was pale but gamely smiling as they struggled together through customs and immigration...

'Business or pleasure?'

'Bit of both, actually –'

...and were stamped into this oddly French-speaking country.

'How can it be thirteen o'clock?' asked Eddie.

'You take off twelve,' he explained. 'It can't really be minus 16 can it? How can it be minus 16? Freezing's 32.'

'Maybe you add 32.'

'What was it on Boxing Day when we left? 104?'

'105.'

'I can't believe it's minus 16 just the other side of that glass. 'Scuse me a sec.'

'They're calling for boarding!'
'No worries. I just want to see how it feels... '
'...So how did it feel? Your nose-hairs have frozen up.'
'Weird. It doesn't feel like cold. Feels like pain. And you can't breathe, your throat just shuts, like trying to breathe a wave. You did bring a thicker coat than that, didn't you?'
'How could I? There wasn't any room left in your suitcase.'
What about *her* suitcase?

Eddie's last-second decision to come had been such a flap: passport, dumping her teaching job, her lease, all her new used furniture – and he didn't remember even asking her to come with him. Surely he wouldn't forget a thing like that. No, he had not invited her. In fact... he'd said no. He recalled solemnly promising to write and ask her over just as soon as he'd had a look around, and he meant it – and yet suddenly there she was, marching onto the plane right behind him. Past him, into his window seat.

But now, on this small, bumpy prop plane making its meaty GARONGA-RONGA-RONGA sound instead of the nervy shriek of the jet, she seemed fine, and with her head next to his as if they were a pair of scared children she peered down on the endless, darkening forest of snow-iced pines.

Then the white curve of a river, here it is, the capital of New Brunswick, the home of Steven's two-year appointment.

The plane banked sickeningly – like their other big trip together, last year, to Cambodia when the crazy pilot, also French-speaking, had stood the 707 on its skinny left wingtip high over Phnom Penh airport and dropped it out of the sky like a shot hawk. But this landing was better.

They thumped down – tyres squeaked, props reversed pitch, engines whined, they rolled to a stop at the end of the narrow runway, facing the trees; noise died, lights dimmed, pre-crash music ended – and waited. The pilot announced: 'Ladeez an' gennelmen, we appear to have arrive in Fodderton unexpectedly.'

And that was it.

Steven unbuckled, gazed at the back view of her bowed head and wondered. Was he really here? And where was here?

As Bob Hughes had said, the Arabs believe the soul cannot travel faster than the speed of a trotting camel. If so, his own soul was still barely trotting out of Sydney Harbour. He would have done his two years and left for home before it arrived.

Home?

Oxford University had been home on his Shell Scholarship eight years ago, and he wasn't sure his soul's camel, exhausted, had ever made it the whole way back to Australia. Perhaps the two had crossed, and his soul had switched camels half-way across the Pacific, and was heading north-east again. He felt closer to Oxford now, closer to London, the real world.

Still nothing. Soothing Muzac started up. Those who'd illegally unclipped and leapt up, wildly relieved to have landed alive, wearied of crouching under the baggage space and sat back down.

'We're two, three hours late,' he told Eddie's twisted back. 'If anyone came to meet us they'd have gone home again for sure.'

She nodded. She had, as they touched down after 12,000 miles in the air, finally succeeded in vomiting into her white paper bag, which she clutched in white fingers. Her plan was to find somewhere to deposit it, then clean her teeth, then die.

Rodman wouldn't be waiting, surely. Much too busy and important to hang round aerodromes. No, they're called airports here.

They'd left Sydney on a blue blazing Boxing Day, after standing on South Head watching the start of the 1969 Sydney-Hobart yacht race, the green-blue harbour raked with the wakes of the pursuit fleet.

And now here they were, seatbacks and tables in the upright position, still buckled in, waiting.

In the distance a small truck flashed its red roof light and buzzed self-importantly towards them. Steps appeared, and they descended into a wind like razor-blades. They were here.

And they were met – although the hours of waiting had rendered their official meeters and greeters, Rodman and Joyce, magnificently, gigglingly drunk.

'Profesh-professor Michael Joyce, I give you the distingwished international expert in, in international expertise, the brilliant young management expert from Down Under, Steven Butts, and his good lady Edwina, was it? O'Malley.'

'On behalf of my colleague and my good self I hereby welcome you both to Fodderton.'

Professor Joyce had merry blue eyes above the smile of a mad actor; someone playing Peter Sellers playing Doctor Strangelove, perhaps. He was all Irish eyes for Eddie, and, like her, was well dressed and so freezing to death. His three-piece silver suit and camel-hair coat flapped in the gusts, contrasting with the beefier Rodman, securely bundled in lumberjack's jacket and farmer's boots. His long silver hair flapped like the peak of Rodman's fleece-lined cap, worn flaps down. Clearly, in Canada the choice was between fashion and survival.

'What've you got in here?' asked Rodman, snatching up the first, weighty suitcase. 'Jars of Vegemite?'

He led them to an oddly-parked Volvo, reached in and extracted a magic wand that he waved over the windows, making the fluffy new snow vanish.

Then he fell into his seat. The others stood tapping on the doors and windows until he noticed and unlocked for them. He seemed to have dozed briefly at the wheel, but in no time they were away and heading for home and a warm bath and sleep, sleep that knits up the ravelled sleeve of...

But almost at once they swung into a tavern, The Oromocto Arms (what's an Oromocto?). Professor Joyce leaned in and confided to Eddie that this was where they' been waiting the whole afternoon, swooping out to meet each plane as they heard it drone overhead.

'So do you feel like something to eat, love?'
'No thanks, Professor Joyce. They fed us every hour.'
Steven nodded. 'I've eaten dinner four times since we left...'
'Eight times,' she said.
'I could go a beer, though.'
They trudged in, and took a small steel table.

For entertainment there was a flickering fluorescent light, and a radio playing commercials for new trucks. Four beers arrived. Oddly, the four beers arrived in bottles. The waitress, as tall as Rodman, snapped them open with a resigned stare at the wall, as if she'd been doing this for them all afternoon, which she had.

Steven reached for his bottle but she beat him to the draw, snatching it up to begin filling his glass. But – just like a woman, he thought, just like Eddie – she failed to tilt the glass first.

Steven could see what was coming – half a glass of froth – and he mimed a tilt, but she solved the problem in her own way by pouring at a trickle, a dribble, like adding oil to a crankcase.

She presented him unsmilingly with a first in his entire life: a completely flat glass of beer. He reached for it, but remembered his manners and stared as the other three glasses were laboriously filled.

'I can't leave the bottles on the table, eh,' she explained, and left with them.

'Is this a Canadian law?'

'We're not real Canadians,' said Rodman. 'I'm originally from London, and of course Mike's a Dubliner so we're guessing, but...'

'Something terrible would happen if she left the bottles with us. Skittles, probably, or throwing them around the room.'

'Or rushing out to return them for the deposit.'

'Or tooting them,' Steven suggested. 'You can make a whole orchestra out of empties.'

'Right! Illegal music,' said Rodman. 'Reminds me. See that piano? If there's a pianist, and a patron starts to sing along, by law the pianist has to switch to another song.'

'You're joking!'

'No, s'true.'

'But what if he knows that one too? What if he knows all the songs?' demanded Steven, who'd played trumpet in a dance band and felt he knew most of them.

He had them there.

'Have to arrest everybody, revoke their – hello! 'Scuse me, there's a chap I know.'

Rodman rose with his glass and headed for the back table.

But the waitress was quick. In two steps she blocked him.

'Patrons are not allowed to move drinks to another table, sir.'

Rodman opened his throat, poured in his beer, burped softly and handed her the glass. Her face did not move; she'd already seen the size of Rodman's tips.

Joyce was still trying to get Eddie to open up. 'Surely you have some strange drinking laws in Australia, lass?'

Eddie fake-sipped her beer, and smiled frothily.

Normally she didn't speak. In Australia there was rarely any need for more than smiles and appreciative noises. Among men, that was. And for some reason she hardly knew any women. But those blue eyes were still looking at her, in a most un-Australian way, almost as if listening. So to be polite she said, 'Absolutely. If someone falls on the floor you're supposed to step around, not on them.' She ate a peanut, and fluttered her lashes.

'You must be tired,' observed Joyce, and merciful minutes later they were driven cautiously back to town. Home.

Home being two nights' paid accommodation at Admiral Beaverbrook Hotel. The overheated hotel room had a bizarre self-emptying bed, but Steven helped drag its over-sprung innerspring onto the floor, then threw himself down beside her as if to sleep the sleep of the damned, the soon-to-be executed.

Next morning, Steven was shown around the FU campus-red brick buildings on a steep hill, presented with his office key, and introduced to a blur of uninterested faces and odd-sounding names, of which the only one he remembered was LeBlanc. There were two LeBlancs, though which was which he at once forgot.

Eddie walked the icy streets in her stylish thin coat, slipped and hurt her back but found a place to live; a basement rental on Rimford Lane with an advertised view. That evening she showed Steven the ad, wondering what a basement view would be.

He snatched the local paper from her.

'My God! Will you look at the used car prices! You can get an MGB for under a thousand bucks! This is like Paradise.'

Snow

It was love at first sight.

The moment Steven saw the little British sports car, perched high on its pneumatic pedestal, Eddie knew he – we – would buy it. With a sharp hiss the hoist began to descend, and his eyes flickered greedily over the spoked wheels with their silver knock-off nuts, the chrome grille, the elegant sweep of the mudguards.

She knew it was a 1966 MGB, just four years old, at a terrific price that Steven, now forcing a buyer's scowl but too late, would try to bring down still more. What she did not know was whether it had a heater. Surely it did. She'd been shivering, on and off, since they arrived the day before. The shivers began in her midriff and shook her briefly like a dog. At least they were indoors now, though barely. Outside, the snow was thickening again and gusts of wind sneaked under the roll-up garage door, making her shuffle her feet in the dance of the freezing ballerina.

Minutes later, she found it had a heater. You could choose comfort or safety: without the defroster on full, you couldn't see out.

When the car began to skid, Steven Butts did not panic. He was an expert at the wheel, which he flung wildly to the left, grunting, till it bumped the stop, and his new car steadied. It was now moving crab-wise downhill, on the snow-dusted Trans-Canada. An oncoming Mack truck hooted its air-horn in appreciation.

Looking through the side window to steer, he held the skid – then caught it when it tried to come back the other way.

'Thing sure doesn't handle like the Nota,' he mentioned in his calmest voice at the bottom of the slope. 'Oversteer. And it's three whole turns lock-to-lock. I need to get a smaller steering wheel, if I'm going to race it.'

'You've only driven it about a mile since you bought it, and it's the first time you've driven in snow, so you're doing awfully well,' said Eddie, staring straight ahead through the struggling wipers.

That was a long speech, for her.

The snow whirled away from an expansion point just ahead. It wasn't so much falling, as hanging about waiting for him to part it.

Their turn-off came up. Oddly, the reflecting signs, where the white snow stuck to them, showed black. Something LANE. This must be it. He slowed, slowed, and turned the wheel to the right.

But the spring-spoked wheel felt light, numb under his new driving gloves. Far from turning right, the car speared straight ahead, seemed to be picking up speed though he knew that was an illusion: he'd locked up his brakes often enough in practice for car races to know what was going on.

Steven knew exactly what to do.

Feet off everything, he coaxed the wheel expertly to the right, feeling for some grip, the master's hands...until the car flew into the roadside ditch, fluffed along like a snow submarine, and came to a quiet halt, buried.

Eddie spoke. 'Understeer,' she said.

Steven cranked it into reverse and spun the wheels briefly.

It was dark. Ahead, a faint headlight glow. And silent, only the ticking of the engine and the struggling wiper blades.

(I think we went off the road, said Eddie, but not aloud. She suddenly needed to pee).

Steven – remembering the threat of carbon monoxide poisoning, a stranded couple found dead in their VW at Mt Perisher, or was it Mt Hotham in Victoria? He'd look it up – switched off the motor, wipers, lights.

The silence was total, like being locked in a cold storage room.

(How far *down* are we? she wondered.)

He reached across and turned on the tiny map-reading light.

Now he could see her folded gloves, and the comforting swell of her new green ski jacket, bulging out as if her breasts were now twice the size, and they were a good size already.

He yanked the rip-cord of the MG's door catch and shoved with his shoulder. The door opened an inch, but snow poured in and he had trouble shutting it, thwarted by snow.

Eddie's door opened a couple of inches, but she got it closed.

(Should she suggest climbing out the windows? But her window was frozen shut.)

'I guess we'd better sit tight for a bit,' Steven instructed. 'They say when your car goes into a river you should wait till it settles.'

'I think we've settled.'

'If the worst comes to the worst I can always unclip the hardtop from inside. Push it up.' He fingered the clip above the windscreen – windshield, they call it here in Canada. It felt frozen. Eddie was great the way she didn't talk too much.

Their first date, she'd hardly said a word, as if quite happy just to be there with him, to listen and learn.

'Shouldn't waste the battery.' He clicked off the map light, put his gloved hand behind her neck and gently, gently leaned her towards him, over the gear stick – what do they call it here, the Shift Column? The accelerator's a throttle, and the silencer's a...a muffler. It's cold... If he's going to teach these Canadians about business he'd better be businesslike, learn the local dialect.

With his left hand he lovingly unzipped her jacket.

The telegram had arrived out of the blue of...Canada. Rodman's job offer had been just talk, but the telegram made it real.

A firm offer. Canada.

Canada he knew from the National Film Board – the government there actually *paid* people to make films, like that dazzling Norman McWhatsis strip-movie of the Oscar Peterson trio, shown at the Sydney University film fest.

What an enlightened country!

And wasn't Peterson a Canadian, not a Yank? Or maybe he became American later, they were pretty well the same place: North America. Canada, the Rockies (or had *they* become American too?), the Mounties who get their man, and snow. Bags of snow, not just the two months of alternating slush and crust at Thredbo, in the Snowy Mountains. *Real* snowy mountains.

As a ski racer, he loved the idea of Canada.

And as a car racer who'd managed to lose his Australian competition license and get stuck with a pathetic Restricted

Licence that only let him compete in hillclimbs and slaloms – *slaloms!* – Steven was hot for a fresh start.

Hillclimbs were wild fun, though not the big time, but he'd left Australia holding the sports car record on every hill in New South Wales, plus the racing car record; on the day his then-girlfriend Linda had managed to unbolt the Nota's elegant mudguards, front and back, he won the open-wheel class as well.

In Canada he could surely pass the medical and restart his racing career. Because (apart from sex, of course, and jazz), driving a racing car was what life was...for.

He was pushing thirty, but the Formula One circus was not just a dream. He could do it. Brabham had done it, had scared them rigid with his Aussie approach to corners.

Here in Canada, Steven would be close to Europe, where he could get his break. The key was earning enough to pay for it: the break, the chance, the trial drive.

And the telegram had offered him a two-year appointment as an Assistant Professor (Professor!) at Fodderton University, on twice his Sydney pay.

So he'd telegrammed 'Yes' without mentioning it to Eddie, took a two-year leave of absence from Auscon, the Personnel Consulting firm – let his beery boss now spend the unending, fly-buzzing afternoons interviewing all those desperate, fast-talking job-seekers and then talking – even faster – into a Dictaphone; sold the car he loved, his Nota Sportsman (which resentfully blew its clutch as the over-eager young buyer ripped it away); and he'd said, as he remembered it, a firm, masculine farewell to Eddie; and then he was off.

So why was Eddie here?

Seated quietly, darkly in the car as he warmed his wicked palms inside her ski jacket. And up her shirt and around her lacy bra, as the snow high above settled on the grave of their plunge, ripples closing over a skipped rock, sunk.

It was all a misunderstanding. He'd never meant her to rent 'his' place on Bent Street. He'd never meant to 'shack up' with her. He'd never meant her to come. Most things with Eddie were

a misunderstanding.
Women in general were so... so... And Eddie in particular.

There was a thump on the car roof. Somebody's boots had landed on the hard top. Eddie's hand withdrew in shock.

He tooted the horn, DIT DIT DIT – DAH DAH DAH – DIT DIT DIT – SOS, if they knew Morse Code.

The boots scuffled around – don't hurt the hard-top, it's only fibreglass – amid muffled shouts. Then magically the MGB moved, rose and floated back. They heard a whirring shriek as someone's tyres spun on ice. The car was now a white translucent dome, they couldn't see a thing, and the wipers were stuck.

Steven punched his door open – and saw big fellows in fleecy jackets like fat shirts, checked, green and white or red and white.

Behind, a truck was backing up, towrope stretched taut. A yellow light flashed. Somebody slammed his door shut again. Strong hands lifted the car, dropped it back on the highway.

Snow slid from the windscreen. Steven scrambled out.

'Thanks for helping,' he shouted. 'Thanks a whole lot, guys.'

'We seen you go in,' said a Canadian giant. He grinned and shook his gloved hand where he'd apparently hurt it.

More shouts. The men climbed back into the ute/pick-up.

Steven turned to where the giant was scooping snow off the MG's windows with his huge paw (watched by Eddie who was trembling, shivering, for some reason).

'What do I owe you guys?' he called.

The giant shook him off.

'No, really.'

'Nah. You would'a done the same for us. It's winter. Better see if she starts. This a little furrin car, eh?'

But the little foreign car would not start. Its starter groaned in a descending scale. A piercing whistle brought the pick-up across the highway, another Canadian hopping out with jumper cables.

'Where's your battery at?'

After searching under the bonnet (no, hood) and in the boot (no, trunk) Steven had to confess he wasn't sure.

'Hop in, we give you a shove.'

And on the third try it started. Behind him Steven glimpsed the three men turning to walk back up the hill to their pick-up. He would have waved but the window still wouldn't open.

That was Canada.

What marvellous, big, tough, kindly people!

Australians would only have raised their beers in ironical salute, and begun taking bets.

Now the snow was falling straight down in heavy flakes, big as postcards. He did the slowest of slow u-turns, waited while a huge snow-plow rushed past at improbably high speed, its blade rumbling and striking sparks from the roadway, a wave of snow soaring off the right side. Then he crept around on the ice ('It was ice, under the snow') into Rimford Lane, went to turn into the driveway of their newly rented place, between the two bare (dead?) trees (maples?) – and halted.

There was no driveway. There was nothing.

A sloping wall of snow instead. When he jumped out and crossed to peer over the wall, he could see the long driveway, driveable, with the warm lights of their rented place glowing, unreachable, at the far end.

The Great Gatsby dived in.

'No problem once we get through this bit of snow,' he explained, crunching it into reverse and backing up.

Wheels spinning, he rushed straight at the wall and hit it hard, the front riding up a little. Then he backed off, staying in his wheel tracks, and with less wheelspin this time hit it harder. He was making some progress.

(One more bump, Eddie's bladder announced, and I'll pee all over his nice leather seat.)

He crunched into it again.

This was fun, the MG's 1800cc four bellowing nicely. Nearly through... On the fifth try he had a good head of speed, the car rode up...and halted on top, seesawing gently. The front wheels were in the air. The back wheels were in the air. But at least it was clear of the road, so they clambered down and began the trek in.

'Turn your back.'
'Why?'
'Turn your back. Please.'
Women were so weird. What was she going to do? Adjust her makeup? Change into a slinky negligee, TA DAH! in a blizzard?

He trudged along the driveway, high-stepping, leaving footholes that should make it easy for Eddie to follow.

All this snow! Enough is enough. His high-stepping recalled a disastrous, pre-season, post-blizzard ski trip, trudging in to the aptly-named Perisher Valley from where the bus ended at well-named Smiggins Hole, having boldly invited the glorious six-foot Zoë Dobson, the darling of Arts III. Zoë of the crinkly eyes and the mouth so wide that when finally, finally, after all the witty chat, after she'd laughed in your face for rolling your eyes up as you closed in, you got to kiss her, her lips seemed to press directly upon your brain. And when... Oh, yes... Oh, no. He cringed.

At Perisher he'd done The Wrong Thing, all right...

'In the mountains everyone carries their own skis,' he'd explained, loading her with the rentals and poles, and her suitcase. (Compromising, he'd taken her heavy white make-up case.)

The going was tough. Zoë complained for half a mile before going ominously silent. When finally he reached Adam Zapenski's hut, dumped his load and turned back for her – she had no skis.

'Where are your skis? Where are your *skis*?'

Zoë said not a word. Neither then, nor for the rest of the long Long Weekend.

She ate, drank, read her detective stories, even smiled; but did not speak, except to Adam, the dapper little ex-Austrian downhill champion – but then, incredibly, she was all over him on the steam train ride back to Sydney.

They're a different species. Ah, Zoë, tall Zoë!

You could kiss her goodnight eye to eye, no bending down, equals. Where was she now? – And where was Eddie?

But this time Eddie was right behind him at the sliding glass door, her breath fuming like a steam train.

She had the apartment key.

The McTavishes lived above, Joe and Grace, and had wanted to hear *all* about Australia, "once yez get all settled in".

But the fabled Canadian Winter (Where Lives Depend On Stopping Colds, according to the wind-swirling Aussie radio commercials for Buckley's Canadiol Mixture, a brew unheard of in Canada) was no friend to keys and locks.

The keys wouldn't line up. His gloves were wet, but anyway, the key wouldn't go in, or wouldn't turn.

They trudged, muttering, round to the front.

At the upstairs front door their landlady Grace, shocked, attacked them both with a broom before she would let them walk through and down, and they felt themselves shedding snow as they cringed through her gleaming house.

'What happened to *you*?' barked Joe with a rather horrid old-man's grin as he walked past, but it was not a question. He denture-grinned again as he walked past. Again.

Smiling fixedly, ever the gracious, Christian hostess, Grace held open the cupboard door that, oddly, led down wooden steps to their basement dwelling. They stepped into her dark cupboard and were gone out of sight, out of mind.

'If the rent is late, even one day late, you're out,' she'd told them earlier, with that keen smile.

But they'd signed, admired the view through their double glass doors, now stuck, down the wooded slope to the mighty Saint John river, now frozen solid. Cars and trucks drove straight across it, and those little snowmobile things buzzed around like water beetles. In spring, they were told, 'All this will be so beautiful. You'll love it here.'

Their new home was big. White walls with nothing on them, a living room with couch and an antique wood-veneer TV.

No bookshelves, but a splendid bathroom, kitchen, bedroom, and a spare room for the cases, trunks and boxes of worldly goods Steven had shipped over, courtesy of the university. And a junk room with a large heater for water or whatever. Here, Steven had balanced a spare door on some cases to make his desk.

They peeled off their wet clothes and stood naked over a rush of hot air from the energetic heater vents. Canadian homes felt like ovens. Beyond the double glass, those silent postcards from the arctic steadily fell.

'You don't think there'll be a problem with the car, stuck out there?' asked Eddie.

'Nah. I'll dig it out in the morning when it clears up. What can I do? And I gather I'm supposed to start teaching tomorrow.'

During the night a strange phone call came in.

A foreign-sounding voice (Arab? Indian? One of those whiney ones) identified itself as Professor Ramadam Goatee, welcomed him to Canada and to FU – then switched tone from hearty to moribund – severe 'flu, not at all well – to ask if Professor Steven would mind taking his class tomorrow at 8am, as, after all, they *were* both teaching the same course: Introduction to Business.

'No way,' said Steven.

'But I am unable to attend, and my entire class will be waiting!'

'Listen, mate, I got troubles of my own.'

'Who was that?' Eddie was too travel-tired to lift her head.

'Some clown at FU wanted me to run his class tomorrow so he could stay in bed. Mahatma Coat. Some name like that. Anyway, I told him I got troubles of my own.'

And he did. In a way he was glad that 'he,' his *alter ego*, was perched perilously out at the end of the driveway, because it took his mind off the looming, thundering snowplow of his confrontation with the university classroom. He'd sat in many of them; too many, over the years.

But he'd never taught. Never taught anyone anything. Eddie was the teacher.

Though he looked forward to learning about his topic, Introduction to Business, he knew nothing about it, never having taken a business course in his life. Not one. So how could he teach it? His field was psychology, plus moral philosophy and English, and one year's French. In a pinch he could probably teach a course on *Women: Why They Never Say Yes*, or *The Self-*

Fulfilling Prophecy Made Easy or on *The Slow In, Fast Out Approach to Race Driving*. But Business? Who cared, anyway?

Insurance salesmen, sweating through their deodorant on the North Shore train. His opposite numbers, men in grey suits, standing, clutching the financial pages while Steven used his sharp eyesight to read the comics on their back pages.

Dean Rodman, acting head of the FU Department of Business Administration, who'd sent the telegram, knew this. Or should have known. Or could have looked it up – Steven *had* sent his CV, as asked – but had appointed him anyway. Why? Simply, he'd met Steven, liked the cut of his jib, and got him appointed.

Steven felt good about this, as long as he didn't think about the other small matter. A very small matter, that hardly mattered.

Steven's novel. An embarrassment all round, but there it was.

The girls on Manly beach, on his and Rodman's second-day stroll together, had brought it up, so he'd mentioned it. Deliberately *en passant*, as if were.

As an Australian, he lived for weekends, but the earlier days of the week, especially all those Tuesdays and Wednesdays, were hard to survive. During the brief ski season this was no problem, as he was unconscious at his desk: the hours of Sunday night driving (or worse, being driven) back from Thredbo cemented a bone-weariness that lasted through to Thursday, when he found himself snatching up the phone to plan the next assault on the unforgiving, twig-infested slopes, and the flexing dance floor of the Copper Kettle.

But when the fickle snow melted to mud and the wealthy team of Austrian ski instructors flew yodelling home to their own winter, there was that long work week to be got through, a day at a time. And one rainy afternoon he hit on a plan.

He'd write a book.

Rather than launch into the rush-hour crowd shoving towards the nearest pub, Steven would shift to his secretary's desk – gaining brownie points if spotted by late-leaving bosses – and from 5 till 6 type up a novel. Become a writer, the Aussie Ian Fleming. Though he couldn't afford a Ferrari (or, maddeningly, an engine rebuild for his currently dust-gathering Nota Sportsman racing car) he could write one.

Two, in fact. His novel, *The Moon is a Cold Bone*, had twin red-red V12 Ferraris (one real, one a replica of the other) plus a little dark-blue U2 that the ex-cop hero uses in his wild, full-opposite-lock attempts to chase down the bad doctor guy (*guys*, in fact: one a clone of the other).

It was a tortured tale that had somehow sprung from Steven's reading of two recent discoveries: the cloning of a piece of asparagus (or was it carrot?), and a 'pleasure centre' located deep in the brains of laboratory rats, who – getting a break for once – would happily keep pressing the bar to stimulate it, ignoring food, drink and even hot female rats, and... There were women.

Young women – girls, really; milky-breasted beauties who were controlled by the evil *real* doctor, who'd craftily implanted tiny electrodes in their brains' pleasure centres, and who kept giving them a remote radio-controlled buzz, so they felt happy about being foster mothers to a new super-race of cloned, fast-maturing female assassins. All cloned from the one beautiful aboriginal super-assassin who had this unbreakable bad habit of smilingly approaching wicked, racist, anti-aboriginal politicians, striking a match, and spraying flaming petrol (gasoline) into their faces.

Yes, that was basically it.

World domination (fry *all* the evil politicians, 'til they give up being bad) through a cloned master-race of lovely, fast-maturing female suicide-hit women.

Sounded reasonable enough.

Hundreds of pages of the ex-cop chasing the wrong twin Ferrari (the getaway cover) up and down the curves of Palm Beach. And admiring the foster-mother-girls' curves on Palm Beach, wondering why they kept twitching happily as they dozed in the sun, and why they would never make small talk with him.

And in the big climax he forced his way into the doctor-doctor's lair, despite a panic attack induced by having a drug-squirting 'bone pointed at him' (the aboriginal touch, there) and, well, what else?

The book ended as he began leisurely working his way through the whole lot of them, yanking out their electrodes and giving them a taste of the real thing.

Steven's novel was rejected swiftly on the grounds that the publisher's reader '...couldn't make head nor tail of it.'

In fact the reader's report was such a fine account of utter bafflement that the agent included a copy for Steven's benefit.

No problem, thought the author.

As autumn moved into winter, the personnel consultant-by-day, novelist-at-five-o'clock, added explanatory hints so broad that even an imbecile could now follow the plot – if that imbecile *read* the thing. Steven photocopied it on Auscon's new clunking machine and sent it off again. But in a cunning, semi-subliminal move to ensure the manuscript would be read right through, and favourably received this time, he inserted pictures.

Playboy was banned in Australia, and *Penthouse* was thought to be an architectural term, but the occasional colour shot of busty nude and as-good-as-nude lovelies could be unearthed, and Steven had artfully pasted the highlights of his personal stash into his book's inside pages.

Back it came, still rejected as 'incoherent' but with all the pictures intact. Aha. Clearly unread.

By contrast, Dean Rodman, when he casually lent him the manuscript as a little something he'd tossed off in a few months of fun, returned it – minus the pictures.

'I liked it,' the Dean said. 'When are you going to finish it?'

(*Finish it?* Had *the Dean* finished it?)

So perhaps that was how Steven got the job in Canada.

Who could say? Getting a job was as mysterious as the start of any other relationship, so it was probably pointless to speculate.

And yet, a psychologist with degrees both domestic and imported, Steven spent much of his time pointlessly speculating.

Relationships were quite a mystery, like weather forecasting, but he was determined, one day, to find out how they worked.

Might even write a book on it. He was, after all, no fool.

A Snowy New Year

The pair of Aussies hunched over the last white plastic table had never seen snow falling out of the sky before. It just kept on coming, flakes rocking gently out of a windless black sky, down past the golden arches and the bright golden '2 Billion Served' sign, on its blood-red background, flaring into their window light.

Snow-softened cars turned slowly into the car park for this, the opening night of the town's first-ever McDonald's.

Munching cheerfully, the Australian aliens stared through the plate glass, warm inside, cold outside. They'd trudged up Regent Street and gone in.

'We've been served, so shouldn't that read two billion and two?' Steven asked Eddie, her face still palely interesting from the long flight.

She nodded, hypnotised by the endless gentleness of the snow. 'This snow,' she mused. Down it came like feathers, feathery down, feathering down. Everything was rounded, unreal as dolls' houses.

'Definitely a snowy year,' said Steven. 'This is the first day of the year, in Fodderton, New Brunswick, so what did you resolve? I resolved to give up making New Year Resolutions.'

'I, ah – you're not supposed to tell, are you?'

'Anyway,' he continued, 'that's only two thousand million. In Australia or England they'd have to serve up two *million* million before they could brag about two billion. Even their gallons are shrivelled, not the full imperial.'

'Is Canada British-style, or American?' Eddie said.

Suddenly he wasn't sure. Research was needed. With a tiny head flick he signalled her to listen in to the down-east Canadians talking at the next table.

'Really coming down, eh?' said a big man, holding his coffee mug in both hands.

His two companions, working sugar into their coffees, nodded in expert agreement.

'They reckon the Trans-Canada's shut down up North but. Snowplows can't even get through, eh? Boys O boys.'

'Out my way, it's yea-high.'

Steven leaned in and caught Eddie's eyes, fully made up as always, lashes and liner.

He pursed his lips and nodded.

On dates they'd liked to listen in to surrounding tables, and this was like a date. Since the night he'd moved in on her, there'd not been many dates. She'd been, somehow, lost.

Would she find herself here? Fodderton seemed an unlikely place to start looking.

She could never go home. Back to Mackintosh Girls' High. As one of her sharper girls had put it, she had burned her britches.

The flashing blue light of a huge, unstoppable snowplow passed, lighting the tops of the swelling snow banks. Then a flashing red light passed, its vehicle unseen.

The outrageous snow, the holiday, and the gala New Year's opening of this, the town's brand new dining establishment (with Free Gifts, the best kind) had the locals in a mildly celebratory mood.

She'd read about McDonald's, America's contribution to utensil-free dining, and Steven had spotted his first golden arches, the celestial bosom, from Honolulu airport, so here was a chance to find what all the excitement was about.

It wasn't the food.

'Place like this wouldn't last five minutes in Australia,' pronounced Steven. 'I didn't want to say anything while you were eating, but hey, the bun wasn't bread – too sweet – the beef wasn't meat, the grilled cheese didn't melt so it wasn't cheese – or grilled. My guess is the fries are greased-up powdered potato pulp. Easily the best part's the tomato sauce, and that's a bit sugary.'

'I think they call it ketchup, eh.'

'I better ketchup, eh?'

Eddie was suddenly back at Newport that magic, cooling evening after a day at Palm Beach and, after making love in 'their' vacant lot, high above the beach, sharing a tin tray of curried shrimps with him, swapping their one plastic fork, ravenous.

Surely he would remember.

'Remember that superb burger we had on the way to Thredbo?' he demanded. 'We were *starving.*'

She remembered, the brief stop in the fog of a dangerous ten-hour drive.

Steven blinked for a while but then smiled his lovely smile.

Yes.

His hair still had snow in it.

Sometimes he looked like a taller Robert Redford, minus the moustache but plus the warty things on his cheek.

She wondered if that biggest warty thing could be squeezed, but they weren't really intimate enough for that. Not yet. True, they'd been living together for a while, but that was sort of an accident. Not a misunderstanding, more... Hard to say what it was. She tried not to think about it.

She spotted a tiny spider and, beaming, coaxed it onto her finger. If the staff saw, they'd lunge at it with insecticide spray, but not even Steven noticed.

'Yes. Yes!' he went on. In public he spoke a little louder than he needed, aware that others could hear his words. 'First there's the big bun, toasted. Then –' he started constructing it in the air. 'Buttered lettuce...*fried* onions, fried on the grill, nearly burnt...*juicy* tomahto.'

'Tomayto.'

'Tomahto'

'Tomayto.'

'Let's call the whole thing off! Then, ah, grated carrot, then TA-DAH! the ground beef, juicy, dripping...'

'Pineapple.'

'*Pineapple!* Nice slice of pineapple. Nice slice of beetroot, so it'll run down your chin and stain your tie red. And on top of that your fried egg, salt, pepper, tomato sauce – ketchup and the buttered top half of your bun. And that, ladies and gentlemen, is what we call a *hamburger.*'

She remembered the crisp bacon he'd forgotten.

'Where's that, eh?' asked one of the three big boys, raising his complimentary can of root beer. 'You from England?'

'Australia,' grinned Steven. 'We're Aussies.'

'Aus*tralia*, now! I had an uncle was in Australia in the war, eh.'

It turned out that everyone had an uncle in Australia in the war, or a sister who'd gone there for a trip and married a fellow from, what is it, the back out?

'Outback.' Australians were popular here.

The car-less pair were even offered a ride home in a four-wheel drive ute (what Canadians suggestively call a pick-up) with monster tires and a snowplow scoop on the front. It bellowed along in low gear, walls of snow either side, the 8-track whining a Country and Western lament about a man who'd lost his girl, his dog and his truck. The heater pumped hot air onto them.

Grinning, the driver tugged off his right glove and thrust his wiggling hand in front of Eddie's face. She smiled politely, swallowing down a kick of nausea. Worse things had been pushed in front of her face, but this was indeed ugly.

'You see that? I lost the ends of all me fingers last month. Even me social finger, eh?'

His mate tittered, peering down at her.

'Gosh. How did you, um, manage that?'

'Adjusting me snowplow blade, it came in on me, pinched 'em right off. Never felt a thing. I wrapped her up in a bit of rag and kept right on plowing. Worked forty-eight hours straight through, did a *lot* of driveways that storm.'

'Made a lot of money, but!' yelled his mate. 'First snowstorm of the season, like this one but with a wind blowing something fierce, boys O boys, freeze the monkeys off a brass ball.'

'– That's my car!' shouted Steven from the back seat, as they passed the snow-lump on the left of the driveway entrance.

'You want I should dig her out?'

'Please.'

Eddie hoped Steven knew to tip these guys, or not to.

The driver lowered the blade and, with a display of insolent skill, carved and clanked and backed and sliced a path from the MGB-shaped snow lump back to the driveway.

'No, no, put your money away. Buy your little lady something nice. You might want to think about buying yourself a real car, too. Those furrin cars never start too good. Buddy of mine had a Volvo? Below minus ten it wouldn't even turn over. Those five bloody wide main bearings, pardon my French, he said it was. He used to kick the thing.'

'On the television,' his mate shouted, 'it says in Sweden the average Volvo lasts eleven and a half years.'

'That's because they never start!' Steven said, and got a good laugh.

'Happy New Year, eh!'

Back inside, showered and plodding around naked, they both realised how tired they were.

Mercifully, making dinner wasn't needed. Making love was out of the question, and that was another first.

Eddie, eagerly hired by the local high school, had a lesson plan to prepare. She toiled away for an hour, her eyes crossing.

By the time she slid open the double window a crack and slipped into the punishing double bed, its Seeley Posturpedic mattress poised on a matching inner-sprung under-mattress, so you needed a seat-belt – one move could roll you onto the floor – Steven was sleeping soundly, with the emphasis on 'sound.'

She'd never heard him snore in Sydney, though she'd watched him dreaming. He was a sad sleeper.

Up above, Joe was taking his first steps on the long nightly march to ward off heart disease.

She would *never* get to sleep, and would look like death warmed up in the morning...

She dreamt she was a kid again, sunning herself on the beach at Dee Why. The sun pressed her hips into the sand, the Pacific breakers rolled majestically in.

But a huge figure, a man, stood in her sun, teasing her , smiling down, blocking her sunlight. He froze her. Her sweat turned cold. She couldn't see his eyes, but knew they were blue.

She woke to a strange voice speaking French in her ear.

Steven had all the blankets, and refused to wake up, even once he was awake.

She twirled the knob but there was no music, just news and frantic advertisements for junk food. (Is pop a soft drink? What are buffalo wings? Steven would know.)

She cooked him breakfast and phoned a taxi/called a cab.

The snowfall had eased, but the wind, now that its raw material was in place, had begun sculpting it into weird, almost beautiful forms.

She stared out at the new shapes that reminded her of surf breakers, frozen, or sand dunes with spray or fine sand blown endlessly back from the crest – but they were not.

They were nothing she'd seen before, and too menacing to be beautiful.

In places they spilled onto the highway, like a sudden beach.

'I've got to get the B started up,' Steven muttered. 'Need to get it towed in to Canadian Tire. So I'll see you back home.'

'Back home, eh?'

They kissed as she clambered out of the cab, lipstick to lip salve, and for the first time, he felt it was almost like being a married couple.

This trip, he felt, wasn't fun anymore, not that getting here had been much fun either. It was work, and work was not quite his cup of tea.

More Snow

The clock radio burst into static and Steven yanked its cord. No news, no radio, all snowed under. New Brunswick whited out.
'How'd you sleep?' he murmured cheerfully, rolling over.
(*You* slept well, she didn't say. I hope this new snoring only happens when it's snowing.)
He saw she hadn't removed all her eye makeup last night; a first. Why did women *wear* that stuff?
'Do you think Joe's going to pace upstairs all night, every night?' she muttered, throatily, one Panda-eye gummed shut.
'God, I hope not. You could hear him, could you?'
(*Hear* him! I can still hear him, and he's stopped.)
'It just went on and on!' she marvelled, shaking her aching head. 'I'd try to get to sleep when the furnace cut in, but then it'd click off and there he was again, like Hamlet's Ghost.'
'Hamlet's *father's* ghost.'
(I'll kill you one day, I'll kill you with a bread knife.)
She rose from the pillow and shook her long, fine, reddish-brown hair. And smiled. 'It's funny,' she said. 'If he stayed on the rug we wouldn't be able to hear him. Or if he kept to the wood floor, so it was continuous, I could get used to it. But every lap he crosses the rug twice, those five steps – it's like the Chinese whatever torture.'
'Grace says he had a heart attack.'
'Yes.' (I hope he has another *right now*.) 'I know, poor old guy.'
'Uh-oh! Now he's putting in a few laps before breakfast. What does he wear – ski boots?'
'Golf shoes.'
After breakfast Canadian-style, loads of grease and the sugar-sweet bread they sold here, they dressed carefully for work. First day on the new job. Eddie's face took forever. Snow had drifted half-way up their sliding glass door and was still falling busily.

Getting to work could be a problem. Did taxis (cabs) come when it was snowing?

A loud knock on their cupboard door. Joe.

'That your little car blocking the snowplow?'

'Yes, you want me to dig it out and move it?'

'Bit late for that. It's been moved. I'm heading downtown, if you'd like a ride.'

As the big wagon surfed out along the drive, which had been plowed but was silting up again, Steven glimpsed a somewhat MGB-shaped lump of snow in behind the snow bank.

No problem. Shovelling it clear would be a good workout.

'Don't they cancel school when it snows?' he asked Joe, who drove cautiously with one hand, the other gripping the buckle of his undone seat belt where it hung from above the door.

'Nah. They did that, the kids'd never get 'em an education.'

And true enough, there they sat, at ten: forty-five young men and women gazing up at the new guy from Austria (Australia – whatever) Professor Steven Butts, as he took the platform for his inaugural lecture.

Scanning the faces, the mass of hair and eyes, Steven noticed with horror that half the Business Department, too, had turned out to hear him. Dean Ted Rodman beamed expectantly up.

Is this thing on? Yes, it was on. He opened by asking if there were any questions. No, there were no questions.

He was on for 50 minutes.

He planned to begin by thanking Dean Rodman but blanked on his name and seemed to recall that, on his return, Rodman had been replaced as Acting Department Head (make that *Acting* Acting Head) by Acting Head somebody else. *Joyce*, that was the name! He thanked Dean Joyce and proceeded to proceed with his lecture on Introduction to Business.

The business of business, he reminded them, is business.

But (sliding into an area where he felt more at home) the ethical considerations of business must be...considered. Always.

He offered a string of examples from his native Australia of unethical business practices and (his own speciality) misleading advertising. He noticed his audience sliding away on principles, but returning whenever he switched his tone to signal an anecdote. 'Thing that happened to me' was the key that caught them. They had no questions but were surprisingly willing to try answering his. Especially, he noted, his rhetorical ones.

One shaggy young man had them all riveted with his story of a bottle of Moosehead Beer (was there really a beer called Moosehead?) that he'd opened – and it had the head of a mouse in it!

'You were lucky it wasn't a moose's head!' Steven quipped, to laughter and even a spatter of applause. This won't be too hard. These nice folk are all inbred, or something. He worked the crowd. From the tight looks on the faculty faces he surmised that working for audience participation was frowned upon, doubtless considered un-academic. But it was working.

He pressed on, stressing the need to think critically and make up one's own mind (ha!) on these matters, and in no time the fusillade of clicking binders signalled that his time was up.

As he left, the faculty avoided him, except for Rodman (that was his name! Rodman!) who slapped his shoulder and muttered, 'High verbal fluency. That's what it is. High verbal fluency.'

It felt like a put-down, but Steven was still high on having survived his first public speech since a school debate back in the fifties, against Bob Hughes and his school's panel of judges. He'd lost that debate, but this lecture felt like a comeback.

Paid to talk – what a concept!

The major victory arrived when Acting Professor Steven Butts slogged through the clearly unending Canadian snow to the campus Bank of Nova Scotia, opened a savings account – and found it already full of Canadian money. This was more like it!

His teaching appointment had begun in the second, 'spring' semester, i.e. winter, but apparently they'd been paying him since before Christmas.

And it got better.

The manager, a stick-figure lady with wondrous red hair and a faintly seductive manner, assured him that he would not have to pay Canadian income tax for the two years, provided that he intended to return to Australia at the end.

'What if I don't go? Do I get stuck with repaying all the tax?'

She smiled. 'Of course not. You just have to assure them that, at this point in time, you had every *intention* of returning.'

'Absolutely. Two years and I'm gone. I'm out of here.'

He wondered. If it would only stop snowing, this was a country you could live in. Nine hours teaching a week, that was only 1.8 hours a day, at $11,700.00 a year (exactly twice his Sydney salary), three terms – semesters – a year, or was it only two?

That makes...money for jam! Let's head to the Faculty Club for a Moosehead with lunch.

Up the hill at Fodderton High, the time-klaxon sounded and Eddie O'Malley entered Hour Three of her 6-hour teaching day. The same lesson repeated five times in a row. Then a different lesson. The group now filing in were listed as the A's. But with her three years of Australian experience, she judged, from the dark-browed look of them, their slow gum-chewing rate and uninterested glances at this brand-new supply teacher, that they were in fact the C's, the 'Opportunity' students, who, given the opportunity, could see lightning and hear thunder. And if they *were* A's, the worst were yet to come.

Eddie gave them all a big smile and welcome, noting the puzzlement as a few tried to place her but failed.

She called the roll. By Day Two she'd know all their names, she was like that. Steven, now, hopeless! Mind like a sieve. It was as if he knew why he was on Earth, but had no idea what all these other people were here for. Including, perhaps, her. Hopeless.

Already far too tired to erase and rewrite all her excellent blackboard notes, she'd left them up from the previous class. By now she had her Introduction to Biology lesson word-perfect, and in fact, half-way through she became fuzzily aware that a talking head was now delivering the lecture, in a resonant, shamefully Australian voice, and that therefore it must be her. She needed lunch. Something. Anything.

Between Periods One and Two she'd managed, by trotting up the locker-lined corridor to the staff room, to grab someone's filthy Snoopy mug off a hook and pour herself some coffee with powdered whitener. It tasted, as a tiny, furiously smoking teacher called Dianne said, watching her face, 'A bit like the stuff you use to clean paint brushes.'

'Yes.' (More like something you sit in to remove a low tattoo.) She smiled and nodded. That was not original. She'd read it and could remember where, and who wrote it, and, if she put her mind to it, probably on what page.

She was like that; unlike the handsome blue-eyed man she'd fallen hopelessly in love with and tailed to Canada. The man who seemed to know nothing, but could always make it up. Brilliantly.

Perhaps that was what they taught at Oxford. Make it up.

Hadn't the Oxford debating team recently defeated Harvard by delivering made-up quotations, which their opponents had wasted their preparation time desperately hunting for?

'You really don't have to do that,' said Dianne as she washed out the Snoopy mug. Oh, yes, she did. Had to. Raised a good Catholic, repeatedly beaten into silence by her chain-smoking mother for 'insolence,' she really *did* have to. Saying 'No' meant trouble. So she had to say 'Yes' when Mr Volen, the rodent-like head of the biology department, informed her that his teachers would take turns to pop in and feed the class hamsters on weekends. Starting with her. This weekend.

As the electronic Klaxon went for the start of another round of Biology, Eddie fell easily into a teaching state she called 'déjà vu all over again' where the talking head did most of the work.

She was good, and had done it all before. Even in Canada, brain-cells had axons, though they lacked the elegant Australian 'e' on the end, and it showed. They had an 'Eh?' or 'Duh,' instead.

Steven though, was still waiting for the opening bell, to meet... The Engineers. His colleagues grinned as they spoke of them. He had faked the business students, but these were a greater unknown. All engineers *had* to take Introduction to Business and the word was that, at least under the terrified Professor Ramadam Goatee and before him, the chattery Acting Acting Head, Professor Michael Joyce, Introduction to Business was a bird course. He could sense, as 300-odd (some very odd) engineering students clumped into the lecture hall, that the attitude was, 'We've shown up, you don't expect us to do any work, do you?'

He struggled on.

'Can you all hear me?'

'NO!'

'Can – you – hear – me – now?'

'NO. Can't hear a word.'

'Was that a dog barking? Where's the dog? I can't see him.'

He was introduced to Jack the Wonder Dog, who attended all engineering classes, handed in his papers on time, and in fact, was well on his way to graduating with his BE: not just a pretty face. A good boy, Jack proffered his mongrel paw which Steven shook, and this improved the atmosphere.

'He runs a sub-three-hour marathon, too,' said Jack's proud seat-mate who, like Jack, was unusually lean for a Canadian.

'But that's only six hours in dog time, isn't it?' said Steven.

'What he say? What he say?'

They were having trouble with the accent. This bunch were not dumb like the business students. Steven resolved to speak slowly, clearly, and straight from the textbook, keeping at least one page ahead of the class for the whole semester. And he did.

This was the class that could get him into trouble, as they became aware what a weirdo he really was, what he really believed in, but for now he was doing rather well. He had plenty of examples of bad management to use, and perhaps it was a mistake to keep taking examples from his recent daily life, but he hadn't yet read the textbook and so forged ahead, groping for material.

Classic example of how *not* to run a meeting: call the whole group together – and then tell them to come and see you *one at a time* if they've got any questions.

Classic example of how *not* to make a presentation: lift the hinged podium, pile your unnumbered lecture notes on top – and then lean on it and make it collapse, magically swallowing all your notes like a magician's trick. For your second trick, place a transparency (upside-down and wrong side up) in the overhead projector, which you adjust so the image runs in a thin slice across the ceiling. Then whine about poor equipment.

Those in the know would recognise Dean Joyce and Professor Goatee at once. Like Steven, they'd seen the pair in hilarious action. Eventually the word could get back...

When he trudged into Canadian Tire, his car was already being towed in and brushed off by a monster boy in once-white overalls. Steven gave his particulars, flashed his International Driver's License and diagnosed his car's problem as a flat battery. As instructed, he settled in to read old copies of *Motor*. Within the hour, Big Boy returned to ask, 'And where would the battery be located on this model, sir?'

'I think it's under the seat, or behind it,' said the proud owner.

Within another hour he was told they had located the battery but that it would not take a charge.

'Looks like she froze, sir.'

'Oh. No problems. Stick in a new one if you've got one.'

Sadly, they did not.

It was a rare, six-volt model – but they ordered one in, urgently.

To make a long story longer, within a week the battery did arrive, it was the correct model and was installed, but there was a problem.

It wouldn't take a charge.

'What do you mean it won't take a charge! Thing's brand new!'

'Well, sir, what happens is, the other battery sucks the charge right out of it. Just like that!'

'What other battery?'

'Oh – there's two batteries, eh? Two six-volt batteries, making that, ah, twelve volts. It's a twelve-volt system. You did know that, didn't you sir? We figured you're a man knows cars, with your international licence and that.'

For an instant he thought they were sending him up, and had already decided to lose control, pick up that metal chair and smash it through the fucking glass window – but then he saw the earnestness on the young man's face. Big Boy was doing his best. It just wasn't very good.

Steven instructed him to order a second battery, SAP, and call him the moment it arrived and was installed.

'Course,' B. B. added, 'if you're planning to run the car in winter you'll need a block heater.'

'Sure. Stick one in.' Whatever it was.

'You got an extension cord sir?'

'What do I need that for?'

'To plug into your block heater.'

'Right. How long do I need?'

'That depends, eh.'

With a vision of the MGB trailing an electrical cord behind it down the highway, Steven called for yet another cab.

This country was not so cheap to live in. Everything had to be warmed up electrically before you could use it.

And strangest were the houses: instead of warming the people, as Australians or Brits did by putting on more clothes, here they warmed the space.

Space heating, it was called.

On entering one of these super-heated buildings (in the FU library you could surely bake bread), a Canadian would remove his coat and go about dressed for summer. In mid-winter.

He wondered how hot it *was* in summer.

If there was a summer.

First there would have to be spring.

The distant, unimaginable spring.

Another Trip

'I heard some fabulous news today.'
'Me, too!'
'No – you first.'
'No, what about? Is the car ready yet?'
'No way. These clowns can't even spell 'tyre' right so don't get your hopes up. No, it's the Business Admin. Society. They're running a trip to Europe in the mid-term break. I get to go free, as a, you know, chaperone. We land in London and I said I'd show the students around my old haunts in Oxford. Then we see France and Holland.'

(But Linda's in London!) Eddie paled and blinked, looking down. She spoke softly. 'I can come too, our breaks are the same week.'

'Gee, I don't know, love. It's a charter thing and it's already all booked and so on. I got in by replacing old Ramadam. He says he doesn't want to fly, doesn't trust any machine made by Man. My bet is he wants to spend the break lying flat on his back staring at the ceiling.'

(You pig! You just want Linda lying flat on her back, don't you.) 'Oh, Okay, then. I just thought it would be nice. You could show me Oxford. I've never been anywhere, and you've been all over the place.'

'Oh, we'll go, we'll go. Just not this trip. Summer we'll go. It's just a hop across the pond. You can practically swim it.'

But now everything changed.

That night they made love and he noticed nothing, no change. But afterwards she did not sleep. She became aware that she'd been sweating ever since they landed in this place, and she was still sweating. It wasn't the blazing, power-to-burn heat in the buildings. It was fear. The fear that she'd lose him to one of his former girlfriends (oddly, she never considered a brand-new,

Canadian one) and would have to go home alone, in disgrace. To confess to her mother that she had been...right.

They were not married, and her mother had suspected that he was 'not the marrying kind'; though she'd spared no effort and no expense to help her only child win this good-looking, bright young man. If Australia had social classes (and only politicians and statesmen pretended it had not), the Anglican Butts were clearly upper-middle, with Humber Hawk, Hillman Minx in their double garage and a ten-metre swimming pool, while the Catholic O'Malleys were good solid middle-middle, with fishing dinghy and Holden. He was a good catch.

Lying staring at the low ceiling, Eddie tried not to think of how much, just how much she and her mother and dad had given her young man. As if he was her last chance. It was almost insulting. She wasn't *that* old! Forget giving him her heart and her virginity – the dinners! The dinners! And later on, the breakfasts!

He would ring on Thursday, sometimes Wednesday, sometimes not until Friday, and she'd be in a panic, jumping at every ring of the phone.

His voice, so off-hand, 'So...why don't we get together this weekend, surf looks good – Friday night?... For tea? Sure your mum doesn't mind?' Eddie still lived at home, so convenient to the high school where she taught – taught now in a happy daze, knowing that he was coming this weekend.

He'd make the long drive from his small dim room with the hot plate in Double Bay across the bridge, flying down through French's Forest (in the days before it had a speed limit) to Mona Vale in his joke car, about as comfortable as a motorbike but faster. Once he picked up two speeding tickets in the one night – different routes, same cop, coming and going. For her.

It was after that that her mother started asking him to sleep over – and why not stay the Saturday night too? It's such a long drive. So dangerous.

Eddie waiting, watching behind full make-up including her trademark twin eyeliner lines to the outsides of her hazel eyes, filled in with a dab of white, listening for him.

A few magpies warbling, after the sudden-death Southern sunset, the dinner waiting in the warming drawer. Warm darkness, and quiet enough to hear the distant breakers boom.

Then the change down, the squeal of tyres, the change up – and her knight in shining Nota was here. Switching off with that sudden silence of a high-comp. engine. She knew cars, though she was nervous about driving herself.

And she'd meet him in the driveway with a brisk, businesslike hug, knowing her parents watched. And her mother turned on the best dinner he'd have all week: roast chicken or lamb chops, salad, beer or white wine, and a tropical fruit salad with ice cream *and* a bowl of whipped cream to slop on as well. He always took seconds, grinning, shaking his head at the amazing generosity of it all. He knew they liked him, and they did.

At first he slept on the living room floor, wrestling with the Burmese cat Garuda, but one afternoon they returned from the beach, shagged out and sunburnt, to find a folding bed (the plastic-and-aluminium garden lounge) set up and neatly made – in Eddie's room. Mrs O'Malley had even rigged up a mosquito net over it – as if that would symbolically separate him from her daughter lying in her narrow bed a mere arm's reach away.

'I thought you'd be more comfortable,' she announced in her always too-loud, nasal voice.

Oh, yes, they were. Agonisingly comfortable, struggling to make love in silence, the house poised, waiting for the first bump or groan. And on that first Sunday morning the hideously embarrassing truth was revealed: he'd somehow pushed one foot through the fibro-plaster wall.

'Can't imagine how that happened,' was all one could say.
'Easily fixed.'

But it was never enough. She had him for weekends, but she never really had him. There were always the others, the Unknown Others, from his past, maybe from work – who knew? He never showed up with lipstick smeared on his cheek or alien panties dangling from the Nota roll bar, and on the beach he never said 'Look at those!' Nothing that could make you throw sand at him, or a brick. But somehow, even when he was there, he was never quite... there.

Certainly he wanted to get into Formula One and become World Champion, somehow, some day.

He told her how close he was, and she believed him.

He'd done racing schools in England. He was the smoothest driver on the track.

He'd had a try-out for *Ecurie Sud* before the legendary old Luke Davison had died at the wheel at Sandown – and then Luke's fast protégé – Ricky Trebilco was it? – had been given the big 2.5 Cooper for the following weekend at Longford, to keep the team alive. And lost a wheel at 160 mph and been killed. That was awful luck. Awful.

Yet Steven still hinted that he was quicker than Ricky had ever been. No evidence, but he kept at it.

But the racing wasn't it.

Simply, she never believed he was in love with her. Not really. And anything, everything she did for him didn't help.

Nothing made any difference.

Letting him get her pregnant would have made no difference.

He'd be off like a shot, and her mother would beat her around the face and the back of the neck like the old days.

She'd gone on The Pill, the early high-dosage one, greeting each day with morning sickness, creeping outside to throw up in the hydrangeas.

And soon the furious row when her mother discovered them, bellowing, 'No daughter of mine...!'

Ghastly.

So then she left home, and then he moved in with her, and even *that* hadn't made the difference.

And here she was in this strange country, unable to sleep, sweating inside and freezing half to death every time she went out the door, and now the pig was going away *again!*

London was not London. London was Linda Austen, his last, or make that next-to-last girlfriend...

Linda had gone to London so that he would follow her! That was the plan. (Men had no idea. They thought they were calling the shots.)

But he'd spent all his overseas trip money on rebuilding his Nota instead, and had missed his cue.

In a straight fight, breast-to-breast with Linda Austen she would lose. She knew she'd lose, and this is why she could not sleep. Could only lie there, shifting carefully from time to time as the sweat made her armpits and legs stick together.

He would never return from London. Ever.

He'd be dancing cheek-to-cheek with blonde Linda.

She'd watched them at his Welcome-Me-Back-From-Oxford party, dancing cheek-to-cheek – knee-to-crotch, more like it.

He'd stay there and she'd be left to pack and slink back, broke and ruined, to Australia and her own room, and her mother so carefully not saying I told you so.

At least her lovely Burmese, Garuda would be there –

'Sorry love!' (He speaks!)

'Sorry, I've been out like a light. I forgot to ask you what *your* good news was. I was going to, but then bam! – are you as buggered as I am?'

'More. I'm beyond buggered. I hardly slept last night, either. It's probably the time change.'

'Bob Hughes says the Arabs, the camels...'

But he was gone again.

Her good news, two free tickets to an ice show Saturday night, soured in her mouth.

Linda would doubtless swim across from London and appear, skating around in that blue, strapless dress of hers, tits on a plate.

Hockey on Ice

'They weren't sure how many people would come, with the blizzard and everything,' Eddie explained as he deftly backed the MG into a parking space. 'That's why I scored the free tickets from Dianne. And it's the opening of the new Ailing Centre. Lord Ailing paid for it, for some reason.'

'He's quite a young guy. I think the university gave him a degree or something,' muttered Steven.

It rose before them, in prefabricated metal, neo-aircraft-hangar style. They crunched across the car park. There must be a way in... Must be...

'Hockey on ice!' he announced as they took their seats. 'What will they think of next? My mother was a terrific hockey player.'

Beside him, three beefy men rose as one and moved further along... to be replaced by a young man in a short skirt. Kilt, really, with rather good legs below and neat jacket above. He smiled.

'Hi! Aren't you freezing?' Eddie smiled back, and Steven grinned too, resisting the usual quip about what do Scots wear under their and so forth.

'What's the special occasion?' Steven asked. 'It's not St Pat's Day is it, I mean Robbie Burns, whatever? – You're not one of the Burns Burnses, are you?'

'No, I just got the jacket made and thought I'd show it off. There's not many special occasions you can wear the stuff. Though we do have Royalty coming, in the spring.'

'Yeah, but this skater guy, he's not exactly the Queen.'

'Dollar Cashton? No, but he's awfully good. You never heard of him in Australia? Bronze medal at the Olympics?'

'Nah. We don't get TV down under, not yet – sorry, I'm being rude. My excuse is my car's got *another* flat battery, had to have a boost to get here. Steven Butts. And this is my whatever, Eddie O'Malley.'

If he'd fumbled that one I'd have thrown him onto the ice, I swear.
'Alan Burns. I'm a lawyer, on the other side of the river.'
'It sounds like "liar" the way you say it.'
'Well – that's my job. You want some lies told with a straight face, I'm your boy.'
The lights dimmed, speakers blared, coloured spotlights swam over the ice and the announcer told the crowd what they were about to see, and what they were seeing!
Cashton appeared last, a smallish figure in black, moved at terrific speed, did an improbably high splits-leap, then another, another, *another* – by now the largish crowd was roaring – and then, picking up pace, headed backwards across the ice, tracked by a greenish spotlight, and –
'Jesus Christ!' said Steven. 'Did you see that!'
'*Did* I!' cried Eddie.
'I told you he was good,' said their new friend.

At intermission Eddie was inexplicably in tears. Apologising, blubbering, obviously deeply moved by the little man in the tragic clown's costume.
Steven though it best to ignore her embarrassment, and began chatting with Alan, but she spoke.
'I'm sorry, I just can't seem to stop crying. My dad used to skate like that. I mean, not the tricks or anything, he was an ice hockey player, captain.'
'Your dad? Old Ernie?'
'I never saw him skate but just once, when I was a kid, he took me to the Glaciarium. He hadn't had the skates on for years, but he suddenly just took off. And he skated just like that. Turns, jumps – people all stopped. He skated like Gene Kelly dances; solid, grounded. And so *fast*. But I could never get him to do it again. He was white. He said "That's enough of that." That was just before he, you know...'
She sobbed, choking.
The two men nodded their heads.
I know Steven thinks I'm nuts. Now Alan does, too.

After the show they hung around, freezing, till the great little man appeared, swept out bare-headed, in a black cloak.

He was surprised they only wanted to thank him, not demand an autograph or item of clothing.

'Are you all coming along to the party?' he asked.

'Of course,' said Alan.

They eventually took Alan's Volvo, as the MGB had caught its flat battery disease again.

'Take two brand-new batteries and call me in the morning, eh?' said Alan. 'Mine starts up fine, even on the hottest days.'

'You've got an MG!'

'A red '66. I've got four winter treads if you'd like them. Studded. Stop on a dime and the guy behind keeps crashing into you at every red light. Fun for all the family and a great way to meet people.'

'Does your Volvo start okay on the really cold mornings?'

'If I keep it plugged in all night, sure. Hydro's really cheap here or we'd still be using horses. I've got two heavy horses, Mo and Old Timer, just in case. You must come out and meet them.'

They swept into the party.

'Hi! Come in and dump your coat on the bed, or come in the bed and take a dump on your coat, whatever,' said a pleasant, plumpish drunk called Robert at the door.

They somehow downed a generous glass of champagne before even getting past the entrance hall, where Steven stood mesmerised by a large picture of a runway at night that gave the 3D illusion of tiny landing lights stretching off to infinity.

They were real lights. He kept reaching around the wall, like a kitten baffled by a ball rolling into a paper bag.

Soon they were magically drunk.

The house was full of people and paintings and dolls – toy dolls. He spent a happy time twanging and playing a big artwork created by hammering hundreds of a nails of various lengths, precisely into a grey plywood backing.

'Will you listen to this thing!' he ordered Eddie, running the back of his nail around the whorls of polished nail heads.

The food was good, too. Lobster from somewhere called PEI. Dollar was in his element, holding forth to an admiring group.

In another room a huge lumberjack-bearded man called Arnold Someone told a long, hilarious story about a moose, his throaty voice emerging from a cloud of cigarette smoke.

He had his audience spellbound, roaring, as if he was some kind of backwoods poet, but Steven, smiling appreciatively, could not understand a word.

Eddie, normally so quiet, was in her element, a rare combination of champagne and sugary confections.

A leech in a silk suit made for her. He opened with the line, 'You have the most extraordinary eyes.'

Eddie shut them tight, and swayed.

'What colour are they? Blue, brown, green or other?'

When she re-opened her other-coloured eyes he was, mercifully, gone.

Linda's are blue, Steven would remember them and I don't care.

She undid one button, just to keep the men on their toes.

In the kitchen, searching for a healing glass of water, Steven found the jovial Robert at the stove, aproned, in the throes of creating a sauce.

'What do you think?' he asked, blowing on the spoon and holding it to Steven's lips. 'A tad heavy on the oregano, or not? And don't tell me it's too sweet. Everybody tells me that.'

'I won't. But whatever you do, don't quit your day job.'

'I'll try not to.'

As Alan drove them home Eddie related her champagne-bold attempt to engage Dollar in small talk.

They'd met briefly at the cake tray and she'd enthused over the house and all its wonderful paintings, by men she'd never heard of; that lovely bowl of flowers by Bobak, the haunting Artful Dodger in a battered top hat by Ross, the chilling silent scream of a seascape by Pratt – and another, very different one also by Pratt, a dead fish in silver foil. In fact, the only thing she hated was the sketch of strawberries.

'And I *love* strawberries,' she'd told Dollar, 'but that's truly tacky. It doesn't belong here.'

'Well, thanks a *lot*, love!' he'd sniffed, swishing away with his crème caramel and silver spoon.

'Silly me! It must have been his favourite.'

'Not necessarily,' said Alan. 'He paints a lot of strawberries. He's in his strawberry phase right now. They sell like hot cakes.'

'NOOO! You mean it was *his*! Oh, my God! I'll have to leave town. It wasn't signed.'

'He probably didn't have time. Robert should get him to autograph it.'

'Who *is* Robert?' asked Steven.

'Premier of the province.'

'Do you think all those people went to what's-his-name's show?' Eddie said. 'They looked like they'd been partying for days, most of them.'

'I'm sure they all meant to, but you know how it is, it's easy to forget things.'

'MY CAR!'

'Not to worry, Steven. It'll start in the spring. Mine does, most years.'

British Racing Green

Next morning his car had sunk deeper into winter, but no car was going to get the better of Steven Butts.

Die (or was it *Der? Das?*) *Regenmeister*, The Rainmaster, he privately called himself, when he splashed, slithered, half spray-blinded to victory in his first and second club races in Victoria, through pouring rain (though there'd been rather a dry spell since). So why should he not become, with a bit of practice... *Die Schneemeister?* These thoughts and hopes motivated him as, panting steam, he glove-shovelled down towards the trunk/boot/bonnet – it had *better* be the trunk end – of his buried car, that contained a dinky car snow-shovel, the longest that would fit.

The trunk lock was, of course, frozen.

Ever the risk-taker where cars were concerned, he unzipped his fly. Nobody was looking so he pissed on the frozen lock. He was right about the 'wind-chill' thing; the wind didn't feel like cold, it stung like pain.

Now he was in, but the battery – both batteries – were still flat. Time had cured nothing.

Hauling in to Canadian Tire on the end of a rope and the end of his tether, he demanded that they check everything; new generator, whatever it takes, whatever it costs: he *had* to have a car that would start. (And next weekend the FUSCC was holding a Midwinter Madness snow slalom in the very Ailing Centre parking lot where he had spent his Saturday morning shovelling. He had joined up and entered already. He did not mention his racing plans to the boys, as they wheeled it inside.)

'You know,' he told the Service Manager, 'in Australia, an MGB like that would cost two thousand, twenty-five hundred easy. I got it for nine hundred.'

The manager paled. 'You paid nine hundred dollars for that vehicle, sir!' Then he forced a smile. 'I'm sure the boys will have you on your way in no time, sir.'

And they did. Everything ship-shape and charging nicely (they sure knew how to charge), he drove out with a flamboyant half-wheelie, did a few bumps and touch-downs along a country road – snow is *slippery* – in good time to collect Eddie at the school, where she'd again been on gerbil-feeding and lab-clean-up roster.

'Well, we've got a car,' he smiled, as she introduced him round the gerbils and locked up the lab.

Right.

'– Oh! Stevie, I met the old character who runs shop here. Jimmy. He's an A-Grade mechanic, likes his booze but he really knows his cars. He says he knows the MGB and his students will do any work on it for free, as a project, if you want to leave it right there. For free! He showed me where to leave it.'

'Ta, but it's fixed. And please, I hate being called Stevie.'

Oh dear, now I've hurt his feelings. Love me, love my car.

But Steven, sweaty snow-covered Steven, maintained his good humour even when the starter produced only a low moan. Flat battery. Even when their attempt at a four- then three-legged push-start, with him hopping in at the last second and banging it into gear, failed for the third time. Snow is *sticky*.

So he left it at the school with the keys in the ignition, exactly where old plastered Jimmy had suggested.

Good luck, guys!

Now he's showing off how good he is under stress. He keeps quoting me that study about how the top racing drivers performed better on the tests when they were deliberately put under stress.

They taxied home with their usual driver, showered, climbed into bed and made love. It went quite well. But for the first time she thought it felt like children clinging together, alone together, warming each other but not just for fun – for survival.

She was noisy – who was it confessed, back in Australia that he only dated Catholic girls because they make more noise? – and maybe they could hear upstairs – but who cared? When finally he cried out, it was the loneliest sound she'd ever heard.

Beyond the window the afternoon snow still fell. It was supposed to have stopped by now. Could it fall forever?

Shouldn't they be building an ark, or a giant sled?
Afterwards she murmured, 'So you're still going to London?'
'Sure. You should come. Bring the gerbils.'
I hate him most when he's making jokes. They're his fancy form of lying. He's even lying to himself. That's 'it' for us and making love, and I mean it.

He slept, Steven Butts, the last of the late brakers, dreaming of driving exploits, the chequered flag waving for him, on his victory lap with the corner workers grinning, waving all their coloured flags at him.
Eddie slept, too.
They slept through dinner.
They slept through the wildest part of the unending snowstorm, and when they awoke, on Sunday morning, the world was new.
'I think it's stopped,' Eddie said.
'I'm starving.'
'Me, too. Sorry about dinner. There wasn't any.'
'If I don't have a pee – oh! It *has* stopped. You're right.'
Clever me.
After breakfast they forced their glass door open, and as its flat-fronted wave of snow began to topple inwards they hurled themselves out into it, like bodysurfers leaping at an incoming breaker – and flew through the fluffy snow bank.
They were free.
Under a blue sky they waded about, flung armfuls of snow, tried and failed to make snowballs, laughed, then hurled themselves on their backs to trace snow angels.
They shoved handfuls down the back of each other's necks, cackling – all this watched from above by dour Grace McTavish and, as he passed the window on each lap, circling husband Joe.

And the car finally started.
Though 'promised for first of the week,' which meant Monday, it took a whole two weeks; what Aussies call a fortnight.

The boys in shop class worked over the electrics, sprayed reeking WD40 in every corner, and sure enough, all was well.

Steven drove it around the car park, and sure enough, all was still well, the ammeter needle holding right where it should.

Steven drove it home – flat battery. And repeat. And again. And so on. Even the A-grade mechanic Jimmy himself was calling it, 'A real head-scratcher, eh?'

Once it had been boosted into life, the little car ran beautifully, and some enthusiastic sideways driving got Steven an outright win, on his last run, in the Midwinter Madness slalom.

None of the car club boys minded that he left it idling between runs; men generally feel uncomfortable about switching off their engines.

He also left the B running for brief shopping stops, and took to parking it on hills, or at least with space ahead for a bunch of volunteers to push-start him.

But it was as if the car had been built to have a flat battery. Jokes about Joseph Lucas, Prince of Darkness came back to him. And Why do the Brits drink warm beer? Because they have Lucas refrigerators.

But the morning prayer, *Please* let there be spark, then the impotent grumbling groan from the 'starter' was getting him down, and even Jimmy and his pit crew were losing interest, rolling their eyes each time he drove Eddie to school and dumped the car there for them, outside the shop, with the keys in it.

Impressively, Eddie solved the mystery. One afternoon as they bounced along a snowy side road she announced, 'Every time we hit a bump the ammeter needle drops down.'

'No, it's only the needle's a bit loose. I thought that might be it, but it's not.'

Oh? Say nothing for a bit. Try again next bump.

'It just did it again! It hits the stop on the left, and I can smell burning, like rubber burning.'

'Really? You sure?'

No, I'm just having a sexual fantasy.

And that was it!

Each time the prop shaft rose on a bump it shorted out the frayed electrical cable linking the twin batteries, one on each side.

When the car was on the level, on the shop floor, nothing. Perfect. Told the problem, Jimmy's crew fixed it as fast as a racing pit stop, and then, to show their area of true competence, volunteered to do the minor bodywork repairs and repaint the car in the colour/color of his choice.

'B.R.G,' he specified. 'British Racing Green.'

'– What the hell colour is that!' he squawked a week later as his grass-green car was proudly revealed.

Two students in grass-green-oversprayed overalls scuttled off and returned with a paint colour chart and thrust it at him.

'But for Christ's sake, British Racing Green is an official colour, dark green, nearly *black*!'

'Not in Canada, Stevie,' said Jimmy, and, pulling a half-pint from his grey dustcoat pocket, took a derisive swig to indicate that the era of free repairs was now officially closed.

Another snowy slalom was held, and he won his class – though on the hairpin turns nobody could beat the Mini Coopers, whipping round their snow-spraying front wheels like a swinging door.

It was time to apply for his Racing License – the whole point, really, of his trip to Canada.

Because he'd lost it in Australia and could never circuit race again without it.

How so?

The Three Stone Trick

There had been a moment when he could have braked late and dived past that irritating Dunlop racing tyre-shod MG TC on the outside, and shut the door on him into the left hander. Into second place. (Or into the ditch, if he slid wide.)

He could have, should have gone for it. On his day Steven's Nota could outbrake anything on any track, certainly this pathetic blaring old TC, with the driver's elbows sticking out, working so hard to wrestle the wriggling car back on line. But this was not his day. (This was at Oran Park back in Australia, three years before.)

For a split second he had a vision of Caution: Don't Make Any Mistakes.

There was a moment when he could have, should have gone for it but he backed off, swore to take him next lap. But there was no next lap. Not for Steven. Ever. And it is so easy, such a cheap shot, to blame someone else for what was his own...not really a mistake, more erring on the side of caution...followed by a spot of bad luck. But the fact was, that morning at six his father had put a curse on him.

'This is a day,' his dressing-gowned father pronounced with a long, agonised face, as Steven, already in his white racing suit, clambered into the Nota to head off to his first race in his newly rebuilt car, 'that you will regret for the rest of your life.'

Thanks, Dad.

For the rest of your life.

Standing by the red-flowering gum tree on the groomed nature strip of the elegant street in the exclusive North Shore suburb, where a car like the yellow sports-racer simply did not belong, Mr Butts watched his boy leave, waving as the blaring exhaust shook the neighbours' Sunday windows.

Thinking back, the man had looked terrified. He'd already watched his only son (the rest were girls), who was supposed to follow the family tradition into The Law, slip down into the perilous lower-class world of grease-monkeys and pit crews and brassy women.

Steven knew this. But what was I supposed to do? he would mutter to himself, jaw clenched. Shut it off and climb back out and say, 'Gee Dad, in that case I won't go. Let's have a cup of tea and a round of golf at Avondale instead?' Dad *knew* it was all I cared about. He *knew* I'd been working all night on the car for five nights in a row. So what happened? It wouldn't happen in a million years, but it did. On the next corner the MG ran wide and clipped the kerb, kicked up three stones, pebbles really. Steven saw them coming, dodged two and the third hit him.

Smack.

He shivered for an instant. Doctor Remulac's waiting room chairs were cold as the ice outside. He was here to get his licence back, and the doctor being a sports car fan himself, it should go well. It had better. The professor's job, the money, Eddie – none of it counted beside this.

Two others waited: a fat mother holding a fat three-year-old with an explosive cough that showed off his pink, down-curved tongue; and a big, square man who waited with his head down, gloved hand clutching his other hand which seemed to be wrapped in a mechanic's rag.

Steven stared across the room at the cover of an old Maclean's: 'Trudeau declares War Measures Act.' That was with his good eye. With his injured eye – and he was wearing his contact lens – it was, it was... Maclean's, and the bright colours of the tank picture, and...possibly 'war.'

This was one tough country, but he could, he would, get his full racing license back, and go racing again.

His reflexes were still razor-sharp.

The floor tiles looked like thin slices of reddish rock with bits of stuff in them. Fossils, or artist's impression of fossils. The red was now the dark red of blood, and Steven saw them as a retina with stone chips embedded, and his heart thudded in his neck.

Flashback: He could slowly wriggle his fingers inside their soft things, but he must not move. He must lie still.

They'd wedged sandbags beside his head so that it could not move. They had murmured something about the danger of a retina detaching if he moved. But what about his feet? The bed was hard, a bench made for backaches, and the blankets tucked in tightly, forcing his feet down, leaving his shoulders out in the cold. He should have got past. He stayed back, waiting for – Oh, No! Seated on the cold plastic chair he felt his head jerk back on his neck. A reflex. Got to watch that.

'Mr Butts?' said Doctor Remulac. 'So... You're one of these crazy racing driver types, eh, from New Zealand? Need a medical to renew your license. Well, let's see what we can find, young man.'

Steven glimpsed the eye chart and began memorising its bottom line but got only half way before he had to turn and sit on the stool.

Reading upside-down, he helped the doctor scribble through the form.

Childhood mumps, measles, chickenpox, the usual: foreskin snipped off for being born, tonsils clipped out for complaining of a sore throat, appendix cut out for mentioning a stomach ache that felt better when he raised his right knee, a broken leg for skiing in slush and a broken finger for surfing in a storm – no need to mention the Amaroo Park accident – incident, rather.

Breathe in, Aah, hold; yes, he had lungs; hard fingers tapped his chest, his back; yes, he had a heart. Rubber squeezed his forearm, hard, harder, hardest, then released in a series of pulsing hisses; yes, the heart pumped. A triangle of hard red rubber on a chromed fancy mallet tapped just below his kneecap and he watched his leg spring into unwilled action, the other one too.

And yes, he was alive all right.

'You're pretty fit.'

'I run.'

'Cover one eye and tell me what this says.'

Steven slapped his left hand over his right eye and read out:

'BRDXFUVEA Printed by J. Pollock and sons, GB.'

'You're joking.'

'No, that's what it says, bottom line.'

Dr. Remulac went closer and inspected the eye chart.

'O...K... Now cover the other eye and tell me what *this* says' – and he switched the eye chart!

The blood ran to Steven's face. This was a nightmare!

Out in the waiting room, the man clutching his hand moaned; a single, loud moan. Steven slapped his right hand over his left eye, sneezed, and performed a brief coughing fit.

'Sorry, I got something in my eye,' he said, head down, rubbing his left eye. He slapped his right hand over his right eye and looked up. '– And it's my not-so-good eye,' he muttered, blinking at the new chart through his now pink left eye.

'E, J, A...' He read laboriously through from the top to the bottom, leaving out the printer's name although, since it was still his good eye, he could read it perfectly.

'We'll put it down as 20/20, though actually it's better than that. You're a healthy young man, fit. Don't go getting yourself smashed up.'

'I'll try to remember that,' grinned Steven. He reached for the signed form.

'That your MGB outside with the wire wheels? I used to have one just like it. Different green though, darker. Could never get the blessed thing to start.'

Now Steven sang aloud, sang the happy blues. He tail-wagged around and roared out, opposite-locking through the snowy turns between high-piled banks.

Oh, I went down to the Saint James Infirmary
I saw my BAAABY there!
She was stretch' out on a long white table
So sweet, so cold, so fair...

This was more like it.

Full opposite lock, holding it balanced on the throttle. If he could find a way down onto the river he could do some practising on the ice, like the immortal Dick Seaman who as a kid used to train in the family saloon on a frozen river, developing such a delicate throttle toe that, when the flag dropped for the pre-war German Grand Prix and 650 Mercedes horsepower clawed at the wet road through those skinny 4 ½ inch wide tyres, he found some grip, got away first – and won for England.

Steven, though starting late, would win for Australia.

But there was no way onto the river. Piled-up wedges of snow, that could only be leapt in movies, blocked him.

Nosing into slush he got stuck once, twice and had to extricate himself, using his patented technique of pushing the car, which already had its wheels spinning in reverse on the choke – and then as it began to move, running back and jumping in before it took off without him. The hard part was running backwards, in snow, behind the advancing open driver's door.

An appreciative toot of horns from the road showed that he'd been watched. The locals didn't have much else to do.

Finding a smooth, empty parking lot upriver, he worked for two hours on his doughnuts, double doughnuts with a twist or a locked up side slide, forward handbrake 360s; and his classic move, his *tour de force*, the backward 180 with a silent change (wheels locked) into first gear half way round, emerging with no loss of speed.

This was what Canada was for.

Even Australia's wet grass cricket fields couldn't match a snow-slick parking lot.

On the track he'd been known for being quick and *not* spinning, ever. Sideways, yes, but he could always flick it straight again.

Race driving is a series of tiny mistakes; perfection is unreachable. Even Stirling Moss, Fangio's equal, admitted he'd never driven a perfect lap – but Steven was determined that if he ever did find himself in a big mistake, a race car lost and spinning, he'd feel right at home.

A couple of three-sixties without hitting anything, changing down and standing on it; that's what would get the big cheer.

A police car came and went.

As the sun set downriver, flaring the ice, a wolf, or perhaps a fox, bolted across the car park right in front of him and took to the ice, where a couple of circling locals chased it with snowmobiles, out of sight.

Cold with sweat, having used half a tank of gas going nowhere, Steven drove thoughtfully back – not really home, but back; past the hospital, towards Eddie and food.

A flashback hit and slowed him.

A siren, rising and falling like pain. Inside a rocking ambulance the siren was loud and continuous, maddening. He was on his back, rolling with the wild driver. His right eye was bandaged but he had not dared open either eye since the stone hit. He knew she was crouching above him; her, Linda Austen, in her role as nurse (she was a nurse) and for an instant he opened his left eye and glimpsed her, pale, staring ahead and struggling to keep her balance as the ambulance lurched towards Parramatta Hospital.

He'd spoken. Promised her he'd quit racing and concentrate on his writing. He'd forgotten this, and remembered it now.

Why the siren, why the big rush?

On arrival the driver slammed open the door and carried him – picked him up and carried him up the steps, at a half-run, into Emergency.

And then everything slowed down.

Flaring white light.

The voices above sounded interested, attentive to their new specimen, and when he managed to open both eyes as ordered, he glimpsed someone with a pencil sketching him and describing what he saw.

'Hematoma,' whatever they were.

Cold water sluicing. Eye-drops and ointment.

Then both eyes were bandaged up and he did not see Linda for many weeks.

Though he felt her. Ah, yes.

She felt so immensely...significant, wonderful, like life itself in the dark shape of a hand, of generous hands placing his eager, trembling fingers on her breasts as she leaned over the bed, and he wanted to cry but was afraid tears might do further damage.

And Eddie (whom he hardly knew: she'd asked him out once, that was it!) showed up, too.

And he felt her breasts: there was no confusing the two women. This was the problem: 'How happy could I be with either, were t'other, dear charmer, away.'

His two girlfriends played hide-and-seek behind the hospital potted palms. Eddie knew nothing of Linda, but Linda tearfully told him that she'd 'had to wait hours till that...woman finally decided to leave' – and then had to play hide-and-seek again with Matron, because night visiting hours were over.

But if there emerged a winner, it was the newcomer, Eddie.

Though having to spend hours on the train and bus (Linda had the family car) Eddie kept showing up, and Linda finally blurted out the words...

There had been earlier words.

A month earlier, he recalled a shouted conversation, over the blare of the Nota's exhaust as he flung it down into Galston Gorge and up through the hairpin turns, home from an earlier hill climb, at Amaroo Park. He'd won, outright, against seriously expensive machinery – cubic dollars – that arrived and went home in painted trailers, and was feeling cocky.

The magic figures stood, blazing in the ferocious sun: 30.28, 29.40, 27.02 FTD. The delicious symmetry of winning. Burnt-faced officials were rolling up the timing cables.

Nobody could take a run and beat him now. It was his day.

He'd finally located Linda inside a sold-out soft drink tent, sitting in the trough of iced water in bra and panties, her face pink. His annoyance switched to desperately wanting her.

'I'm sorry I didn't watch you. I'm so hot. Did you win?'
'Sure I won.'
'That's wonderful! Good for you. I'm dying of thirst –'
'But Linda! There's a drinking fountain just outside!'
'Steven, you know I can't drink from public fountains. I'm sorry, I just can't.'

'You're insane. You're really, really insane.'

Down into Galston Gorge, ghost gums and red sandstone, the air on their faces cooled for a moment as he announced, cockily, that last night someone had rung him up, some girl he didn't even know, Eddie somebody.

'I know the one. She's the brown-haired witch with the make-up like a Chinese doll.'

'Well, anyhow, she wanted to know if I'd come to some Commem Ball with her at the Roundhouse this Friday. I said I'd ring her back.'

'– Well, don't ask *me*. Just do what you jolly well like.'

He whipped back to second for the three uphill hairpins, getting the power on early.

'Don't be cross, Snooks,' he yelled. 'If you don't want me to go, I'll say no.'

'She fancies you!'

'I don't particularly fancy her, though. I don't go for all that eye make-up, and she's got no tits.'

Linda took a deep breath and shrieked, 'SHE'S GOT *ENORMOUS* TITS!'

A hitchhiker's head whirled, followed the little car out of sight.

(Really? He honestly hadn't noticed, the one time he'd seen her – at Thredbo Downhill Club, holding forth about how she was supposed to be a dancer. And he didn't like her voice. Resonant, Australian. He loved hearing Linda speak, though. Like him, she affected an English gentleness. Just to hear her voice in his head made him hard. And the lovely things she said! 'You've got a nice phallus,' she once declared. She must have got the word from a medical textbook; he'd never heard it used in broad daylight before.)

But in the hospital darkness the soft-spoken words, wet with tears, were simply, 'You know I've been talking about going to England? Well, I'm not getting any younger, I can't put it off forever.'

She had given him the best years of his life.

He filled the car at 50 cents a gallon, slid sideways into Rimford Lane, down the driveway and made a neat handbrake turn into his parking spot.

'You look like you've been having fun,' said Eddie with a huge smile that didn't quite reach her eyes. 'Your dinner's ready, or do you want to have a shower first?'

Ever since he had announced that he was visiting London in the mid-term break, Eddie had been...off-balance. Trying too hard, or something.

Still, she had nothing to worry about.

He was only going for a week.

'Funny thing happened to me,' he said. 'I was doing wheelies in a car park and the cops pulled in and asked to see my license. And I handed over my racing driver's licence application! I don't think they were too impressed.'

Eddie grinned.

He didn't think she'd be too impressed by the story about the wolf, or fox, being chased by the buzzing snowmobiles, their headlights bobbing on the ice. She had a soft spot for animals.

Long Flight

He was in limbo, in the sulphurous city of Saint John. Waiting. No one could be this tired and live. He'd had a bad last night, Eddie in tears, her back shaking the bed.

The weeks leading up to this break, this mid-term, had worn him down, keeping a page ahead of his classes in the textbook and a jump ahead of Eddie's moods.

Now she was getting headaches she called 'meegraines,' that clouded her eyes; but she refused to take 'drugs.' Whenever he turned on a light she'd moan gently.

Professor Rodman had quietly asked him to take over his Tuesday night 'Resistance to Change' seminar for a few weeks, while he was consulting 'Stateside,' but Steven had said no.

Sorry, no can do.

His refusal was a major tactical error, like the Indy 500 drivers sticking to their front-engined cars even after they'd seen Jimmy Clark in the Lotus, but how could he have known that?

And how could he have accepted? Dean Joyce had already quietly asked him to run *his* Tuesday night 'Intro. to Marketing' course at their sister campus in the reeking, pulp mill-infested city of Saint John, and he'd said yes.

It paid extra, plus a dinner allowance.

He hadn't mentioned that to Rodman, in case there was some professional rivalry or academic jealousy or whatever.

Academics were touchy.

The Saint John business students were, if anything, of even lower wattage than the Fodderton ones. The first night, he asked them, 'How can you stand the smell? Why doesn't anyone complain?' but they just shrugged. 'You get used to it, sir.'

But he never got used to it. It repelled him.

So the best thing about Saint John was the drive home, away from the place. Every Tuesday night, late, he was on the road for two hours driving fast; four hours if it snowed. Excellent driving practice, hurtling along like Eric 'On the Roof' Carlson, though bitterly cold; one frigid, windy night he had noticed the tip of his nose getting frostbitten, and now it tingled oddly in any icy wind.

And here he sat, slumped, stuck in Saint John, of all places. At least he had a window seat. He pinched his nose, which seemed to have fallen asleep.

The chartered bus down to the 'Port City' had been delayed by a freakish snowstorm, the plane by a freakish windstorm.

He was dead before takeoff – the whole flight-load of Bus. Admin. Society students moribund, but now and then bellowing out phrases like, 'I wanna go ho-oome,' 'Are we there yet?' and 'We're going the whole way overland, right?' as the icy plane taxied around the greater Saint John area.

He considered scratching some Robbie Burns on the plane's window glass:

We came na here to view your works
In hopes to be made wise
But only, lest we gae to Hell
It shall be no surprise

Finally, they rose. Now, as their charter flight roared and whined through the night sky, Rodman was asleep with his big mouth open, drooling into the proofs of his new book, *Management by Collectives,* which Steven had agreed to read, and had: correcting all the typos but declining to comment, as 'It's really not my field,' to Rodman's obvious annoyance.

'Well, you *are* teaching the subject,' he had barked.

'Yes, but I haven't read everything in the field yet. For all I know it's all been said before.' (Wrong answer. It had, much of it. A plagiarism suit was being mounted against his earlier *Management by Directives,* even as Steven spoke these foolish words.)

Acting Dean Joyce was again giggling drunk, his prematurely white head of hair swinging from side to side as he entertained girl students left and right.

But Steven was beyond fatigue.

As the old 707 flapped its wings across the Atlantic its vibration entered his skull – propped by a toy pillow against the cool curve of the window frame – and drilled the aching cavity of his brain. A song from Hell was alive and well and living in the pulp of his head, singing around and around like a stuck needle. It was a childhood advertising ditty that, when he was overtired, surfaced from some neural kink to join him.

I like Aeroplane Jellyyy! it squeaked in chorus,
Aeroplane Jelly for me!
I like it for dinner
I like it for tea
A little each day is a good recipe.
The something is something

The something is ahh... He could never decide whether not quite knowing the lyrics was more infuriating than knowing them, or less. He really should have paid more attention as a kid. Or less. *It's made from pure fruit juice...* He could never say that bit as a kid.

That's one reason why
I like Aeroplane Jelly
AEROPLANE JELLY FOR MEEEE!

Then a moment's peace, during which he groped for sleep, knowing it was hopeless; his sore neck had already woken him once and now refused to support the weight of his head. Then, up from the depths of childhood...

I like Aeroplane Jelly...

He gave up. Lie back and think of England.

Oxford ('*Punting through a thousand years of blossom*', he had written somewhere). Oxford and London.

Oxford had been the absence of Lynn, Linda's precursor, the one whose eyes, whose soft voice he never let himself think about or he would surely go mad.

But Linda. Linda was London.

Linda's last words, her little confession, or boast, sitting so prettily beside him in the car outside her parents' house, the night before she flew away, 'overseas,' four years back.

Bragging of what she had achieved in her bed the night before that. Seven? *Seven* times in a row? Had she made it up to drive him mad (his cock had leapt to stunned attention, as it did now, just at the thought) or was he losing her on the very night they invented champagne, the night she sprang into full sexual blossom? Clearly it was his cue to say something, do something, but what?

Propose? Get married? What – and be miserable like his parents? It hadn't worked for them. Already, by twelve years old, lying in the darkness, head stuffed under the pillow, trying not to hear their endless muffled, then raised, crescendo of voices behind the wall, he'd vowed he would never marry. 'You *never* –' 'I *always* –' and him a kid in bed, terrified as the shouting tore down the walls of his world.

No. Keep clear of the Tender Trap. He would never marry. He had sworn. No fool, he.

And yet he'd stayed on, living at home even after returning from Oxford. The shouting was not so bad now. And home was cheap. And his mother loved him.

But why not get his own place, move away from the parental roof (and fridge and swimming pool and Ping-Pong Room)? What! With the Nota in desperate need of a new oil cooler for the next race? He couldn't afford to, and neither could Linda. She was living at home to save for her big trip – it was no secret; every Australian girl takes the Big Trip. But as she had murmured in her sweet, sweet-breathed voice, after an evening of passion on the vinyl-sticky lay-back seats of his mosquito-infested old Peugeot 403 (sold to buy the Nota), 'I'm not at my best in a car.'

In London, he assumed, she would have a bed.

She'd certainly be pleased to see him.

He hadn't written, planning to surprise her with a phone call on arrival.

God! If they had only had a bed, back then! The nearest they ever came was a couch.

The flight droned on into night, and his brain refused to shut down, feeding him chips of quotation and memory: Straight on to morning, East is East and West is West (how true!) and so we beat off, boats against the current, borne back ceaselessly into... Hands squeezed into his lap, he would have liked to somehow clamber over Rodman's sprawled form and slouch to the washroom to jerk off, but it was too much trouble.

The vibration reminded him of...yes, the Nota, with its oversized engine bolted directly to the space frame, turning the whole car into a hundred-and-ten horsepower vibrator.

Linda loved the car. After a long trip she would sit with her head down and murmur, 'Just a minute: I'm still buzzing.'

That Sunday they sat, with his Amaroo Park trophy wedged into the tiny space between the seats (that and his pockets were the extent of the luggage capacity, though for races he bungee-strapped an oil can to the roll bar and, for picnics, an Esky).

As they sat, buzzing peaceably outside her parents' house, breathing in the cool Jacaranda-scented evening, Mrs Austen emerged, all gracious smiles and set hair, and invited Steven in for a little something to eat.

Dinner was impressive, served with endless 'Excuse me's' and 'Would you care for a little more roast pumpkin?' and he ate his fill, conscious his nails needed a good clip-and-clean.

After a luscious passion-fruit Pavlova that burst in the mouth, and Nescafe served in floral china with cream, Mrs Austen steered her daughter off to the girls-only washing up and Mr A, after an orgy of throat-clearing, re-opened the subject of Steven's Intentions.

'Gloria and I were saying to each other last night, it's over three years now, you've been our daughter's young man.'

'Mmm hmm.' (Doesn't time pass quickly when you're having fun?)

'She's very fond of you, you know.'

'I know. Yes. And I'm very fond of her.' (*Very* fond of her. No, it was true. Actually I love her. Better not admit it, though; look where it leads.)

'And we've had you in our home, and we're delighted to do so...'

'Thank you.'

'Not at all, but quite frankly, man to man...'

Clarence Austen's small, hobbitty hands fiddled with his saccharin dispenser. Then his blue eyes, alarmingly Linda's eyes, looked up and caught Steven's.

'We were asking ourselves what are your...actual intentions towards our daughter Linda? She's twenty-three now, as you know. And you'd be...twenty-six?'

(Was she? He'd thought her about twenty.)

What could he say? The immediate truth? That his intention was to lay her down on a perfect bed and screw her relentlessly, watching her swollen breasts bob back and forth on her chest that glowed brighter and brighter red until she came and kept on coming for ever, her nervous system completely in his power? So that he could – what? Wheelspin away in the Nota, leaving her permanently incandescent? That the Austen's youngest daughter was the living subject of an experiment in sexual ecstasy, and coming along quite nicely, thank you? That after their last petting session she had been unable to fit her breasts back into her bra. 'Look what you're *doing* to me!' she cried, staring down appalled. Then suddenly kissed him again, feeding on his mouth. But perhaps Mr Austen didn't need to know the details.

Still, having said his piece the father seemed to feel better, and they moved on into tiny talk about ever-rising property taxes, before repairing to the sitting room to watch the Dean Martin show, Steven toying unseen with his girl's little finger.

And then, miraculously, the Austens bowed and nodded off to bed. Presumably to give him time to propose.

He squirmed and writhed as the plane rushed on, but his mind rewound four years and was replaying that night. At least it beat the Aeroplane Jelly theme. Why is remembered pleasure so painful? Was it that...though he could remember what happened, and in what order, he could never again actually feel it, actually *be* there? If he could get back, back before the accident, back onto that soft, golden couch...

Linda had bounced up and made a pot of tea.

A wall clock ticked slow seconds.

Sipping, gazing at him, her fingers seemed to tremble, and abruptly she rattled her cup into her saucer and grabbed his head down onto her breasts. He'd never known her so hot and passionate. Rage, fear — why was she suddenly like this? He felt giddy, watching her fingers fly down her buttons, reach back to her triple bra catch, staring; and her breasts dropped into his waiting hands. She was mad, a crazy woman, staring at him, wriggling out of her panties.

He unzipped his fly and then incredibly there they were, sitting side by side on the sofa, with her skirt up and her leg somehow over his, and his cock right inside her, moving, writhing together until she was coming, coming, come with a gripping, squeezing orgasm that made him come too — in — space — out — of — time.

The room returned, the clock started up again, and he realized that she must have had one of those...a vaginal orgasm. He'd read up on the subject. Gosh.

He pulled out and zipped himself up, she speed-buttoned her blouse without attempting the bra business; and they sat side by side and finished their tea, possessed by the mad certainty that her parents had somehow entered and stood against the wall watching, with quiet interest, as their daughter performed.

And now, unbelievably, it was back to Aeroplane Jelly time. Steven loathed jelly.

In hospital he'd spoon-slung it blindly round the ward. The dreadful ditty circled his brain three times, but on the fourth run-through, inspiration struck. From some deep unconscious pocket of resistance sprang the truth.

'THE QUALITY'S HIGH AS THE NAME WILL IMPLY!' he roared aloud.

Heads twitched, and beside him Professor Rodman stirred and rubbed drool from his lip before settling back, his huge feet splayed.

Steven squeezed his neck, wriggled his socked feet against the metal footrest, then raised it and slid the feet underneath.

Dean Joyce's white head was sideways on a student shoulder. The entire plane was asleep, including both pilots, and he was stuck awake. He untangled his headset and clamped it on his ears. Nothing. Nothing. Nothing. A French channel.

He listened in for a while, typical *beaucoup d'ado* about nothing.

Of course, being Australian-educated he spoke French, and had been startled to find that in bilingual Canada nobody seemed to, except students from the province next door, who specialised in spectacularly bad English.

When in class he referred experimentally to '*La Belle Province*' instead of 'Keebeck' he got dumbly cross faces, but also a tiny speckle of Francophone applause.

Now someone called Charles Bois was introduced, and at the first, wailing guitar intro, Steven sat up, riveted, his mouth open.

He'd never heard anything like it.

By the end of the song he was sobbing, drooling worse, or better, than Professor Rodman.

It was *his* song the unknown French-Canadian balladeer was singing. His song.

O it was a long, long, long flight baby
It took almost all night long baby
And it seemed to me like eternity
When I walked along through London City
Nobody was talking anymore
Nobody was laughing anymore
Nobody was singing on Piccadilly
Nobody was working in factory

...And again. And again, and something about:

So I went on old Campton Street
And bought a pair of new big glossy shoes
And I heard that the Beatles
Gave their clothes to people
Who broke their windows...
O it was a long, long, long long flight baby...
So I took a cab

An old black cab
And went away
Alone on the wrong side of the road.

And he wept for his lost vision, the ruined right eye that showed him the moon in double vision, just there to the right of the real, crystal-sharp moon.

How would he drive to win among all the ghost cars, hovering and bouncing there, just to the right of the real ones?

But he could and he would!

Jimmy Palmer had done it, becoming New Zealand champion and winning brilliantly at Warwick Farm before the Sydney officials discovered (how? how?) that he had monocular vision and was therefore unsafe at any speed.

Jimmy Palmer, Mr Smooth, never lost a car in his life, *unsafe?* – and passed a special regulation banning him for life.

...Which took out Steven, except for hillclimbs.

Never mind that Steven had shown them the articles on perception, proving that binocular rivalry only helps distance judgement for objects less than a metre away.

Beyond that, one eye's as good as two. Sidney Allard had won the 1950 Monte Carlo Rally with one eye – not that anybody else knew, at the time.

'The other drivers wouldn't like having a guy on the track with a blind side, mate.' (Why not? Wouldn't he be easier to pass?)

But he would get a fresh start, would get back on track in Canada, Steven reminded himself, as he flew away from it.

2B Denbigh Place

The bus roared along on the right–left–side of the road, and when they'd all checked into an immense railway hotel redolent of cabbage-flavoured insecticide, he made the call.
'It's me.'

Meanwhile, Eddie O'Malley would not taking this lying down. Encouraged by little Dianne, she signed on for Intermediate Ballet at the Y and bellied up to the barre, sweating and fretting about her lost form.

'And!' cried the teacher, helpfully, and to discreetly meaningless piano accompaniment by a plumpish young lady called Sally, a dozen pairs of turned-out kneecaps began to sink as a dozen elbows rose.

In the back row Eddie glared straight ahead, a picture of sweaty elegance, neck stretched high, tailbone stretched low, sinking, sinking as the arms described their time-honoured pattern – then rising, rising, the trembling hands opening 'like a flower.'

By the fourth repeat every face had a rosy glow, and all nipples were up. Like life, and most things that other people can do, it's harder than it looks.

'You're good,' whispered Dianne, straining for more turnout or, failing that, a cigarette.

And she was.

Certainly she knew all the moves, and could move fast. Sneaking off daily to Borovansky-Skully ballet classes, an artistic truancy known to her father but kept from her mother, had extended her 3-year Biology BA at Sydney University to a 5-year stint. She was as ballet-mad as Steven was about driving.

The difference was, he had no idea. He only knew she liked dancing.

First position, Second Position, Third Position one way, Third Position the other way, and then? Correct! Fourth Position. The awkward Fourth Position, one kneecap pointing north-east and the other, a step behind or in front, north-west (in Dianne's case, north-north westward).

Fourth open, Fourth closed, and then...the dreaded Fifth Position, with the feet together but reversed, the cripple-maker, the one that really separates the sheep from the goats, the girls from the wannabes.

On the front line a slim youngster in candy-pink leotard and lime-green tights shuffled her toe-shoes together, one pointing due east and the other west, and was instantly hated by all.

Miss Duckie's cane (she had a hip problem) tapped round behind Eddie, inspecting her efforts like a master butcher or slave trader. Above the room's perfumed sourness of sweat, Eddie could smell her teacher's scent. The piano rippling around the edges of an almost-recognisable tune, down she went. Up she came. Down she went again. Miss Duckie seemed to make a tiny, throaty sound of approval and Eddie's heart sang.

'Not so stiff!' she commanded, causing Eddie to start as if whacked on the back of the neck.

'Your neck!' she commanded. 'Long neck, long! But not stiff!'

It should perhaps have occurred to her that Eddie, in her long years of training, might have heard these words before. Somehow, the long flight to this strange new land of ice and snow had neither removed the tension from Eddie's neck nor restored the right eyesight of her absent, untrustworthy, worthless turd of a boyfriend. Her heartbeat rose.

Miss Duckie, in an attack of kindness, neglected to command her not to sweat so much. She would bring it up next time. Miss O'Malley, clearly, would be back.

And after an hour of pulsing in the vertical plane, the group of eleven females plus two questionables were released and permitted to actually dance across the floor, from corner to corner of the little mirrored room. Eddie, in guilt-black, followed the candy-cane girl who seemed to weigh approximately nothing.

'You can really jump!' marvelled Dianne as they stood outside in Sixth Position, where ballet dancers stand about dressed like bag ladies, smoking.

'Thanks!' said Eddie. 'Actually, I was a high jumper at the convent. Did five feet two, when I was just five feet.'

'Five foot two, eyes of blue...!' sang Dianne, happily waving her cigarette in the freezing air, and so Eddie didn't get a chance to tell her about the day after, when Sister Twinem had called her in and banned her from all further high jumping, to 'protect your virtue,' whatever that could have meant.

Miss Duckie emerged and began struggling to start her snowy Morris Minor. English cars seem smaller here, like toys, thought Eddie, who noticed cars.

Dianne had a vast, butt-sour generic V8 which sneezed instantly into life, and they next bellied up to the bar in the Admiral Beaverbrook Hotel, crunching pretzels and sipping Golden Cadillacs.

Dianne leaned in for fresh gossip, and once Eddie began spilling the beans she couldn't seem to stop.

'The prick's meeting some old girlfriend of his in London, right now, as we speak...always been like this – once, I was dancing in this revue, the Northern Lights, *Rip Off and Refund* – he wrote it, actually – and he was supposed to drive me home afterwards, it's miles, and yes I will, thanks, and he shows up with the leading lady with some bullshit about her car had a hole in the petrol tank. Right!'

'Right!'

'Right, and I ended up having to phone my poor old Dad to come out and drive me home. And he was *royally* pissed, I mean really –'

'Steven?'

'No, my dad. Steven doesn't care, it's like water off a duck's hind leg, all he thinks about is winning the next race. He should get a pit babe, with the hair like, you know...' (Like Dianne's hair, in fact.) 'And another thing –' But by now she was talking to Alan Burns, who had drifted in, in a beautiful grey silk three-piece suit, fresh from work, and she was telling him what a shit, a real shit her boyfriend was and is and always will be.

Alan was buying her coffees but they too tasted like Golden Cadillacs, and then he was holding her sweaty hand pleasantly as she explained that she couldn't trust Steven, couldn't go home to her father and old 'Told You So' her mother, couldn't stay here and it was all over anyway, they would never get married and the guy was a, a cad, that's what he was.

'He must have some good points,' said Alan, grinning, and as if for something to say, 'Is he well hung?'

'Is he well *hung*? How would I know?' The bar went very quiet.

'You mean, you never looked?' (Had the barman actually turned down the Musac?)

'Of course I've looked. It's just it's the only one I've seen. I've got no comparison. It's about, oh...'

The entire bar leaned forward on their stools as she held her hands about so far apart.

'When it's hard,' she explained.

'I should *think* so,' said the slim young man on the end.

'You're a very lucky girl. I'm going to drive you home,' said Alan, and did. And kissed her hard, confusingly, once. But not until they were well out of sight of any peering McTavishes.

He wore his new camelhair coat like a cloak, and it was not impossible that he greyed his hair, just on the temples.

As she waved him goodnight he salaamed beautifully to her, but with the hands held rather too far apart.

His Volvo tore away, swaying as if the driver was giggling his head off.

'It hasn't got any bigger!' shouted Linda Austen above the warm hubbub of the Prince of Wales, as Steven emerged from the Gents. The hubbub cut. Heads turned like hairy sunflowers toward the blushing sun. His eyes widened, his neck tightened and his head gave a tiny shake.

'I love you, too,' he said when he reached her. 'Have another drink.'

His voice felt thick, as if English cooking ale and jetlag had shrunk his brain to the size of a pea under a mattress.

He remembered what a pathologically cheap drunk, a 'two-pot screamer' this well-brought-up young lady was, how wine would loosen her plump lips. Once, after a party – but that'd be telling tales, and it *was* only once. And it ended before it got going.

She was so lovely. She was lovely when she wept goodbye, four years ago, but this afternoon, dashing out from the Turkish Importer's place where she worked, she was lovelier still.

Her blonde hair was cut boyishly short and she looked ten years younger, a girl. A girl who was now fumbling out a Pall Mall cigarette.

'You don't smoke!' he cried. (In his bedtime fantasies of Linda he always buried his face in the sweet, crushed-biscuity smell of her fine, fair hair. Would it smell smoky now?)

'I can do anything I like,' she grinned, cocking the cigarette up at an angle. 'You can't tell me what to do.' But now she was heading out the door. He dashed after her.

She felt like walking. The sun had died and the London evening was dank but it was not actually raining. Small cars whizzed around on sidelights, their drivers too mean or impoverished to use up their headlights. They passed under a floodlit white archway that led towards some park – geography, like names, being a weak point with Steven – and soon she was clipping along with that happy energy of hers that delighted him.

But now he had to pee again. Once you start, it's hard to stop. When he emerged from behind the stout, leafless English oak, Linda's mouth was hanging open.

'Oh, I'm sorry! I meant your cheap Japanese *bladder*!'

'Oh... I love you too,' he repeated, and it was true.

Her little paw in his, they walked on.

She chattered away about this and that and he savoured her newly English accent.

He'd always enjoyed her voice.

She seemed, oddly, to be talking about books she'd read, plays she'd seen, even The Rinse Cycle or some such that went on for days like a cricket match, but he was full and could take in no more, only nod. In the middle of his life he was lost in a dark wood.

His day had been surreal.

He'd been volunteered to supervise the students' educational visit to Oxford, and had dozed in the coach up the familiar A40, dreaming that he was awake on a plane, trying to get to sleep, but being waked, then put to sleep again by a pimply business student who talked at him quietly non-stop, who felt the English really had something to offer, sir, all that history and so on, sir; talk about your old buildings.

He woke as they descended Headington Hill and recalled the nightmare of his first arrival in Oxford, the brakes fading on his little Peugeot motorbike as gravity swept him down into his city of dreams. And he was back. In the city that built his mind, such as it was. In traffic. As the bus ground over Magdalen Bridge (Ah, memory! May Day! May Day!) and down the High, he stood and announced that he was going to tell them exactly where and when they would meet to depart, and told them, loudly told them what he had told them – and when the bus stopped, ran for it.

They were still behind him as he entered the portals of his old college, named after the brass door knocker that had been stolen only a century or three before.

They immediately trampled across the sacred emerald grass of the 'Old' (Sixteen Something) Quad to explore a staircase – the very grass on which he and Rob and Hugh had played a forbidden game of midnight croquet, lit by Hugh's angled desk lamp, with muffled mallets.

'Canadians,' he explained to the porter – who recognised him from eight years ago!

'Oh, yes, sir. You were the young gentleman from Australia, stroked the second boat. We won, did we not, sir?'

He was, he had, and we did. It was still 'we.' He had never recovered from Oxford, and never would. A familiar gowned, book-clutching don crossed the grass as dons may, and glimpsed his face (Ah, is that not the large colonial who insisted the proposition 'All swans are white' is absurd in the antipodes, where, he claims, red-beaked, swan-shaped birds are black in colour?) but kept his head down, perambulating, raven-like. All ravens are black.

An impulse from the past swept him back inside the porter's lodge where his left hand, possessed, swung up to the top left pigeon-hole, *his* mail slot, and reached in, as it had every day for these two years, for a bluebird, an aerogramme from... her.

Lynn.

Surely there was a last one that he had somehow missed, that would explain everything.

There was nothing.

He slipped out.

Rounding the Radcliffe Camera, Steven had rid himself of all but a dedicated half-dozen, whom he led into the most famous library in the world, of which one of them had heard, past the Sheldonian, where he insisted they study the restored, acid-eaten stone faces of Roman emperors, pointed them towards the most famous bookshop in the world, of which none of them had heard – and then made a dash the other way, under the Bridge of Sighs, and vanished left into the wings, down the shoulder-width lane that opens into... the best, and best-hidden pub in Oxford, his Home Turf.

Sipping, he glowered at girls. Oxford had failed him. No, he'd got his degree, his convertible BA that matures effortlessly into an MA with the passage of a few idle years. (When some antique parliament had passed a new law restricting its membership to MAs, the wise men of Oxford had leapt this hurdle by converting all their bachelors into masters.)

Steven had left the city of dreaming spires, of perspiring dreams, believing he'd got a second or even a first. A week later, the news of his disgraceful third-class degree, when he read it in Central Park in a borrowed *New York Times*, hit him like a falling Steinway, another Oxford wound from which he'd never recover.

He was happier there, and unhappier there, than ever before or since. He was alive. But – apart from the Janet Incident three years before – he was a virgin there, and after two years of his best efforts, he was still a virgin when he left.

True, he *had* talked a few young ladies into his college bed, and even, one memorable night after being locked out of his own college, and not yet knowing about that spot behind the church graveyard for climbing in over the stone wall, had talked himself into a young lady's bed. But no go. The ladies, without ever actually saying Yes, seemed willing, but he was afraid of being unable, or he was able but so fearful of pregnancy as to find himself unwilling. Or he was so urgently able as to be willing – but then *they* took fright and became unable. He was forever cycling home wondering why it hadn't worked out.

One English rose, warm in his arms and under the spell of his big hands had leapt from his college bed, crying, 'If you only knew how you make me *feel*.' And, shaking with suppressed lust, the sheet-wrapped beauty spooned instant coffee into his unwashed mug, added warm water from the basin tap and stood gulping it down, forcing herself not to look back at his comely, naked body now standing hard upon her. What's a gentleman to do, but keep apologising and wait for better times?

The thought of using any kind of force he found more of an anaphrodisiac even than the thought of unwanted 'childers, childers everywhere.' Worse, the tender trap of marriage. Not for him.

Cringing, he recalled the chemist's near Carfax that he'd been trotting past when he suddenly remembered he was out of sticky tape, so slipped in and asked for some. Durex Tape, as it's called in Australia. How was he to know that Durex means contraceptives in this country?

'You know, clear sticky tape, for wrapping round things. Durex.' The salesgirl had coloured and fled.

'…What sorts of things do you wish to wrap, sir?' asked the pharmacist. The idea was novel as an erection aid perhaps, he reflected, leaving.

So pigs would fly long before Steven Butts strolled into some chemists to demand, 'So – what sizes do your condoms come in?'

And of course, the first night after he left Oxford, the very first night, he got laid. That only proved that fiction is stranger than truth, though truth should be strange enough for anyone. So to speak.

So his beer with Linda was not his first of the day. English pub food being far stranger even than truth, he had not eaten. The Scotch eggs kept reminding him of a glass jar he had seen in a Saigon restaurant containing alcohol and an assortment of foetuses, various small white shapes that a real Man's Man would publicly order and gulp invigoratingly down, if the live monkey brains, eaten with a spoon like a boiled egg, were off the menu.

Walking deliciously in step he began telling Linda this, but oddly veered off in the middle, perhaps to avoid the word 'foetus.' But then he stepped into the old 'we' trap.

'Funny thing happened to me last year. Robert sent me this weird telegram, "WILL MEET YOU AT PHNOM PEN AERODROME 20-12-68 TO JOIN HUGH ON TOUR ANGKOR WAT THEN SAIGON LOVE." So of course, when Oxford calls! A chance to see my two Brasenose buddies – you knew Rob was at the British Consulate and Hugh the New Zealand Embassy –'

'I think it was the British Embassy, actually, in Saigon.' (How did she know this stuff? In Australia she'd never known anything about anything, except what he'd taught her. Once she'd said, 'You speak foreign languages so beautifully,' and she didn't even speak any!)

'So when we – I landed –'

'She went with you, didn't she!'

'Who?'

'Miss Big-Tits.'

'Which one? Edwina? Yes, she insisted on coming, and it worked out rather well – she'd studied those jungle temples, and you know me, I can get lost on a ferry. I assume you know where you're going, by the way.'

'No idea. I'm just enjoying the walk.'

'Well, so it was quite a trip.'

He held off from giving her the full, riveting account of Prince Sihanouk's speech, his gorgeous dancing daughter and the elephants, and how on New Year's Eve 1968, on the main street of Cambodia's capital the three Brasenose men had bumped into Jim, a fourth Brasenose man – and had celebrated the New Year together, all four.

After studying the region for a year, Jim said he hoped Cambodia's troubles were behind it now, and they had toasted the promising country in scotch and soda. Nobody had heard of Pol Pot – nobody but the locals, who were now beginning to suspect that Applied Marxism means sacrificing everyone to the Common Good, which in practice means killing everyone who does not agree with Applied Marxism. Roughly one in five in the end, a new record for self-genocide.

No longer holding hands, the lovers were now out of the woods and into London proper, though strangely, passing no sign of food. He remembered how she used to love the garlic prawns, served deafeningly, sizzling on a hot plate, in that Spanish place beside the Sydney Town Hall.

Under a streetlight she halted and turned to him.

'She came with you to Canada, didn't she!'

'Well, yes, but the thing was, I never asked her to. In fact – sounds a bit mean to say this, but she borrowed the air fare from me and I think she's forgotten about it. Hasn't mentioned it. She's working in the local high school.'

'Are you two married? Engaged?'

'Eddie and me? You know me. I'm not the marrying kind. I mean your parents seem happy enough married, but mine, you've seen how they can't even get through a meal without Mum having to run out of the room. Not my idea of fun. Anyway, racing drivers don't get married, do they? Is there a Mrs Fangio knitting in the pits?'

'Pat Moss.'

'She's his sister.'

They walked on. She promised to make him something to eat when they got there, wherever there was.

'So how was your trip back to Oxford? You never took me to Oxford, you stinker.'

'I will though, I will. Just not with the Bus. Admin. bunch. We'll go, just you and me –'

'But how was it? They can't be *that* bad.'

'Oh? They all followed me into Brasenose. I told them the whole place had been bombed flat by the Germans in both world wars, and painstakingly rebuilt. That impressed them. I kept trying to find something to hold their attention long enough for me to scoot away. I told them to watch out for dons, as they all carry weapons. But they kept catching up to me. So you know those heads of the Roman emperors round the Sheldonian?'

'They *were* rebuilt.' (She *did* know them!)

'Right. The car fumes ate their faces off. Well, I made a little speech, in my best Pommy voice: "Oxford has a long tradition of honouring her famous racing drivers," I told them. "The first head you see is that of Richard 'Dave' Seaman, an Oxford man, who defeated the German might on their home ground, winning the European Grand Prix, pre-war. Unfortunately he had to use a Mercedes-Benz to do it. Oh, and he was killed next time he raced there."

'They wanted to know who had killed him so I explained, "Ecktually, poor chap killed himself. He'd been hooking his inside wheels over a curb at the Carousel to hold him in as he whipped around. One lap he missed. Next to him we have Graham 'Joe' Hill, world champion, another Oxford man, though he raced under the colours of the London Rowing Club. Then the two brilliant Rodriquez brothers, Pedro and Ricardo, both Oxford men, double Firsts in Classics. Jimbo Clark, the unbeatable Scot. Jocelyn Rindt, who read Modern Languages." And so on. Then I waved a tenner in the air and bellowed, "Anyone who can correctly identify all twelve heads, wins this. Reference shop over there!" Pointed towards Blackwells, and took off in the other direction. I still know my way around Oxford, though I've been lost ever since I left the place.'

There was a pause.

'You don't know what day tomorrow is, do you?'

No, he had no idea, and she wasn't going to tell him either. Some woman's thing.

They halted again, this time in front of a barred shop chock-full of clocks. 'My boyfriend makes clocks.'

'That's what he does?'

'No, he's a town planner, but he makes beautiful little clocks. I've got an alarm clock he made. He's a clockmaker, and he's a stinker. Took me to a party last Saturday and spent the whole night dancing with some girl in a red dress. I told him to buzz off.'

Steven tried not to grin at the notion of this happy little idiot tweezing a tiny cogwheel into some cuckoo clock. All Brits were short. Their ancient doorways were low, making him feel larger than life.

But then he remembered: Linda loved that kind of little stuff.

Once, in an attempt to escape her life as a registered home nurse, paid to watch people sicken and die in the comfort of their own homes, she had begun manufacturing, for sale, small wooden tables with a red and gold chessboard painted on the top. She bought the tables, sanded and varnished them, and then painted in each of the sixty-four squares by hand. Then she hand-painted the chessmen. It took forever.

He'd come upon her hunched in the garage, dipping her little brush, and would have to wait till she finished before he could start. And in the end nobody bought a single table, though there was great public interest in picking them up, inspecting them closely, pointing out smudges and asking what colours she had other than red and gold. He should have bought one. He really should have. Her new clockmaker boyfriend would have bought one, which perhaps gave him the edge.

But she had called him a stinker, a good sign. She'd told him to get lost. They crossed a square and entered a tiny, hidden street that seemed closed at both ends, her key clicked in the door and she pushed ahead.

'Come on in. My humble abode. My flatmate's away for two days. She's the really nutty one.'

An Awkward Moment

He was shocked by how small the bathroom, how rough the toilet paper, how stringy the towels and how minimal Linda's cosmetics. She did however appear to be in excellent health, and on The Pill, which she'd never been while he knew her.

The living room, which, rather suggestively, contained both a couch and a bed, had a gas fire which popped into life and began heating itself.

The other door led presumably into the mystery flatmate's domain.

The kitchen was in one corner and did not really exist. It *was* the corner, and here Linda busied herself with two aluminium saucepans, a hotplate and the original Edwardian toaster, improbably quickly producing a welcome dinner of hot meat and vegetables.

They sat like campers, eating delightedly off their knees. For dessert, biscuits.

'They call these cookies in Canada,' he explained.

There was even some red wine, though it was served at room temperature – that is, stone cold. Steven offered to help wash up but she shooed him back to the couch.

Music played, a baroque piece he did not know.

'Mozart?'

'Vivaldi, actually. I used to call him Vival-dye.'

He spotted the music case.

'So who plays the cello?'

'We both do.'

This flat-mate must be quite the musical one.

'Who reads all the books?'

'Me. I read at work. There's not a lot to do and the boss wants me to be happy. I think he fancies me.'

'Me, too. I've always fancied you.'

As the temperature rose she dimmed the lights and sat beside him. They looked at each other, smiling, and not saying a lot. Not saying a *lot*. He wanted her so much now that his whole body had a faint tremor, and her pale blue eyes seemed to be vibrating too.

They were alone, Steven and Linda, within leaping distance of a bed.

The record ended, she flipped it, returned and kissed him on the mouth. This was something new! A hungry tongue kiss! Luscious, with a bold nose and a hint of biscuit. She'd never French-kissed him before, not for want of trying but she couldn't.

'Wow,' he panted, coming up for air, and nearly added, 'Marry me!' as a joke.

'I got my tongue-tie snipped,' she grinned, and poked her wicked pink tongue at him. Before, the best she could do was spread a curve of tongue towards him, the underside held down by an intriguing red thread. 'I was at an Aussie dentist here – they're all Aussies – and he said "I'll snip this." I said "Don't! I won't be able to talk properly!" but he went ahead and did it.'

'You talk beautifully. I love your voice. I think you might have even had a bit of a lisp before, but it's gone.'

'Do you think I sound like a Pommy? Jill says so.'

'Who's Jill when she's at home?'

Linda gestured towards the locked door.

Then they went back to kissing, warming each other with their hands. The moment arrived, the bed beckoned.

'I'm sorry!' cried Linda, leaping to her feet. 'I can't!' She was in tears. 'I just can't. I thought I could take you straight inside...' (This, he recalled, was from some ancient nurses' book she must have read once, possibly Freud, whom she'd called 'Frood,' some notion that the *mature* woman doesn't need any clitoral stimulation first, that it's an 'infantile' form of sexuality that, worse, blocks her from the Real Thing.)

What poppycock!

Neither Steven nor the good Doctor Freud could have suspected that the Real Thing might have been, in this case and on this particular couch...rage.

(Ah yes, there he sat, immortal, the later Freud, half his jaw gone to bone cancer, chain-smoking to the end, his cigar wired firmly into place, that plumber of the human soul, the worldly judge of maturity.)

'I'm sorry,' she wailed, her face wet. 'I've thought about you so much and now I thought I could, but I can't.'

'That's fine, love. It's okay. We don't have to do anything. Really. Here...'

And he held her like a sister as she sobbed her heart out, apologising through her tears.

When the storm passed she made the classic nice cup of tea and they sat, sipping in silence.

The room had warmed and he realized that in England heat costs money, unlike Canada where it pours into buildings free. Like water over the dam in fact; when Rodman had complained of his 'Hydro' bill, he had thought it must be for water.

He felt calm, his hard-on had almost gone damply down and he felt proud of himself, the gentleman, not forcing the issue.

He put down his tea cup and, leaning, kissed her cheek.

'You want me to go?' he murmured into her perfect ear, and chilled to feel the tiny nod of assent.

He smiled, rose – no hard-on, now – said he'd phone her tomorrow at work.

She helped him on with his coat – this *was* surreal, like being onstage in a dream – and he thanked her and strangely shook her hand at the door, then twitched towards a goodnight kiss but stopped himself, holding the evil thought that if he played his cards right there was no way she'd be able to let him go.

Then he was at the bottom of the stairs, guessing a left turn.

Then he was off, three steps into London before she called his name.

He swept back into her arms, his hands full of her breasts, and they climbed into the narrow bed and made love.

There was an awkward moment when he found himself lying on her left side – he made love right-handed – but he deftly rolled over, saving the blankets, and settled in.

All in good time his hand left her breasts and trickled down her belly as he suckled her so-familiar nipple that even tasted of her. (How different she felt from Eddie, how softly yielding, unmuscular; a cheek-to-cheek waltzer, not a competitive jitterbugger.)

She was gorgeous like a goddess, and his middle fingertip gently circled the familiar pleasure spot (she had no word for it and he was unsure of the pronunciation himself and kept meaning to look it up), knowing that she didn't like too direct a touch at first.

And when she had recovered from the infantile climax which she called 'break,' as in 'You're making...me...brea...k,' and of which the great Freud so sternly disapproved, and was contentedly waiting for him to slide into her, she murmured,

'You haven't forgotten how to make a girl feel nice.'

'How could I ever forget?' he smiled, wondered briefly what kind of idiot her boyfriend must be, and then he was hot, flinging back the blankets and surfing, moving too swiftly out of his mind and depth.

As he felt the wave lifting him, cresting, he backed off, waited a pulse or two, then began again. And again.

And had to once more, but then he was safely aboard and moving fast, with an overstuffed, numbskull hard-on, riding endlessly and easily forever.

Once, in the early days, she had thanked him, thanked him! for giving her such a 'nice long time.'

How could he forget what he had remembered, alone in bed, a hundred, a thousand times? (And Katoomba, surely she lay in bed and remembered Katoomba, where everything went according to Freud.)

Below him in her narrow cot she glowed like a sunset beach, like a peach, sun and sunburn and sunstroke, and in the end the wave rose unbearably high and he picked up the suicidal pace – and as it dumped him into oblivion he reared back and roared.

To hell with the neighbours. They already knew his name. Screw them.

'Gosh,' she said, after a decent, deep-breathing pause. Then, 'I think it *has*, you know. And not your bladder,' and then, 'I know it's an awful thing to say but I would just love another cup of tea...' – but then she fell back on his arm and was asleep.

He kissed her sleeping, swollen mouth – another first.

His own eyes were closing and he could feel, where their bellies touched, a delicious warmth spreading, as if they were joining like Siamese twins, joining in sleep.

They slept together, slippery with sweat but they slept well – until a frantic Teutonic alarm clock woke them. It was early. He had a pee and when he returned she was still in bed, tousled, smiling at him.

'I set it early,' she said. 'I like to have a little cuddle before I go to work.'

He obliged, catching an instantaneous break – had she started before him? and plunging ashore, thrilled by her glowing, growing sexiness. He assumed that the 'little cuddle' was her own work (seven times!) and did not involve the idiot clock-making boyfriend, who was, after all, a faithless stinker.

Again, she felt so different from Eddie, who was all muscle and tension.

Linda was like salt water, like sand.

He adored the soft curve of her belly, down to that blonde bush, natural, fair; only her lover knew for sure.

He could have spent the whole day – but she had to get up.

He, too, had to get going, for the breakfast meeting back at the hotel. And what was it about today being a special day? She shrugged when he asked her again.

They gulped tea and then they were off and running.

A Special Day

Back in the land of snow and ice, no transatlantic phone call came in. And as is well known to the waiting classes, silence speaks louder than words. Eddie found her students particularly annoying, except for a golden-haired boy called Jackman who kept blowing her subliminal kisses from the back row, and despite bad skin was, somehow, unnervingly attractive. As she waited for Dianne after school, Jackman strode up and asked her if she skied, and invited her to ski with the school team this weekend. They would pick her up on Saturday morning after gerbil duty.

Steven, unable to share the old black cab's front seat because there wasn't one, only a space for his non-luggage, was driven along in state of high, royal excitement, supremely self-confident, buzzing with happiness and badly in need of a shower.

As he dashed up the hotel's front steps he met Dean Joyce, poised at the top.

'Ah! Thank God. We were wondering where you'd got to. The bus for Cambridge leaves in about three minutes and we assume you're going to show the lads around.'

'No way! I showed them Oxford yesterday. Isn't it your turn?' He was feeling good, cocky, lucky, or he would never have flatly refused his boss, the man holding the key to his salary, promotion, tenure – the key to the formula race car he planned to buy, in fact.

Joyce shrugged elegantly. 'I'd love to, but I have to buy books.'

'I'm sure they'd have a book shop in this Cambridge place.'

The acting Acting Dean shook his fashionably grey locks. His fashionably grey three-piece suit contrasted with Steven's unshaven, unwashed, slept-in and shagged-out look.

'Rodman, then.'

'Says he has to buy shoes. You know he has those extra-large feet. The boys *loved* your tour of Oxford yesterday, they're asking for you. The girls, too. You're a bit of a hit. Did you *really* tell them Alice-in-Wonderland Alice –'

'Liddell.'

'– posed in the altogether for Louis Carroll?'

'Charles Dodgson, yes. She did. He liked to photograph nude little girls, to show their innocence in exhibitions. You *know* it's true, because not a single student believed me. "Aw, that's a bit rough, sir," they said, but I told them, "Those were rough times. You couldn't support yourself just by being brilliant at mathematics." "Was she really all *that* brilliant sir?" –'

'Now you're pulling *my* leg.'

'C'mon Mike, you knew I was an Aussie when you hired me –'

'*I* never – I mean we're delighted to have you on board –'

'But you *know* we're untrustworthy. Okay. I'll take 'em there but they'll never get back alive.'

'Good man. They're in the bus waiting for you as we speak. You can put your lunch on expenses. Oh, and did you really tell them the Radcliffe Camera was the first stone camera ever built?'

But Steven was gone. He stormed into his room, took a cold shower, the day's ration of hot being exhausted by all the dirty (or was it clean?) Canadians, trotted downstairs – and smelt the breakfast before he saw it. Bacon and eggs. Toast and marmalade.

His mouth watered. Breakfast, the one meal the British know how to cook.

Grinning, he settled in and ordered the lot. Eggs, sausages dipped in Worcestershire sauce, chips dipped in the egg yolk, toast triangles extracted from those wire toast-coolers and dipped in the tea. More tea. More toast. Then he sauntered back to his room and cleaned his teeth.

But it was no use. The tour coach was still there, idling smokily away, the cloth-capped driver happily idling away his morning with the racing times.

There was something to be said for Cambridge, but being an Oxford man Steven didn't know what it was.

For Oxonians it was 'an unidentified university somewhere in England,' the place where they punt from the wrong end of the boat, teetering on the built-up deck end, and, perversely, play the annual tiddlywinks challenge kneeling, instead of in the correct, Oxford position of lying prone.

On arrival, to bore the students rigid, Steven began reading straight from the brochure, and soon they were all gone.

Being top dog, he'd chosen an early departure time, and by the time it arrived many were already asleep on the bus.

Certainly, he was.

No fool, he'd phoned Linda and told her where he was. 'You haven't taken me there either, you stinker.'

He would meet her, he promised, and swoop her out for dinner, restaurant of her choice. The trouble was that tomorrow they all leave for Amsterdam... No, of course he'd rather stay. Holland was rather flat, and he'd done it. On his Shell Scholars' junket in the old days, had he not stayed at the Grand Hotel Krasnapolski in Amsterdam, and bathed in a bathtub so long he could do tumble-turns at each end?...

'You mean stay... tonight? God, really? Would you have me? I'll tell 'em screw Amsterdam, tell 'em I have to buy books and shoes and things, I'll check out tonight.'

So they dined with two suitcases.

She'd chosen Spanish. An old guitarist hunched over his instrument like a blue Picasso. She had chosen the 'El Greco,' which he explained was Spanish for The Greek, but she already knew that. She seemed to know an alarming amount now, for a young lady who'd never even passed her Matric. He could still make her laugh, but he had lost the knack of making her blink in utter incomprehension. Worse, she was quicker on the uptake now, as if her mind had woken from a long antipodean snooze and was ravenous to catch up.

After telling his Alice Liddell story, he even posed the stickiest, trickiest riddle of all, Carroll's 'Why is a raven like a writing desk?' and she beamed, her mouth wet with her water, 'Because it's got drawers.' And reminded him that they call crows 'rooks' here.

He blinked, twice. 'I know. But your Pommy crows can't sing properly, not like the real Aussie crows, with that tragic, hard-done-by overhead wail.' He did it, the authentic Aussie crow, and the flamenco guitarist, delighted, picked up the beat.

'We do the best we can,' said Linda.

The sizzling din of garlic shrimps on a hot plate took them back to the bad old days, and they ate in selfish, shellfish silence. There was something about Sydney Town Hall, and that area, and the rattle of Spanish dancing, that picked at Steven's memories, but what *was* it?

'So what is it that's so special about today?'

But she only shrugged, and her smallish pale blue eyes for a time would not look up from under the fine eyebrows that he loved, had always loved. Her fingers twirled the stem of her water glass and then she blinked up and announced, 'I've changed my mind. Yes, let's have a bottle of booze. Hell, you're only young once.'

'Champers?'

'Yes, what a lovely thought. Why mourn when you can celebrate? It's a birthday.'

'Signor? Champagne, *por favor*. Whose birthday?'

'... Our daughter's birthday.'

Steven knocked his water glass but snatched it out of the air before it could fall and smash.

He was hoarse as he spoke.

'How, how do you know it was a girl?'

'Oh, come on, Steven, with all the girls in your family and mine...'

He nodded, blinking hard. She was right. It *would* have been a girl, and it would have been...five years old today. She. A little five-year-old girl with blue eyes and fair hair and a thin face. He was strangling; the past had his throat in a noose, a garrotte, dragging him back.

The champagne arrived right on cue to ruin the poignant, ruined moment, and as the waiter performed the mystic fertility ceremony of removing a cork, holding the bottle at the standard ejaculatory angle, Steven's mind swung him backwards, five years to the day, when she was already dead.

To his office, staring blindly at reports, his heart thudding, waiting for his phone to ring. It would be Linda.

They had agreed that when she'd had it done, out in Bondi, she would phone and he'd fly to her side by taxi. No, he couldn't be there; the address was secret and she'd even been told to park around the corner. And bring two hundred pounds in an envelope. It was her money – of course he had offered, but she'd insisted it was her fault, she would handle it.

As for having the child? They'd never even considered it, or at least he hadn't. Anyway, it wasn't a child, it was a mistake.

A freak of nature, proof that some women – one woman – could succeed in ovulating while menstruating.

At 'Vatican Roulette' the house had won again. There were no words to use for discussion, only snatches of slang. He knew a 'D and C' stood for dilation and curettage, but of what?

As instructed, he'd phoned her doctor's number from Wynyard ramp, people pushing past, and heard, 'Yes, Mr Wilson, the test result was positive.' (Positive?) Ah. *Positive*. He coughed and heard himself croak, 'Is there any chance you could recommend someone who could do something about it?'

The line clicked and went dead.

He visited his own doctor and was shown the door. Procuring an 'illegal operation' in Sydney in the Sixties, and thus avoiding the 'knitting needle brigade,' was easy if you knew how, but who knew how? You couldn't ask without telling.

On behalf of a 'friend' he asked the company's first-aider, and was chilled when the man grinned broadly and announced that he did it himself. 'Perfectly safe, mate. No worries.' And this from a man with the handwriting of a child.

Then Linda said she'd got the number, from a nurse acquaintance, of the place in Bondi. The Place. All real doctors.

The official rumour was, someone told Steven much later, the Sydney police knew all about it; they even dropped in from time to time, and more than doughnuts changed hands. But the policy was to leave well enough alone. Illegal, immoral, an outrage to Church and State and a thorn in the side of their common hope for unending expansion – but better than nothing. 'Nothing' meant tipsy women found bleeding in the street, claiming to have fallen, muttering 'No,' they'd be fine if they could 'just have a ciggie, love' – but they weren't, and many died.

When the contraceptive pill – instantly called The Pill – arrived, Australian women took to the thing, in its brutally high-dosage form, faster than any nation on Earth. But hundreds, thousands couldn't seem to get the hang of taking it every single day, and wailed that if they did, they felt cheap, as if they had to have sex any time 'he' wanted it, or every single day. And there was nobody around to tell them, 'No, you don't. Says who?'

Woman's Day began boldly to publish letters from women whose boyfriends came round every night to supervise the Taking of The Pill before heading off to the pub.

Still, the thing did work – despite the side effects of lowering sexual desire while raising the risk of death by thrombosis and so forth. And there was weight gain, though this began in the breasts, so who was complaining? Not the men.

But for Steven and Linda, then, there was – what?

One evening Linda gaily produced a paper bag full of condoms.

'Where'd you get these?'

'The hospital. You've got me stealing for you now.'

The concept was sound, and condoms work well on penises that don't mind having a too-tight rubbery ring rolled down them, but Steven found his was not one of these.

He tried his muttering best, but soon the very sight of an approaching condom would make his hard-on shrink like a candle in a blowtorch, so all he could offer was his hand in...romance.

There was something called an IUD or UDI, and something else called a Dutch Cap. Perhaps the man wore it religiously (i.e. while praying) and the woman laughed her head off, then they shook hands and went home.

As a joke there was the 'glass of water,' taken not before, not during, not after, but instead of. Oh, ho ho ho.

Not so funny to the city fathers was the sight of the Kings Cross prostitutes cocking a leg over the upright nozzle of the

Hyde Park drinking fountain by the war memorial, to douche. In the interests of public health, the offending nozzles were swiftly redesigned, removing even that small hope of getting off scot-free, as it were.

There were also, his red-faced inquiries revealed, small white fizzy pills that were guaranteed not to work 20% of the time, but, as the first female pharmacist he had ever seen barked at his receding, cringing back, 'Only if inserted before each occasion. That's, *each* occasion.' One night he woke sweating from a dream in which a Germanic voice kept reciting:

Hickory dickory duck
You're really out of luck.

This left masturbation, probably the all-time, all-round favourite. Or what the books called 'mutual masturbation,' whatever that was. He was never clear whether the woman was supposed to do it to him before, during, or after – and how? He would be embarrassed, having to show Linda what a vigorous, manly rubbing was needed, and for how long, to do the job. It wasn't like caressing a shampoo bottle on TV.

Oral sex? He adored it. And Linda, unlike any woman he had ever known, smelt and tasted as sweet as an orchid. It was impossible, but she did.

Oral sex... – on him? Well now, that would have been too amazing for words, but he just couldn't reach. Pulling his head down, down, he didn't get close. Lying on his back, rolling his legs over his head and then walking his feet down his bedroom wall, with the Complete Shakespeare under his head, he could just...just kiss the big hard head of his cock, but that was as far as it went. An interesting feeling, unforgettable, but a real pain in the neck. Hard to breathe, too. It was tantalisingly not-quite-impossible, like kissing your own elbow or writing a book and getting it published. At Sydney University in Psych. IV he'd read up 'A Case of Auto-Fellatio' which sadly gave no instructions, though it revealed that 'the practice had been begun in early childhood and had continued into adulthood.'

He'd probably left his run too late.

As for someone *else* sucking on his cock, that would have been a wet dream woken up, but nobody had... Although one night, after a party, after a few drinks – but that was another story and more humiliating still.

Speaking...hypothetically, what should a gentleman do if a young lady with whom he has been – unexpectedly, out of the blue – intimate, then invites him to her farewell, Going Overseas party and greets him with the whispered news that she has just had her medical (no, not Linda, of course not, but a nurse, too) and found that she has 'a social disease'?

A what?

'A social disease, so you'd better get yourself tested.' The gentleman thanks her for her honesty but then, after the party, finds his own girlfriend – unexpectedly – lowering her tipsy face into his lap. What does he say, as she fumbles for his zipper? Naturally, he will do The Right Thing. But what is it?

So here they sat, facing each other over the wreckage of fine dining, Linda and Steven, fully clothed, hearts pounding, unable to speak. 'Their daughter' was all there was to say. The champagne tasted like grape dust. Their waiter, a tiny man in a tiny black suit, slid forward and with a half-smile of reassurance topped up their celebratory glasses. Drink up. Forget. But it was too late.

Their thoughts had slid away from each other and half-way back around the world. And the flamenco guitarist, strumming and wailing as to a demon lover finally jogged Steven's mind to the end of the story:

His office phone had rung.

'It's me. It's all done. Will you come and collect me now?'

'Are you all right? You sound –'

'I'm fine, I'm just a bit woozy still. Will you –'

'I'm coming right away. I love you. I'm coming right away.'

He galloped down the seven flights and onto the taxi rank. The March day was blazing hot. When he gave the Bondi street address the driver turned sideways and looked at him with the beginnings of a smile, but decided against the wisecrack comment and drove him, fast, in merciful silence. Steven felt calm, still, with the solid relief of having handled a rough situation with dignity.

The Austen family car, a pale blue Falcon, stood alone on a wide street of square, brick buildings, somehow like a de Chirico painting in perspective. She should have moved it into the shade. As he jogged up he could see her sitting in the passenger's seat. He climbed in and kissed her cheek. She was sweating but surprisingly cheerful.

'I'm fine, just a bit sleepy. Can we go now?'

The place itself was around the corner – he never saw it – and the job had been done professionally and well. Her only complaint was that the head nurse, afterwards, when she was desperate to lie down and have a sleep, insisted that she get up and dressed. Now. No, not in a moment, NOW! And, when she was so thirsty for a kind word, anything, turned rather nasty.

'I never, ever want to see you in here again,' were her parting words.

They had an afternoon together. What did they *do*? He couldn't remember. Did they sit in the Botanical Gardens? But he recalled the evening. A Chinese meal at Dixon Street and then the show he'd booked tickets for, Luisillo and his Spanish Dancers. That was it, the Spanish connection. A tiny man in black stamping his masculinity all over the stage of the Prince Edward.

And afterwards, in the parked Falcon, right in front of the theatre she announced that for some reason the abortion made her feel sexy, so he reached up her dress, pressed aside the sanitary napkin she had been told to wear, and easily made her 'break.' Then he drove her home. She was good as new.

Better in fact, because the next time he saw her, her breasts had swollen and begun to lactate.

'It's awful,' she said. 'Every time I lean forward they stain the front of my dress. I was washing up with Mum and I saw the stains. She hadn't seen, but I rushed off and had to put cotton wool inside my bra. It's not really milk yet, it's some sort of fluid.'

And sitting in his family car she showed him her breasts,

moon-white, faintly blue-veined under the streetlight, swollen, superb – but she put them away again before he could suck on her now darker nipples, sip her – what was it? Would it taste good, like melted vanilla ice-cream or somehow bad, cheesy, like blue-veined wheels of cheese? He never found out, because she saw her own doctor next day who prescribed some pills that stopped the flow.

And that was the end of it, never spoken of again, never, a sworn secret to the grave. There was not one word about it in his diary or his journal. Ever.

He never told a soul, nobody, and again, felt proud of his absolute trustworthiness in the matter.

Yet here she was bringing it up, a five-year old dead daughter, as real as the tiny man in black who was now inserting their champagne bottle into the ice bucket, upside-down in case they had missed the fact that it was empty.

They took a taxi home. He still had a full wallet with English pounds at two dollars each, and on his next trip they were only a dollar, everything was twice as cheap (or the other way round).

And after another cup of tea, and yet another pee, he descended the steps to find her already in her bed and beautifully asleep. The couch would not do.

He eased into bed behind her and lay still, her warmth mingling with flamenco music in his head.

His jetlag seemed to have returned, and he had trouble getting to sleep.

He was so happy, and so uncomfortable...

He was dreaming saltwater dreams, *Barque sur l'océan* unravelling gently in his mind, those blue-green southern rollers slipping over his head till he caught one, boy on a dolphin on a wave, and rode it gently in to break on the shore.

Breakers rolling, rolling in to break on the shore...

When the appalling alarm sounded the call to arms she rolled his way and hugged him deliciously.

'You know what happens when you dream, when you go into REM sleep...?'

'Sure. My eyes wiggle around. Every ninety minutes or so right through the night. What?'

'You get hard. Your thing kept bumping into me and waking me up.'

'I don't remember that!'

'Of course not, dopey. It's only when you're asleep.'

'That's like the one about the guy with such a huge cock that whenever he got an erection, the blood flowed away from his head and he passed out. Anyway, sorry about that, I didn't mean to wake you. You should have woken me!'

'Why? It was nice. Now I want you again. I'm afraid you're habit-forming.'

'Got to have a pee first.'

'No. Now!'

And now it was.

And then he got his pee but when he returned Linda insisted they had time for at least another 'quickie' and they did, though he would have needed a lot more time to get off. Men need time.

He heard the door click behind her and, realising that he was still in a bed, rolled over onto his back and fell asleep...

She was sitting on his bed leaning over him. As he woke he could have sworn she had lightly brushed his cock.

'Cup of tea, whoever you are?' she said, in a dry Australian voice. 'Thanks. You're...Jill.' She smiled down at him, green eyes in a tanned face. He'd seen those eyes before.

'You're *that* Jill!'

'Why? Did Paul-the-Prick tell you to look me up, look after me if you ever got to London? I bet he did. I just bet he did.'

Come to think of it, he had. At the time, it was usual.

Steven himself had written to his Oxford friend Robert when Linda left. 'Look after her, Rob.'

And Robert had, although Linda's letters reported that his heart wasn't in it because he was hopelessly in love with a black girl – *the* black girl – from Oxford, who kept refusing to marry him. He'd now left for Africa.

Just before leaving, when Steven was over in his car-racing buddy Paul's Paddington flat, taping his great jazz records for the trip, the phone had rung.

It was Paul, from work, sounding very man-to-man serious.

'Steve, I need to ask you a favour. That sounds like Coltrane. Get the Aussie jazz too, there's some Freddie Logan and even a Julian Lee somewhere. Steve, you remember Jill Bacon, the love of my life?'

'Absolutely. Didn't she go to England last year to study Psych?'

'Study something, anyway. I'm going over to marry her one of these days. I'm looking at a job with Qantas, and they give you free flights after you've been with them a couple of years. Make sure you tape the Col Nolan, Canada needs Col Nolan. If you bump into Jill, tell her I love her and I'll always love her. And... look after her, mate. Look after her.'

There was almost a choke in his voice as he hung up.

That Jill.

A Day on the Hill

The gerbils fed and watered, Eddie met the long-haired Jackman and off they drove in his mother's no-name sub-compact to meet the ski team. There was one problem. They had to rent a van, he explained, a 12-passenger, and the rental company wouldn't rent to Jackman, whom they knew, or to anyone else under 21. Eddie was over 21, but as she confessed, flustered, 'I don't drive.'

'No problem. You only have to sign, for the insurance and stuff. No hassles. One of us'll drive.'

The freshly-washed blue van gleamed in the car park of Randal's Rentals.

'See your driver's licence, please.'

'Here's my Passport for ID. I don't have a driver's licence.'

The clerk looked up slowly, holding himself back. 'Customer Relations' said a small voice in his head, his manager's voice. He wiped a large hand across his brow to clear away the cobwebs.

'So... and... How're you going to drive the van without a license, eh?'

'I'm not going to drive it. I just want to rent it. We're planning to sit in it in the car park and enjoy the sun. Maybe play the radio, maybe not. It's what we do. We're a van-rental group.'

'Like a cult,' added Jackman, and the rest of the team nodded in solemn confirmation.

With the shiny new key she fumbled the rear doors open and the ski team loaded in their costly, ski-bagged Heads, Fischers and Rossignols, plus her cheap pair of wooden Arlbergs. Then they all sat in the van, did up their seat belts and listened to the radio. After ten minutes the clerk had lost interest in watching them, so they all got out, including Eddie, and began pushing the van out of the car park. No problem, nothing unlawful, nobody at the wheel. In time they were out of sight, out of mind, and gone.

Jackman drove fast and excitedly, up the river, across the dam, up a frighteningly steep hill, the back tires whirring, and across the maple syrup ridge, past the suggestively-named 'sugaring off' huts, where the local tabby cats sport extra toes, some even extra feet, and march proudly about on top of the snow. So far so good. They didn't crash until the turnoff to Crabbe Mountain. Jackman turned right and the van turned right but he kept the back wheels spinning and the van kept turning right. Turned right around, in fact, and then fell off the road.

'That's it! I'm driving,' said Eddie, and did. 'You guys are hopeless. When it oversteers you've got to lift off. And get your opposite lock on *fast* – but be ready to wrap it off just as fast... You don't have a clue what I'm talking about, do you!'

A mile further along, wrestling the van up the icy ruts she added, through clenched teeth, 'Neither do I.'

She parked successfully on the third try, they unloaded, stubbed out those awful sweet weed-smelling cigarettes, and suited up with much kicking of ski boots in the small, over-packed lodge that already reeked of fried onions, hotdogs and damp clothing. Then they skied away, yodelling and yelling, leaving her standing there in her old blue Arlbergs.

She poled cautiously off, and found that she still skied well.

Her only problem was that her sunglasses kept sliding off her nose, which some Sydney hopeful had once called her 'fine Etruscan profile.' She envied Steven the way his stayed on, though she was constantly annoying him by reaching across to straighten them up. He had one ear higher than the other, but which one?

The Canadian snow hissed dryly under her antique boots as she descended the gentle road between maples, curving left and right, getting a rhythm going, then dancing, a delicious left-right mambo, and now finding that the faster, the easier to turn.

She soared up the snow bank on one side, down and across to the other side, slaloming through the clenched beginners. Steven will love this. The road opened out, gloriously.

Perhaps Canada would work out for them after all, this strange country where they drive on the wrong side of the road, where your reflex to flick the light switch down to turn it on leaves you in the dark, petrol is 'gas' and their oversize cars don't have a bonnet or a boot.

Waiting for the T-bar she could watch the steep side of the hill, where the ski team were warming up. They were maniacs.

Jackman appeared first, bouncing from mogul to mogul under minimal control. Tom Cane, their top racer showed how it was done. Parson then showed how it wasn't. Parson's sister descended in her controlled, stemming style that surprisingly had won her a full shelf of junior trophies. John Dobson was looking good, quite pleased with himself – until he caught an edge and shot past on a tilt, obscenely fighting to get his airborne ski down from behind his ear. (Pride cometh...thought Eddie, as gravity finally won.) Mary Kendrick descended, mostly side-slipping, eyes out on stalks, and most of the others avoided the mine-field of that side.

Landry, clearly stoned, flew straight down the well-named fall line, his long yellow pony-tail streaming behind him, and went upside down right opposite where Eddie was lining up for the lift.

Like a thrown rag doll he cartwheeled by, rolled to a stop, staggered to his boots – and bowed to his delighted, muffled-clapping audience.

He clambered back up to his point of departure from his skis, which were neatly stuck in and crossed, X marks the spot where the elaborate accident had begun to unfold. He stamped into his skis, found his flung pole – but continued searching.

Suddenly Eddie spotted his mirrored sunglasses, stuck in the peak of his final mogul, pointed, waved – and whistled. She had a good whistle. He looked up, blew her a kiss and her heart sang.

She was happy to stay on the intermediate side of the hill, and by lunch time realized that in her whole life she'd never skied better.

'So where'd you learn to ski so good?' asked Jackman, open-chewing a hotdog. (They all seemed to chew with their mouths open. Oh, well, different strokes...) 'Chasing Steven, I guess.'

'Not in Australia but. Do they *have* snow in Australia?'

'Snow? We ski on sand dunes. They're really high, and you get terribly hot, but sometimes, when the tide's in...'

'You're shitting me, right? You got snow in Australia. Where is it? Ayer's Rock?'

'A place called the — wait for it — Snowy Mountains. Bigger than the whole of Switzerland, actually. But it's not good snow like here. Most weekends it's either raining and slush, or ice, or a sort of mixture of snow and grass.'

He was listening, nodding, chewing.

'At Thredbo — that's where we skied, about eleven hours drive from Sydney, nine if Steven's driving — the lower slopes have a sort of path of plastic doormats you take. Unless you like skiing mud.'

'You'd be a good racer.'

'No, thanks. I just like to bumble along, do my own thing.' And later, bumbling happily along she recalled that perfect day at Thredbo, skiing the lower slopes with Steven skiing the upper runs, skiing the whole day with the certainty that, that night, he would come to her, in her bunk, and for her first time ever, they would make love. How she had seized his buttocks and pulled him towards her, and afterwards he had murmured, oddly, 'You're so...*brave*!'

Well. It was a risk, but her doctor got her on the pill before anything happened, thank God. Thank Harry. Harry, her amiably half-drunk family doctor.

The sun set into the river, a half-moon rose and she drove them slowly back to Fodderton. And kept going, after a brief stop to collect a change of clothes and give a cheery wave to the McTavish faces, both crowded in the upper window. The plan now was to party at the Kendrick's cottage, down on the lake, maybe stay overnight. How they would all fit into a cottage was answered when their headlights swung out of the trees and lit the place. It was a suburban house on the lake shore.

Though the place had two fridges and a freezer, the boys kept to tradition by joyously ramming all their beer bottles into the snowbank. Eddie had seen this done before and delighted in the sight of the late drinkers digging deep for the elusive last bottle, only their Greb boots visible, kicking above the grave of so many 2-4s. Empties were boxed for return, ashed into by the endless cigarettes, or mournfully tooted upon, so unlike back home where they were usually hurled into the bush at passing wildlife.

The plan was to party hearty out of doors, under the moon, and soon firewood was being carted *out* of the house to build a bonfire in the snow. Inside the house, the featured feature was a display of the outdoors, in the post-Magritte form of a full-grown birch tree that rose, encased in a cylinder of thermal glass, in the centre of the living room; and branched out through the roof.

'What happens if the tree dies?' she asked Mary. 'Will you have to tear down the house and rebuild it round a new tree?'

Mary seemed embarrassed by her family's uncool opulence. She was a quiet one, Mary Kendricks of Kendricks Motors, like her mother, who had quietly handed her the cottage keys. So unlike her roaring father, who knew nothing about all this.

'If dad finds out, he'll kill me,' she said, which Eddie amplified.

'Guys! GUYS!' Her whistle worked beautifully, though she'd learned she could not employ it at school without attracting the Principal, the Grey Ghost himself, prowling the corridors of learning.

'If Mr Kendricks finds a lot of mess he'll murder his only daughter, so let's keep it clean, shall we?'

Drink kept appearing in her hand, in everybody's hands. The hardwood fire blazed and crackled, raising emphatic smoke-signals towards the half moon. Party Here. Party Now. Picnic tables and heavy lawn furniture, apparently designed to use the most wood possible per chair, were dug out and dragged up from the shore. Bags of ghastly sour-bubble-gum-flavoured chips were passed around. A stinky spit-wet cigarette was passed around, and Eddie, who didn't smoke, politely passed it on twice before she woke up to what it was.

'Just for interest, that's pot isn't it? Cannabis?'

'Nope,' said Parson, preparing its replacement. 'It's just a Marlborough with hash oil. You've got to go to Halifax to get decent grass. Stuff they sell at school's goldenrod.'

'Goldenrod – that's the good stuff, right?' she inquired, but they only snickered until someone explained that it was a weed that grows on the railway tracks.

'I mean weed. Weed's pot, right? Right?'

Where had she been all her life?

With no wind-chill, the fire kept at least the front parts of their bodies warm. Its yellow flames glowed out onto the white sheet of the lake. Strange songs were sung, more advertising jingle than campfire song, gross jokes told, or befuddledly attempted, and Eddie grinned in the darkness, and enjoyed her fruit-juice drink.

Jackman leapt up, yelling, 'Let's do wheelies on the lake!' but Eddie only grinned again, knowing she had locked the van and stuck the keys down her bra, where they would be safe. The boys rattled the rented van's door locks and kicked the tires for a while, but then returned. No worries.

Some food would be nice.

Ta Dah! Meat appeared and was dumped before them, and Mary and Dobson handed round an assortment of toasting forks and forked sticks, to allow the true savages to at least burn their meat (mercifully pre-cooked) in the flames before dousing it in sauce and wolfing it down. Corn, too, appeared, and defrosted white bread with briefly microwaved butter. Jumbo tubs of parti-coloured ice cream followed, and hot Sarah Lee cakes, as a number of the troops now had the 'mad munchies' and would otherwise have ransacked the house for cookies. Bad coffee.

Eddie was telling them about Australian men, a sorry lot. How she had developed her strong arms wrestling off surf club types in parked cars, and usually ended up, after a date, having to walk home. One night she had been ordered out of the car and had walked home, in full party dress, from North Head, arriving just in time for breakfast. Her mother hadn't said a word but her father had red rage in his eyes.

She was tempted to tell them a joke on the subject, but wasn't sure she could remember the whole punch line. Something about the farmer's daughter who was a paraplegic, and the travelling salesman, something or other. Oh, yes! The next morning the farmer shook his hand and called him a real gentleman, because, because, 'You brought her home. Most blokes, when they're finished they just leave her hanging on the fence and I have to go out and get her.' Something like that. She'd never have got through it, though.

But Steven, Steven was a real gentleman.

'You love him, don't you,' one of the girls marvelled.

'Sure do. He's a bit of a shit and he only really cares about his racing cars, but I love him. I love him,' she repeated, and began to sob.

She shared in the next round of illegal breathing, just to be a sport – they were all so *young* – and later found herself giggling quietly, wondering what their dog, if they had a dog, thought of the tree in the glass case.

Then talk turned to sex, and as if on cue, the sky darkened – the moon had already swung behind black clouds – and snow began falling. Big, soft flakes, falling into the flames, falling onto their faces. Wet on the tongue. If you looked straight up you knew you were flying, flying into the universe.

Later she heard herself telling them about being thrown out of the confessional at ten. They were all ears as she related her awful, true story. They had been ordered to confess, but at ten she couldn't think of anything she had done wrong – apart from using little flowers, lilies of the field, to play with herself, which was surely not a sin. But then she remembered the phrase, 'Impure Thoughts.'

'Father, I have had Impure Thoughts.'

'What were these Impure Thoughts, my child?'

But there she stuck. She thought wildly of saying something about her puppy but was now completely out of ideas and sat there, sweating, in her confessional dress.

'Well, my child?'

'Impure Thoughts about my puppy.'

She could hear the priest breathing faster, losing his temper, and suddenly he hissed. 'Get out of my confessional!'

She knew she had done something so wrong that it could never be forgiven.

So that was it, really, for her Catholicism.

But *why?* Why did he kick you out? They all wanted to know.

'God knows. I think he thought I was sending him up or something. You know, taking the mickey out of him. But at the time...'

'Like, wow!'

Jackman then theorized that the priest was real ticked off at missing out on a juicy bit of sex gossip, but nobody had any other suggestions.

However, they had heard her out, and that felt comforting.

Steven had heard the story many times, but she never quite got that he had *got* it.

She sensed that the psychologist in him really believed she had remembered it wrong, or misinterpreted what really happened, or misheard it in the first place – which is probably why she had to keep on telling him the story.

But the Fodderton High Ski Team had listened, patiently, and they had heard her.

That Jill

'You were one of Paul-the-Prick's motor racing buddies, weren't you! I think I saw your legs sticking out from under his car once – who the fuck *are* you, anyway?'

'Steven Butts. How do you do. Thanks for the cuppa. I'm a friend of Linda's.' (Wow! This woman was Impatience in a Pantsuit.)

'I sort of gathered that, snoring away in her bed. Well – sorry if I was a bit sharp there. I, aagh, you wouldn't want to know.'

'No, really. Please tell me. I'm not going anywhere.' (He wasn't, either, not with the roaring hard-on he was trying to keep down with his cup and saucer.) He saw the airline tag on her case from...Hel? Hell? Helvetica?

And she told him the story. She had just had a break-up, the final break-up, with her Greek boyfriend in Athens. Steven nodded, in full listening mode.

'I just couldn't face having to go through the big emotional yelling showdown scene thing one more time. They expect you to do it regularly. The Big Scene. It's expected. I couldn't be bothered. After two years? That's enough. Piss on 'em – now I've *got* to have a bath before I die. Did you leave any hot water?'

'I haven't used any.' (I'm in enough hot water as it is, he nearly said.) 'But maybe you could leave yours in when you're finished? I'm sticky as hell.'

'Right you are.' Though clearly mad, she was not hard to talk to. He was remembering now.

'So did you ever get your masters in Psych?' he called.

'Sure. Got it here.'

Wow.

'And you play the cello?'

'Not me, mate.'

And right on cue, a knock on the door. Not quite a knock, more a tentative tapping, an apologetic, questioning sort of knock. TATA...TA?

'This'll be interesting,' said Jill and opened up. In tiptoed a red-haired young man in a mackintosh, who flashed a look of stark terror as he saw Steven reclining bare-chested, armpits-to-the-breeze in the bed, centre stage. All in all, he handled it rather well. Pretending that the man in the bed was only an apparition, he strode across to the cello case, lifted it, plucked up the music stand too, and then stood addressing Jill, who was now leaning against the doorway, delightedly waiting.

'Got the day off,' said Hugh Streeves-Grevesby. 'Thought I'd do my practice while herself's at work.'

'Go for it,' said Jill. 'You might as well practice in my room, All my crap's still in here.' After selecting a small, elegant bag from the growing suitcase collection, she set off bathroom-wards.

Steven rattled his empty cup back into his saucer and lay back, the two mad people gone, his erection gone. A pee would be nice. The perfumed bed was still nice.

The luscious tones of a cello warming up began emerging from behind the closed door. The bloke was good, alarmingly good. He began playing one of the few cello pieces, apart from *The Swan*, that Steven recognised, having read about it in some book and looked it up: the second, slow movement of Shostakovich's First Concerto. He sat up in bed to listen. Such... such emotion.

Not quite his cup of tea, though. His kind of music was more *Over the Rainbow*, Maynard Ferguson's trumpet climbing into the sky on EmArcy's *Dimensions*. No, more to the point: the stern, rising blare of a well-tuned Cosworth four-banger. Or a flat six, the meaty bellow of a racing Porsche 911. A mob of Repco-Holden straight sixes sounded sweet music too, chasing each other up and down Mount Panorama at Bathurst. Such sweet thunder. No – the 250F Maserati at Bathurst! The ultimate six.

Or a V8, and not one of those dumb, woofling boat anchors the Americans seem to worship, but the Aussie Repco, the little engine that 'Black Jack' Brabham got the local spare-parts company to put together, that won him the World Championship. Twice. Or the ultimate Horsepower Concerto, the sound that Steven had read about and now heard in dreams, the scream of the V12 Ferraris down the three-mile straight at Le Mans at night.

Bet the guy straddling his little cello drives a Morris Minor. If at all. Hugh Whatever-Hyphen. Tootle-OO, Hugh.

Jogging with Jill. She ran like a girl but, surprisingly, seemed to be keeping up. She had insisted on coming, sensibly pointing out that he'd get lost at the first turn (how did she know that?) and that, like him, if she didn't get some exercise soon she would go crazy. 'Apeshit' was the term she used. They were circling some park with a pond, the damp grass still green, under immensely old trees with bare branches like charcoal sketches on the sky.

An ancient man in a cloth coat was flapping along, desperate to fly a huge box kite, but there was no wind. Round the cold grey pond, other ancient men were shooing their model yachts away. But there was no wind. Had there been wind, they would have thought they were frozen and all gone home to drink tea.

Jill was trying to keep some weird monologue going but was not quite fit enough. Unconsciously, Steven picked up the pace, and soon she was quiet. She wore stretchable signal-bright petrochemical derivatives, and her perfumed fumes rose with her core temperature, while Steven had chosen a more natural-fibre look, and smelt increasingly like a mob of wet sheep.

He tried not to think of that clean, mag-wheeled blue Mini Cooper they had trotted past, parked right outside the flat. Its oversized add-on chrome tailpipe announced that the owner was suffering from exhaust-pipe envy. A fool. And the 'I (heart) my cello' sticker pronounced him, to Steven's way of thinking, an idiot. Probably got a pet name for his cello, like 'Mastroiani,' he sneered to himself. 'This is my cello Mastroiani.' Dickhead.

Side by side they circled clockwise. Approaching anticlockwise was a plump figure who had clearly, as he'd read somewhere, 'mastered the difficult skill of running at walking pace.' Steven recognised him, with the small mental kick of seeing someone in the wrong place, the wrong hemisphere.

'It's Clive Jones!'

'James.'

'OK, Clive James then. Gate-crashed my twenty-first. Knew who he was, read him in *Honi*. Seen him onstage, Union Revues. Never met him, still haven't. Barbecue at our place at twenty-two Boomerang. You know, playroom, swimming pool blasted out of a rock. Wisteria out. Full moon. Night Teddy McAlpine – remember Teddy, the Libertarian in the Psych Department?'

'Sure. Fat.'

'Night Teddy came dressed as a cardinal. Stood on a rock over the pool. Pontificated. Malediction. Anyway. Up by the fire, I heard Clive Jones holding forth. "The Butts have got plenty of money," he announced. "But they use it well." Well, thank *you*. Hi, Clive!'

But Mrs Jones' boy kept his bald head down, soldiering on.

'Hi Clive!' said Jill and the effect was instantaneous. The head snapped up and his legs, relieved, halted under him.

'Mole! What're you doing here?'

'Walking my dog, what does it look like?' Jogging on the spot she looked around. 'Damn! He's got away *again*.'

'Hi Clive! I don't think we've actually met –'

'Haven't seen you around for ever, Mole! You still doing those fake interviews for a crust?'

'Keeps me off the street. Gotta keep going or I'll cramp up. See you on the telly!'

'Always a treat! Say hi to the lovely Linda.'

He ordered his legs back into motion.

'Got one for you,' called Jill as Clive got under way, 'Perseus and the Monster.'

'Andromeda.' He was quick. They left him.

'He's trying to get some astronomy series going,' she explained.

'Do you know *everyone*?'

'I don't know you. Amazing we both spent four years at Sydney. And never bumped into each other.'

'I was before your time. Older and wiser than I look.'

'Might have seen you, though. *En passant*. Read a study somewhere says "Love at First Sight" never *is*.'

'First sight. Yeah. Read that, too. First sight of you was at Paul's. Must confess I liked that dress with the square holes. Round the waist. Kept trying to peek in. Not in love with you, though.'
'Not in love with you, either. Don't worry about it.'
And they picked up the pace.
...Then slowed as another figure approached, this one having mastered the even more difficult art of walking at running speed. Tall, theatrically handsome.
'Hi Harry!' said Jill, but he only glanced up and waved vacantly.
'Some old boyfriend?'
'Hell, no. That was Harry Bumphreys.'
'Really? I *love* him. I should chase after him, get his autograph.'
They walked on at walking pace, agreeing that the creator of Bazza McKenzie was an Australian comic genius. For years he'd had the English wittily using traditional Aussie slang that the Aussies hadn't even heard of yet.
'Clive Jones writes hilarious stuff but Bumphreys *is* hilarious.'
'Linda can't stand him. She says his damn Edna's a bit too like her mum for comfort.'
'Edna *is* her mum. Miss Moonie Ponds herself. You know I went to school with Harry Bumphreys? Camberwell Grammar. He was ahead of me and I never heard the stories about him till years later. I guess they tried to hush it up. We *had* to attend the inter-school football matches, and apparently he'd sit with his back to the play, knitting.'
'He's brave as Ned Kelly.'
'Funnier, too. What was that show of his called, at the Phillip Street theatre? *Nice of you to Come?*'
'*A Nice Night's Entertainment.* God that was a funny show! I kept crossing my legs and praying. By the end there wasn't a dry seat in the house.'
'Remember when he said, "Of course, the Catholics get all the good locations, don't they!" It was like lancing a boil –'
'Boiling a lance –'
'The audience was on the floor.'

'Hands and knees!'

'Hands and knees! My sister and I went backstage afterwards.' He shook his head, smiling at the memory. 'She wanted to give him a bunch of gladioli she'd brought. He was very nice, took them graciously, said, "Of course, they're eternal." Nobody else around. I think he scares people off, hurling those glads around like javelins. Otherwise they'd give him a knighthood. Eddie hates him, says he's like Clive Jones, too smart for his own good. Woody Allen ditto.'

'Who's Eddie?'

'My, ah, buddy in Canada.'

'He's a guy? You're full of surprises. No?... Oh!' Her grin burst through. 'Miss Big Tits!'

They halted under an oak that was chained to a heavy park bench, presumably to discourage theft.

Back in Canada nobody bothered to steal the trees – they were free for the taking. Back at FU, even on the frigid mid-winter nights they kept hearing the chainsaw whine of the amateur logger who was felling the campus maples and pines, a few at a time, just for the pleasure of yelling 'Timber!' and watching them topple. Likely a drunken student, but nobody was too concerned; there were plenty more trees where they came from.

Cut down a tree, plant a seedling, wait a hundred years and you could cut it down again. FU's Professor of Logging could diagram the process for you.

Steven stretched his calves, as if trying to push down the oak, alerting a patrolling constable.

Then they both stretched, using the bench. Jill was flushed and – and impressively supple. The girl could do the splits forwards, backwards, sideways, doubtless on her head. Steven tried not to stare, and said nothing, maintaining the frown of the serious stretcher at work.

Then: 'Boy, you can really *stretch*,' he said, as her forehead settled down on one shin.

'It just feels so nice. I do it all the time.'

It was all so smooth and easy, and abruptly he thought of

Eddie doing her ballet stretches, sweating and grimacing. And when Eddie lifted her leg to the front or the side, or especially to the back, it didn't go very high.

Ballet dancers were supposed to be loose; he'd seen one youngster – in a class Eddie dragged him to – enter late. She'd duck-waddled up to the barre, kicked the back of her head with one foot, kicked the back of her head with the other foot, and announced, 'I'm ready.'

Poor Eddie was never quite ready. Tight.

As they jogged back, his runner's high let silly rhymes go around in his head, and he recalled Spike Milligan's poem about Soldier Neddy, who, unlike Soldier Freddie, was never ready.

'*...so while Soldier Freddie was standing at attention at six o'clock in the morning in the pouring rain being ready and steady,*
Soldier Neddy
Was home in beddy.'

A Long Night

Eddie found an empty room and slipped into the bottom bunk. The room, the Kendrick house was now totally dark. But someone had followed her in and sat on the bunk, wanting to continue the conversation about sex. He had that self-pitying tone she despised, but he sounded close to tears and was convinced that she, as his biology teacher and a woman, had the answer.

'I'm seventeen next week,' he snivelled, 'and I've never done it with a girl, and it's driving me crazy. I'm a laughing-stock.'

'There isn't any rush,' she said kindly, slipping back out to sit beside him. The room felt steadier with her feet on the floor. 'I was twenty-four.'

'But I'm a guy! And for guys, it gets real rough. It gets hard all the time and it hurts, I mean it really hurts.'

Soft murmurs of agreement drifted from the darkness.

'Blue balls,' someone prompted.

'What on earth are blue balls?'

'Like you can't get anyone to sleep with you so your balls swell up and they go blue, and they ache like you wouldn't believe.'

'But...all you have to do is, you know, relieve yourself.'

There was a long silence.

'How?'

'Well, personally, I just put myself under the tap.' Stunned silence. 'In the bathtub. I've been doing it forever. When I was little we had this gas heater with the long spout. You had to light a match and toss it in and it went FFOOMP! and used to scare me. Anyway, the warm water came out in a thin stream, well into the bathtub. And it landed right between my legs, right on that spot. And it made me, you know, have an orgasm.'

Everyone wanted to know, urgently, where that spot was. But she couldn't remember its name to save her life. Carborundum? Ginglimus? Clytemnestra.... She went scientific: 'It's located, ah, ventrally of the urethra. Ventrally of the vagina'

(Vageena? *V*a*g*ina? Nobody ever said these words aloud.)
'Which way's ventrally?'
'Towards the front.'
'But which front? I mean if your girl's lying on her front, which side is ventrally?'
'Nearest the belly button, the navel. Okay? So from the front, heading dorsally, it goes – ah, the spot, then the urethra, where you pee – *we* pee, then the, ah, vageena, with its *labia majora* and its *labia minora...*' (Except that my *minora* are a bit too *majora* for me) 'then a little space, I don't know its name, and then the anus. Then the coccyx,' she added, pleased at having got through it.
'The *what?*'
'Tailbone,' someone prompted.
Eddie felt good, fizzy. She felt an urge to recite, 'The naming of parts is a difficult matter, it isn't just one of your party-time games...' but bit her tongue.
Outside the snow fell, muffling all sound. Only breathing could be heard, and deep in the house, fridges and freezers worked hard to keep their temperature the same as outside. Some skiers were sleeping but nobody snored.
'So – that Eureka thing in the bathtub, how long did it take?'
'No time. Straight away – I heard Mum coming once and shot back so hard I banged my head. Anyway, that's how *I* do it. Nowadays, I have to sort of scrunch down the bath with my legs up in the air to get under the faucet. Usually after I've let the water out. It's so easy it's not even worth talking about. You guys should try it. If my thing stuck out like yours I'd use the shower.'
'Like a cold shower?'
'No, hot. Not too hot, not too cold, just right.'
'Can you do it standing up?'
'Well, yes, but I feel pretty silly.'
'It doesn't work for guys,' someone said, mournfully.
'Well, okay, so just grab it and rub it up and down. I know *that* works. Steven does it a bit when he thinks I'm not looking.'
The longest pause yet. A breathing pause.
'Oh, come *on!*' she said. They couldn't be *that* clueless.

The young man sitting beside her took her right hand and placed it gently on his cock, which was stiff, and she gave it a comforting squeeze. He took it out and she gripped it – what tiny cocks Canadians had, like thumbs! Was it the cold? – and cheerfully rubbed it up and down, counting aloud.

'One, two, three – twelve, that's all you get – four, five, six...'

Somehow, counting aloud made it less embarrassing.

'Eleven, twelve. Okay.' There was a shuffling forward. '*Okay*,' she said resignedly. 'Next customer. Anyone says a word, *one word*, they're disqualified.'

Another little cock slid into her hand in the thick darkness. 'No – other side. Sit on my left,' and she began counting, rubbing cheerfully and not really counting every stroke, but counting.

'...ten, eleven, twelve.'

Another, smallest yet, gave a series of quick pulses on three, and by twelve was, oddly, losing its stiffness. She was glad that no slime had come oozing out; her hand stayed dry. How convenient to be a guy and not to get all damp when you got excited.

The next person sat down, she had no idea who, and presented his stiff offering. She was pretty sure these guys all knew how to relieve themselves and were just playing dumb, but it was a friendly little ritual, and they seemed to enjoy it. She was being a good sport. Probably they would all have liked to make love to her but that wasn't going to happen. That was definitely not going to happen. She rubbed hard and counted him out.

Your arm could get tired.

Another pair of legs shuffled up, as if with underpants round its ankles, and he sat beside her, his arm loosely round her shoulder as she did her dirty dozen ritual or lesson or whatever it was. With her eyes shut felt best. She felt, it felt better. The dark was comfortingly sensual.

The next was a surprise. There was no cock. It was a girl.

Undaunted, Eddie licked her page-turning finger and just rubbed away at the sensitive spot, but the result was odd. The little thing began to recede and shrank back inside its hood by twelve, as if it hated it, though the girl's hips were vibrating as if *she*, on the other hand, rather liked it.

Clearly Eddie had a lot to learn.

Another, then a softie. She was getting better at it, though.

The next cock in her hand felt exactly like Steven's. Exactly.

In a dreamy way it actually *was* Steven's, and when she reached a slow twelve she bowed her head and gave it a little appreciative kiss on its smooth knob...which swelled so gratefully under her lips that she opened her jaws and slid slowly down it.

Like a fireman sliding down a brass pole, but it had interesting texture and shape – until it hit the back of her throat and triggered a retch.

'Sorry.' She tasted her last drink, orange and rum, then: 'That's enough. Sorry, that's it. Really. I've got to get some sleep.'

They were good about it. They shuffled out. Never again.

(And surprisingly, back at school she was never teased about this night – always prepared, primed to blush, but it was never mentioned again.)

Nor would she ever try that with Steven's cock: what a surprise, that retch! Her throat still burned with the acid, and she hoped desperately it hadn't burned whoever-it-was's knob.

But there was something else... She had felt, she was sure she had felt, the lightest, dearest touch on the back of her head, the faintest hand pressure downwards – but instantly withdrawn when she got into trouble. So tentative, so...loving.

Almost a touch of love. If only Steven had such delicacy, such...sensitivity?

She could still feel the phantom hand on her nape as her head weighed into her pillow. She dreamt of a sunrise at her favourite beach, the sun-god rising from the Pacific and sending its first orange ray across, through the small ripples to her. Steven was there. But when she woke it was still snowing, and from her window she saw the trees wrapped in snow like winter blossoms, and the van cocooned. Mary Kendrick had slept in the upper bunk. Oh. Didn't realise anyone was up there.

She felt fine. On the wall opposite her bed hung a beautifully framed picture, which she inspected with a chronic dope-smoker's attention to detail. A tall man in black robes stood blessing a group of kneeling Redskins, with canoes and piled-up supplies in the background. There was something...slime on his face so she got a tissue and wiped it carefully, though it left a faint halo of stain around his head.

Inset were two smaller scenes, Indians inexplicably carrying their canoe, and Indians in a canoe hurtling over a high waterfall, perhaps to show how badly they needed guidance from the white man in black.

'Father Brebeuf' or some such was written underneath, in a childish hand. The picture's dimensions suggested the top part of a calendar, perhaps for Kendrick Motors. It looked old.

She hoped Mr Kendrick would never notice the faint stain, because Steven had talked of him as a possible sponsor for his formula racing car campaign: the MGB was only a start.

And tonight Steven would be home.

They spooned in the children's breakfasts that Canadians love.

(Down Under it was a real meal, often with steak and eggs; certainly bacon.)

The Morning Cry of the Skier was heard: 'Let's get there before the powder's all gone!' and she tossed Jackman the keys – poor Steven could never catch anything – knowing there was a mass of shovelling before the van was in any danger of moving. A posse attacked it, Don Quixote-style, with brooms.

Others approached the day by climbing on the house roof and doing stunt-man falls into the snow drift.

She laughed as Parson, shot in the belly by Cane, staggered backwards and flew yowling through the air – and later emerged like an Abdominal Snowman, still shot, but clutching the last of the beer bottles. He snapped off the cap in his perfect front teeth and held it aloft, the Statue of Libertines? Her mind was generating puns and she ordered it to stop trying to be punny. Lowest form. And no more drugs; silly.

As Parson drank the half-frozen beer, Eddie prayed he'd not chipped a tooth; you're supposed to use the molars. She noticed teeth. The last of the pre-fluoride generation, she envied the flawless whiteness of these kids' proud smiles. Mind you, they were all from well-off families. In her Health Class she had seen some horror-show mouths from the other side of the river.

The dozy ones, who only cringed and blushed when she breezily asked, 'Hands up those who had breakfast this morning?' or who had managed only a Coke and a candy bar, often had appalling teeth, with goalie gaps or, unbelievably, dentures.

She had pretty fifteen-year-old twin sisters with a full set of dentures, upper and lower.

'Me dad said, "Get 'em all out early and like you'll never have any trouble,"' one had lisped in explanation. Already the twins' jaws were caving in. Later Dianne, the sociologist, had explained that Welfare didn't stretch to dental expenses. Welfare, then, was the Dole, Pogey. And no, even if the twins' father stayed sober – a major challenge – he couldn't get work, because when you're a logger and the trees are coming down faster than they're going up, nobody needs you. (Was *that* who kept taking down the FU trees in the dead of night? Was it him, keeping his hand in?)

Nobody needed the fishermen either, though the sea was still jumping with fish. It was all mechanised away. As Dianne lowered her voice to explain, over the whole province lay the dead hand of K.C. Irving, the lumber/oil/shipping magnate who so splendidly kept alive the nineteenth century Robber-Baron tradition.

This was all new to Eddie, though her grandfather had been a fierce Labour man and parliamentarian, so she recognised a few of the terms. But no jargon was needed when Dianne gave her one clear example: one fall, a raft of K.C's branded logs floating down river broke up and scattered. And all that winter, which was killing cold, K.C. had his men out scouting through New Brunswickers' woodpiles. And if they found a single branded log, they pressed charges and had the man arrested. And still do. Nobody has dared touch a K.C. Irving log since. They'll freeze to death rather than touch one.

A different story: Dianne's brother, in the Government (the only place with steady jobs, it seemed), swore he called on one career welfare family who kept bitching that they needed more (free) fuel oil, they were freezing, couldn't keep the house warm – and found a porthole-sized hole punched through the wall.

'Why don't you fix it?' he asked the head of the household.

'*You* fix the fickin' thing,' he was told. 'It's your fickin house!' Dirt floor, colour TV. This was a strange province, all right.

And as she chauffeured them cautiously out and headed upriver, she asked what the faint smell of rotten eggs was.

'That's K.C. The Irving pulp and paper mill at Saint John,' said Tom Cane. She rather liked his hair, a cap of brown feathers.

'But that's twenty, thirty miles away!'

He nodded. 'On a clear day you can smell forever. Imagine if you lived there. They used to have this tourist trap called The Reversing Falls, the tide comes in so fast it flows up the rapids, it really does. You know about our sixty-foot tides in the Bay of Fundy?'

'Sure.'

'Well, old K.C. thought, Here's the perfect, God-given spot for my mill. It'll wash the effluent away four times a day. Perfect.'

'So did it work?'

'Not really. You just get a great wad of foam moving back and forth. Amazing how any salmon can get through it but they do. You can watch it from the bridge, one of the seven wonders of the world – or you *could* until the acid fumes dissolved the steel.'

Jackman chipped in. 'So the city paid to rebuild the whole bridge, and the next week it blew up!'

'That's right! The Irving gas station right next to the bridge went up and took it out again.'

Eddie was getting the idea.

'So the city paid to fix it again, right?'

'Bridge *and* the gas station. Sometimes,' mused Tom, 'it's hard to believe you're living in the Nineteenth century.'

'I hear it's the Twentieth.'

'NOOO!'

'Don't make me laugh when I'm driving.'

As they worked their way back towards Crabbe Mountain she realised that whatever had happened last night, they had either forgotten or had somehow agreed not to talk about it. It had entered the region of myth, the pretend-forgotten domain of matters too important, too…to bear thinking about.

Jackman tried to break the peace by asking, out of the blue, 'Mrs Butts, why do guys have nipples?'

She took her eyes off the road for only a second to shush him. It was over. (Good question though: she had no idea why; probably an evolutionary mistake.)

He made one more try before getting the message: 'Eddie, in the bath... what do you think about?'

'Nothing,' she said, truthfully, and shushed him once more, thoroughly, the effort nearly landing them all in the ditch.

Tonight Steven would be home, and she couldn't wait to tell him about her driving the van. About the kids, too. Anything about sex caught his interest. He had always shown an unflattering lack of sexual jealousy towards her. Not that he'd had any reason, since she first laid eyes on the handsome bastard, but it was irritating. He really didn't mind. Or care, more like it.

Or care.

She'd never skied powder before and was astonished by its swiftness, the lovely quiet swish. She laughed as she merged into it, and was grateful for help in collecting her scattered equipment each time. But then she got the timing: it was a graceful, patient up-and-down dance, and at lunchtime the boys agreed that they had never, ever seen a first-timer pick it up so fast.

'Wait till you see Steven,' she said. 'He'll probably ski it backwards.'

The whole team cheerfully pushed the van back into the rental car park, and the clerk expressed sarcastic surprise that they had managed to put 195 miles onto it without driving anywhere.

'Oh, that. Wheelspin,' explained Jackman.

They paid with a credit card, something Eddie had never seen.

'Who actually gets the bill?' she asked, but nobody seemed sure. The school, or somebody's father. Whatever.

Linda Comes Home

'Let's head for home,' said Jill. 'I'd hate to get *too* healthy.'
Home.
Where was home? Steven followed her, but spotted Harrods and insisted on a detour. He trotted, reeking, in the door to buy splendid floppy green towels for Linda.

(Naturally, when that evening he handed Linda the big parcel she said, 'Gosh – I don't get quite *that* wet.' '– For Jill too,' he said. It seemed only fair.)

This time Jill gallantly let him have the first bath and all the meagre hot water, and then used his. The tiny tinny radio played *A Day in the Life* and he felt like 'a lucky man who made the grade.'

He rang Linda at work and told her all the news.

She sounded delighted he was getting on so well with her roommate, who, before her trip to Athens, had been very 'down in the dumps. I think she broke up with the big fellow. Too much emotion needed. She'll ask you to do one of her questionnaires, next. Please don't say no. The rent money's coming up.'

Steven said yes, and was all prepared to be brilliant and witty, but Jill surprised him:

'No need to do the questions, I can do that. I just need you to sign that you did it on such and such a date, so I get paid. I just can't seem to do the signatures.'

'How do you know what to put in the answers?'

'Oh, they're easy. I know what they want to hear.'

His professional hackles rose. This was not Social Psychology research as he knew it from Sydney and Oxford, nor Marketing Research which he had done, with methodological rigour, for three years.

This was academic fraud, and he found he was close, very close to saying, 'Sorry Jill, I just can't.'

But he just did. She was unsurprised.

In revenge for her corrupting him he asked an impertinent question.

'Tell me, do Greeks do it, you know... Or is that just a myth?'

'Greek style?'

'Yes, Greek Style, or is that just a myth?'

'You mean did my Greek boyfriend do me Greek Style? Is that what you want to know?'

'Yes. Did he?'

'Gee. I can't tell you – I never looked.'

'Never look back, eh?'

'Exactly.'

She was so funny. He liked her a lot.

After lunch, white bread sandwiches with margarine and mystery spread, she proposed an outing to view the Nolans, and was impressed that he knew she meant the Ned Kelly series. But how could an Australian not know! Sidney Nolan, yet another dazzling export to London.

Not that the Aussies seemed as impressed as the Poms.

The 'cultural cringe' made it obligatory to say a fond farewell to any obvious talent with, 'So, we're not good enough for yiz, are we?' and then, years later, to welcome home the triumphantly returning artist with, 'So, yiz all washed up now, couldn't make it overseas. Don't say we didn't tell you.'

Ned Kelly, the Don Quixote of Oz, their Irish knight in bullet-dented armour who stood against the troopers, both pistols blazing, and refused to bend – until they broke the rules and shot out his knees.

'Such is life,' he had sighed on the scaffold, and Australians have worshipped him ever since. Now the Brits were getting their chance.

Arriving at the gallery steps, Jill had to drag him away from admiring the four-cylinder engine of a rakishly-parked Honda CB-750 motorbike ('That's a thing of *real* beauty') and in they went.

The paintings were huge, thoughtful, disturbingly beautiful. Jill seemed to know her painters.

He wondered what it meant, the helmet eye-slot having no head behind, just air.

'It means just that,' she said quietly, pointing back at the painting, and he felt bad about the 'airhead' joke he had just bitten off. She knew her stuff.

Then he scored one. A familiar head of hair that could only belong to Bob Hughes strode past, surely en route to New York to make his name as a pointillist.

'Hey, it's another genius Aussie, Rupert, ah, Hughes. I know him.'

'Why don't you talk to him, them?'

'Don't know him all *that* well. I was envious as hell of the guy at Sydney. He really *is* a genius. *And* he stole my girlfriend in Arts 1, the almond-eyed Doll Bryan, became an almoner. I can still remember one of his poems from *Honi* - a*n ageing man is but a paltry thing, a tattered coat upon a stick, unless he clap his hands and sing...* Wow! Where does he *get* this stuff?'

'I've read it somewhere. I think Geoff Lehmann wrote it.'

'You know I went to school with Geoff? We both debated against Hughes in the school finals. Rupe stammered like a bastard and went minutes overtime but they *still* gave him more points than me. Catholic judges.'

'Try to get over it, old fellow.'

He did, and again they drifted through the Australian dreamtime.

But then she wanted to see the Brigitte Riley exhibition as well, and this was a different kettle of worms entirely.

The Englishwoman had selected precise colour combinations, and thin lines, to produce, within minutes of beginning to stare at the horrid things, the optical illusion of a migraine attack.

Luckily Jill hated them too, and when Steven whispered that he had a headache and that he *never* got headaches, they left, found a small cafe, and drank a large what-the-English-call-coffee.

She didn't want her water, and when he poured hers into his empty glass and momentarily missed, she asked, quietly, what was the matter with his eyesight.

'It's monocular,' he confessed, to his surprise. And to hers, as she knew he was a racing driver. He hated feeling clumsy, mopping at the spilt water. He really only felt graceful at the wheel of a racing car.

They spent rather a long time not talking.

She wore ivory nail polish and drummed on the little table while not talking. Then she took his hand and his heart leapt.

Suddenly he felt so lucky, so happy; he could do anything and everything was possible. Her traffic-light green eyes looked sorrowfully into his and for a moment he was sure she was about to propose a quickie.

'Steven,' she said, 'I'm very fond of her and she loves you very much, you dickhead.'

'Who – Linda?'

'WHO ELSE, YOU FUCKHEAD!'

The diners looked up, briefly.

Then they went home. As she let them in he recognised the strains of the time-honoured cello piece, played without any noticeable vibrato. *The Swan*. The earnest player stopped short and stuffed the lovely, red-varnished instrument away.

Jill vanished, and Steven did The Right Thing and swept Linda out to dinner. Italian.

Afterwards she walked him across some bridge, over the mighty river that Oxonians call the 'Lower Cherwell.'

They halted at her favourite place in all London, the concrete patio of the new Festival Hall.

The Thames gleamed like a Turner canvas on fire.

Already she'd seen such wonderful shows there...

An asterisk hung in the air between them. (*If only you could have seen them *with* me.)

She wished she could get out of London into the country some time, a day in the country. She wasn't complaining, but a day out of London would be so nice.

He added two silent asterisks.

(*He would love, he would *love* to rent a Mini and take her driving into the country tomorrow; *and the best possible place would be Brands Hatch to watch practice for the big race on Sunday.)

But, unbelievably, tomorrow was Saturday and he had to join the flight home.

– And impossibly, the alarm failed to go off. He woke beside the sleeping Linda, the clock steadily, guiltlessly ticking, saw the time, blinked, dry-mouthed, checked it against his bedside watch – and erupted. He was up and running. Packing. Dressing. Trying to pee faster. Unshaven, unwashed, almost unhinged he got it all done – Jill had volunteered to dash out and hail a taxi – he took one sip from the cup of tea Linda held out with shaking hands, gave her a kiss. And was gone.

'Hugh must have done something to the alarm. It's set right. I'm so sorry,' were her last words, before he turned and bolted down the steps of 2B Denbigh Place.

(And did not know, could not have guessed that the highest he would ever climb those steps again, in his life, would be to the second-last step.)

Linda stood on the top step. Jill swung the taxi door open and he kissed her cheek but missed and got her wide mouth instead. (Was that a blue Mini Cooper, parked?) The taxi driver did a gentle U-turn, almost in its own length – these things must have more lock than a Lotus 27 – and, cruising along, his cap nodded thoughtfully as Steven shouted the looming flight time, insisting that if he missed his charter he would have to pay full fare on the next flight, whenever that was.

'So you need that plane, Guv.' (Did he say 'Guv'?)

'Desperately,' said Steven, but for one moment he thought how nice it would be to miss the plane and just do another of those improbable U-turns, back to breakfast with Linda and Jill. That sip of tea badly needed more of the same.

'If I'm going to risk me licence it's going to cost you a ten quid honorarium.' (Did he say 'honorarium'?)

'Ten quid it is then. No problem.'

The driver double-shuffled the Austin back to second and floored it, and they were off, as they say, like an Australian simile.

The man was good. On every roundabout the horizon tilted and the tyres moaned.

As he sprinted through Heathrow terminal Steven wished he had held his heavy coat instead of wearing it; steam was rising.

Along the moving walkway, slipstream from his seven-league strides cooled his face, but once his feet hit the carpet again it was pure nightmare, as if the walkway had reversed direction under him. A smooth-haired attendant at the empty boarding counter saw his steaming approach and snatched up her phone. A male attendant ran with him down an endless corridor, down steps – and then he was on a bus.

This driver was good, too.

They approached a plane – Air Canada!

Standing on the tarmac he could see both pilots looking down at him and slowly, slowly shaking their capped heads. No? But the bus has left!

Then a thin ladder unhinged and descended and up he went, luggage and all.

England, clearly, was pleased to see him go.

Canada welcomed him with a roar of laughter.

'Slept in, did you, sir?'

'Swinging London a bit hard to leave, eh?'

'You sure like to make an entrance.'

'Sorry about that, guys. Thanks for waiting.'

He stripped to a damp T-shirt and sat, panting, between two business students, male, who were reminiscing. Amsterdam, it seemed, had not been a popular choice. Holland had turned out to be even flatter than expected and its food was uneatable, 'gross.' In fact they hadn't had a decent burger since leaving home. One Amsterdam dinner had had sixteen courses – but there was nothing you could eat!

'They just kept bringing these little dishes of hot stuff, I mean hot so it burned your tongue. And there were like little mystery meat things you were supposed to dip in peanut butter stuff.'

The hostel beds had been hard, hard foam mattresses, and they were sure some glad to be heading home. (And when finally the plane did touch down on Canadian tarmac the whole group burst into song: *Let's all go – To A and W...* It was burger time again.)

But for Steven, something was happening in flight, something disturbingly painful, like an approaching toothache or nausea. He was not going home. He was going away. Home is where the heart is. These few London days with Linda had been, he realised, the first time he had ever had, well, enough sex. (Eddie didn't count. Weekends only, too much course preparation, too exhausted.) No, enough...calm, continuous happiness, knowing he was loved and wanted.

By two women, that was the thing.

That was why he'd been so deliriously happy, so lucky and confident. Being attractive to a woman makes you attractive to women. He sensed this blessing on him, like a perfume.

He knew now that he could have Jill, on her bed in her unseen bedroom, any time he wanted her. And he did want her. She was his kind of woman: smart, fit, brave as Ned Kelly.

Yet all that joy, that rich possibility he felt beginning to turn inside him, like the walkway reversing direction, and he knew he was going...mad. He must be mad.

How else could he even *imagine* settling in with his beloved Linda – and boffing her best friend on the side?

After three days?

And after a full week, who?

Some of those Oxford girls who had been so close before but no cigar? They must have London flats by now.

Plus any pretty jogger he happened to meet in Hyde Park? Why not do it in the trees?

He was a threat to himself and others, fit to be tied up. He was a philanderer, he really was.

Like in the book, incurable.

It was a sickness, emotional sickness.

If only... If only he had managed to find a lover, a partner, some dream girl as interested in sex as he was, during all those dead years of studying at school, at Sydney and then Oxford, becoming a bachelor of useless arts, master of none.

God knows he had tried, cursing God for His little practical joke, forever hiding the lightness, the enlightenment, the *relief* that would free him from the sex-storm of his mind, that would let him *get on with it*. Would let him keep his nose down and see the page he was supposed to be studying, at home or, worse, in the library – free from the flashing, shadowy images of...temptation?

No, not temptation. Girls.

He wasn't resisting temptation; it was resisting him.

And doing the relief job himself didn't quite hit the spot: the polarity of the electric charge was somehow wrong, short circuit sparks instead of the – the one, true, shared illumination – though he did discover, all on his own as a schoolkid, that doing it with the other hand made it feel like someone else. The first time, anyway.

The theoretical backing for this empirical finding was revealed in a strange book called *Sexual Perfection* that his blonde older sister had stolen from the public library; this dog-eared bible advocated 'Karezza': long, leisurely love-makings, snake-like copulations to fully neutralise the opposing electrical polarities of Male and Female.

Riveted, he'd learned that the reason newly-weds squabble so much is that they screw too often and for not nearly long enough – not that this was of practical help to him.

Every night in his narrow bed the young Steven fell asleep through a rosy, fresh dream-fantasy, set in some familiar part of the neighbourhood, of bumping into The One, the friendly, usually fair-haired, girl who every night in her narrow bed fell asleep through a dream-fantasy of bumping into...him.

But he always woke alone, his cock tapping tentatively at his navel like some one-eyed beggar at the door of an impossible Hellfire club, while the rooster next door announced its own confident presence.

Someone was getting his share, though it was nobody he knew at his all-boys school. Like the true Enlightened Ones, those who knew did not say, while those who did not know talked a blue streak.

As a teenager he was blessed with plenty of low-numbered foreplay, beginning after his final year school dance, but no actual play. No body game. Petting, wonderful, dreamy kissing, delirious above-the-waist, around-the-bra petting with a succession of mermaids in his father's Humber Hawk.

Plenty of delicious chaperoned evenings of cheek-to-cheek dancing in the gloom to *La Mer*, hip-to-hip and, in the turns, unmistakably thigh-to-crotch, and even, once, a drive-in. But every North Shore girl had a sort of built-in sprinkler system that flung cold water on the proceedings whenever her body heat climbed too pleasurably high.

True, he was a heat-seeking missile, part of him, and would in no way have treated them well – though who knows?

But there was treachery on the other side too, and in one case, virgin-to-virgin treachery. The one serious prospect for intercourse was good old organ-playing, high-diving Connie Small from Strathfield, in first year arts, who cheerfully petted both high and low – but then stunned him by announcing one evening, on the North Shore train (though she lived in the opposite direction) that she was pregnant.

Pregnant.

By him.

'A bit must have got on your finger.'

It turned out that she wasn't, of course; he reasoned that it was a nasty trick to keep him from drifting away, because the evening before, on Wynyard Station, he'd agreed, okay, he'd see her tomorrow, but refused to specify where and at what time. 'Around' was not good enough. She'd broken into furious tears.

Yet oddly, he stayed with her, and finally she graduated (magically, without opening a book), and left for Hong Kong to make her fortune in the sheet music copying trade. And did.

But the fear was in him.

And it swelled in Arts II, when that mysterious woman took him home to meet her parents and then, on their wall-to-wall

Axminster, took him. Did he do her or did she do him? Who did it and who was it done to? But when it was done it was done, and, the pregnancy scare in full flight, flapping like a mad bird, he was done for. Her (genuine) madness had infected him.

Or if, during those two years in the City of Dreaming Spires – dreaming, now in more educated detail, of getting laid – he had succeeded, even once. How could he have tried harder? Easy: pay for it. But the sensible notion of paying for it repelled him.

He couldn't imagine getting it up and on with someone who wasn't mad for him. That would be as unthinkable as 'dropping' a girl. Just telling her you never wanted to see her again. Impossible cruelty. Other men could, and bragged of it. He couldn't. Girls were sensitive creatures.

Lovely creatures. So different, and so the same.

Hat-Trick Sunday had turned Sydney into a magic kingdom for him – just before he left it for an endless winter. The over-friendly Julie, the silken-breasted Rebecca, and his own dear, maddening Eddie, last but not least. (Or was it least but not last?)

Lost. He must be mad.

The flight droned on, bearing him away from London. He was, he was insane, a mad man. An Engineer of Women's Hearts, the Celestial Plumber himself. No! Plumbing. He was mere plumbing, a vessel for muscular twitches and glandular squirts.

Every spring, he was reminded: every spring, he fell in love. *Oh, boy! He didn't notice that the lights had changed.* The Lightning Rod of Lust. Mind over matter: at the thought of that now-dead Sunday so well spent, he felt himself unravelling, unravelling. It was getting harder all the time. Dizzying. He snapped down his drinks tray. You break it you bought it.

The plane bumped and jumped.

Something dark was scratching at the lid of his mind, some monster roaring behind glass.

No, not feeling bad about Eddie. She was okay.

She didn't need to know.

Marry in haste, repent at leisure.

Love is a many-splendoured thing.

You may see a stranger.
A thousand songs urging you to fall in love, but then what? Then what?
Blue moon. The Tender Trap.
And who to ask?
Sigmund Freud, the wired cigar smoker?
Woman's Weekly? Woman's Day? Makin' Whoopee. Must be the Season of the Witch.
He had a decision to make.
Tea for Two?
He had to choose...something.

Suddenly it was all up. He snatched for his white paper bag and vomited. He inspected the peanut-flavoured orange mess and added to it, reaching, retching deeper.

'Gross!' said the students in unison.

Hours later (or was it earlier?), standing glazed in the plane's rocking toilet he had the urge to look over his shoulder, and there, in the mirror, someone looked over his shoulder back at Steven. Someone with a white, haunted face, like the Vincent van Gogh self-portrait, Vincent torn between the church and painting.

Steven was torn between the need to sit down and the need to stand up. He shook.

Time to sit down. Where had all this begun?

O Lucky Day

1969 had been a good year for sleeping, but tonight Steven Butts could not get himself to sleep. He was too happy.

He lay back beside his faintly snoring sleeping partner and live-in girlfriend, Eddie O'Malley, grinning at the ceiling through closed eyes, reviewing his day.

The day he died he'd surely remember today, Hat-Trick Sunday, first Sunday in October, the day his luck turned around.

Passing headlights slid by the drawn blinds and over his eyelids. Yet another Holden, Australia's own car, heading busily down Bent Street towards the Sydney Harbour Bridge.

Poor fool. Steven noted the driver's sloppy gear change with satisfaction. The worse others drove, the better he felt, for driving was his thing.

– Had been his thing. Steven Butts had known he was unlucky since 1966. What are your chances, when driving a racing car, of ducking two pebbles kicked up at once by the car in front and then getting hit, smack, by the third one? It was sheer bad luck. A hundred times since then, plucked from dreams or lying half-awake, he had ducked his head, dodging that third missile. And since then, everything bad that happened was solid further evidence of his unluckiness, everything good an anomaly. But today his luck had changed. From drooping at half-mast, his personal pennant was faffling away in a whole new wind.

Today had begun as a fine spring Sunday, the IllawarraFlame Trees glowing lipstick red, the Jacarandas dropping their blue-blossom shadows on suburban lawns, churchgoers in their Sunday best, before a salad lunch, a change into whites for their game of lawn bowls, and for the younger set, tennis.

And for Steven, WOW!

In the dark he smiled his secret up at the ceiling.

Eddie snuggled towards him, fumbling and mumbling in sleep. She had to teach the brats tomorrow. He could sleep in, because his management conference out at Manly didn't start till ten.

He closed his eyes with the self-satisfied 'amen' of a man who had got lucky, a man who had spent the morning, the late afternoon, and just now, making love.

Sleep would be nice. The cars kept on coming. The more sporty drivers changed down for the notorious right-hander, messily, easing out the whinnying clutch, and he rated them all. Nobody could heel-and-toe to save their life. He could. He could, indeed. The Bent Street bend, with the bump right on the apex, was his.

Then another Holden, an FJ with a Lukey 'Arrest Me' muffler flew down the one-way hill, fast, way too fast – his eyes snapped open – braked hard, blipped down to second, squealed into the corner, bouncing towards disaster – and bellowed away with that fruity straight-six tone. And a snap change into top. Nice. Must be a Driver. Steven was a Driver, had held a full race licence – until the bastards took it away, that is, but he would win it back or die in the attempt. Time was passing and Formula One drivers get started in their early twenties, not their late, though Fangio was forty.

Now he was lying wide awake and Eddie was definitely snoring, sadly but with dignity. Such a dear girl. He had worried, as he did it, that he might feel...guilty? Or, worse, that she would somehow find out, but no. No future in confessing – or in bragging to anyone either, not that he was the boff-and-tell type. Soul of discretion. A gentleman. He would sit on his delightful knowledge, lie in its afterglow.

Julie Pearl had warm, dark brown eyes, light brown hair and skied like a man. Was it only three weekends ago, that moonless Saturday night, the last of the ski season, he had barefooted down the Thredbo Downhill Club stairs, late, in the wee hours, for a glass of water...and sensed somebody lying on the sheepskin rug, half-lit by the flickering fire? And had approached, courteously, smiling, as to a strange animal, holding his glass of water, heart thudding, and seen it must be that girl Julie, on her back, with a reflective brandy? And blinked at her breasts pushing improbably high beneath her white, fire-lit turtleneck? And startlingly, she hadn't seemed at all annoyed by his intrusion on her quiet moment, but in fact smiled at him.

No, they hadn't actually been introduced yet, but on the ski lift he'd twisted back to follow her cherry-red ski outfit skimming down through the dwindling snow, alone past Middle Station, dodging and leaping the patches of rising twigs and bushes and ski-wrecking gravel – sticks and stones wouldn't break *her* bones – and then schussing the final steep slope on the blue plastic mats.

That was her.

And after club dinner, over Carols' wondrous transparent strudel, he'd defended her when she reached out to take a turn at reading aloud from the club copy of *Catch 22*, though the club president, a Sydney Uni lawyer type, had pronounced that, 'Allowing a woman to read would constitute altogether too, ah, too unconscionable a departure from club tradition.'

The pompous fool thought he was being amusing.

He handed on the sacred book to another tittering lawyer type, who read of General Dreedle's nurse, her nipples like Bing cherries. 'Like *Bing* cherries,' the president echoed, in a reverent tone, glowering at the upstart Julie Pearl.

The fireplace crackled and fired a spark. This was not a time for talk. And in no time, grinning like kids, Steven and Julie crept upstairs and clambered into his lower bunk in the dark, breathing men's dormitory. Rearing up he banged his head hard on the wood of the upper bunk and they collapsed, shaking, stifling each other's giggles. The darkness was total, enveloping like a blanket, and yet he could just see a glint of merriment in her dark eyes as he recovered his dignity…

So before today, Steven had made love to Julie Pearl exactly once, although, come to think of it, he had come twice, once as he slid inside and then somehow, choosing to ignore this false start, again at the end. (Was it something about her? A knack?) She was most appreciative and seemed to know exactly what she was doing. They moved in silence, though by the end the dormitory breathing had changed: men were awake now, erect and miserable. And when she had kissed him wetly on the mouth and flitted off to the women's dorm, he grinned at the underside of the upper, presidential bunk, and dozed off. After a decent interval, feet and legs emerged and half the men crept downstairs for a pee and a cold glass of water.

To tell the awkward truth, he'd been a late and unlucky starter in the love-making business.

Raised as a young gentleman, he would never dream of forcing unwanted attentions on a young lady, and if the girls he adored *did* want his attentions they never said so, having perhaps been raised to play a waiting game too.

So it was not until second year Arts that he met someone: fast-talking, fast-smoking, wildly intellectual Janet, with the gold-flecked green eyes like kaleidoscopes under a black monobrow, who took him home to her parents' big house for dinner and afterwards, after coffee in tiny cups and Cointreau in tiny glasses, on the parental couch with the MJQ rippling from the Black Box, said so. And took him.

They descended to the carpet, and after a flurry of undressing he was stunned by how outrageously *easy* it was, but a few thudding heartbeats later his mind filled with the dread words, 'Unwanted Pregnancy.' He heard his voice hoarsely apologising, as he pulled out and painted her belly –'Sorry to do this to you,' meaning the early pull-out, of course – though what she thought she did not say. Once she got her cigarette going she refused to believe it was his first time, though.

'A bloke with your looks? Nah,' so that was flattering, in a way.

But the next time they did it she clambered on top, wild-eyed, and locked in he came inside her (twice) and sure enough, the Curse of the Missed Period, the big scare, the nightly phone calls with her sobbing on the line, him pulling faces, eye-rolling but unable to hang up, had somehow... numbed him. The scare ended, but the third time (in her 'safe' period) he could not rise to the occasion, and retired on the spot from trying again.

To hell with the whole business. For years he numbly bore the self-diagnosis of the term his psychology textbook had presented him with: 'erectile dysfunction,' acute, now turning chronic. (No problem when performing solo, of course.)

Driving home from Thredbo that Sunday night (Julie Pearl had flown back) the fog of the twisty Alpine Highway changing to steady rain around Cooma, Steven felt unaccountably happy, and the thought struck him that if he ever *had* been erectively dysfunctional, whatever that was, he was now cured.

Then, after another eight hours of country roads, halting, wipers slapping, for the notorious one-way bridge on the main highway linking Sydney and Melbourne, he was back in Sydney for another weary work week.

The reports, the endless, meaningless reports. A psychologist by training, Steven was doomed to dictate personnel reports on perfectly normal executives all wanting the same job, *and* he was working on his racing car and rehearsing most evenings for a play. Eyes shut, he dictated yet another report, hoping that his secretary wouldn't notice that it was identical to the three before, only the name and position changed.

At last the Dictaphone tape was full and he handed it over, removed the saucer from on top of his heavy cup of stone-cold tea, swigged it — and woke up. He had to see Julie again, *had* to. He charmed her phone number out of the ski club secretary, and shutting his glass door, dialled with a shaky finger. As her phone rang he panicked: finding a time and place for a date would be tricky, with rehearsals, and he *was* living with Eddie. But the swelling problem burst when her breezy answer sang into his ear.

'Oh, Steven, that would be nice, but I'm engaged to be married, to John, you know, John?...' (He did: too-tall, business-body type, a rotten, slow-but-unsteady skier when he managed to get a weekend off, rich enough to keep buying Julie new skis and new ski outfits.) '...And it looks like we're getting married next month.'

'Oh... Well —' (After the wedding? he nearly, nearly said, choking it back.) 'Congratulations — or no, you don't say that to the bride-to-be. Um. Good luck, lots of good luck. Really. John's a very lucky man.'

So. He had given her a call, but too late.
He'd been beaten to it.
Interestingly, it never for a moment occurred to him to feel jealous, or envious of too-tall John, who skied like a girl.

He envied him the silver Porsche 911 linked to his key ring perhaps, but Julie? Could he even have thought of saying, 'No, no! Marry me instead. I love you'?

Never, though he liked her a lot, she had that great knack in bed, her father was a professor at the Uni, she was funny and fearless on skis – but marriage? Never.

The thought of marriage never occurred to him. He'd dismissed the idea years ago.

Why not just go on and on and on as he was? Things were opening up and the Nota, his racing car, was finally running like a dream.

And that was it, except for the phone call at work last Friday. It was Julie. Julie was miserable. She was in bed with the 'flu and going mad with boredom. Couldn't even read. Could he pop round and cheer her up? He would see what he could do.

So on this Sunday morning, as Eddie was doing last night's dishes – she hated doing them straight after the meal – he announced that he had car business, the Nota was misfiring, probably just ignition, better go see Robbie, he'll be working on his Bugatti-Holden for sure – Oh, and that he'll go straight on to the rehearsal at Rebecca Cohen's place afterwards, they're doing a full walk-through – so – See you when I see you.

From the open window Eddie watched him descend the steps, wave once, quickly, his little-boy wave-and-smile.

She watched him clamber elegantly into the funny little yellow sports-racing car that was their transportation and the love of his life. A motorbike would have been more comfortable, a motor scooter luxurious. She had to sit with her knees over the battery full of acid, and once when he was escorting her to her girlfriend's wedding, to keep her neat he'd had her first climb into a plastic garbage bag, before lowering her into her bucket seat and strapping her in.

She watched the love of her life strap on his gold crash helmet, fire up the engine (it had a toggle switch instead of a key but nobody would steal it: nobody else could get it to start), snap down his visor, deftly back out, then tighten his four-point racing harness and roar away. It *was* misfiring.

It was misfiring fruitily because he kept the choke pulled out until out of earshot, and then buzzed through the quiet Sunday morning streets, a man on a mission of mercy. Back at the window Eddie heard the note change. She knew what an ignition misfire sounded like: sharp, not fruity. She was not dumb, just pretended to be – to herself. Otherwise she would have heard and seen too much that hurt. She was as dumb as she needed to be, dumb enough to forget instantly what she had heard, that he must have been driving with the choke yanked out, so there was no need to entertain the niggling suspicion that this lovely man she was in love with, for whom she had given up everything, was a jerk. Possibly, even, a prick.

She could of course phone Robbie, a cheerful little mechanical genius she rather liked, Robbie who had got into big trouble and had to move on, after he told a wealthy client with a blown-up Mercedes engine that he could fix it at a quarter the quoted cost, with more power and guaranteed better fuel economy. And had, too – until the horrified owner found he was now driving a Mercedes-Holden. But of course she would not phone him.

She gazed across the oval towards the little bay with its yachts and a pair of submarines. The married couple down the street, doctors, emerged with their tribe of stray cats circling, tails high, and shepherded them down to the long-jump pit where they did their business in the sand. Well trained, for cats.

On landing, any actual long jumper would have really been in it, but nobody ever jumped into the pit. Except me, she thought. She was in it, for sure.

She turned back to clean up and prepare Monday's lessons.

Julie Pearl's skinny young brother let him in, showed him into the sick room, and after some chit chat about cricket, a game Steven detested, made himself scarce. The bride-to-be lay back with thick, sweaty blonde hair and a mild fever. He brought her a glass of water. He kissed her hot brow and remembered something about Humbert Humbert enjoying his feverish Lolita (in *venus calorifica* was it?) before getting round to calling in the doctor.

Julie patted the bed and he sat.

'I'd hate you to catch my 'flu,' she said, but Steven wouldn't. He was invincible. He peeled off his clothes and tumbled into her warm sheets. She smelt of costly perfume. He was outrageously lucky. He couldn't catch anything, and didn't.

She was subdued afterwards but thanked him for cheering her up. Now she felt like a nap, so he kissed her brow again. He topped up her glass of water.

The rehearsal, for a staged reading with the local amateur players, went well.

The older couple were near-professional level, both secretly convinced that they would have lit up the professional stage in their day had things only been different, and so on.

Steven was one half of the romantic young couple, circling wittily, warily around each other and, at one point, their book-arms intertwined, kissing – a dry, lipsticky affair, far from romantic. It was his first stage kiss and he worried that he might look unconvincing. Once, at Uni, a girl had burst into merry laughter as he approached for the goodnight kiss, his eyes rolling heavenward, but luckily she had explained why, so he'd changed his technique.

He rather liked the look of his leading lady, tall, black-haired Rebecca, but he had seen her acting and she couldn't. Couldn't act for toffee. More to the point, she acted her heart out, but you couldn't bear to watch her – odd, since she was nothing like that when just being herself. She was nice. She liked Steven. When the older couple left she asked him to stay on for lunch and made him a sandwich. Some kind of ham substitute, lettuce, and Velveeta on white bread. He would have liked butter as well – Eddie was always generous with the butter – but didn't ask, as he suspected she would produce margarine, which he detested.

They sipped their strong Lipton's tea, and she suggested they rehearse a bit more, but when they reached the kissing scene, things fell apart rather. His hands roved to her marvellous breasts, she unhooked her bra, removed it, letting him glimpse that it was a 38C, then they lay on the red carpet of her parental home and copulated, loudly, for quite a long time.

Then they had another pot of tea.

Sydney's North Shore being a maniac driver's paradise, Steven drove back to Bent Street like, as they say, a man repossessed. Tap dancing in the cockpit he revelled in the engine's song.

The bucket seat pressed hard against his left side, his right side, as he tossed the little car into the familiar corners, Steven Butts, last of the late brakers.

He double-shuffled down to second and fed the power on, his largish feet playing the tiny pedals like an organist.

They were holy pedals.

They were the very pedals that Colin Chapman had trod in his personal Lotus 11, to win his class at Le Mans, 1960. The Nota had been rebuilt from that actual Lotus (imported and wrecked in its first Australian race), though of course the Coventry Climax engine had long since come and gone.

The front axles, also holy, Chapman had manufactured by sawing a Ford Prefect's front axle in half and mounting each half on a central swivel, which, supported by the famous Chapman Strut (a shock absorber wrapped in a coil spring) created independent front suspension.

The problem, as Steven discovered the first time he drove the Nota (five minutes before he bought it), was that the front wheels then became independent of the normal rules of geometry.

On bumps, the tops of the wheels tilted inwards, and on rebound, outwards, so that at speed the front end had a mind of its own, skittering all over the road.

Unless you were very good.

Steven was very good.

He drove in a cold fury, using every inch of his side, the left side, of the road. Only once did his back wheel overlap a double white line by about an inch, and he cursed himself. Sloppy.

'Did Robbie fix your misfire?' Eddie asked him when he arrived back in time for Sunday dinner.

'Oh, actually the thing seemed to fix itself. I guess it was just the plugs were fouled up and they unfouled themselves once I got going. Thing's running like a charm now. Took it for a burn.'

Back home with his Eddie, Steven was absurdly, ludicrously happy. Delighted with himself.

After an excellent baked dinner, with fruit salad and cream for dessert, they went to bed early and for a moment he wondered if he would, or should, or could make love again.

But then the thought of his possible hat-trick surged in as a sudden turn-on, and, though his girlfriend Eddie at first seemed in two minds about it, she soon got caught up and he made love to her – being careful not to try any new tricks he'd just picked up – as if his life depended on it.

Now she was dead asleep, and her snoring had settled into a soft lament.

Thank God *he* wouldn't have to face her little monsters tomorrow.

The cars had petered out, and Steven was finally, finally sinking into a rosy new world of possibilities.

Monday's conference, for example. It could really be the start of something. Anything at the office would be an improvement.

As a good Australian, Steven was no fan of work.

He lived for weekends, especially those with a motor race.

Work was to earn money to buy parts to make the Nota go faster, or, lately, to go at all.

He'd just had the engine completely rebuilt, emptying his savings account, and now, predictably, the clutch was complaining and the gearbox groaning under the strain of all these fresh horses.

But the future, as the founder of his company had confidently noted in a recent speech, lay ahead. And Steven had volunteered to attend, 'audit' and report back on Canada's Professor Ted Rodman's ground-breaking new three-day 'MBD' seminar.

Perhaps Canada lay ahead, thought Steven, lying back, still grinning all over.

An expert is defined as someone from overseas.

Professor, now Dean, Ted Rodman, author of the influential *Management by Directives* (MBD) had flown into Sydney in a blizzard of brochures, to run his influential training course of the same initials. And Steven's boss at Auscon, a beery businessman who mistrusted all psychologists, the younger the worse, had called him in to suggest he attend. Not just as a participant but as a Trainer-Trainee.

'So Stevie I want you to check it out, behind the scenes, see if Auscon should get into bed with this bloke.'

'Run it in Australia under license?'

'Or not. The Old Man's pretty hot on it. Circulated twenty copies of the MBD book but I'd bet my right knacker he hasn't read it yet.'

'I read it,' said Steven. 'Wanted to see what all the fuss is about.'

'And?'

'This Godman/Rodman character does a great line in bullshit 'n buzz-words but he's got no hard research data. He even claims it's now for "other people" to do the research, prove him right. At their expense. You gotta say this for him though, he's arrogant.'

'Okay. Your baby.'

So, on Monday morning Steven buzzed out to Manly, parked the most un-executive-looking Nota well clear of the conference hotel, and attended Day One of the three-day seminar. Afterwards he told Rodman what he thought of it. Not much.

'You see, Ned –'

'Ted.'

'Ted, I did your Management Mode questionnaire three times: before you came, Day One and this morning – scored it and got three different results.'

They were strolling under the pines, looking down at the Manly beach and its womanly figures sun baking.

'How 'd you get the scoring key?'

'Worked it out; it's just a, b, d right through, right? So unless my management style switches around every time a cloud comes over the sun, what you have here is an unreliable test. Your reliability coefficient is squat, and as you know, until a test is reliable it's not even worth asking the question, "Is it Valid?"'

'Of course. But it's not for me to do the –'

'Sure it is. You're the one claiming it measures what it claims to measure. From my tiny bit of experience in Sensitivity Training seminars, my guess is that the managers who put themselves down as the most democratic, Theory Y, people-centred types are generally the most hard-headed bastards of all. And the poor characters who are forever apologising for being too fascistic and directive are, in fact, the sweethearts. Like bores: bores are boring because they honestly think they're interesting.'

'So… How'd you like to come and work with us at Fodderton U? I'm doing a bit of recruitment, to justify my trip. You'd be on a two-year assistant professorship, possibly tax-free. The students aren't too bright, but I think you'd like it.'

And it was as simple as that.

He was a driver, not a professor, but the teaching business might help him with his career, help him to meet sponsors, to win himself a paid ride.

He stepped over the Nota's tiny joke 'doors' and strapped himself into this little aluminium coffin-on-wheels where he felt so utterly at home.

He swung into Bent Street, accelerated, whipped it back a gear for the chicane, pulled up into the carport, blipped and switched off, the engine cutting dead with that high-compression, light-flywheel way he loved. It started the same way, in a hurry to get going.

He told Eddie right off, bragging really, and she seemed strangely upset. It was only a two-year appointment, after all. Surely she could manage to do without him for that long. But she didn't seem to see it that way.

Still, she was not coming with him, that much was clear.

And he assured her that he would write, would telegram or even phone her, as soon as he'd had a look around the place.

He wondered what Canadian girls were like.

In winter, did they wear fur coats and tennis racquets on their feet like Eskimos? Was it true that Eskimo men insisted on lending their wives to any visitor sharing the igloo, and it was bad manners to refuse?

Or was that only in Alaska, which he suspected was not part of Canada at all?

He'd find out, he'd tell Eddie the lay of the land, and then they could make a decision of some kind.

She might want to come over after a year or so.

He realized that getting away from Eddie – for a while – was exactly what he wanted.

The thought of sleeping beside her, in the same bed, every night for ever and ever was...discouraging. Appalling, now that he thought of it.

She asked if he had the job offer in writing, and his escapist balloon deflated.

No, it was only talk, only hot air – and when he asked Rodman the next day, yes, it was provisional only, conditional upon departmental approval.

He'd need to put in a CV.

His great white hope melted away.

So it wasn't really going to happen, and if it did, she wasn't coming.

The End

'Will you marry me?' asked a sweating Steven, still clutching his airline suitcase, and Eddie nodded fast without thinking.

Spring in the Air

Even his car had changed. Left plugged in during his long week away, the MG had melted a moat of snow around itself, rather like the skiers' bonfire. Resentfully it had begun to rust, earth-brown spots now bubbling through its rear mudguards. Ace mechanic Jimmy had warned him to expect this, that the road salt here dissolves to hydrochloric acid and that his car, being Positive Earth, becomes a giant electrolyte. The only solution, he claimed, is to let the boys weld a big slab hunk of steel underneath it and let *that* rust away. Steven had declined. But the thing did start, and he drove in to work.

He knew he was in faintly bad odour with the Acting Dean for having lost one at Cambridge.

The unfortunate lad, a loner, had apparently been trusting the Cambridge clocks, or perhaps the sundials, to tell the time, and had missed the bus by a full hour.

'But Good God, didn't you call the roll?' the Dean had hissed at him, smelling faintly of fear through his after-shave.

'Sorry, I'm not too good with names. I assumed they knew they'd be coming back on the bus, not signing up for advanced study. He got back okay on the train, I hope.'

'Eventually – but surely you got them to *write* an attendance list?'

'Have you ever tried to read their writing?'

Joyce seemed to have had a total sense-of-humour failure, though Rodman was supportive, and on their safe arrival home had announced to Eddie, heartily and unprompted, 'Steven behaved himself beautifully in London. We all had a splendid trip.'

It was true. But in flight, Steven had made his decision. For once, just for once in his life, he was going to do The Right Thing. The Right Thing was to put somebody else first, for once.

Once ought to do it. 'You never, ever think of anyone but yourself!' his mother would hissingly scold him when the squeaking floor boards woke her as he tiptoed in late through the dark house. But this would prove her wrong, once and for all.

He was clear of his home now, he reflected, but could hardly send Eddie back home to *her* mother, shamed and disgraced.

They could hardly stay as they were, either, with tension and, he reasoned, Repressed Catholic Guilt cramping Eddie's style in bed. That was... a consideration, but his true motive *was* altruistic.

He was thinking of her. It was what she wanted.

And once he'd made an honest woman of her, the good days would return, her natural lust would blossom, as in those wondrous weekends on Palm Beach, soaking up the delirious morning sun and then roaring in the old A30 (his short-lived street car, with the hot Holden engine) up to their pet vacant lot in the bush, to hump on the camp mattress that he used to strap underneath his surfboard on the car roof, Eddie naked under him in sunglasses.

The right decision. Tough – but right.

And he could hardly do a U-turn, pack his things and take the long flight back to London, though that *was* the first choice. Leave his students staring at the vacant podium. Move back in with Linda. Get a job in London – the British Institute of Management? His old ski buddy Johnno was running it now...

No.

There was no engagement ring – the Ringmeister had forgotten this important detail – but the proposal, made in the terminal at first sight, was instantly accepted, and the only thing now was to cut to the marriage itself. He suddenly remembered that once, years back, he had spent a whole miserable lunch hour eying the engagement rings in George Street jewellers, convinced that he ought to propose to Linda Austen. He liked the ruby surrounded by diamonds best, but to actually buy the thing was impossible. Out of the question. Expensive, too.

So just the marriage, now.

No wedding, absolutely not.

No parents and in-laws flying 12,000 miles to complain about the arrangements. No arrangements.

All he had to arrange was the civil marriage itself. Phoning from work, he asked the Provincial Government switchboard operator how to go about getting married. It seemed a simple question. After a range of transfers and considerable background discussion, including chuckles and even shouting, he got someone who knew.

Steven explained that he'd never been married before and needed to know the drill, in detail.

Aware she was speaking to a foreigner, the clerk was careful to list everything he would need: a bride, proper identification for her and him, some money – it was something of a bargain – and an appointment three weeks minimum after publishing the banns.

'The what?' (*Bands?*)

'The wedding banns.' (He *was* a foreigner.)

'Like the rings?'

'No, sir, the banns, the wedding announcement, placed in the local paper, so that if any man hath any reason why these two should not be joined together in holy –'

'But we're from Australia. I don't know that the *Daily Gleaner* is so widely read in Sydney.'

'Our paper is just fine, sir. We can arrange the banns. I'll see when Judge Grogan is available...'

And it was as good as done.

After a trying three weeks, the happy day arrived.

Already the long arm of the O'Malleys had presented them with a huge Kenmore washer and dryer, and the Butts clan had sent a card.

Eddie, in a lovely floral dress with hat, fully made up and glowing, and her husband-to-be in his new three-piece wedding suit of deep plum, his now-too-long hair gleaming, extricated themselves from the cocoon-like MG and strode down the river-bank into the magistrate's office.

Side by side they stood, a handsome couple.

– And fell to pieces at the first question.

'*Witnesses?* Nobody told me I had to bring witnesses. Haven't you got any witnesses we can use? *I don't know anybody here!* We're Australians!'

The shrug.

They turned and marched out – and the first couple they saw, strolling down Queen Street, they knew. It was an older student of Steven's, a Scot, with his fiercely-cute young wife.

'Angus!' (The human mind, under stress, can surprise even itself.) 'Would you like to be our witnesses, so we can get married? Right now?'

'Delighted!'

All signed in, and the clerk, relieved and smiling, stretched forward her freshly-manicured hand and said the magic words.

'May I have the license, please?'

Steven handed it over.

'I'm sorry,' she said, 'I meant the Marriage License.'

Consternation. Pandemonium. Uproar.

'*Nobody* told me I had to get a Marriage License! I *told* the government lady I'd never got married before, we must have gone over it three times, she never said a *word* about a Marriage Licence!'

Everyone talked at once for a while except for Eddie, who quietly drifted out the door and was gone. The clerk was pale, in a panic now because in ten minutes time her judge would arrive and she would have to explain that they were dealing with foreigners, and send him away again. He would not be a happy judge, not at three on a Friday afternoon. She took charge. Flapping both manicured hands for silence she snatched up the phone and pleaded in a desperate whisper, half crouching for emphasis. She hung up and straightened.

'They've agreed to waive the waiting period. Here's the thing. Here's what you have to do. They close at three. If you can get yourself up to the fourth floor they'll be waiting for you, they'll give you one. Okay?'

'Fourth floor of where?' asked Steven, but already the Scot was propelling him out the door and firing him off across Queen

Street towards the gleaming glass windows of the Provincial Government building. Now he had his racing vision: everything was clear. He sprinted past the Playhouse, where stage hands struggled to load twelve-foot flats for *Anne of Green Gables*, one at a time, in through a side door.

Fighting his way up like a salmon through the Reversing Falls, Steven cleared the departing, heavily-deodorised government employees, sprinted the length of a nightmare corridor, swung through a glass door – and met more dismayed faces.

'Here I am! It's me!'

'But – where's the bride?'

'Just a tick. Nobody said I needed her. Back in a sec.'

The cooler air felt good as he re-crossed the car park, sprinted over Queen Street and headed downriver. Snow had been cleared from the dead grass, to remind folk that Spring was always a possibility, and a number of brave souls were walking their dogs.

'Scuse me,' he asked one, 'You happen to see a lady in a hat come past here, throw herself in the river?'

The man thought hard, but shook his head.

'When would that have been?'

'In the last ten minutes.'

No, he was almost certain not.

Now Steven was standing, yelling out her name.

He would embarrass her out of hiding.

He no longer wanted to get married and neither did she, but the problem was that Professor Rodman had volunteered to throw them a small wedding party, and this was already in progress. So he needed her.

Screw the wedding, but they would have to arrive and at least *pretend* to be married. Maybe they could get married some other time.

He bellowed her name, as he'd bellowed it once in the hot, insect-drilling jungles of Cambodia, that day they got separated among the stone temples. And it worked. She emerged from behind a monster dying elm, her face black with rage and ruined mascara. He pleaded. He apologised. He pleaded. He held her hand – and they ran like the wind. For a woman in high heels she could cover ground. The stagehands with the wood-and-canvas flat, now securely stuck, turned their heads to watch them go.

The Department of Births, Deaths and Marriages had stayed behind, grinning, to watch the drama.

In their official capacity, they informed Eddie of Steven's exact age, and Steven of Eddie's exact age – he was too dispirited even to quip, 'What? You told me you were twelve!' – and sold him the license for a mere five dollars.

The judge appeared on cue and did the job.

The civil wording was something of a let-down, no love, honour and obey, nothing much, just I hereby in my capacity as a judge hereby say these words. And that was it.

Except for the brief problem with the ring. It was a fine solid gold affair of carved vine leaves, not cheap, a sort of engagement-wedding combo that Eddie had chosen.

And it was the right size.

But somehow in all the agitation, rage and running around, Eddie's ring finger had swollen, so it wouldn't go on.

'Push!' she hissed, red-faced, and Steven pushed, with a twist – and it cleared the knuckle. (Why did he suddenly want to run out barking mad and jump in – on – the river?)

They thanked Angus and the cute Jenny – who, in the swing of things, invited them round for a wedding dinner, in their trailer home, for eight. It would only be burgers but she had guessed that Steven had not planned anything beyond the marriage itself, the main event.

She was right.

For him it was, after all, the end.

Wedding Party

Back at Rodman's the party was roaring, and they had to knock twice before anyone heard. Then the door was shoved open and they were met by a skunk. The skunk – fat, glossy, and splendidly skunk-patterned – waddled towards them, seemed a little hard-of-seeing, and began ominously to turn its back.

'It's okay, she's been de-scented,' bellowed its owner – former truckie, now head of FU's Psych Department and unquestionably a good bloke – and turned back to his academic shouting match with a smaller but determined opponent.

Eddie fell to her knees. Clearly she'd be happy playing with the skunk for the next hour or two.

The old house was huge. Every wall of every room had floor-to-ceiling bookshelves, and most tables held fresh volumes piled up, shining, unopened. The publishers were generous to academics. Steven clawed his way in through controversy, wrangling and full academic discourse, to the big old kitchen – an Australian party habit – where he swung open the fridge and downed a Moosehead beer.

A stranger swung into his face and told him a beer tale, swearing it was true.

This American salmon fisherman, you see, had ordered a beer at the newly-opened Mactaquac Lodge (another provincial money-losing venture to boost tourism) and was offered a choice of Canadian brews. Indigant, he demanded an *American* beer, and when the bartender said they didn't have any, made the mistake of saying, 'Gimme the nearest thing you got to it!' So the bartender handed him a glass of water.

'Me, I would have pissed in the glass,' said Steven but the man was already on his second joke. Soon Steven was getting hoarse just listening. He juggled a white wine to his bride, now on excellent terms with the skunk, who wore the standard black, with a separating white stripe. He decided he would have his racing car painted in skunk pattern, instead of his former favourite, the orange of Denny Hulme's F1 mount – which he might take over yet, if he could wrangle a test drive and prove quicker even than the burly Kiwi.

Rodman shook his hand and shrugged off the possibility of quieting this bunch to make any announcement. Joyce, too, offered his heartiest congratulations, if Steven read his lips right.

Back in the kitchen he was forced to meet a fellow Australian, guarding the fridge. But this was an odd little whiskery fellow, introduced as 'Professor Somebody, the eminent Augustinian – and Flat Earther.' This seemed to Steven to be taking medieval studies a bit *too* far – he wondered if the worthy professor applied leeches when he felt a plague coming on. But perhaps it was just a sort of joke. Or deadly serious – so hard to tell with academics.

The man seemed to believe he'd invented the Flat Earth Society, and Steven was tempted to tell him there's nothing new under the sun.

At Oxford he had himself attended the founding Planoterrestrialist's meeting, to scout for loony girls, at which the keynote speaker made his case and then threw himself open for questions. 'But, sir,' quavered a don (or somebody doing a don's voice), 'if the Earth is indeed flat, then *what is on the other side?* – 'Sir,' the speaker replied with a self-satisfied, humourless smile, 'I am not here to deal in idle speculation.'

The kitchen was too loud for Steven to tell his story and he didn't want to hurt the man's feelings. Professor Ramadam Goatee then spotted him and shuffled up to complain bitterly about the work load and the unrelenting pressure of preparing the required nine hours of lectures a week, week after week.

Again, Steven didn't want to hurt his feelings by pointing out that there is another way: if you ask questions, and get your class involved, you don't have to talk non-stop. You can listen. But he did say, shout rather, as his parting line, 'I'm teaching thirteen hours a week!' Goatee heard, but disagreed.

He took his bride another white wine spritzer, persuaded her to part with her skunk and, amid continued full and free exchange of academic views, the pair left for the wedding dinner.

They had never entered a trailer park before, and cruised around the maze of permanently temporary structures misnamed 'Mobile Homes,' their small garden shrubs neatly hessian-wrapped against winter, until, on the third pass, they saw an odd sight. On the top step, outside his rectangular residence stood a bare-kneed figure brandishing a sword. It was the angelic Angus, in full kilt and regalia, waving them in.

The wedding dinner was excellent, Eddie was thawing out and Steven sipped unaccustomed single-malt Scotch, and began to feel lucky again, for the first time since London. Jenny was cute but his own wife (wife!) was every bit as cute, wore her dress much better than Angus wore his – and he, too, was now a married man. Angus seemed delighted, as if every new member of the marriage club supported his own decision to join.

Jenny produced a tiny flash camera for the official wedding photo, and Angus handed over his ceremonial sword for the cutting of the cake. In fact it was a hamburger bun (nobody had told Steven to bring a cake) but the idea was good, and the photo turned out surprisingly well. It had the look of history. Enlarged and mounted, it was mailed expensively to the baffled parents-in-law, with a feeble, jokey try at an explanation.

The wedding night, however, was not a success. They made the mistake of tapping on the McTavishes' door and announcing that they had just got married – and were very nearly evicted on the spot, for *not* having been married before. Grace was deeply offended... 'Living under our roof in an unmarried state,' and Joe chimed in, 'Got a good mind to throw you both out into the snow right this very minute.'

Lying miserably in bed, listening to their pounding hearts, Steven stated the obvious: 'I guess these God-fearing folk could never let it in that we were *not* married. Very small minds, Catholics.'

(Small minds, big tits? You just married one, you twit.)

'You don't *know* they're Catholics. Not everything's The Church's fault. They're just getting on a bit, and they're, they're...'

'New Brunswickers, sure. So in a way you can do anything you like here and nobody'll suspect you. Thick as bricks. Must be that spruce budworm spray they drench 'em in every year. *Spray 'em again, oh, spray 'em again, the locals are restless so spray 'em again!'* He was on a roll, now. 'The little budworms'd *never* suspect that, I don't know, that their Premier could be gay, or that their newspaper doesn't tell 'em the whole truth, or that, I don't know, some wheeler-dealer up from the States's going to take them for twenty million dollars and just walk away laughing. Or that FU names their new library after K.C. Irving's wife and he *still* doesn't give them a cent. Or –'

'Go to sleep. You're getting yourself worked up over nothing.'

He kissed her and she said good night again. Again.

This marriage thing would take a little work, he saw.

He should do the dishes more regularly.

True, he was earning nearly twice her salary, but all the same, he really should still help out more.

And he should be a better listener.

Maybe she'd talk more, if he was a better listener.

Overhead, from their separate solitudes they heard the pacing, floor...carpet...floor, of their landlord, keeping heart-attack at bay.

He was moving faster than usual, clearly a worried man.

'He's really clipping along,' muttered Steven, trying to break the ice.

'Night,' said Eddie, and rolled over.

Class Act

News.

Some treasury minister called Laporte was kidnapped by some Quebeckers who believed in greater freedom, stuffed into the trunk of a car and, when nobody in the government would pay any ransom money, found dead.

Steven read the news, stunned by what seemed a most un-Canadian next move: the Prime Minister, that liberal Trudeau chap from Quebec, sent in the tanks to quell the 'State of Anticipated Insurrection.'

'Anticipated?' By whom? Did it mean the General Uprising that hadn't started yet, but that *he* said *he* expected? He unleashed the troopers, who joyfully kicked in doors and roughed up the known homosexuals and political big-talkers – but especially, as Steven heard later, the homosexuals and the artists.

As a card-carrying Australian, he felt he had to speak out, and opened his Management of the Enterprise class with a few words.

'So tell me, are you chaps aware that as of midnight last night, any one of you can be arrested and held in jail, *without being charged with anything*, for three months? Hands up those who knew that.'

Seven hands rose gingerly, though two fell back down when their owners saw how weak the overall response was.

'Okay, so it seems to be news to you, but trust me, it's true. I'll say it again.' And he did. 'What's it called?'

'The War Measures Act, sir.'

'Good! Now...does anyone have a problem with that?'

Incredibly, nobody did, and they explained to him why not: it was only in Quebec, and who cares about Quebec?

'No, not so! You could be arrested here in New Brunswick too, and held in jail for three months without being charged with anything.'

'But sir! Why would anyone want to arrest *us*?'

Why indeed.

Reminding himself that stupidity is not an indictable offence, he began the lesson for today.

Effective Supervision. Hah!

Although the set textbook was new to him, as were the three or four management texts he'd managed to skim through in preparation for sharing his expertise with the engineering students, he'd found that they all taught the same thing. Perhaps they all copied from the same, *Ur*-textbook on Effective Supervision. In a nutshell, Be Nice and You'll get Better Results.

This made sense to Steven. All his psychological training had stressed that one should *reward* desired behaviour and *not reward* undesired behaviour. Punishing it was a bit tricky, and had some odd effects: shocked rats freezing on the take-off platform, their feet sizzling – or else fixating on their first, dumb response of, say, always jumping left when the buzzer sounds.

But reward the good and don't reward the bad: simple as that.

This shiningly obvious notion – which he himself believed utterly – he found a hard sell. Every case study calling for management action seemed to generate the same front-row response: The Grin. 'Fire him!'

'Fire who?'

'The guy who's screwing up.'

A variant was, 'Kick the bastard out!' Sometimes, when a hand shot up and, delighted, he called upon it – 'YES!' he would wince to hear, 'Give him one chance to smarten up, and *then* fire him.'

But that was about as far as they'd go towards the textbook model. When he reminded them that in a unionised company it was extremely hard and expensive to fire someone, he was met with The Shrug. Well – unions!

Well – what was so wrong with unions? His father had reviled them almost nightly, and Steven had always seen himself more as management than as blue-collar labourer, more officer than man, but at Oxford he'd been impressed by a couple of union take-overs of dying companies.

The Glaswegian shipbuilders, all laid off because nobody, not even Australia, wanted to buy the ferry they were half-way through building, had locked themselves in and, with a burst of released energy, had completed the last vessel – unpaid! Rogue suppliers kept delivering materials at dead of night, while management, their own pensions intact, fluttered about trying to stop them working.

And later, when the Norton-Villiers company went under, another group of brave workers obstinately kept on building the superb Norton motorbikes, unpaid, and discovering that left alone they were able to do everything – except market them, of course. They even offered to buy the company, but were refused; it would have made management look bad.

All this had changed Steven's tune. Not that he had ever been a union member, of course. And union leaders did sound an uneducated lot.

How hard it is to teach someone about something they're sure they already know! he mused.

As some teacher had written, probably in a suicide note, 'It's not what they don't know; it's what they know that ain't so.' For the first time, his teaching job began to feel like work, like pushing a giant snowball up a hill.

But here Eddie was a real help. She reminded him that he was being paid a huge salary, tax-free, just to teach.

It wasn't like *her* job, where the students had to actually *learn* new stuff. All her husband had to do was stand up and talk, which he already did, she smiled, 'brilliantly.' She had a point.

Best of all, while his wife was grading term tests and mutteringly marking assignments, he was, right now, settled back reading *Road and Track*, because Joyce had awarded him a 'Teaching Assistant,' an earnest young engineer who graded all the papers for him at startling speed.

Steven had looked over a number at random, and found he agreed with the grades. The guy was brilliant. Well, perhaps they were all brilliant – but not at hearing what Steven was trying to tell them.

The notion of actually listening to what employees had to say and acting on it was so foreign to North American ears that, though they learned to say the words, and to provide the right exam responses, they never for a second considered trying it out themselves.

It was absurdly...feminine?

Like the catechism or the Ten Commandments, the Word was the thing, and a wonderful thing – but business was business.

Steven noticed that preaching about effective management sent them into a coma but that he could rouse them quickly by shifting his tone of voice to signal a story.

They seemed impressed that he had experience in what they called the 'real world.'

His first was that he had helped to run a week-long 'Sensitivity Training' course for a group of Australian Gas Company managers whose world was about to shift with the switch-over from deadly coal-gas to sweet-smelling natural gas, and who, in the view of their General Manager, were not up to the job of remaking themselves, and needed the course to 'unfreeze' them.

Their first three sullen days inside the beachside motel were spent recovering from the insult of being sent on such a course, muttering that it was the Manager, not them, who needed it.

But towards the end, solidarity overcame some of the sting from this vote of no-confidence, and they took to the course work rather well.

It was about – what else? – effective management.

But there was one player – Steven could still hear his voice – who was the most hard-nosed, unblinking bastard (the class loved the word 'bastard'), impossible to deal with, not worth talking to, the classic 'My Way or the Highway' manager.

And this clown *loved* the course content.

He became a total convert to *talking* about the need to be sensitive, to *listen* actively, to give *full* consideration to *all* ideas, no matter where or who they come from.

Steven's point was that in a follow-up, he learned that this character had appointed himself Sensitivity Training Manager for the whole organisation, spoke constantly on the subject, ran unauthorised courses and saw himself as Mr Sensitivity himself.

Meanwhile, the other managers agreed that he was now even more of a hard-nosed bastard than ever.

From this, Steven had devised Butts' Law: The more open-minded people believe they are, the more closed-minded they are. It's the ones who fret that they're not listening hard enough, worry that they may be missing valuable suggestions, who are the open-minded ones. The others are bastards.

His company, Auscon, continued to use and praise their trademark diagnostic tests, but Steven privately took the high self-ratings for sensitivity and reversed them.

(Most of Butts' Laws were inverse: Fast in, slow out. His Law of Familial Closeness scored the O'Malleys at 12,000 and his own, three-sister family at a grand total of 34,200 – miles from parents, that is.)

His students enjoyed the story – but hated any conclusion, any moral. He's trying to preach at us again. He always goes too far, gets pushy.

His Japanese Management story was a brief one.

He'd been hired to report on the image of Japanese products in Australia, did a survey and wrote the report: in a word, they stank. Flimsy, 'tinny,' junk. Their shop tools? Junk.

Almost everyone interviewed remembered a cheap Japanese clockwork toy that had either clattered to bits or stuck in the mystical, mysteriously culpable stasis of being 'overwound.' ('You must have overwound it.')

He scored a trip down to Melbourne to hand-deliver his report to the Japanese Consulate building.

He knocked, a hand emerged and received the six copies, the door closed. And that was it.

'They always pay, but you never hear anything back,' his own manager explained.

But where was Steven's feedback, his...grade?

Suddenly an engineering student had a question, 'Why would they pay you good money to tell them their stuff was junk?'

'Well – is it possible they were trying to improve it?... Well? Show of hands?'

Opinion was divided, in what now seemed the familiar Canadian way, between those who didn't know and those who didn't care.

Soon Steven began to enjoy that most Australian pastime, 'taking the mickey' out of his tame flock, by searching for the simplest, dumbest question that would, he bet himself, stump them every time.

'So – today's true case study is Buick Motors, early days. Somehow or other, the piston rings are being installed in such a way that they keep breaking, and wrecking the engines. Complaints pouring in. Bankruptcy looming. Management desperate. If they can't stop the piston rings breaking they're all out of a job. Question: What should they do? Who do they call in?'

Then, after ten minutes of heated class discussion, he reveals the startling answer: they ask the man who installs the piston rings. He tells management that he needs a flat-sided screwdriver to install them properly, instead of the slightly wedge-bladed one they gave him. *Now* what should they do?

'Fire him!'

'Give him one chance to straighten up and then kick the bastard out!'

Uh huh.

'What! Be *nice* to him! You're joking, right!'

'How about giving him the right screwdriver? Anyway, that's what they in fact decided to do, and Buick Motors was saved. So what can we learn from this?'

'...?'

'Anyone?'

And so it went.

He resolved that if he ever ran a company, he would at least try out the Japanese technique of listening. (It was really the American Technique, but without the wink. Would it work in a marriage?) But no, he still had no interest in business, even now that he was teaching the subject. Money, except for buying racing cars, was uninspiring stuff – who cares?

Adding it up, studying the hourly stock prices, seemed such a sad waste of a life.

Driving a bargain was degrading, driving a racing car the noblest art.

What men or gods are these...?

Human behaviour *was* interesting though; he was sure he was interested in behaviour, even though people were something of a disappointment. He'd studied psychology to solve his parents, and had taken six long years to give it up.

He'd love to know how people work, though work itself was for dullards: a true Australian lived for the two-day holiday. Saturday was practice, Sunday was race day. The little matter of working all night on the car didn't count as work: it was just what had to be done. When the flag drops, your tyres had better be smoking.

At the time, American companies were fighting each other off to do business with the amazing Japanese, and Professor Butts kept reading articles about how maddeningly inscrutable the Asians were to negotiate with: you'd convince one set of managers, think you had a deal – but the next day another set would show up and you'd have to convince *them*.

'Time means nothing to these guys. Meanwhile, the American manager is itching to get home to start selling his board and his people on the new idea, the new concept.

And yet, somehow, a month after the final bows and handshakes, the Japanese company is going full tilt in action while the American one's still arguing the point, or hearing mutterings about strike inaction.'

'It's easy for the Japs: they don't have unions,' shouted one of his brighter students.

'You're right. So...next question: how would you feel if you joined a company that promised, no, *guaranteed* you lifetime employment, steady advancement based on merit, an exercise break every hour, basketball games in the lunch break – but no union? Oh, and you have to sing the company song every morning? How would you feel?'

They would feel, it was clear from their looks, very, very uneasy. They hated unions but hated companies even more. They wanted to work for themselves.

Then, a toothy challenge: 'Sir, I bet you drive one of those little imports.'

'You win. But from what I read, my next car will definitely be Japanese. That 240Z Datsun is only $4,000 and it's got 150 horsepower. How many V8s have got 150 horsepower?'

The Grin. A small but hairy figure in the red FU leather jacket, whose name, improbably, was Stu, stood up to make his announcement:

'*My* V8 puts out four hundred fifty!'

He had him there.

Too late Steven remembered the car, an immense, orange object with fins and foot-wide rear tires, clearly designed to go straight.

On the front it bore the timely warning: DODGE.

That night he took his bride to a special Playhouse showing, a one-night stand, of *I am Curious – Yellow*, advertised as uncensored and uncut, due to an oversight in the provincial Canadian censorship code (it had been banned everywhere else across the country).

Not much of a film, but the idea was exciting, for in Australia such movies were only shown 'overseas.'

Not much of a honeymoon outing either, though it trumped *Anne of Green Gables*.

The next day, *the very next day*, as he passed the Playhouse theatre he found it dark, closed, and apparently being demolished.

Roaring machines were attacking its rear end.

Was this the censor's wrath for showing one lousy sex movie?

What kind of province was this, in what kind of a country?

Another Wedding

Another wedding? Spring in London?

His old Oxford pal Robert was tying the knot, with an English rose, Lady Caroline Somebody-Somebody whom he'd just met. Apparently Africa had not (or perhaps had) offered him a replacement for the black girl of his dreams.

The Butts accepted. It would be a nice holiday, a sort of honeymoon trip.

They booked tickets, writing separate cheques. Barbie, the campus bank manager, kept urging them to open a joint bank account but never offered any reason why.

Eddie agreed it was easier to 'keep track' with separate accounts, while Steven was alarmed at the thought that she could spend all her own money and then go ahead and spend his. There was still no mention of repaying the air fare from Australia that he had lent her, and he felt annoyed to find himself still stewing over it. Not that she had married him to get out of paying him back, not at all, and yet...

The sticky point was that he'd never actually invited her to accompany him to Canada. She'd invited herself. True, he could have said no when she asked for the loan, but – he didn't want to upset her.

They always split the groceries, reaching into their matching leather wallets whenever the kitty ran low, but he paid all the rent, having some slim notion in the back of his head that if they ever *did* get a divorce, he would not have to pay so much alimony if he could prove he had always paid more than his share.

As the driver in the family, he chauffeured her about, waited in the car, freezing even in his new ankle-length Afghanistan cameldriver's coat, on their weekly mammoth shopping runs to the new Dominion store.

He knew he should go inside and help but he couldn't, he just couldn't. It was mainly because of the meat. Somehow, the blazing lights and walls of 'Processed Meat' gave him the willies.

And there were too many choices, all identical but in different packages. A dozen types of bread but no – *bread*. Two dozen over-sugared cereals. How could a man choose?

He resolutely did the dishes until she begged him to let her, confessing that the wild way he did them drove her mental. She liked to pre-rinse and then soapily massage each item before post-rinsing it and assembling a Chinese puzzle of stacked dishes, never the same twice, that stood like a porcelain card house, daring him to try to remove one to dry it. So he didn't dry up either – not that he'd dried up before: draining was clearly the efficient way to go, and ergonomic efficiency his latest thing.

Noticing more and more that she had a knack of never doing the same thing twice, never having 'a place for everything and everything in its place,' never putting her tools away, as it were, he began to suspect that she was mad. Not insane, but definitely...cracked. A neurotic.

This would help explain her shrivelled interest in sex.

Now that they were married, she seemed to have more menstrual periods, monthly as an absolute minimum – but every weekend, more like.

Spring had come at last. Daffodils waved in the fields, the woods sparkled with bluebells, blossoms shone and birds sang lustily.

In Canada the icy wind still blew razorblade necklaces, and back home in Australia it was autumn and the yellow poplars shivered. But now Steven was in England, his second home really (his mother was from Nottingham), though in his whole life he'd spent only two years there. Now two years plus a week.

As best man, his job was to deliver Robert, dressed, ambulatory and with the ring in his pocket, to the altar. This he did. There had been only one dodgy moment the night before, overlooking the Thames, when his old Oxford friend confided that this was all a horrible mistake – but he could easily get away.

Over that fence, down the wall, swing out along the underside of the bridge, drop onto the deck of that freighter, downriver, out into the Channel – gone. No problems, they'd never catch him.

Lie low for a few years. Steven nodded, and suggested another cognac instead.

But he wondered... She was a perfectly nice girl, with one of those unspeakable Uppah Claws accents – he wondered if she continued to sound like that in bed, but didn't know his best friend well enough to ask. (English men – unlike the women – are rather prudish, he had decided, based on his one memorable occasion of being silently assaulted by an English girl in the back seat of her parents' car, as they drove him, hitch-hiking back from France, from Dover back to London.)

Marriage, though? Where was the point? Married himself, he still didn't see it. It seemed like an admission of failure, a suicide of the spirit, the funeral of love. He assured and reassured his old friend that he was doing The Right Thing, time he tied the knot, a beautiful girl (rich, too), the day (today!) would be a triumph. He could hear himself convincingly making it up, but what are best friends for, if not to lie to?

No, not true; he *wanted* to tell Robert to do the brave thing: run like hell, don't stick around waiting for the troopers to shoot out your knees...but a strange paralysis was upon him. He was not, was far from, being himself. Frozen in union, his numbed body yearned, his cock tugged him, swivelled him like a compass needle towards 2B Denbigh Place. With every shared sip from the big cognac bottle he tasted the bitter certainty that Robert should, right now, be hand-over-handing under the bridge (a mountaineer, he could do it, too). And that he, the old Steven, should be sprinting through the streets towards the warm breathing body of...Linda Austen. For once, he knew precisely how to get there.

Big Ben struck once.

Steven knew the coming day would hurt, but had no idea how much it would hurt. No, not hurt; nothing hurts numbness. Wound.

Robert was muttering something about, 'I did it for you,' but it was the drink talking and Steven got an old black cabdriver to take them home down Crampton Street.

Eddie was asleep, after her day of shopping at Harrods. He guessed she'd chosen a gift appropriately costly, useless and non-returnable. Earlier she had been threatening to have her lovely long hair 'cut off' at Harrods, but he saw it was only trimmed, sprawled across the king-size hotel pillow.

He stared out the window, in what he knew, *knew*, was the direction of 2B Denbigh Place – and across the air-well, was startled to see a man and a woman enter a bright room, swiftly remove their clothes, almost leap onto the bed, and, after a moment, pull down the blind.

But before tugging down the blind, the woman had gazed out into the night, as if searching for a friendly sign, as if desperate for one last look at the outside world. She might have seen him, looking across, but probably not. He was in darkness. He slid into bed, holding that thought in his hand.

'Whether 'tis nobler in the mind to suffer...'

The wedding was everything Steven and Eddie's was not. Everyone who was anyone was there, along with a few who were really someone. The gentlemen held their red cummerbunded bellies in, the women their white bosoms out. Indeterminate organ music seeped from the historic church as the costumed wedding guests climbed the steps, conversing in that oddly fearful, expectant tone, as if midway between a funeral and some kind of high-risk circus act that could easily end in death.

The handsome couple, Steven and Robert, approached the altar and stood by Carolyn and her titled dad. The magic words were spoken, ring produced, declaration made. How bizarre, thought Steven. One second before the, 'I hereby pronounce' line was pronounced, Robert was single. One second afterwards, he was not. The word was indeed a magical force. And the setting, the unyielding stones, the organ, the very echo itself made this a significant event.

Now it was over. His duties done, he withdrew – and saw a face. She was seated directly opposite him. Linda Austen, in a blue dress. She must have entered late. He stared at her, expressionless, and she stared across at him. He could see the glint of light beneath her blue eyes. He was frozen, staring at her staring back at him, when someone squeezed his arm and he had to do something, but had no idea what it was.

On they swept to the reception, he got to kiss the apple-scented, beautifully-maned bride, who already seemed rather older than her bridegroom (*groom*? Doesn't a groom groom...horses?). Robert, like Steven, was a bit of a Peter Pan himself.

Clearly the tone was celebration. Crust-free sandwiches and champagne swirled about in hired hands, and for once the music was danceable. Robert made a truly appalling speech (... 'I'd like to thank my mother for having me – instead of, I don't know, a sherry bottle or something.'), so appalling that the drummer helped him end it with a TA-*Dum*!, and there was dancing. Eddie felt elegant and light in Steven's arms, but over her shoulder his eyes were scanning the faces; no sign of her. She can't have come.

He had to make a speech and made it ('Accustomed as I am to public speaking, the first time I ever saw Robert he was drunk – actually, the last time I saw him he was drunk...') earning a TA-*Dum Chhh!*

The big band picked all the right numbers, from dreaming Glen Miller to wake-up Latin Jazz, and he danced his shoes off, with Eddie, with a couple of bridesmaids, one bride, and, for a while there, with himself, in a killer *Tequila*. Then a proper meal was served, with good South African wine and then, incredibly, it was evening. Night, even.

And there she was.

Linda Austen, tipsy. Flushed. Gorgeous

'Linda! Ah, Eddie, I'd like you to meet, you remember, don't you?'

'Linda Austen. Oh – yes, we met at Steven's party.' (Oh – yes, and Linda had burst into tears there, too, to see Eddie's arms around her Steven. 'All I could see,' she had sobbed into Steven's shoulder after Eddie went palely home, 'were those red fingernails, those claws around your back, I'm so sorry.')

And on memory's cue Linda burst into tears again. She was

sobbing now and within an inch of wailing.

'I'm so *sorry*,' she gulped. 'I told myself I wasn't going to cry and now –' Robert appeared and gallantly swept her away onto the dance floor but it was heavy, damp going, and when Linda had downed yet another champagne, he touched Steven's arm and murmured, 'You take her home in a taxi, old chap. She's a bit upset. I'll – I'll see Edwina back to the hotel and see you there in, what? Half an hour?'

In the taxi Steven sat beside her, holding her small, warm, familiar hand, and willed himself not to feel his heart breaking inside his rib cage. The taxi stopped at a red light, waited. The light changed and it moved on, the driver changed gears...

I heard the news today. Oh, boy!

There was nothing to say, but at least she had stopped crying. She seemed to have gotten over it. He could even be a little proud of himself, being so...English about it all, such a gentleman, doing The Right Thing. Escorting her home. She would be all right.

'This is it!' he told the driver. 'Right here.'

He looked into her face, pale in the dim light, and kissed her once, lightly and well on the tears. And walked her up the steps to her door and left her there, fumbling for her keys, as he got back into the taxi – and had to hold his body back, forcibly, from throwing itself out the door and up the steps again.

Back at their hotel Robert and Eddie had not gone outside but were waiting for him. She had been crying.

Robert murmured in his ear, 'I'm *so* glad you came back. You did The Right Thing to come back.'

He felt light, almost cheerful, as if hollow, convincing himself that Yes, he had done The Right Thing but knowing he had done the wrong, the unforgivably Wrong one.

Spring

The first day of Eastern Canada's spring dawned deep and soft and even. An ocean of snow had fallen as they slept.
It was a school day but there was no chance the schools would be open after such a monster fall.
Already the wind was picking up, peeling snow off the top of the dunes like surf blown back by an off-shore wind. Thank the Snow God, the god of a hard-earned day off.
Still warm in bed they rolled towards each other and, for the first time in many weeks, made love. (How different she felt from Linda, so solid, urgent, almost an opponent. 'Harder,' she urged through gritted teeth, where Linda had murmured once, afterwards, 'Please don't bump me so hard. I'm really delicate there.')
Afterwards they slept through breakfast and rose, stretching and yawning, for brunch at home. They sipped Melitta drip coffee with whipped cream and munched Eddie's toasted whole-wheat BLTs, dripping and grinning like a couple of kids.
Their big jar of black Vegemite, which had alerted Canadian Customs ('You *eat* this stuff?' 'We spread it on our toast. All Australians do,') was down to its final scrapings, but they were going Canadian. Pancakes with maple syrup and sausages still seemed an odd mixture of main course and dessert but they were adapting, and had given up trying to persuade waitresses to bring their steak before they'd finished up their little salad plate.
Through the double-paned glass door, they watched the sparrows digging.
Feather-fluffed little black-chinned sparrows, down from Churchill, double-kicked madly at the snow cone that had formed on the big flower pot just outside, working their way down to the sunflower seeds Eddie had left them. They seemed so jolly, in the 15-below windchill.
After brunch she planned to take out the now-full glass bowl of bacon fat and wedge it into the fork of the maple.

'It says in *The Gleaner* that birds love fat, especially in winter.'
'Me too,' munched Steven. 'I'll take it out.'
But as he snow-waded towards the bare tree, he was struck by a tiny bolt of lightning that froze him. A midget bird landed, with a 'Ting!' on the rim of the glass bowl he was carrying, looked him boldly in the eye with its gleaming black eyes, as if daring him to move a muscle, then dipped for beak-full of fat. And, bending its knee-ankles to spring, shot away. Steven became aware that he was now perched on one leg with his mouth hanging open. Rewinding his mental tapes he saw that it wore a black cap. From high in the tree it announced its name: 'Chickadee-dee-dee.'

Back it came, and three more times, filling him with a joy he had never known. He couldn't wait to get back inside to tell Eddie, though she had seen it all through the glass. She was pointing back, behind him. He turned to see a crow in a blue suit. Dazzling blue, but still a crow, it stuffed its head into the goody bowl and gave an ugly shriek of apparent delight. A bit coarse perhaps, for the bluebird of happiness, but spectacularly coloured. A blue crow – this was odder than a black swan. He should notify the Oxford philosophers. What a day!

School had not been cancelled.

When Eddie showed up on Monday, bright and early, she was called to the Principal's office. She read the eyes of the staff watching her go in.

The Grey Ghost smiled his thin-lipped smile and told her she was no longer with the school. Terminated. Sacked. Fired. Let go. Her reported unwillingness to feed the gerbils was one thing, but this flagrant, unexcused absence was quite another. Her classes had been re-assigned. Should she wish to lodge a protest, her union delegate was available at this number. He slid a slip of paper across his desk.

Eddie was in shock. When she called the number all she could do was blubber. But that evening, at her meeting with the delegate, a tall, thin lawyer-about-town (much praised by Alan Burns) her Irish-Australian blood rose to her face and she announced her intention to fight for her job.

Together they faced the Grey Ghost once more, in his office – he was an even whiter shade of pale and not smiling at all.

This was not over.

Then she told Steven she was going to fight to get her job back, but in the meantime she would make good use of her time off, which could be months.

Steven, on hearing this, swallowed but said the Right Thing, that he supported her decision every inch of the way.

Losing her income was a bit of a blow, though, and it felt like a...a trick; he recalled the cartoon bride cutting herself a thick slice of wedding cake, with a cry of 'Whacko! No more diets!'

But Eddie swore, tearfully, that what she *really* wanted to do – and this was news to him – was dance.

What *he* really wanted to do was get the MG in shape for the first race of the season at Debert, the airfield circuit in Nova Scotia, and there was work to be done.

The kids at Fodderton High were appalled at so abruptly losing one of their favourite teachers, that cool, crazy lady from Australia, and sprang into political action, complaining loudly and bitterly to each other.

After a week or so, the ski team and their buddies vowed to do something about it, and did.

Party Time

There was a tinny banging sound. Someone was banging on the glass door. Whoever it was must have trudged around through all the snow. Eddie stepped out of the shower, skilfully twisted a green towel round her wet head and another round her middle, and peeped out.

It was Jackman, standing in the snow, beaming, holding a huge case of beer before him. She unclicked the door and slid it back. Snow poured in and so did Jackman, Landry, Parson, his sister Mary, Dobson and Cane, and a snowy tribe of new faces.

'We came to cheer you up,' announced Jackman.

'Hi, guys,' said Steven, peeling off his headphones from which be-bop trumpet still sizzled.

'Come on in. Looks like a good night for a party.'

And it was. The dancers sang along as Jethro Tull thundered out his advice to 'poor old Aqualung' ('snot running down his nose...eyeing little girls with bad intent'). Steve'n Eddie showed how it was done, and then the kids showed how it *is* done, as Santana and Buddy Miles led the charge into joyous bacchanalia.

Eddie trotted upstairs to warn the McTavishes that they were having a little impromptu party, but their unsurprised landlord and lady smiled and nodded with surprising warmth, and insisted that it was perfectly all right with them, as long as they were having fun. Eddie assured them that they were.

The odd burning oregano smell of marijuana softened the endless cigarettes – for these young athletes, to party was to smoke – and the beer-cap flipping games became earnest. As non-smokers, the Butts did not toke, but nobody seemed to mind them just saying no. Now it was Janis Joplin offering yet another little piece of her heart to Big Brother and the Holding Company, as a jumbo bag of chips was snatched from someone's suspiciously-rustling packsack and circulated, like a rapid-fire communion of lost souls.

Luckily Eddie had just bought cheese, and this went down fast and well among the *Hot Rats* fans. Steven kept turning the Hi-Fi down a touch when the pieces he hated were on, like the endless footling guitar solos from the Allman Brothers, but Parson, who as always bragged boringly about how many and what varieties of upper, downer and mystery pill he had taken in how short a time, kept cranking it back up.

'*Pie!*' The cry went up from the kitchen. Someone had found a frozen apple pie that Eddie hadn't considered. By now the post-grass 'mad munchies' were setting in. She at once slid it in the oven at 450 degrees and stood guard until the hot apple pie smell had the howling gang ringing the kitchen like wolves.

'All right!' she announced, taking charge. 'I will now hand out your implements.'

Armed with teaspoons and assorted blunt instruments including an eggbeater, the mob waited for the countdown. The pie was placed centrally on the kitchen floor. On 'Go!' hungry hell broke loose. Bits of apple pie flew through the air and the foil dish shot away like a Frisbee. A surprising number got some in their mouth. So much for dessert.

Tom Cane, nicknamed 'OD,' drank beer until he suddenly passed out, still seated on the couch with his eyes shut and half a bottle in his hand. Somebody removed the bottle and drank it. Burped.

But that was the last beer. Snowy-haired drift diggers confirmed it. The marijuana was gone and so was the hash oil, and crawling around on the carpet unearthed nothing smokeable. So that was it for the drugs.

But then – consternation! They had run out of cigarettes. Action was now unavoidable. A posse was formed, led by Parson, to plunge out into the snowstorm which had just restarted. Out of sight, out of their minds. The glass door slammed shut and the posse were gone. Peace. The mellow trance of Pink Floyd filled their smoky cave: *Wish You Were Here*.

Steven found himself wedged pleasantly between lovely twin sisters, chattering across him. When he put his arms round their shoulders they neither minded nor responded. Nor, perhaps, noticed. Their jolly green eyes met across him. He focussed on the lyrics: *We're just two lost souls swimming in a fish bowl, year after year... Wish you were here.* Like all pop lyrics it made no sense – unless they were swimming in separate bowls – but perhaps that was the point.

'The point,' he announced, 'is that there *is* no point.' The sisters nodded – at sixteen they were so many years ahead of the thirty-two-year-old that in his whole life he would never quite catch up. *Shine on you crazy diamond.* Every song was so damn full of advice. The amplified man with the mike told you what to do, or the woman told you how she felt. *And did we tell you the name of the game, boy, it's called Riding the Gravy Train.*

With Parson gone, he was keeping the volume low – those poor McTavishes had *said* it was okay, but midnight had come and gone. The cigarette scouting party had not returned.

Eddie beckoned him over to ask what he thought of her students, 'the Stop and Go Twins.' A woman who could never remember a punchline, she then told him the full, hilarious story of where they got their name.

The previous summer they had signed on with a road-repair crew and been planted, one at each end, with the STOP/GO signs. Sadly, they were unused to acting independently, so there were either long, long traffic pauses – not that the lead drivers complained, staring at their gorgeous faces under the yellow hard hats – or else all hell breaking loose. So the besotted foreman had to whistle them in for briefing.

'When your sister turns her sign so the GO side faces you, you have to turn yours so your STOP side faces her. Okay? You'll do fine.'

And after that, they did. The only problem was cars halting in shock as they saw the second twin – or pulling U-turns to take another run through. But they lasted the whole summer and were rehired for next.

'Same in class,' said Eddie. 'They're a few bricks short of a full load.'

'But they're built like brick shit-houses,' whispered Steven. 'They'll go far.'

He slipped on his own favourite 10-inch LP, Clifford Brown blowing *Jordu*, his solo as well constructed as an intelligent conversation, and the party began to dissolve.

He and Eddie dumped the ashtrays, decided to leave the rest – the kids had taken the refundable empties – and went to bed...

A sudden blast of noise.

'Party time!'

Parson had returned and put on the Allman Brothers at peak volume.

Steven leapt up and handled it diplomatically, steered him around and out and up through the snow.

Parson was feeling no pain, unlike Steven, who stood barefoot on the ice just long enough to watch the cheerful student start off in his parents' white Mercedes – and he waved it a cheerful goodnight as he scampered back to bed.

In the clear blue-and-white morning there could be seen a white Mercedes lying on its roof, blocking the curving driveway.

Parson was fine.

The Butts were evicted.

Canadian Tyre

Moving all their stuff to the new, upper-story place by sports car took an impressive number of trips, even after Steven had removed its hard top (a farcically complex procedure needing at least two skilled assistants) and had shivered back and forth in his camel driver's coat, the little car bulging with boxes, trunks and such roped-on oddments as Eddie's new Rossignol *Stratos*. His final load was, of course, the hard top.

This resettlement had put his car preparations behind, so now he swung into action. After daily phone calls, two of the four 5½ inch-rimmed wire wheels he had ordered arrived, so he collected them from the CN railroad yards, had Michelin Xs mounted, and, since the car was a bit of an understeerer anyway, put the wider rims on the front. Still no sign of the roll bar, though.

'The item has definitely left the other end but has not as yet arrived here at this end, sir,' was the daily refrain, on the phone and in person. On a hunch, he finally thundered down to the CN yards yet again, marched in behind the counter and did a search. And there it was.

'Is *that* what you mean by a roll bar, eh? We was looking for something much bigger, wasn't we, boys?'

After jamming it in place he wished the thing *were* bigger. When he sat in the car, his gold crash helmet domed well above it. Eddie thought it looked very nice, very racy, but he snapped at her.

'Right! It's perfect. If the car goes upside-down the road'll only grind my helmet down to about, oh, the top of my ears. Perfect! For midgets.'

Dashing away after delivering his lecture on Managerial Strategy (not to be confused with Managerial Tactics) he got the local machine shop to fabricate him four steel blocks, about the size of half-bricks, drilled for the long bolts he would now need, and mounted the roll bar on top of them. The blocks cost a few dollars, the bolts a small fortune.

'You're not in any great rush for these, eh?' the machinist had asked, and the desperate Steven slipped into an Australianism that he had never used before:

'Listen, mate. I'm busier than a one-legged man in an arse-kicking contest!'

That made the point, otherwise he was going to be busier than a one-armed paper-hanger. He had noticed that his Englishness dissolved under pressure, and the pressure was rising.

His four-point racing harness now made him feel very much the racing driver, though he had to click off the safety release whenever he wanted to look behind or park. But he was looking forward now, his race entries posted in, his dreams full of late braking, smooth heel-and-toe downshifts and getting the power on early, early, the key to the quick lap.

The sports car club held its Spring Fling slalom, this one on the tarmac of Canadian Tire's car park, and he won again, though not until his third and final run, by holding it scarily close to valve-bounce revs in second, to get the time he needed. (A fourth run was cancelled when snow flurries started down.)

'But you always look so *slow*!' said a couple of wankers-on, music to his ears. 'What's your secret, eh?'

'Special racing engine,' he lied. They were nice kids, but being Australian you never give a straight answer unless you're being paid, and certainly not then.

There were some hot cars and surprisingly quick drivers. A Lotus Cortina was ferociously fast round the pylons but always managed to clip one and score the two-second penalty. Someone called Morris produced, of all things, a full-race Mini Cooper on race tires and was hilarious to watch, lurching and whizzing about in a flail of red witches' hat cones, lost in a car park. No doubt he would do better on the race track.

Alan Burns had his polished MGB and was predictably hopeless. But the big threat was another MGB. Full-race. Freshly built up over the winter by its immense driver, Paul Miles, who was mercifully only using 5000 revs on its new engine. He seemed to know what he was doing though, and was not pleased when Steven's final time beat his by a tenth.

'Well, what do you expect!' he roared, jovially. 'Bald snow tires don't have a lot of grip, eh!' And true enough, he was running on bald snow tires.

That night Steven suddenly sat up in bed.

'Wait a minute!' he announced into the darkness.

'What is it, Stevie?'

'Bald snow tires are better than *my* tires! They're like racing slicks, and I bet they're soft rubber too. And I'm Steven. Or Steve.'

'Of course. How right you are. Let's go back to sleep, shall we?'

She checked that he had not sneaked her necessary open-a-crack window shut. He had, so she waited till his first snore and sneaked it open.

She could feel him slipping away. It was one thing for her to be jealous of Linda Austen, and all the others she wasn't supposed to know about. But being jealous of a rusty little green car? Ridiculous!

In her dreams she was on the hot sand of Whale Beach...

– She checked that her window was still open a crack – No, the bastard had shut it on her again, so she sneaked it open again.

As for getting back to sleep, the overhead march had been replaced by the urgent ding-ding-dinging of the open Regent Street rail crossing, which now started up, a sure sign that a train was approaching, was crossing, or had just crossed. This warning symphony, performed twenty times a night, irritated her – but it enraged Steven, who told her he had tried but failed to get his engineers to see how absurd it all was.

'Why does CN need to warn people that the train has just gone past?' he had demanded of them. 'Why doesn't the bell stop?'

The shrug. That's the way it is. The way it's done is the way it is.

'No but really, guys. From a communication point of view,

what's the bell *for*?'

'To warn cars there's a train coming,' they chorused, masters of the obvious.

'But why's it so goddam loud? The train's not coming through my bedroom!'

Joyously they explained that with the car windows and the music up, you can't even hear it.

'So if you can't hear it what's the point of it? Is it for people who drive with their eyes shut, who can't see the flashing red lights?'

He had them for a moment, so he pressed on, Socrates closing in on some hapless Greek cutie. 'So tell me, when you see the flashing lights start, do you stop dead?'

Not really. They mostly slowed and looked for the train. If there was no train coming they'd cross – Canadian trains can take a week to pass. But if there *was*, they stopped. Steven was relieved to hear it, but soldiered on.

'OK. So a red stop light means stop, and you stop; but a pair of flashing red lights means: slow right down and watch for trains. It's *supposed* to stop you but it doesn't. So here's my question: why doesn't CN use an ordinary traffic light to stop cars?'

They had him here. 'Because it's a *railway crossing*, Sir!' (Sheesh! Don't they have trains in Australia?) 'You don't *have* to stop. Nobody's going to run into the side of a train when they can see it right in front of them!'

'You're right. But what if they *can't* see it? I did some research on this. Did you know two hundred people a year in Canada are killed running into the side of trains?'

'They must be blind.' They had a good laugh at these dead Dodos.

'No. You can't see the side of a train at night. It's invisible. Other night I'm driving back from Saint John in the rain, I come round a corner and ahead there's a sort of grey mass across the road, like a fog. I hit the brakes and it was a train. It was a train! I'm skidding, I got stopped two feet short of the tracks.' (A lie; it had been five car lengths.) 'So I called CN head office and told them their rolling stock needs reflectors on the side, to stop drivers running into it.'

'Bet they loved that, Sir!'

'They hung up on me. Thought I was a crank...which brings us to our next topic, Resistance to Change. Have you all read the article I set, "Gunnery at Sea"?'

A setback! A compression test at Canadian Tire revealed that cylinder three was a dud. Could they manage an engine rebuild? They nodded. Absolutely.

Could they do it in a week? Hey, they could do it in a couple of days...once they got the parts, that is. From Halifax.

How long would it take to get the parts? Oh, depends, Sir. Could be a couple of days, could be a couple of weeks. Longer. Depends if they have to be back-ordered or not.

Steven made a decision. 'Order me a new engine. A complete short block. You know, everything except the head, the carbies and so on. Phone it in now and make it a Rush. Okay?'

'Short...block...for an MGB –'

'Sixty-six.'

'Nineteen...sixty-six.' Steven watched the bruise-black fingernail trace its way through the parts number book. The call was made. Yes, the part was indeed in stock. Rush delivery.

He was in for a lot of money, close to a thousand dollars by the time it was in and running. But the racing starts in two weeks! An easy decision.

In one week the part was in. His heart was thudding as he approached the order desk.

'Yessir, Mr Bute I have the part you ordered, I have it right here for you, Mr Bute' – and handed across the counter a cardboard box big enough to hold a distributor cap.

Big Paul Miles had a great belly laugh at this story, but volunteered the information that a garage in Moncton did shave cylinder heads. A sixteenth of an inch off the head gives a huge boost in compression (8.8:1 to a sexy 10:1) and torque. Confirming this in the hot-up book, Steven roared away down the Saint John river.

Eddie was now able, for the first time in her life, to devote herself to her first love, modern dance. The ballet classes were getting her back into shape and she had attended the first, informal class of a strange new modern dancer in town, up from New York. Jane Gotham had just left Merce Cunningham. Merce *Cunningham*. The dazzling Merce Cunningham Company!

Who knew the full story? Perhaps she was simply past it. ('Old dancers,' as Balanchine had famously pronounced, 'should go away and die.') Ms Gotham still had fine, wide-set eyes, with, perhaps, a glint of madness in their gaze, though below them, the face had collapsed rather. Her swift-moving, fully trained body, that could still do anything and everything, did look too thin for comfort. Alarmingly thin, in fact. Eddie had never seen her eat. There might have been drugs. Certainly, on the bell curve of Normality she was out on the skinny end branches, first one and then the other, switching from gloom to rage like a faulty electrical switch. But then, she *was* an artist. Eddie understood, being an artist herself.

Abruptly, halfway into her third 'master class,' Jane sat them all down on the cold wood floor and unfolded her vision. She would, they would, put on a show. They would give Fodderton a chance to see what modern dance was all about. It would take place in the Playhouse (which, it turned out was being renovated, not demolished). She was considering calling it *Undertow*. No, she did not need alternative suggestions. She would of course be performing herself, but, if they were willing to work harder than they had ever worked in their lives, so would they.

Eddie was now possessed. In their new place, which she had chosen for its wooden, not carpet-on-painted-concrete floor, she rolled away the rugs, had large mirrors delivered, and began filling the space with dance. Day after day, and at night in bed, she was creating a modest little solo to the strains of Ravel.

The body of a man with the horns and pointed ears of a goat – not a pretty picture even without his hairy haunches, skinny hoofed legs and tail, but the word itself, 'faun' was the thing, not the goat-smelling reality.

And the dance was good, well structured. Eddie, when she danced, became another creature, certainly not goat-like or ballet fairy-like – but not Eddie-like either.

Simply, a different creature. Neither a man nor a woman. She felt it, and glancing in the mirror she knew that others would see it too.

Jane Gotham saw it, in silence.

Her only response was to take up smoking. No one had seen her smoke before.

The others applauded and congratulated Eddie.

'Beautiful,' was the word. 'Truly beautiful.'

The phone was ringing, ringing.

'Christ, what time is it?' demanded Steven as he stumbled to their newly-installed wall phone. 'Who's this?... It's for you. You might ask your dance buddies not to phone you at midnight. Some of us have to work.'

Eddie returned to the bed in shock. She was beyond tears, stunned. Steven was trying to be supportive and sympathetic but kept falling asleep. He knew he *had* to stay awake for her but his brow kept sliding down over his eyes...

Apparently what Eddie had done was too 'balletic,' too 'pretty-pretty' and 'as artistic director of Undertow I have made an executive decision that it will not appear in my show. Over my dead body.'

The Moncton Experience

Down the Saint John, still frozen – God, what a climate! – freeze you limp – someone had called it, 'Nine months of winter, three months of bad sledding,' the little car droned along, the blare from its minimal silencer/muffler falling behind in the icy air.

Foot to the floor.

Steven felt the warm, spiritual inner excitement a man feels when he knows his car will have more horsepower on the return trip.

Up over the new bridge, tyres moaning through the delirious series of curves past the sombre religious settlement.

He imagined the Baptists all in there not drinking, not dancing and not fornicating together as one, and gave them a celebratory toot, too too toot.

He skimmed along between the rich pine forests – or what look like pine forests (when he stopped the car and, after a pee, crunched in deeper, he was shocked to find only a thin wall of trees, left there for public relations. Behind, was all clearcut).

The Irving dynasty's relations with the public were becoming clearer all the time. He wondered how long before the forests of the whole province were turned into paper money for them.

Back on the road he swiftly forgot all this, and then – Moncton. There was one thing to be said about Moncton: it's easy to get lost in. Finally he found the garage, the service station, and once more explained what he wanted doing: a sixteenth of an inch shaved off the head.

A problem: they couldn't get onto it right away, this fellow had just brought his Chevy back with a complaint, and 'We have to put our customers first I'm sure you'd agree, sir.' Steven hated being called 'sir,' but not as much as he hated the prospect of having to spend a night in – Moncton.

...And a second night.

The man who does the heads, his daughter is very sick, the doctors don't know what it is. They're doing tests.

But on that second evening he was hit by another thunderbolt, and this one struck him right in the groin. In the Jug Milk stores of Fodderton, while shopping for what was, to him, hilariously called 'Homo Milk,' he spotted a few fetching magazines with titles like GENT – and BUF, which he learned, on speed-reading the thing, stood for 'Big Up Front.'

'Ah, and I think I'll take this,' he muttered, Joe Casual.

Gingerly placed, backside up, on the Jug Milk counter atop his pair of plastic milk bags, it was snatched up and its alarming cleavage studied closely (for some reason the Canadian price was always in tiny print) before being slipped into the obligatory brown paper bag, in case...in case he began reading it on the spot, moaning, and becoming uncontrollable, who knows?

He'd never seen such magazines before.

Australian Customs banned and confiscated *Penthouse*, and their finest minds were only now debating whether the occasional issue of *Playboy* might be allowed in – for the articles – or would its hedonistic philosophy wreak havoc on the body politic?

Topless Aussie sunbathing yes, but *pictures* of topless *Yankee* sunbathers! It was a risk.

Here and now in the brave New World, Steven found he could buy, and easily afford, these glossy monthlies, philosophy-free, devoted to photos of large-breasted women.

The women were not quite his type perhaps, with huge hair and some odd habits such as licking their own shoulders. Some wore a pair of big black ink spots over their nipples, and they all had one over their crotches. But their shamelessness touched him. One looked straight at the camera with a huge smile.

And the boldest ones (as, seated on the toilet, he studied the tiny advertising photos) were even approaching, with open mouths, the black ink spots of their unsmiling male partner.

But it was the tits he went for. Every issue they seemed to go up a bra size, and he was fascinated.

He'd read in *Time* about a slim stripper called Carol Doda who had volunteered to have her breasts injected with silicone, progressively expanding them, to the roaring delight of her public – eventually they named the strip joint after her, or maybe they just gave it to her. 'Now every girl can be as big as she dreams,' the dream woman had cooed to the *Time* reporter, and Steven had wondered just how big a girl's dreams could get.

So this evening, in this small Mom 'n Pop store beside Moncton railway, Mom in attendance, he was not buying milk, had already bought a Mars bar and was flipping swiftly, dazed, through the best collection of one-handed reading matter he had ever seen. And was caught.

'Sir, ARE YOU BUYING OR READING?'
(How dare she!)
'I'm buying, I'm just deciding which one to buy.'
'WE'RE NOT A LIBRARY, YOU KNOW.'
He plucked out the final magazine – and saw her.
Chesty Morgan.

The cover showed a blonde woman, with good legs, posed beside a pedestal, gazing goddess-like upwards, her plump breasts hanging... well below her navel. Almost down to her black spot.

'They've...finally gone and done it,' he confusedly thought, and came in his pants, an orgasm of astonishing sweetness and warmth.

Clearly, he was buying.

In the morning his car was pronounced, 'Ready for you to pick up, they're just finishing it off for you now, sir,' and he lost his temper.

'This bloody job better been done right, I've been waiting long enough. You did take the sixteenth off the head, right, no more? Just a sixteenth? If the valves start hitting the pistons when I torque down the head you're gonna wish you'd never seen me.'

Absolutely. They looked as if they were already wishing that. Definitely no more than a sixteenth. If anything, a tad less.

He drew out his wallet. Paused.

'How much less?'

Mechanic and manager were vague, insisting that he would be very satisfied. Steven marched backstage, found the man who operated the head milling machine and asked him.

'A thou,' he said, not looking up.

'A thou less than a sixteenth?'

'No, a thou. We took a thou off your head. We just skimmed your head. Why'd anyone want to take a sixteenth off? There'd be nothing left.'

Fuming, Steven drove home in a car that had precisely the same horsepower as when he had left.

He'd just have to drive harder, that's all.

Race Day

Debert was an abandoned military airfield.

Not a building stood, and grass sprouted through the cracked concrete of the paddock area. The military rented it to the Atlantic car clubs whenever they asked. They had to. To refuse would only have raised suspicions. Suspicions and doubts.

For there were already suspicions, murmured over many beers, that the place was not abandoned at all, but housed, deep underground, some top-secret electronic surveillance complex, a whole city with spy planes, a maze of subterranean roads and – who would know? – maybe a racing circuit of their own. Maybe squadrons of pit babes. The FU Sports Car Club liked the idea of the squadrons of uniformed pit babes.

Did the sworn-to-secrecy underground workers wait till the racing noises overhead died away, and then abandon their UFO repairs and surface, to run hot laps in hot mystery vehicles? For a locked-up, unused airfield it did show a surprising range of fresh rubber marks, both straight and curved. Perhaps they smuggled in drugs on off-days.

As he swung the MG into the paddock, Steven noted that every other team's car had arrived on a trailer. Some of the racing cars even had advertising on them (not allowed in purist Australia).

'Let's hope we don't have to go home on a trailer,' he told Eddie, his team.

'Just take it easy, love. It's your first race.'

'I will, I promise.'

But already the adrenaline was rocket-fuelling him into that pre-race state of sharpness. He was never so alive. He saw everything now, every blade of grass, an early bee struggling to get its motor going, a dark cricket. The pale spring sky was filled with light, not the ground-glass glitter of a Southern sky perhaps, but it did have its own Canadian-style light, and he was hungry for light.

Swiftly he unloaded the boot/trunk, stuck on his plastic numbers, taped up his headlights and that was it: the car was as ready as it could be. He had arrived dressed for battle, in his white racing suit with full name and blood type, so that if push came to shove, the track marshals would know what name to call him by – STAY WITH US MR BUTTS! – or at worst, describe him.

Crouching over a hand mirror he inserted his hard contact lens, which always stung and left him with a bloodshot right eye, though it did improve his view into the right side mirror.

Across in the snow-flattened grass, a spotty bird he'd not seen before was pip-pipping in alarm and doing an Academy Award-winning impression of a bird with a broken wing. So were two others, which struck him as more than a coincidence.

Overhead, above the rumble of engines warming up, he heard a hoarse bark, like an unusually cheerful Australian crow, and watched an immense raven cruise by – or was it a remote controlled spy plane? It seemed ominous either way, but as he had so wittily told his students, 'It's unlucky to be superstitious.'

Deep inside, he still thought himself unlucky. Black Sunday in 1966, when the three stones flew up had confirmed it, though Hat-Trick Sunday, he thought, might have taken off the curse. But once in 1965? – 64? late, at a party at lucky Paul's, an unnecessarily tall young man from Melbourne had gone around the group doing his party trick of diagnosing them as Lucky or Unlucky. Had stared into Steven's bright blue eyes and paled.

'Unlucky,' he had whispered into his ear, and moved on to the luckier waiting girls.

The new guy from Down Under circulated among the drivers, each struggling with last-minute preparations, greeting those he knew, wishing them good luck, witty and insulting and making them laugh. Paul Miles, who was a doctor in his spare time, was applying his stethoscope to his giant SU carburettors to balance them. Steven made obvious wisecracks and moved on. People liked him. He felt at home. He felt ten feet tall.

One more thing. The trickiest part of racing at Debert is

finding somewhere to pee. There are no trees; it was enough to make a dog howl. In the end Steven had to piss against his own car. And another thing. Irritating, but he was always too nervous to wear cotton underpants under his fireproof Nomex long underwear. Cotton burns. Elastic burns fiercely. So now, after a hasty shake he was reminded of this omission, his super-sensitivity extending to a dribble-burn down his right inner thigh. Nobody said racing is a comfortable sport: it's grace under pressure.

As a new licence-holder, Steven was required to turn half a dozen laps, observed from behind by Max Someone, the Senior Instructor.

'The new boy's right on line but he's a bit of a snail,' he heard Max tell the officials, but his card was signed and he was in. He practised and qualified slowly, too – third slowest; how many laps his old engine had in it at peak revs was the question.

The standing start of a motor race is the most exciting few seconds in the entire sporting world. And Steven was good. He had studied the three starts before his race. The Official Starter, in blazer, cravat and yachting cap, had walked across the track in front of the pack of yowling cars, kept walking – suddenly leapt in the air, half-turning, and dropped the flag.

Then the field had moved off, drivers deafened by the mayhem all around, struggling against wheelspin, swerving for any opening gap.

Not for Steven, sitting at the back of the grid, out of sight, out of mind. He had no intention of starting when the flag dropped. He would pop the clutch the instant he saw the starter's knee bend – you can't jump in the air without bending your knee first.

As the big flag swept down, his MG was already blaring up the left side of the grid. The starter saw him coming and sprang back.

The man was certainly agile. Snapping it into second, Steven hoped he hadn't run over his cap.

He grabbed third, slotted into the pack and barged across as far as he could before braking for the sharp left-hander.

At the hairpin he was fifth. Next lap, fourth.

The trouble was the long back straight. The noisy Volvo ahead had more horsepower, certainly much more 'cubic noise,' and its driver was sharp, with quick hands. And there were still two more MGs and a stove-hot yellow Sprite just ahead of the Volvo.

Lap after lap it was follow-the-leader.

Something would have to be done.

Late braking was no longer the answer: the late drums on the rear had faded to a memory (along with the oil pressure) and Steven kept having that attention-getting, middle-pedal-to-the-metal feeling, pumping twice – and next lap, four times – before the hairpin. With a grunt he abandoned his textbook smooth-driving style and started driving like a man possessed, like a man whose car was definitely going home on a trailer: red line/snap shift, red line/snap shift, that pulled the Volvo back a length or two. Two laps to go.

Now something would really have to be done.

At the end of the back straight was a right-hand sweeper – then a quick brake/change down to third for the left-right-left chicane. The chicanes were made up of haybales which you weren't supposed to hit 'unless you really have to.' On the final lap, after omitting the part about braking and changing down to third, Steven really had to.

He felt he was driving through a haystack, but when the flying hay cleared, he was already at 6000 rpm in top, rocketing towards the next chicane, easily overhauling the Volvo and a pretty blue B from Nova Scotia.

When the next hay explosion cleared, using the wipers this time, he was up beside the racing B of Paul Miles (mercifully still not using his new car's full revs), iron-manned him into the right-hander, and was second. Two corners to the finish.

He'd finish second.

... Or would have, but the Sprite driver, perhaps mesmerised by all the exploding haystacks in his mirror, ran wide on the next left-hander, yanked it back, then found himself going sideways on full right lock, while watching a green machine looming up from nowhere. Cornering on its rims, listing a good fifteen degree to starboard, the mystery B clawed its way by, flicked onto the other lock and — was that a regal, backhand wave from the cockpit? went on to win. By about half an MG-length, over a hard-revving Miles coming up unseen on his right side.

The chequered flag looked nice, very nice. The starter had safely recovered his cap. Steven was crying as he cruised his victory lap. Miles, in his Right-Hand-Drive Car, crossed over and came up on his left. They briefly clasped hands down the back straight.

The prettiest sight in the whole racing world is the flag marshals waving all their flags together on a victory lap: yellow, green, blue, red-and-yellow striped for oil.

Now he was grinning, even though the lovely flag colours were smeared through tears. The waving at the demolished chicane corner might have been less than wildly enthusiastic, as they were lugging new hay-bales into position, and there may even have been a finger, but surely it meant: Number One.

Eddie was impressed. She had a migraine, but she was still impressed, and hugged him hard, fiercely.

'You smell like a pig,' she said brightly.

Max Somebody, the official from Halifax, took him aside for a little chat, asked him about his past racing and so on. For a moment Steven feared he was going to be disqualified, for cap-running-over or haybale-abuse, but Max was grinning too delightedly for that. Steven mentioned, truthfully, that when he left Oz he held all the hillclimb records in New South Wales — but added, modestly, 'the boys have probably broken them all by now, they're a pretty fierce mob.'

In the end Max asked for his licence and signed it three times with three illegible dates, which made it a full license. And invited Steven to co-drive with him in the Eastern Endurance Series.

This was more like it.

Driving home, dicing with a couple of FU kids in a Sunbeam Tiger V8 round the sweeping curves, Steven felt as happy as he had ever felt in this strange new country.

Even the car felt happy.

Its brakes and oil pressure had returned – racing destroys the breed, all right – and the evening air blowing his uncut hair forward felt sexy on the nape of his neck.

Eddie, slumped, holding her felt hat on with both hands, spoke without looking up:

'We might have to buy us a real car for next winter.'

Maybe, but Steven would be co-driving a very real car at Sanair, Quebec next month: the evil purple Triumph Spitfire with the husky overhead-cam Cortina motor and the wide Firestone slicks. The dreaded, ominously-named... Cortfire!

It was a start.

Because of the chaos of preparing for the race, they were behind in the shopping, their jumbo fridge bright with empty space. Instead of heading home to wash off his sweat and soothe his cramping limbs – racing knocks the body about – Steven agreed to turn uphill, and swung towards fluorescent-blazing Dominion, now open for Sunday shopping.

When finally Eddie staggered out with the rattle-wheeled shopping cart, each of their huge shopping expeditions being an attempt to end forever the need for shopping expeditions, he sprang from the car, plucked out the six giant brown paper bags and loaded them away. Then he jogged the ill-handling cart back to its ramp.

But at their back door, aching, desperate now for that hot bath and oblivion, he blundered badly.

The problem was the way Eddie did things. She had no sense of efficiency. He was sure that if there was a harder way to do something, she would find it. And she wouldn't stick with it, either: if she washed up from left to right one day, she would switch over the next. Her most-used utensils were buried deep, her most decorative ones artfully deployed over every working surface. The can opener vanished daily.

In his bachelor days he'd had every tool in readiness; breadboard and bread knife out, his pop-up toaster permanently plugged in, his steam iron (he ironed his own shirts) pre-loaded with water and standing on his ironing board. By contrast, Eddie, if she couldn't manage to fold and hide their new ironing board, would doubtless stick a bowl of roses on the thing.

He was reminded of the Dada iron with the metal spikes on it: *made* for her.

With Steven, it was toilet roll on the right way round, toothbrush, toothpaste tube with top firmly on, razor soaking in anti-rust, brush in lather soap – everything ready for action.

With Eddie, pretty well everything lay where she had last used it. He'd once found her pen for her – on top of the fridge!

As a kid his favourite film, the film that changed his life, was *Cheaper by the Dozen*, a heart-warmer about the founder of Work Study, a man who ran his home on efficiency-expert lines.

It worked, and his twelve children, and his like-minded wife, had adored him! That's what a real father would be like, thought little Steven, sitting in the darkness of the Hoyts Suburban Theatre rolling Jaffas around his tongue for as long as he could before having to crunch them.

Firm but fair, the man was adored.

So that was how to be adored.

Eddie now stood at the screen door holding it open for him as he approached bearing a 'lazy man's load' of three huge bags instead of two.

His load, with all the eggs, was beginning to slip – but then, instead of stepping out of the way, she switched tactics and tried to fumble two bags from him.

'MOVE OUT OF MY WAY!' he commanded, and she shut down as if he'd hit her with a brick.

'GET OUT OF MY WAY!'

Gravity

Though they were still living together in the same house, they were no longer a couple. He threw himself more into his work and his racing.

His work became harder, not easier, as the semester wore on, but finally it was done, and he'd survived the engineers.

Revenge is sweet.

The exams were in, and the graduating mechanical engineers, for their final practical assignment were to race soap-box derby cars down the university hill.

Their machines were impressively well made, of welded steel tubing, fibreglass and, in a pinch, wood. No two were the same, though they'd had to use standard wheels. In paired starts, they flew down the long, steep hill past Steven as he walked up.

At the start, he looked over the machinery.

The one built by Stu, the 450 horsepower Dodge owner, was a masterpiece of lightweight construction, a spidery, chromed space-frame with minimal aerodynamics, obviously relying on light weight for its speed. Which it did not have. Although first off the line, by half-way down the course it was always caught and passed.

'Stu! How yer doing, mate? Listen, you a betting man? Who's got the fastest time so far?' (The scowling Stu flicked his thumb at a cart next to him, a primal, boxy all-wood number.) 'Listen, Stu, lend me your machine for one run and I'll bet you your car against mine I can beat him.'

'You haven't even got a car!'

'Sure I have. Right over there. Class winner at Debert last weekend. It's a 1966 MGB.'

'Like I say, you haven't got a *car*. You want my Dodge you gotta shoot me first.'

'Okay, ten bucks.'

'Ten bucks it is.'

'Scuse me a second, I'm freezing.'

When he returned from his car he wore his huge Afghanistan coat and was strangely hunched over.

'Bit of a gut ache mate, but no worries. Let's get into this thing.'

He lowered himself painfully into Stu's machine, flipped down the visor on his crash helmet, and let himself be wheeled into precise position for the gravity drag.

As the flag dropped and the wheels were released he began jerking madly forwards and backwards like a railway velocipede, one of those Push-Me-Pull-Yous, which gave him a half-length lead, then lay back – and won by two lengths.

The tow car driver reminded him that the run was unofficial, didn't count, before tossing him the rope to be towed back up the hill. Returning from his car without his coat but with his hand out, he was pleased to accept the ten dollars, even in change.

Trophies were nice but money was better. He was now a pro.

'It's all in the driver, mate. It's all in the driver.'

Stu said not a word.

Returning to his car he found a black-haired professor with red lipstick – he had seen her in the Faculty Club – leaning against it.

'Rose Russell, Chem. You're that new business-body from Australia.'

'I'm not businesslike at all, really. I just teach it. My background's psychology. I want to be a racing driver when I grow up.'

'I noticed. You're quite the lad. One day you'll have a real car. How come you went so much faster than everybody else? It's just my scientific mind talking, I'm not questioning your superior character and so on.'

'Should hope not.' He leaned in. 'Special racing engine. I'll show you but you've got to swear not to tell anyone in the Engineering department. Anyone, not even your boyfriend. Not even your boyfriend's girlfriend. Nobody.'

'It's okay, I'm married. My lips are sealed.'

He clicked open the small trunk of his car and pointed to his tools.

'That copper hammer, for the knock-off wheel nuts? Must weigh six pounds. I had it in my left coat pocket, with all those spanners, sorry, wrenches. Those socket wrenches? Right pocket. Sweating that they were all going to fall through. Pants pockets? Full of stones. Even had some lead wheel weights on me. But the big horsepower boost was that hydraulic jack.'

'I shudder to think where you put that.'

'Right. Held it on my guts the whole way.'

'But...when you drop two objects from the top of the Leaning Tower of Pisa, the heavier one doesn't hit the ground first!'

'You're right. If it was a *falling* race I wouldn't have bothered with the jack. Damn thing kept bouncing on my nuts.'

She was fun. She had a filthy chuckle. They both drove down to the Beaverbrook, which he called the Beaverbrain, an unintended joke, for a drink and a chat. She wanted to know what 'Knock-off wheel nuts' were and he explained that when you belt them with a hammer they come off in your hand. She raised elegant eyebrows and blinked rapidly at him. She had too much mascara and a dirty mind. A dirty mind, as some T-shirt author has written, is a terrible thing to waste, so he forged ahead.

'When you're in a hurry, like in a race pit-stop, you can get it to come off in one hit.'

'Ugh. Sounds a bit brutal to me. Still, don't knock it if you haven't... Where can I get me one of those knock-off hammers?'

'Gee. Canadian Tyre lingerie department, I guess. You know, in Australia "knock off" means to quit work. I had no idea it meant anything different here. My first class I asked them, "So what time do you guys knock off?"'

'I can imagine the reaction. It *is* rather a personal question.'

'Exactly. Stunned mullets.'

'Scuse me?'

'Another Australian expression. It means "Stunned mullets."'

'Oh, I see. Fish. After you hit them with your thing.'

'Knock-off hammer.'

She sucked on her cigarette, considerately squirted it out the far side of her mouth, and burst into that filthy chuckle of hers. He joined in. Half the bar joined in.

She could drink, too.

The next day, the very next day, there was a tap at his office door. Professor Butts had a closed door policy and was deep in his In-Tray, wading through a foot of turgid administrivia that had piled up, unread, during the desperate days of teaching. One day, he swore, he would invent the New, Improved Butts In-Basket that would regularly invert, flipping the older, now urgent material up to the top. And would, if untouched for longer than a pre-set period, say a month, flop to the side, sliding everything into the round file, the WPB.

'Come in,' he bellowed, swivelling his chair. And in walked Rose Russell. Behind her he caught a glint of departmental secretarial spectacles, peering over their IBM Selectrics.

Assistant Professor Russell shut the door, trudged towards him and slumped into a chair. She was as low as she had been high the day before. She told him she didn't sleep well and she drank too much coffee. And Pepsi. She loved her flat Pepsi. First thing in the morning she went to the fridge and she had to have her Pepsi. Coke, she didn't like the taste of; it had to be Pepsi. She bought those huge new bottles, you know the ones? He didn't, but he nodded.

The conversation was circling, like flies around something nasty, and he sat, nodding, his training in Clinical and Abnormal Psychology to the fore now, his admiration for the big-eared father of Non-Directive therapy urging him to sit. And nod.

'Mm hmm... So you're having trouble sleeping...'

'I'm having trouble everything. This place. Did I tell you Matt and I were a joint appointment? But they made him Associate Professor – so we wouldn't have any arguments, the Dean told him.'

'Mm hmm. And you're still an Assistant...'

But that wasn't it. And slowly, painfully, out it came, extruded in little bits, sighs, fragments – and fast, long, witty bursts of insight. This was a hyper-intelligent woman who was convinced that she had ruined her life, or at least her love life, by some kind of unspecified wildness in her youth.

'Sixty men,' she muttered, looking away.

'Mm hmm... What about them?'

'Yes. What about them? *Sixty men.* I've had sixty men, don't you think that's too many men?'

'Is that a lot?...' He honestly didn't know. He'd only had one, himself; one man and thirteen women.

'... I mean I don't know the average for American women – you *are* American, aren't you.'

'Well, it certainly wouldn't be sixty!'

'Mm hmm.'

'Do you have any Pepsi?'

'Hmm mm, sorry.' He would get some in. He offered her the metal WPB as an ashtray.

She talked on, about how badly everything was going, and how her PhD research, on organochlorides – she was one of two chloride experts in the world – was stuck for want of a grant for some hugely costly gas chromatograph equipment – and her car's falling to bits and her department head hates her because she's a woman and the worst thing is, she can only get off when her husband (who was in line for Departmental Head) goes down on her and it's so *unfair* on him...'

'Mm Hmm. That's a lot of issues... Why is it unfair?' (An invisible Rogerian hand clamped over his mouth but too late. No judgements; listen.)

'Because I won't do it back to him, I just can't, but he's so good about it and I feel so *awful* for him.' Now the mascara was smearing again.

Of course! Rose. She's a Catholic. Therefore guilt. He kept this insight to himself. Kept his professional hands to himself too, he didn't want his office filled with sobbing, clutching embraces.

There was more, much more – but towards the end she said something that kicked him in the guts. Oddly it didn't seem to worry her – she just mentioned it as another piece in the puzzle of why her life was a mess. At Yale she was four years a postgrad. And for the whole four years her supervisor was – sexually abusing her, would be the term.

The man would take her down into the departmental basement and do her. All the time, and he was a big man, whatever that meant. No, she didn't enjoy it, but she took it as normal, part of the price of working under such a brilliant man. It was usual.

'Not in my experience,' he had to tell her. 'It's not normal in my experience.'

Not at Oxford, not that there were many girls round. At Sydney one Psych prof, it's true, reportedly began sleeping with one of his girl students, and married her; but this graduate-student abuse business appalled him. It seemed a total abuse of power.

She saw that he was roused, and thanked him for hearing her out, she felt much better – she looked better, and he observed that she looked as if she felt as if she looked better, too.

He thanked her for having confidence in him, for being so open, and showed her to the door, catching another secretarial glimpse over the Selectrics.

Standing at his window he watched her bounce into her battered Bug and whiz away, swinging the door shut on the move.

He stood there for a long time.

Had that been for real?

Was she really in psychic pain, compulsively telling her sad story to see if he, the new boy in town, could help her?

Or did she just plan to make him Man Sixty-One?

If so, she could forget it. He was not as dumb as he looked.

Who knows?

The next day, the *very next day*, a firm knock sounded on his door, and in strode...acting Acting Dean Joyce. Nervous.
'G'day Mike, what can I do for you?'
'Ah! Oh, well, Steven I'm just calling to ask if I have your support in the election.'
'What election? Oh – the one for permanent Dean!'
'Yes, the Departmental Deanship. I can rely on your support?'
'Well...' (This *was* tricky: the man's only qualification for the administrative post seemed to be that he obviously wanted it. As for his administrative ability, he couldn't, as they say, raffle a duck.) 'We've called in three other candidates haven't we, Mike? Outsiders?'

Steven seemed to remember that detail from the ill-tempered shouting match of the last Departmental Meeting, in which Professor Kline (Finance) had accused Professor Rodman of illicit use of the departmental photocopier, for 'Thousands and thousands of pages!' in the writing of his latest book. A charge loudly denied: 'I paid for every single photocopy I made!' – a claim easily checked, though nobody even glanced towards the secretary, who would surely have known; why ruin a fruitful source of academic animosity?

'Yes, three. Flying in next week. But as you know one of them looks hopeless, we're only bringing him in because we're all curious about what a chap with a 4.0 average looks like.'
'Well, naturally you have my support in principle, but I'd have to see them first, wouldn't I? I mean, what if one of them turns out to be Superman on ten bucks a day?'
'But quite apart from that, I can count on your support?'
(The man truly was clueless.) 'Absolutely, of course.'
'So I can count on your vote?'
'So the best of luck for the Deanship. I'm sure you're the man for the job – and you're doing it now, for heaven's sake.'

'Excellent, excellent... So. How are you settling in?'

'Fine. Now term's over I'm finally getting my books organised.'

Joyce eyed the six rows of books, announced, 'I've read this one! Excellent!' and turned to leave. Happily? He didn't seem too happy, and Steven felt the slight dryness of mouth that followed any consideration of his future with the Department of Business Administration, FU.

His support for Joyce would put him out of favour with the rest of the rebellious department (not one of whom wanted the job himself) including those he was already out of favour with for being 'Rodman's boy.' Worse, by agreeing to teach at FU Saint John, he was now seen to have swung over to the latest enemy.

He'd had to piece all this together from hints and dark looks. It seems that by opening a small sister campus in the reeking port city, FU had stuck in the thin end of a wedge that was now being pounded on by the good Port City fathers and the fathers of FU-in-Saint John students, who were only now becoming aware that second-and third-year courses were available only in Fodderton, sixty miles up the road. This was too much for them. Why should our sons (and a few daughters) be forced to leave their homes and travel this dangerous route to complete their education? It smacked of discrimination. What has Fodderton got that we haven't got? (The answer being, FU.) The thin end of the wedge was ripening into a can of worms, so to speak, and, too late, the big cheeses of FU smelt the approaching rat.

Expansion of the sister campus to match big brother would, we learned, cost 'only twenty, thirty mill. or so' of government money.

'For that kind of money,' Professor Kline thundered, his diaphragm jerking his belly, 'we could bus them up here every day of the week for free.'

'For that kind of money we could bring them in by personal helicopter,' squeaked Professor Twine (accounting) in support.

Steven's problem was that he rather liked the smaller classes, and far superior coffee, of the sister campus. Also he had made a friend or two there, including a flamboyant English teacher (Science Fiction, of all things!) who wore pink ties and was founder, and presumably sole member, of The Pink Monday Society. And the lone Business Admin. teacher down there, a pleasant fellow whose name nobody seemed to know, who drove up to attend every Departmental Meeting, often dashing in late to make his sole comment, an apology for his lateness.

A memo had arrived suggesting that perhaps meetings could alternate between Fodderton and Saint John. Departmental outrage ensued. Everyone but Steven and the other long-distance driver sat quietly, amazed at how a roomful of men all in total agreement can still keep attacking each other. Then Rodman, who had some organisational skill, asked the silent ones what they thought. Steven spoke up.

'Well...it'd be good PR.'

In retrospect it must have been his unthinking use of the term 'PR' that triggered the explosion. He was still close enough to his job in advertising, the one before his job in consulting, to think an expression like 'free gifts' was normal.

'Good PR. GOOD PR!' screeched Professor Twine.

'Why don't you go back to selling soap or whatever it is you do!' barked Professor Kline.

This was not a good sign for continued long-term employment.

Wisely, Steven resolved to keep quiet in all further meetings, and did.

But he didn't leave it there.

The secretary having declined any further minute-taking, claiming that it worsened her migraines, Steven, who'd always taken the new-style Action Minutes in his advertising job, offered his services. This would be his quiet revenge.

So instead of transcribing the usual full history of Who Said What and Who Disagreed and Said What in Reply, he now merely recorded – and circulated the same day – a neatly typed list of Who Had Agreed to Do What, and By When. Thus the minutes were blank – except for little things he himself kept volunteering to do, and doing.

Two meetings later the secretary returned, presumably having chosen migraine and heartburn over unemployment.

So the acting Acting-and-soon-to-be-Dean Dean Joyce left Steven's office, firmly shutting the door, and Steven heard him knocking on Professor Goatee's door, although nobody had seen Goatee for some time, not even his students, a few of whom were puzzled by the seemingly random spread of their final grades.

Then his own door swung open and in dashed Rose Russell, high as a kite.

'I've got the car, I've got us something to eat, and I talked Malcolm into lending us his cottage on the lake. Come on.'

Malcolm who? Had he missed a step in this process? Was she in the right office? She was tugging at his sleeve, a naughty girl dragging her big brother into the stolen boat – what was going on here?

Baffled, he snatched up his coat and followed. For once, the Eyes Secretarial were downcast, not watching.

Her car was a pigsty on wheels and she drove fast and badly downriver, swerving to a stop only once to pick up cigarettes.

'You don't, do you?'

'Smoke? No. I tried for a while when I was twelve, but I just couldn't get the hang of it. Maybe if we'd had cigarettes instead of rolled-up filter paper... And then our gym teacher, a little guy, chain-smoker, told us, "the fag shortens yer wind and stunts yer growth," so that was it for me.' (Where the hell were they going?)

'You're lucky.'

'Maybe... Tell me, why don't smokers ever buy enough? You guys always keep running out, and then it's an emergency. Climbing Mount Everest, you'd have to keep dashing down to Base Camp to borrow half a pack. Why not just buy a year's worth? At least a carton?'

'Good question, Professor. I never want to buy too many at a time or I'd smoke them all. It's sort of how we limit ourselves.'

This exhausted the conversation for a while. Considerately, she did not light up in the car, even though it *was* her car, and officially driver's domain. He sort of liked her, liked her bare legs under the wheel, her long pianist's fingers draped over it, wondered about her unseen breasts – knowing that sometimes, under winter clothes you can be surprised: perky little tits can poke out while seriously desirable bosoms may offer no hint of their glorious bulk.

Most of all he liked the way she liked...him. And who knows? If they ended up in the sack, with all her experience she might do something wild like straddle him, or even, if he was fantastically lucky, touch the pair of erogenous zones on his chest. Once, years ago, in the front seat of his father's car, a girl had halted their tongue-kisses for long enough to solemnly unbutton his shirt and apply her mouth, her tongue, her tiny nipping teeth to his left nipple and then his right. She never did it again and neither did anyone else. Ignored by all but their owner, his nipples, in a pinch, would glow redly on his chest, bigger than those of some girls he had petted (especially the left one, as he was a right-hander). But no takers so far. He began to feel lucky again.

Without signalling, Rose swung off the highway and they bounced down towards a lake, passing a huge, out-of-place place that appeared to have a birch tree growing through its roof. Some nuts had recently held a winter bonfire on the beach. They swung into a side track and halted. The cabin. She rattled the key. The place had better have heat.

The idea seemed to be to make love. Steven felt some pressure to hurry up, as his lover-to-be was clearly dying for a cigarette. It was a shade shabby, her jumping his bones within a month, within a month of his marriage, but then, she was a fruitcake and seemed keen, and what man can resist a clear, no-holds-barred invitation? Not him, as he slipped between the clean sheets (which she had brought in a pillowcase) and held her trembling, unfamiliar body in his arms.

Her breasts were very nice. In fact, though no athlete, she was constructed on the American film-star plan: slim waist, long legs, which she wrapped delightedly around him. She seemed ready to go, but he decided to take his time, to be a gentleman on the

European plan – but with the secret knowledge he had picked up Down Under. He had discovered the clitoris. Others had found it before and since, of course, but he claimed co-discoverer status and would now show off his expertise.

His fingertip control did not come off quite as planned, not even on the supersensitive upper left side, the 'Gee!' spot, so after a while he kissed her, cheerfully burrowed down the bed, kissing his way down her flat belly, and kissed her again.

'Oh, yes! When Matt does that it gets me off for sure! Oh, yes please!'

The trouble now was that he made another discovery. Smokers taste of smoke everywhere. Still, his pride was on the line and he beavered away for quite a while before rising like a Greek god and sliding into her.

After a few long, gently accelerating strokes she cried out.

'Oh! I know what you're like! You're one of these people who can go on *for ever*!'

This confused him slightly, as a faintly back-handed compliment, but he was now having a splendid time and, enjoying the image of himself as quite the Don Juan, he humped away for twenty minutes or so, then picked up the pace and howled like a delighted wolf as he finished it. His part of it, anyway.

After a pause, during which she did not smoke a cigarette, she asked a very odd question:

'What's your recovery time?'

He had no idea what she was talking about. Then...

'Oh, uh, I don't know.'

The question had never arisen before.

They ate their rather odd, packaged food picnic, with raw red wine, but there was no water in the cottage taps and what he desperately wanted was a simple glass of water.

Then home they went. It had been fun. She had not sucked on, kissed, rubbed, touched, inspected or even appeared aware of his cock, and he had the odd impression that, for all her talk, she was a little shy in that area. She confirmed this by telling him a bawdy tale. Once, after she was known to have slept with black men, a girlfriend asked her, 'Is it true that their things really are bigger?' and she had had to admit that she honestly couldn't say. She'd never looked.

That night, Number Sixty-One wanted Eddie but she wanted sleep. He lay thinking, hard. He had thought it was a joke, the 'Not tonight dear, I have a headache,' but it was no joke.

Women had headaches all the time. When they got together they compared, not washing powders, but painkillers.

Not in Eddie's case though. She had a horror of painkillers, having convinced herself that if she took too many now, they would become ineffective against some terrible, unnameable pain in the future.

Or perhaps, he reasoned, having been deformed by Catholicism, she believed that pain and suffering were the mark of the Good Woman... Rose, too, was a Catholic. It was obvious: she sinned. But she had seemed...sinned out? As numbed as Eddie was super-sensitive... Maybe it was just all those cigarettes. Maybe they stunted your sex-life too, in which case he *was* luckier that her amusingly sarcastic husband... He had a vision of Rose's delicate, sensitive membranes clogged with tar, deadened with ash. She'd let slip that she had just ordered a mail-order vibrator kit from the States and was petrified that her husband, the tightly grinning Matt, would open the package. It would need, Steven thought, big batteries.

He lay there pleased, pleasing himself, though a touch annoyed that – from now on – he'd have to tiptoe through life being careful not to Wake the Baby, the baby of his wife's current headache. Even a groan, or the soft puff of a Kleenex box could do it...

His wife was always on the lookout for good cakes, and he drove her to a freshly-opened pastry shop she'd read about, in the bustling Saturday market.

They nodded to the Premier, who was standing in front of the counter, having already selected his cakes, then asked for coffees and sat down at a tiny metal table. A young woman entered with two knee-highs, girls of three or four, maybe five – Steven wasn't good with kids' ages. But he and Eddie watched, delighted, as the small pig-tailed one pressed her nose to the glass case, made her choice and confidently banged her tiny hand on the glass, while the other began trying to scale the sloping counter.

The mother caught the couple's ear-to-ear smiles as they sat and watched her children.

She shrugged and said, 'Wild women!'

It was a moment together, a private joke to be shared.

Wild Women.

Children were so cute, other people's children. Though strongly opposed to abortion – after all, it *is* murder – they agreed that if somehow Eddie got pregnant she would have one.

An abortion.

Neck Problems

Eddie was unable to talk about anything of deep importance to her; the words stuck in her throat, so instead of that, she held imaginary conversations with people she knew.

They listened well and never gave her any advice. This one was with Dianne. It was another shopping story.

I'd just finished another marathon shop at Dominion and Himself was sitting in the car listening to the wireless – the Consumer World is too much for his delicate sensitivities. I got him his favourite peanut butter though just the smell of that stuff makes me gag. He at least had the decency to pack it all in the boot and then off he trots to return the cart.

The time before, we'd got in a mix-up at our back door and he yelled at me just for trying to help. I knew he was trying to be on his best behaviour now, but when he came back he started on me. Why was I standing out in the cold? I should have got in the car. Well, how was I to know the door was unlocked? And on the way home this, and that – I can never remember what it's about, I just go blank, but he was telling me what to do and – I get these headaches in the back of my neck, and suddenly I had the worst one ever.

I couldn't breathe. It was like I was strangling. I gave a sort of cough and a choke, and he stopped the car and tried to rub my neck. It was hard as wood, and tears were spurting out and I thought I was going to die. I honestly thought I was going to die.

He said all kinds of nice things to me then and my neck let go a bit, and I remember I yelled 'STOP PUTTING THINGS DOWN MY THROAT! STOP TELLING ME WHAT TO DO!' Or maybe I just thought it.

He said I'd been scarlet, and he was scared I'd up and die on him. Anyway, we got home and he ran me a hot bath and I lay in it, so weak, so light I thought I'd never be able to get out ever again. Now he definitely thinks I'm crazy.

Steven hypothesised that his wife might have been force-fed in her infancy. She'd been born three months premature, covered, she claimed, in black hair (though nothing people said about their infancy could be trusted).

Force-fed or...sexually abused?... She'd never mentioned it.

Not her father, surely. Ernie adored her and he really was a sweet guy, not religious or anything suspicious like that.

And certainly not Steven. He'd been a perfect gentleman on their first date and still was. Well...admittedly on their first date, as she'd reminded him but in a laughing way, he had his hand down her top *and* up her dress (he'd forgotten that bit) but it was many months before they actually made love, and as for forcing his thing down her throat, never.

Never... There was one thing, though.

Perhaps because she was such a know-it-all, she'd once been so dogmatic about some scientific matter – he forgot the details but he knew she was wrong and he was right, something about physics and centripetal force, that he had said, 'I bet you a blow job it *is*,' and she shook hands on it.

She knew what a blow job was, because earlier she had joked about what she *thought* it was, and how it was just as well she hadn't tried it. Like blowing up a balloon it isn't.

Anyway, he won the bet but it was as if she'd forgotten all about it, so he never pressed the point, as it were.

But how could you forget a thing like that, unless there was some...kink in your head?

La Danse Moderne

Rehearsals for *Undertow* were not going well.

The refurbished Playhouse now had a superb upstairs rehearsal room, with a sprung wood floor, mirrors and ballet barres.

In this magical space (which she believed she was getting for free) Jane Gotham spent her days weaving her tapestry of moves and intertwining steps, her imaginary dancers swooping round the floor doing everything that ballet dancers do except wear shoes, turn out their feet, lift each other, or jump. Jumping was out, for this was modern dance. Just as well because her cast, when they were finally assembled (mostly from Miss Duckie's academy), were young and not notably male, and she did not intend to send a boy on a man's errand.

In her mind, rehearsals were going well. But on the floor, fighting time, that enemy of the performing arts, they were barely going at all. With a mere month to showtime, she had almost no show to show. More and more she would sulk creatively while her cast improvised to her chosen music, which they did, self-delightedly, with Eddie Butts, the fountain of ideas with the unfortunate stiff neck, forever pushing, pushing to take over. Creativity was a wonderful thing, but Jane wanted there to be no doubt whose creativity it was: hers.

And she was not getting the support she expected.

Publicity took time.

When Eddie and Dianne heard she had been tramping round the cold streets sticking posters on elm trees and in shop windows, they helped out, but too little too late. (Why had she not just *asked* them? Because they should have known.)

Costumes. Music. Publicity. Tickets. Front-of-house. Tech. Crew.

It all came to a head the day she tried to get the Technical Director, Marcel, to tape *Shaft*. One hundred and twelve bars of *Shaft*, then cut.

It had to be one hundred and twelve bars because Jane had drawn up huge cardboard sheets with random numbers, in four-bar sequences, each number representing a sharp, dramatic move she had created – a different series of moves for each dancer. She agreed to leave the sheets lying on stage, 'so you won't have to memorise them the way *we* would have.' (Merce would have had no trouble, even to a John Cage piece for abused piano.)

This was a relief.

The effect was of concentrated, random madness to a beat, and Steven, watching a rehearsal and taking a few photographs, liked it the best. But he couldn't understand why Jane, watching, was shrieking and yelling, and kept storming over to switch off the pounding music – and then having to start from the beginning, as there was no way to tell where they were.

'You keep just making it *up*!' she shrieked, her voice cracking.

Eddie told him later that Jane could not understand why nobody could follow the counts.

'Well, of course not,' said Steven, who had played the piece, from sheet music, in the Oxford Big Band. 'You can't count it in fours: it's not *in* fours, it keeps switching on you.'

Marcel couldn't count it either. The LP turned, the big tape rolled, and Jane doggedly counted aloud in fours, 'Eighty, two-three-four, Eighty-one, two-three-four' while the wah-wah guitar whacked along in fives and sixes, but her voice always faded out just as the magic number approached...and then she would turn on him.

'Why didn't you STOP IT?'

And he lifted the needle and started again.

After Steven had observed this for two hours the manager, jovial William LeBlanc, walked in and pointed out, rightly, that Marcel was in fact the best TD in Canada, and that, as she was paying him by the hour she'd better get her ass into gear. Which she did, storming out in a whiff of cigarette smoke.

Steven, studying human nature from the background, now took his cue.

He stepped forward and handed Marcel his stopwatch.

'It's seven minutes forty-two seconds, actually. I timed it the one time she ran it right through on stage. Eddie tells me they're all going bananas.'

'Ah. Thanks.' Resetting the big tape machine Marcel noted, 'Now I won't have to kill her.'

Two nights later *The King and I* opened, to show off the newly-added fly tower, the boxy structure on top of every theatre that gives the scenery flats somewhere to go when the stage-hands haul them up on counterweighted ropes. In every theatre but the original Fodderton Playhouse, that is. Rumour had it that the patroness, Lady Beaverbrook, on being shown the Playhouse architect's drawings, had called the thing on top 'ghastly' and crossed it off with her gold pencil. Thus it was not added till she was safely dead, or at least in London, and her disapproval less likely.

So now, for the first time, Steven saw his wife dance with an audience. She had a tiny part as a court dancer who emerges stage right to a glorious golden-toned backdrop, and does fake Indian moves in a spot that too swiftly fades.

She was riveting!

She looked so beautiful, not like his wife at all. For her moment she actually gripped the audience – he heard their silence – and he told her so afterwards, her stage makeup still on, making her larger than life.

Sadly, she was only a one-night stand-in.

After opening night Eddie was replaced by an authentic Indian girl who, as she was quick to point out, couldn't dance her way out of a paper bag, but who looked the part and was signed up for the whole run and round-the-province tour.

But *Undertow* was the big thing.

A one-night stand against the provincial philistines, it was to set Fodderton on its ear. At least that was the plan.

'Who needs New York!' Jane would cry out from time to time.

Slowly it dawned on Steven that Eddie's hobby of dance was as important to her as his own guts-and-all charge to the forefront of the motor-racing world.

No wonder she was being so difficult about it. He resolved to be even more considerate in the future.

In bed she no longer seemed to want to make love, and as he couldn't imagine getting it on, or even getting hard, with someone who didn't want him, and didn't like to keep bothering her, he heard himself telling her to let him know if she ever *did* feel like it again.

He murmured he was quite happy just to suck on her breasts, and was – until one night she pushed him away, saying that it felt like 'something clinging to her, hanging off her' and no, she didn't like it.

Something? Didn't like it? Now? Or ever?

It was confusing.

He tried not to think about it.

The main thing to think about was the race coming up.

Ol' Man River

Not that they were unhappy. They were busy, and keeping fit, and having some magical moments together in this strange new country.

One clear night they went outside to investigate a greenish tinge in the sky, and the Aurora Borealis was putting on a show right above their heads. Twisted rainbows of red, faint yellow and green hung trembling in the sky, shedding and renewing light. They watched till their necks got sore.

'It's so beautiful,' Eddie breathed, but Steven, who was reminded of celestial strips of bacon, or the hanging folds of crystallised stuff inside the caves at Jenolan, thought a more accurate word was 'hideous.' Impressive – but hideous.

Early one Sunday morning they had stood on the ice banks of the Saint John as the spring thaw began, listening to the ice crystals chinking together; a delicate tinkling, ice in drinks, chandeliers, intimate promise of a new life. Of change.

And now the promise was coming true. With a midnight bang the ice broke up (the locals bet on the date) and began to grind seaward, jamming great chunks under the steel bridge. Steven went down to watch the bridge spans straining, the pressure building up. Workmen on the closed bridge hacked and poked like whalers, dynamite was brought in – and finally the ice jam cleared and the watchers cheered. The old bridge had survived another spring and the danger was past.

Roll on spring. A couple of days later, returning from Alan Burns' place on the far side of the fast-flowing, full river, Steven was startled to find himself driving through water. It seemed to be bubbling out of the manhole covers in the road – it *was*, spurting out of them. Surely the road was not below river level! He reached the river. It *was*.

This was absurd. What sort of river can rise three feet while he's having two Moosehead beers, a single malt Scotch and a packet of chocolate biscuits with the cheerful, if faintly boring Alan?

He twisted the radio dial and sure enough, the bridge is now closed and drivers are warned not to attempt... He continued on, downriver. At least the high highway bridge would be open. The problem was to reach it. The drainage system was working well now, draining the river onto the land. One manhole cover had popped up: that would have killed the MG. He drove on, slowly, his feet wet, hoping the rubber distributor cap cover he had just installed knew its job. A truck passed coming the other way, making waves, the driver forcefully waving.

Now his car was alone on the deepening road. Ahead, too far ahead, the rising bridge approach. But the male must go through. Damn the torpedoes – a U-turn would probably scupper him anyway, and the car would float downstream for a while and then – already it felt light. He remembered one drunken afternoon by the Cherwell, outside Oxford, when they tried to see if Hugh's VW Beetle really would, as rumoured, float. Perhaps it would have, if they'd known to seal the 'heater' outlets first, but they hadn't, and it didn't. The MG's motor was misfiring now but at least it still...ran...didn't run.

Oh.

Off with the lights.

Into first.

Starter.

Crank forward. Pause. And again. And again.

...Emerging like a green prehistoric creature from the cold slime onto dry road. Dried everything off, and Bless the Prince of Darkness, it coughed into life and he drove home.

'The trouble with Alan,' he told Eddie, 'What makes him so annoying – and I like the guy – is he won't admit he's gay.'

'Are you sure he is?'

'Of course. But he won't say so because if the word got out he'd lose his law practice for sure. And I can't *ask* him if he's gay because then he'd have to lie to me, and that'd put a kink in our friendship. Which is screwed anyway because he doesn't trust me enough to keep my mouth shut. Which I would if he'd give me the chance, but he won't.'

Eddie thought this through.

'Maybe it's because he's a lawyer. You know, "Liar".'

'No, he's not dishonest. I'd trust him with my life, I really would. And he likes me. Over the Scotch he did open up a bit, told me he's seen *Cabaret* seven times. Seven! I asked what was his favourite bit and – no surprise – he said it's when Sally What's-It finally confesses that she's been sleeping with the gorgeous guy for months, and her boyfriend says, "So have I." He *loves* that bit. He roared with laughter.'

'Maybe he likes boys *and* girls then.'

'No – but maybe he likes boyish girls. I told him my favourite bit in books was in Nabokov's *Ada* – Rose Russell gave it to me to read – where the narrator has been screwing his sister Ada – pun on ardour – pretty well every day since she was a little girl, and ignoring his youngest sister who's insanely mad for him. But at the end of his life he finds that Ada had been cheerfully screwing her little sister daily, too – couldn't get enough of it.'

'That's gross. She must have been a nymphomaniac.'

'Beautiful, too.'

'What *is* it with you men! You're what Buck Turgidson calls a "deviated pervert." Much worse than Alan.'

'No, at least I admit it.'

'I think you're *proud* of it.'

The next morning the phone rang and of all people it was Rose Russell, in tears.

'Eddie? Could you come around and help us with the piano?'

'Of course, of course... What's wrong with it?'

'Could you come right away?'

'Of course.'

They roared downriver, parked where the barricades and flashing vehicle lights halted them, and walked on. Rose had called just as Eddie was pouring their coffee, so she had tipped it back into a big thermos. They might appreciate a fresh coffee, whatever their piano trouble was.

'My God!'

Turning down into the lane they could see the Russell's big old farmhouse, surrounded not by its acre of struggling lawn and fruit trees but by a lake. All the way out to the river was now a lake, of grey, flat, cold-looking water. And it *was* cold, too, as they waded ankle-deep towards the front steps, normally three, now one. The water looked still, but it pressed oddly against them, a strange, steady push like an ocean rip. They held hands, frightened by such a display of sudden, mysterious force, and pushed towards the marooned house.

The other Professor Russell, Matt, emerged with a damp cardboard carton and surged past them in hip-length waders, grinning. He wore a permanent 'Don't hit me' grin, which a little thing like his house going under could not dampen. Nothing could. A skilled undertaker would struggle to get the face looking serious, but the grin would surely snap back into place half-way through the funeral service. He looked deathly cold.

'Hi, guys! Great Spring cleaning, eh? I'll be back in a minute, make yourself at...home.'

'Matt, you look soaked. You been swimming or what, mate?'

The man was shivering under his grin.

'Had to do a bit of scuba diving in the basement, trying to shut off the power,' he called back over his twitching shoulder.

They kicked their wet feet and walked in. The water was just lapping the top step now. One good ripple and it would flow in over the wall-to-wall carpet.

'It's us!' they called.

Rose appeared, black bags under her eyes.

'Isn't this great! We just got the new carpet, and I got the piano tuned just in time.'

They both hugged her hard, feeling her shock, her cold, and Eddie poured the coffee.

'We've had ours – here. Just leave a bit for Matt.'

She drank two mugs, swallowing the too-hot fluid between

coughs. 'How does the water come up so *fast*?' said Eddie. 'It's not even raining.'

'It's tidal.'

(Tidal? A river...tidal?)

Matt returned, polished off the coffee – by now Steven would have killed for a sip but clearly these two had been working all night.

Then: the new piano, Rose's Christmas present, her pride and joy. Matt confessed, still grinning, to having a bad back, so Steven was dispatched to haul in six concrete blocks, a monumentally miserable task. Rose, her circulation restored by the caffeine, crouched before her piano and did a credible Bessie Smith *Backwater Blues*. Steven, splashing up the steps heard,

Well, he rowed a little boat about five mile 'cross the stream and later,

...Cos my house fell down I ain't got no place to go. Instantly she swung into *The Song of the Volga Boatmen*. She had a lovely mezzo voice, like a chain-smoking, whisky-slugging Joan Sutherland, and Eddie joined in. So did Matt.

'This is like a wake,' grunted Steven, struggling in with wet concrete block number three.

'Wake's a good word for it,' grinned his supervisor Matt.

For an instant Steven wondered if Matt knew...if Rose had... No. That would be *too* weird, even for Fodderton. The good Professor was blissfully ignorant. If anything, he seemed to be enjoying the way their suffering had thrown them both – all – together.

Niggers all work on de Mississippi... Rose started up, and when she reached the low notes, the *Ol' Man River* notes, she could actually sing them, unlike Eddie and Matt. Steven could have but was too out of breath to try, as he hauled in the last block and dumped it on the dampening carpet.

'Tote dat barge, lift dat bale!' she commanded. 'Tote dat block, lift dis piano!'

'Screw you,' said Steven. 'My hands are frigid. Those blocks are like ice blocks. Where can I put my hands to warm 'em up? Who's got a warm heart?'

'Here. Cold hands, warm heart.'
'Thanks, but I'd better do it with my wife. This flood may be biblical.'
'AAAAH! They're freezing, Steve! Use your hot head.'
'... Okay. Now where do you want this piano, Professor?'
'On top of the concrete blocks.'
'I'm really sorry about my back,' beamed Matt. 'The Doc says there's one disc could pop out like spitting a watermelon seed.'
'O – kay – so Eddie's as strong as a horse. The Butts'll lift one end and then the Russells slide the first block underneath. No probs. Here we go...'
'IT WON'T GO. IT WON'T MOVE! PUT IT BACK DOWN AGAIN.'
'Sheesh! I think my hernia just got a hernia. You okay, love?'
'I'll never dance again, but hey!'
'Do a dry run. Give it a good shove.'
'It sticks on the carpet.'
'You wouldn't rather just take up the flute?'
'Sweetheart, do we have any plastic, so the block will slide?'
'How do we get the plastic under the piano?'
'No worries. Eddie'll lift it.'
'Could we use a lever?'
'What – to hit me, make *me* lift it?'

While Matt trotted off to get a plastic garbage bag, Rose crouched and began playing again, the Volga Boatmen.

'No! Something light. Something uplifting.'

She switched to music hall.

She was good. It didn't matter that the carpet now had tiny ripples in it as the tide rolled in over the swirling Chinese wool pattern.

Then, 'Pull! Pull! Push!' They got the piano an unsteady block-width off the floor. One end, anyway.

'Hey! Either I've worn myself out or this end is heavier.'
'Of course. It's got all the bass notes in it.'

But they managed: Eddie red-faced, Steven panting.

'Nice work, you got it up eight inches. Now I can play

standing up. But we've got to get it up another sixteen, according to the flood forecast.'

'No worries. We need a volunteer to stand holding the concrete block – I'll lift it first and hand it over, okay? Then when we get the piano up, you topple forwards and put the block in place. Candidates?'

But Rose couldn't and Matt wouldn't, so he handed Eddie the block and struggled to lift his end solo, but failed.

'Get it up!'

'Shove it in!'

They gave up, panting.

'Was it good for you?'

'What *is* it with you guys! Talk about dirty minds.'

Matt didn't seem to get it.

Now they were standing on wet carpet, stumped.

'Hate to change the subject,' said Steven, 'but you know there's a dead horse in your back yard?'

They rushed to the side window to look. Wedged against two apple trees was a big bloated animal, floating on its side.

'It's a cow,' pronounced Eddie. 'No – no udder, it's more like a deer.'

'It's too ugly,' said Steven. 'It's like the world's ugliest horse. Could it be a moose?'

'No horns,' grinned Matt, 'Don't moose have a huge rack?'

You should know about horns, thought Steven, but said not a word.

'Bull moose,' said Eddie the expert. 'Horns fall off after the mating season. They're only for show.'

Then they went back and stared at the piano. Rose was too miserable to play.

Steven tried a feeble joke about it being a Yamaha, and if they could just get the thing started up, but it died. They were cold and all shivering now.

The door squelched open and in came Alan Burns with Parson's sister.

'Can we watch?' he asked cheekily.

'Be our guest,' said Steven. 'We're trying to get these concrete blocks out from under Rose's Yamaha, so we can build a raft out of the blocks, and float off downstream. She's going to accompany us on the piano.'

'Figures – or we could just stick the piano up on the blocks and get the fuck out of here.'

'Oh, *that's* no fun!'

But they did, and did. Halfway to the high ground, Rose halted and looked back at her home, the grey water lapping now at the front verandah, and burst into loud sobs. Matt, oddly, did not comfort her, and Steven yearned to but felt he couldn't, shouldn't. Finally she splashed, apologizing after them.

Standing where the road dipped gently into water they stood, two by two, and all looked back. The big white, weatherboard ark of a farmhouse, which they knew had cost the Russells their life's savings and then some, looked, if anything, absurd; like a symbol of marriage on the rocks.

Among the vans and four-wheel-drive trucks the MG looked like a plaything, and distinguished itself by refusing to start. Flat battery. Steven knew what it was: as the thing rusted away, a decent earth became harder to find, like an addict's useable vein. He now carried jumper cables and hooked them to the Volvo, but groping in the inaccessible darkness behind the rear seats (for legless, headless infants only) must have attached them wrong way round, because a sudden spurt of battery acid splashed and burnt a hole in his favourite Afghan coat. They gave up and push-started the little car, Eddie regaling them with the story of their first date in the Nota.

'It was actually a wedding so I'm all dolled up, and Steven shows up in this miniature yellow racing car. It's got no handbrake so he has to turn it off. It would never start so he orders me to get in and push the clutch down while he pushes, but I couldn't get it down, and we were late so *he* climbs in and I push. Well, it's got this roll bar, which I think was only there for people to push on, so I push away until it gets rolling. But then when it coughs into life it backfires! This great cloud of oily smoke right over me! So I had to go back inside and change, while he keeps revving it up outside.'

'And you stayed with him!'

'I got my revenge – I married him!'

Blue rental van, Volvo and sports car headed back into town, halting only once for the lead drivers to dash inside a Jug Milk and buy one pack of cigarettes each. After that the Professors Russell drove slowly; concentrating, Steven assumed, on their smoking.

They assembled at the Fox's place, the third floor of a prosperous sea captain's house, wisely built well above the river, where the Russells were to stay till the waters receded.

From the packed van they extracted only two small, damp-looking suitcases and headed upstairs, everyone else following, hoping for food. Merlin Fox, a small, hyperactive physics professor opened up, took in the situation at a glance and called back to his wife, the lissom Inge.

'Six for hot showers and lunch, darling.'

He cranked up the thermostat and heartily hugged both women and the girl as if he were the one in need of warming up. Steven had always thought him a fruitcake, but now enjoyed his hearty, Nottingham-accented hospitality. And the man was brilliant: there was even talk of a Nobel prize in his future. He looked wired enough to work all night and come bouncing in for breakfast.

Steven felt a faint twinge of envy: their host had first-class degrees, prizes and medals hanging on the walls, whereas Steven had always, secretly, thought of himself as a rather dim fellow with an MA from Oxford. One day, if he put his mind to it, he might be a dim fellow with a PhD. But dim, forgetful, muddled. Not dumb, but not bright either. Fast behind the wheel though. Take on Rupe Hughes or Clive Jones any day of the week.

Enter Inge.

'Velcome.'

Now Steven was *really* envious. She was complex to describe. Not that she was a beauty, but in her simple black dress, with her simple, expensive haircut she had style, class, and a deliberate, killer smile framing a provocative overbite.

She hugged Rose and showed her to the bathroom. Matt, Steven noted, stood shivering outside it. The house was non-smoking but they could all smell that Rose had lit up in there. And now Merlin surprised Steven, and probably Eddie too, by swinging into the open-plan kitchen and preparing the lunch. Inge watched critically, but clearly he was going to do the job.

'You think he lost a bet or something?' he whispered to Eddie. 'Think she found him in bed with a graduate student?'

'Don't be ridiculous,' she hissed. 'Some men like to cook.'

'I *love* to –'

'I don't mean cheese on burnt toast.'

He did seem to know what he was doing. Professor Fox could open a wine bottle, pour, slip quiche into their counter-top Braun oven, chop vegetables and slice bread, all without losing the thread of his monologue about the joys of British politics.

Clearly the little guy adored his wife, who was a government librarian. He'd just bought her a light blue Porsche 914, 'Because she looks so good in a sports car.'

Unused to drinking at lunch, the Butts were soon happily quiet, enjoying the dozy comfort of the furniture. Eddie had never tasted Juniper Schnapps before, and took to it like a cat to sardine oil, her pink tongue licking the bottom of her glass, which Inge, with a dirty, Joel Grey *Cabaret* chuckle, kept refilling. Alan and Parson's sister, who had sipped a Schnapps but hated it, had had to leave.

'Our token Canadians had to go do a toke somewhere,' said Merlin.

Inge disagreed. 'Alan's just protecting his reputation.'

'Oh, so you knew he was gay?' blurted Steven, trying to make conversation.

'*Is* he?' Inge thought for a moment, then murmured, just loud enough for Steven to hear, 'He *was* awfully rough.' (Did she really say 'was'?)

'Are lawyers not supposed to, to smoke dope?' asked Eddie,

mortified at Steven's blabbermouth comment.

'Not in court anyway, I don't think,' said Merlin, whose eyes seemed to shine behind his thick glasses whenever he looked Eddie's way.

Steven felt that he should feel jealous, but never did. He could never remember having felt jealousy, and this puzzled him. Envy, but not jealousy. Perhaps he just didn't care enough. Or perhaps all his jealousy got used up that day after he returned from Oxford and called on... The One, precursor of all, the beauteous Lynn, who came breezing out to open the door and had obviously, as her shining eyes and flushed cheeks, and her swollen lips, nothing as crass as smeared lipstick, obviously just been...

And he'd turned and walked away from his life...

He was dozing off, but now an industrial noise from the kitchen woke him.

Inge, who was a Berliner and so not easy to please, concocted the coffee using the all-Braun battery of gadgets, and it was superb but didn't really sober or wake anybody up. Especially the two marooned professors, who were now asleep, with their heads together on the couch back, like the twin faces of comedy and tragedy.

Everyone, even the sleepers, enjoyed listening to the velvet of their hostess's voice, like a solo cello complaining at length about a swan, or attempting to spell Shostakovich, so she chattered on, but Steven realised that what she was telling was, in fact, an increasingly touching story.

Her family had escaped wartime Germany, getting through borders by using her. As the littlest, she was trained as the designated crier. Whenever the authorities began hesitating over their dubious papers and passes, on a signal squeeze from her mother, little Inge would burst into piteous wails, unstoppable, louder and louder, the mother screeching at her to stop, until the racket became so unbearable that clearly they had to be either shot, or else pushed through and out into darkness. They were not shot. She had cried her way across Europe.

Steven reflected that she looked all cried out, dry-eyed and acid, as she compared – unfavourably – every aspect of Fodderton with the broad, civilised streets of Berlin. The ghastly food here, the undrinkable wine and deadly beer, the shrivelled culture in general.

'Ze sign says, "Welcome to Fodderton, City of Stately Elms" ...but ven you get here, all ze elm trees are dead from Dutch Elm Disease!'

An unworthy part of his brain labelled her as a complainer, and this was good, for he had observed, while necking with young ladies in the family Humber Hawk, during his virginal Sydney Uni. years, that the ones who complained non-stop about their friends, their parents, teachers and citizens, often let him put his hand on their breast, while the cheerful uncomplaining ones simply pushed it away and kept the conversation going.

But then the phone rang – Merlin answered.

'It's for you, darling, I can hardly hear them.'

She returned, pale.

'Vater is getting into my library. The fools can't get the sump pump to verk. Can ve go down and see vot ve can do?'

The lower reaches of University Avenue could now only be navigated by canoe. In waders and gumboots they pushed across the cold, sobering water. The railway underpass, now in its third day of fame on the front page of *The Daily Gleaner*, held the deepest water in town, so they clambered up and across the line, past the lovely imitation cathedral and Robbie Burns statue – and could now see a puzzling line of people linking the closed Provincial Library to the Playhouse. It was a bucket brigade. They were passing something from hand to hand.

'It's books!'

Inge crouched at the low basement window and got the full story. Water had started seeping in early that morning, shutting down the electrical pump. Then, when the lower shelves of historical books and records began soaking up the current news, an attempt was made to contact somebody in authority for instructions.

Two members of the Legislature were called at home, but both decided that they could not possibly take the responsibility for deciding to allow any documents to be removed from the library itself, suggesting that the library call the Premier (who was known to be holidaying in Tunisia). And no, they could not come down to see for themselves. Far too busy. With the flood.

This sounded about right for politicians, thought the Butts, neither of whom ever voted for anybody, following the Australian dictum that, 'Whoever you vote for, a politician gets in.'

But as the water rose, some unknown hero had simply kicked in the basement window, clambered down into the freezing dark and started handing out the books. Swiftly a human chain formed, and the sopping books, irreplaceable records of the province's past, hand-to-handed across the car-park to be laid, like drowning victims, on the Playhouse lobby floor.

Steven was now handing off to a determined Inge, who was swinging away and handing to Eddie.

Merlin was inside, having relieved a big potato-farmer, who now emerged almost too frozen and exhausted to acknowledge the cheers.

For the second time that day they sang the song of the Volga boatmen, and it was a happy day, a very happy day, sons and daughters of the New Brunswick soil toiling together to save the treasures and screw the politicians. Kids joined in and they all sang commercial jingles.

A police car pulled up. They half-expected to be all arrested, but instead the cop joined in for a solid half-hour before having to return for de-briefing or doughnuts or whatever.

Of all Steven's memories of Fodderton, this day stood out – and the thrill he felt a fortnight later at the Russell's welcome home dinner, gazing into the candlelit, wine-glow faces of Eddie, Rose and Inge Fox, chattering so tipsily together.

Knowing he he'd had them all.

And deliciously knowing that they didn't know.

Eddie Takes Over

Dianne was beginning to annoy her. The continual invitations to join the 'Women's Circle,' whatever it was, were irritating her, because she had no interest in a bunch of women sitting around talking, did not see herself as a Faculty Wife, was deep in *Undertow* rehearsals, and rebelled on principle at the thought of attending anything that could involve baking. She told her friend Dianne most of this, but the only response was an increase in urgency.

'Oh, please come. I'm making a Death by Chocolate cake, we'd *love* to have you, it's at my place this Wednesday, all you have to bring is a plate.'

So she went. There seemed no other way to halt the invitations, and she suspected that Dianne must have promised someone – perhaps the Circle – that she would get Eddie there. Dianne met her at the door, looked oddly at her empty Fiesta-pattern plate and told her she really needn't have.

Dianne's small apartment, hers since her marriage to the older Professor of Logging had dissolved, was cosy, its walls glimmering with a gentle, diffuse light, a Through-the-Looking-Glass feeling.

'It's like silver foil,' Eddie marvelled, stroking the cool surface.
'It *is*,' gushed Dianne. 'I hated the forest wallpaper with such a passion, one night I ran out and bought about a million rolls of silver foil and just stuck it over the walls. Now I love it. Only problem was, I silvered over the power sockets, and the first time I plugged the vacuum in through the foil, foom! Blew everything.'

'Bet that taught you not to use the vacuum again.'
'Absolutely. Come and meet everybody. They're dying to meet you.'

Rose was there but not Inge. The women were bright, slim faculty wives plus some heavier types who sat on the couch knitting furiously, as if for some personal war effort. Eddie recalled the convent tale of the French Revolution, the women who sat knitting, their needles clicking as the guillotined men's heads bounced, one by one, into the wicker basket right in front of them. These Faculty Women, too, seemed to be waiting for something to be guillotined. She was glad now that Steven's half-joking threat to come with her had been vetoed by a horrified Dianne.

As instructed, she introduced herself.

'Hi! I'm Eddie, Steven Butts' wife.'

'We don't need to know that,' growled one of the knitters. 'It's who *you* are that carries weight.' Then she looked up with a wide 'Sorry, I've *got* to say that' smile, which however did not reach her eyes.

Someone asked her if, being from 'Down Under' she had ever met Romaine Greer, brandishing a flaccid copy of the paperback, with its woman's-body-with-convenient-handles cover.

'No, but Steven has. They were at Uni together.' Which was again the wrong answer.

Then free-for-all discussion opened up, a frothy mix of politics, gossip and learned discourse, and Eddie rather enjoyed it. What a change, what freedom from know-it-all Australian men! All her life, it seemed, she had sat quietly while 'the boys' wagged their nicotine-stained fingers in the air and barked out their free advice for the government of the day, 'Aorta,' as in 'Aorta do something about the roads. The taxes. The abos, the outrageous price of petrol...' Chain-smoking, beer-guzzling men who read nothing but the racing form and would never even bother to vote: pay the fine instead, a small price to pay for keeping their grievances intact.

She was again sitting quietly, but at least this was worth listening to. Then, urged to 'share,' she told them this, and encouraged by the smiles and nods and fuelled by the best chocolate cake since her mother's, she told her Sydney Uni story. A Labour politician, a union man, had addressed the first-years in the vast, tiered barn of Wallace Theatre. He was a little bloke in tweeds who paced up and down, haranguing them, beginning his every statement with 'The plain fact of the matter is...'

'That's what they want you to think,' he would snarl. 'The plain fact of the matter is, is that...'

There were a few ironical cries of 'What about the workers?' but then, about twenty minutes into his speech, he began yet another pronouncement.

'Hey!' called a voice from the back. 'What about the plain fact of the matter?'

The whole theatre had exploded, and he had stormed off, shaking his fist at 'Youse bunch of over-educated poofters.' Rose burst into her hearty, filthy cackle, the ladies tittered politely – but clearly you had to be there.

And still they listened.

Nobody had ever listened to her like this. Was it a trick to get her baking for them? She told them about Jane Gotham modern dance show, coming only too soon to the Playhouse.

'Women dancing some man's steps,' muttered the other knitter.

'Actually, no. It's all women. No men at all. Just a couple of, you know, homos.'

In the sudden silence she could hear those needles clicking.

Dianne rattled in with tea, made with teabags and warm water in the undrinkable diner manner that always reminded Eddie how far from home she was. Some sipped Scotch, one lifted an immense personal bottle of Bourbon, whatever that was, and Rose drank Pepsi after Pepsi, having perhaps brought in a truckload.

The group commented on Dianne's books, which included *Oriental Love Positions*, though no one but Eddie seemed to notice the background, the silver wallpaper, in whose soft light the cosy evening swam.

'Didn't think I'd ever see *you* here,' murmured Rose, burping Pepsi-sweetened smoker's breath.

'What's going on?' she hissed back.

'Far as I can tell, if we've *got* a husband they all want us to leave the bastard. Dianne's left hers and Lucy's given hers some sort of ultimatum, a smarten-up-by date. I hear Inge came home a week early from Berlin and found some grad student washing her blonde hair and singing *Snowbird* – flat – so now Merlin's on his best behaviour. It's only my second time here but last week they started talking about love between a woman and a woman. '

'I don't think I need to come back.'

'Don't think I do, either.'

They balanced on the couch end, listening in to the circle's inner circle, who were chewing over something that had happened at the last meeting. It seemed that the topic of discussion had been Sex and Power, how the best climax is the one you give yourself – well, obviously – and Dianne had unwisely asked how long it *should* take to get yourself off.

Five to fifteen minutes seemed the consensus, until a first-timer called Sally (not here tonight) threw them all into shock by saying, 'Fifteen *minutes*! I can do it in fifteen seconds. Of course, I know exactly what to do.'

'In her dreams!' burst Rose.

In her bathtub perhaps, mused Eddie, assuming that this Sally person knew about the healing power of a stream of warm water, and was, if anything, a bit slow. But she wisely said not a word. The only Sally she knew was Miss Duckie's portly pianist, and it can't have been *that* Sally.

Rose drove her home in the ash-reeking Bug.

Steven had been unpleasantly surprised that Rose now showed no desire to jump his bones a second time, and when he gently inquired why on earth not, she confessed that, 'You know too much, you know what's going on, actually you make me feel a bit...embarrassed,' and that she preferred young men who 'haven't a clue.' (Surely she didn't mean students!) With them she could really be, in her word, 'lewd' – and she said how fond she was of Eddie.

Eddie.

Eddie was the problem, with her menstruating-more-than-monthly migraines and her obsession with this dance show – and here she was cropping up again, always part of the problem.

Inge didn't want a return match either, though with no mention of lewdness, only of Eddie.

He pointed out that they didn't have to *tell* Eddie, but she only shrugged, and rolled her marvellous eyes Berlin-wards.

What he didn't know was what the Women's Circle knew: what Dianne had hissed in Eddie's ear as the Absolute Truth. (And Eddie agreed that she had a point.)

We Always Know.

We *Always* Know.

At dance rehearsal the following afternoon, Dianne seemed frosty towards Eddie. She handed back Eddie's plate, which she had forgotten, then turned away. They all warmed up, practised a few moves...warmed up some more.

Warmed up some more.

No Jane.

Lately their leader had been increasingly distant, but now here she was, gone.

'Anybody heard from her?'

Carol raised her head from gently bumping it against the floor while installed in her wide second position, the sideways split she was so proud of, and shook a vacant 'No.'

After a pause the beautiful Lucy emerged from contemplating her waist-length hair in the mirror and said, oh, yes, Jane had spoken to her the night before last.

She slid back into the mirror, but Dianne insisted on knowing what they had talked about.

'Oh...we didn't really talk *about* anything. I said to John after, I think she's pissed, as a matter of fact. She was going on and on about this locked room at the top of the stairs, where she's staying. How it's full of illegal drugs, or why else would it be locked? People go up and down the stairs all night but they take their boots off so you can't hear them, something like that. I wasn't really listening; it was just, you know, Jane.'

'Anyone got her home number?'

'I'd be happy to give us a run-through,' said Eddie, 'but if she walks in in the middle she'll have a willy. Could someone give her a ring?'

'A call? I'll call her.'

But when Dianne returned she was frowning.

'Her phone's been disconnected,' she quietly told Eddie. 'I asked William and Bob but they haven't seen her since Tuesday night, late. William joked about how much money she owes the theatre already, how our show better pack 'em in. He said she'd been using his phone, trying to get bookings for a tour of the province, but nobody was the least bit interested. She'd even called the mayors of all the towns, lecturing them about the need for culture. Then she gave William the real Jane treatment for not promoting her for the Playhouse subscription season, but he kept telling her he'd have to see her show first.'

The music tapes were on the machine, so Eddie clapped her hands for attention, and ran the rehearsal, pushing them hard.

Afterwards she told them they had done well and the show would be a big hit – but that they must remember it *is* a show.

'So when something goes wrong – and it will – or you lose your place or lose the count or your bra falls off on the stage, I don't want to see it in your face. Remember, you dance with your face. No mugging, no pulling faces; it's not ballet, but there's going to be four hundred and ten people looking at your face, and if they see panic, they'll stop loving the show.' (*Our show. My show.*)

And it was true; when Eddie danced you had to watch her face: she was transformed, a goddess – though her body, her slightly stiff movements, the nape of her neck (where her mother used to hit her) still left a lot to be desired.

Her migraine was clutching her neck like a giant bird as she stood waiting for Dianne to bring the car around.

But Dianne did not come and did not come.

Where *is* she?

And then she did appear, on foot and in tears. 'She's gone!' she wailed, and sat down on the steps with her face in her hands.

'Gone where?'

Then Bob appeared, waddling up, his overalls bulging with tools. He was not noted for subtlety or tact.

'She's gone all right. The RCMP just called us back. They're cutting her down as we speak. So who's in charge now?'

Eddie told Steven the appalling news, and then stayed in the shower till the hot water ran out. When she emerged, pink and wilted, she announced that the show must go on, that she herself would direct it, and that it would be dedicated to the memory of Jane Gotham. Instead of being called *Undertow* it would be called *Spring Fling*.

Also, she wanted Steven to be in it.

'It needs men. You're a man. It needs you.'

Stunned by her logic he said, 'Sure! Anything. Long as it's not on a race weekend.'

Off to the Races

That Sunday, early, he roared down to the one-day race meeting at the new abandoned airfield circuit just outside Saint John.

In his newly-appointed capacity as Assistant Instructor he found, to his delight, that he'd drive the students' cars for a few instructive laps, with them belted in, white-knuckled, beside him.

Finally they'd be allowed to drive their own smoking, clicking cars, and would chauffeur the four fast-talking instructors ('NOW! HIT IT! NOW! EASY!') and in the afternoon they'd race each other while the instructors looked on, by turns wincing and cackling at their earnest efforts.

For some reason he had always found the wheel-twirling of less-than-competent drivers hilarious, and had often heard himself chuckling at some newcomer's undignified struggles to keep his twitching car on the track, before Steven passed or lapped him.

What a treat! This was finally teaching something worth teaching.

Max lined up the instructors for a Le Mans-type start to chose their cars, and Steven out-sprinted the field to a silver Datsun 240Z with racing rubber. As he climbed in beside its proud, nervous owner, it still had that new car smell.

He loved hearing himself talk calmly as he flung the pale, helmeted owner's pride and joy from one side to the other round the chicane, before winding it up to a sweet-sounding 112 mph in third and squeezing the brakes, quietly explaining himself.

'Blip down to second, off the brakes, turn it in, firm but smooth, set it up, feed the throttle, unwind it, and GO! You can win your race.'

His next seat was a stink-bug green Mazda rotary that wound up like a turbine – he slightly over-revved it, and had the owner screeching.

'Sorry, mate. How many horsepower's this thing supposed to have?'

'Seventy-five.'

'The Japs've been pulling your leg. It's got more like a hundred and twenty. Thing goes like a mad dog. You can win your race.'

This was the life! Now he was sitting in a Yank Tank hemi in exciting McLaren tangerine with automatic transmission. He got it moving and stood on it, wondering what would happen next. What happened was visual: a row of carburettor flaps at the back of the power bulge snapped open. There was a whooshing, sucking sound. And then the whole front reared up and shoved him hard into the seat back.

Braking for the right-hander, he immediately felt the problem. 'You can definitely win the race. But only if you brake where I tell you... here!'

'But we're only half-way down the straight!'

'And gently, gently. Then lift off, then brake a bit more. Just like this. Just like this.'

And he did, and he won. He thanked Steven for the coaching – a thing no Fodderton student had ever done, and then a little light went on.

'Hey! You're my brother's teacher. Stu? Little guy about yea high.'

'I'm a driver. Nobody's really a *teacher*. It's just what we do to make a buck for what we *really* do.'

As the Dodge-owner's brother walked proudly off with his tinpot trophy, his skinny girlfriend in the yellow jump-suit, like an anorexic banana, leaning against him for support, Steven thought about what he had heard himself say. As a kid he'd only wanted one big thing: to drive, just once, a racing car. But having driven one (ten laps for ten pounds, in the Cooper Formula Junior at the racing school outside Oxford) he wanted to drive it again.

And again, to practice, to improve, to break the one-minute-fifteen barrier. It was like tennis, not like going to heaven.

Then as a young man he'd wanted one big, impossible thing: to make love to a girl... That *was* like going to Heaven, but only on a brief trip. And it, too, was like tennis. You need to go on playing. Another game, another set.

He had still not recovered, and was sure never would, from making love – once – with Inge Fox.

First, she was very good at it.

'It takes zo...long...to make love,' she had observed, referring to the days of courting, of small talk and chat before she felt ready to do it.

'It's zo...easy to come,' she revealed, as they finally settled down to do it. All she had to do was squeeze her thighs together – 'I 'ave very strong muscles,' she explained – so, to her polite inquiry as to whether to squeeze now or wait till the post-coital period, when presumably nothing much is going on, Steven advised, 'Now, if you like. You choose. You might again, later.'

She nodded. He had apparently said The Right Thing.

'It does feel nice, after.'

She leisurely removed her clothes, and as each elegant, pricey garment fell away he was dazzled. She was one of those women who are at their best naked. In the dim light of the Fox apartment (Merlin was off delivering a research paper) her skin glowed like radioactive lemon juice. And the two lovers complemented and complimented each other to perfection.

He groaned as he entered her – 'Oh, No!' – held back, and explained that she had what he called a magic cunt, that seems to have a curve, or another pair of lips, just inside.

Then she told him, 'I can feel you right up under my heart,' and he thought, surely not. He pulled out and laid his cock up against her belly, and it *did* go up rather further above her navel than he would have predicted. Then, tempted by her lovely breasts, he had her squeeze them together, straddled her waist...and slipped between. This was, impossibly, even more sumptuous. She held her dark nipples just so.

'Vait! Just a second!' She reached for her glasses and put them on, the better to watch the red head of his cock popping out of her cleavage at the end of each stroke.

'Such a lovely view,' she murmured, gazing into her cleavage, and really seemed to mean it. Though he knew, from Rose, that Inge had a steady girlfriend, she did seem to enjoy men, perhaps as a nice change from the real thing.

He left the valley of lust for the original magic cave, finished loudly, she drove off to work, badly, in the Porsche – but when he called her the next day it was over. Because of Eddie. She couldn't do it to Eddie.

But it was not over. Not for him. Never. Strangely, she had left him with a clear impression of his right hand on her flat belly. Not a memory either, but an actual impression – he could *feel* his hand on her belly. Right...there. For days and nights, for weeks he felt her skin under his hand, unfading, tattooed like the ghost outline of a cave painter's hand on the inside of his skull, as if some pleasure-torturer's electrode kept stimulating that exact region of his brain. If she, too could feel his ghost hand on her belly she would surely run to her Porsche and rush to him, but apparently not. He needed to...to... Desperately.

Why do certain memories of pleasure linger as pain? he asked himself, squinting up at a high vapour trail heading east. Memories of *real* pain fade to nothing.

With an animal roar the last race started up, blanking his memories. Car racing now seemed both a cause and a cure for his horniness; the excitement aroused and finally overwhelmed, just as cancer cures smoking.

Waiting tensely for the lead cars to reappear, he recalled the *Cabaret* MC demanding, in that marvellous Teutonic voice,

'Vere are your troubless now?'

The Cortfire had failed to appear at the track, as the engine was missing. That is, it didn't have one.

When he asked Max what happened to its engine the big man shrugged, looked away, then admitted, 'We had to put it back.'

'Back where?'

'Back where it came from, but it's all under control, we'll have a fresh engine for the six-hour Endurance at Sanair. '

Intrigued, Steven chatted with the two beefy mechanics in Max's pit crew, the three of them making up Halifax's 'Triple E

Speed Shop.' Big Hal just grinned, but Big Al explained, as to a babe in the woods.

'You know what a California Tune-Up is?'

'Sure. You wipe the spark plugs clean and fit a weaker return spring on the throttle.'

'And charge seventy-five bucks, right. A New York Tune-Up?'

'...Nope. Beats me.'

'It's a street job. You back your VW Bug or Kombi up to a nice new VW, and if you're good, fifteen minutes later you drive away with your car all tuned up, and the other poor bastard wonders why his car's running like shit.'

'So...a *Halifax* Tune-Up, ah, the customer brings his Cortina in for a tune-up, right.'

'Special rate if he leaves it with us over the weekend,' added Hal.

'And you stick it in the Cortfire and rev the guts out of it, and it's running better than ever when he gets it back, right?'

'Something like that. We make sure he's happy, anyway.'

Steven was happy, anyway.

And how pleasant to be able to fire up the MG and just do a circuit waving goodbyes and cruise away, without having first to sit in the dirt and take his 1/4' wrench to those 72-spoke wheels to retighten them! Wearing out other people's cars, not his own, was clearly the way to go.

He drove, wondering why racing made him so horny. Seeing a car crash just made him sick, and being in one himself (the family Humber, a tightening bend) had only made him desperate to pee. But there it was. There it was...

Beating off while driving a car (auto-eroticism?) takes a bit of doing but it can be achieved. Steering briefly with the knees is the key, while the left hand clamps the pulsing handkerchief.

But this time he was caught out by a shocking blare from behind. Pre-climactic deafness may let even a truck tailgate unheard, and in an open cockpit (cock-pit?), one's joystick, and the whole obscene scene may be viewed from the moral high ground.

Grabbing the other stick he snapped it down to third, floored it and got clear, but the thrill was lost, the moment gone forever. Should have given him the finger, the mother trucker.

Mothers never let a guy have a bit of fun. *Very* embarrassing moment.

When he later stopped to pee in the woods, the passing trucker blared again, gesturing 'Wanker' unmistakably with his hand. This time Steven did give him the finger, 'Screw You!' and felt better. There are few pleasures like giving someone the finger, thought Professor Butts.

Eddie was delighted when he wrangled her free use of the new, never-used dance studio in the FU Athletic Centre for rehearsals, in return for her running an 'unofficial' beginners' modern dance class, twice a week – unpaid of course, as she lacked the required degree. FU had been unable to mount a dance program, as none of their fully-qualified Phys. Ed. professors knew how to teach one. And qualifications were what counted; the university had just laid off the coach of their Championship-winning soccer team, on learning he had only a bachelor's degree.

Working well together, the Butts moved out the boxes of hockey equipment stored in the studio, tracked down the key to unlock the new, unused piano, scraped off the gum, swept and mopped the beautiful, glowing sprung wood floor.

Eddie needed men, real men, and now that she was *persona grata* in the Centre she went hunting for them and snared three beauties: a gymnast, a body builder and a diver, all willing to help out with her Playhouse *Spring Fling* show.

At the first beginners' class-cum-audition she worked on teaching them to walk across the floor.

This was not easy as the gymnast walked like a gymnast, the diver like a diver, and so on. Steven walked like a racing driver, which was close but not good enough. She wanted them to walk like men, for her new piece.

'Aren't you going to do your little solo to the Debussy?' asked Dianne.

'Nope. It's out. Jane said over her dead body, and I don't want her spinning in her grave. But we need a big piece to finish off. We'll open with *Shaft*, and close with this new one... I'm thinking of calling it *Shafted Again*.'

Steven was rather proud of his legs, and when Eddie presented him with black Danskin tights to rehearse in, he was impressed by how shapely they looked in the studio mirrors. Pulling on his tights, down in the echoing slam and bellow of the FU guys' locker room, though, took character. Standing in a black dance belt (a too-tight jock strap) among liniment-reeking body-builders, sweat-sour hockey types, shaved water polo men and after-shaved gymnasts, he did stand out rather, and was unsure whether to act over-friendly or over-distant.

Screw them, he resolved, just focussing on getting the stretchy material over his heels without laddering, and yanking it up, in a masculine way, to the crotch, wrinkle-free. The other men in Eddie's production either obstinately wore gym shorts or seemed to arrive pre-tighted.

Now she was trying to teach them to walk, not like men, but like some kind of predatory science-fiction monster, slowly advancing, step by measured step. Like men, as she still put it. All the women were learning something else, writhing around in a heap, like a truckload of drugged creatures, slowly waking up to their predicament. An arm would rise here, a foot there.

'Do we get any lifts?' Thompson the bodybuilder demanded.

'Sure do.'

And they did, trying out various approaches to getting a young lady off the ground and into the air.

'Jesus Christ!' panted Thompson, 'What do you *weigh*?'

Lucy's wondrous eyes widened, and after her standard pause for thought, she whispered, 'A hundred and nineteen and a half.'

'No way! Hey! Eddie, these women are like a ton of bricks. I bench press two forty, but these women stick to the floor.'

'I know. It's because they're dead. Now listen up, girls.'

And she explained that on stage, the co-operative corpse must continue to act dead with the face, but that the limbs press up from the floor as the predator lifts her, then the knees subtly straighten and the feet sharply point to get them up and aloft.

Timing.

'The guys have a lot of lifting to do, and they're not all as strong as Thompson here. Steven, what's your bench-press?'

'About a hundred and twenty on a good day, after I've had my Wheaties. It's not just the weight: they wiggle.'

'Right. No wiggling.'

On went the throbbing Herbie Hancock tape and rehearsal resumed, with, crowding the doorway but clearly too scared to enter, a whispering profusion of Phys. Ed. students.

Steven had never seen – certainly never touched – so many women in his life. So much possibility. The Stop and Go twins, their lovely moon-white, cheek-boned faces gleaming above their lovely moon-white bodies were, of course, a fantasy in double vision – but they only lasted one rehearsal. All that stuff to remember. Lucy's bum-length brown hair, the mere sight of it swinging, turned him into a hair fetishist on the spot, while Carol's wide-angle split made him an instant pervert, mentally having her practice it naked on the Butts' glass-topped dining-room table, to see with his own eye just how deep it went.

But oddly, the *look* of them, when about five minutes into the warm-ups, their nipples all rose in unison as if on a pheromone signal, was more exciting than the feel. They felt, they were, hard, sweating, hard-working bodies, each powered by the deep biological engine of its fierce desire to look beautiful.

Perhaps that was why he needed to race: to look beautiful in a car, in his white Nomex costume, showing off his grace under pressure. As a dancer he sensed he was stiff and near-clumsy – though with proper training he knew he would do as well – no, *better*, than his wife. She was a natural performer but a restricted dancer. What a trier, though!

He knew that as a choreographer she was making it up as she went along. He knew because she'd told him. She was making up this dance on the fly. It was terrifying.

She no longer slept, and hardly ate.

The pile of female victims squirmed and slowly woke up. They untangled themselves, and rolled away to escape.

But the men, watching from the corners, moved inexorably in, picked them up and dumped them, slowly, slowly, back in the central pile.

This development was not popular. A number of mascara'd eyes rolled.

'It's so pointless,' announced Dianne, amid nodding heads. 'We start in the middle of the stage and we all end up back there. It's pointless. It's got no dramatic point.'

'You're right,' said Eddie, sweat beading her brow and upper lip. 'You've made a good point. And it's got a new title. It's now *The Men*.'

By the end of the rehearsal Steven's back groaned. His arms were putty. He couldn't lift another finger. As he entered the steamy concrete pit of the showers he prayed for the balmy touch of hot water. But today the most embarrassing thing happened.

For a man, he was sure, there can be nothing – nothing – more embarrassing than getting a hard-on in public. It had never happened to him or to anyone he knew, and yet it held that ultimate, primal fear: pointing, public exposure and group guffaws.

He adjusted the newly installed high-tech, counter-intuitive replacement for a simple hot tap plus a cold tap, testing the warmth on his hand, not too cold, just a tad too hot, ahh...and slumped under the healing warmth. And turned...

A pale young man with a hairless chest was slumped under his steam-hot shower, in a sort of Donatello David droop, the water playing on the back of his neck, his head down, long wet golden hair, and a cock that was too long for him. It hung straight down, as long and thick as a banana but not curved and not yellow with spots; it was reddish with a brown friction-burn below the knob. A lot of hard work had gone into that cock.

Steven only glanced and looked away, but the damage was done. He felt the blood leave his head and flow into the head of his cock, the familiar lengthening downwards, which was not a visible problem – he'd read somewhere that some men's (black men's?) cocks still point at the floor even when they're erect, and had thought how convenient – followed by the familiar slow rise, which was. A problem. How to solve it? He whirled to face the wall, composing his mind to purer thoughts. But of what?

He hadn't had any impure thoughts, just noticed that the slim young guy opposite was hung with the cock of a big, over-sexed middle-aged man.

Think of England. Of tile manufacture.

It was getting worse. Someone could come in. His towel was outside. He focussed on the high-tech tap. The blue arrow, for cold, pointed to the left. A cold shower! Yes. He swung the lever to the left – and leapt from the scalding water. His cock bobbing comically, he dashed for his towel, leaving the nozzle spurting steam.

By the time he reached his locker, among the hockey men and other mouth-breathing towel-snappers, all was well. He made a mental note. Cold showers don't work but boiling water does the trick. He simply had to tell Eddie, who laughed uproariously at his tale. Later, in the car, she asked,

'So who was the young guy with the huge thing?'

'I don't know. I might have seen him skiing once, but I don't know his name.'

'Was it John?'

'John who?'

'Dobson. You *know* you're not too good with names. Maybe if you cared about people you'd remember their names.'

'Who's John Dobson?'

'One of the ski team guys.'

'Does he have long blonde hair, really long?'

'Nope. That's Landry, and it wouldn't be him.'

'Why not?' he wondered.

'I don't know – it just doesn't sound like him, somehow. Was he a really good-looking guy?'

'I don't know. I never saw his face.'

Show Time

'Okay, you're fired. You're out of the show. I mean it.' Eddie was like a mad woman.

'What are you talking about? You *know* I'm racing the weekend after next. You said it was going to be on week nights.'

'Well, now it's Friday and Saturday night too. Three nights plus a matinee Saturday. And you're out. I'll get – I'll get Bob to do it if I have to.'

'Bob? In his overalls?'

'Well, at least I can trust him to show up. He's reliable.'

'But he's a joke!'

'No, you're the joke. You've got no idea what this means to me. At Jane's funeral I made a vow –'

'And you don't know what this race at Sanair means to *me*. It's my big start. Everybody'll be there. This hotshot, what's his name Gilles Villeneuve's driving an Atlantic, so they'll all be there to watch him, and it's my chance.'

'Great. Splendid. Good for you. All the very best.'

'Can I still do the opening night show?'

'No, but you better be there with a big bouquet of roses or I swear I'll step forward and make a speech about what a self-centred shit you really are.'

'*Me!* Have you looked in the mirror lately?'

The two weeks felt like two days. Eddie constantly on thephone, soothing, negotiating, pleading, appeasing, demanding. Listening in, he thought she should be teaching his management course: she could really manage. She had her new lifting-body, a ski racer called John. For some reason the Playhouse staff were now right behind the project and Marcel had got in forty new lamps from somewhere (he never seemed to buy, hire or even borrow, but he always produced) to give her a blaze of new lighting effects.

It was the technical rehearsal. Steven watched from the lighting booth, fascinated by the subtlety, the attention to detail, as Marcel paced about on stage, trailing a telephone cord linked to the headphones of Sally Somebody, temporarily running the lighting board. Her long pianist's fingers moved over the 707-cockpit controls of the dimmer board as delicately as she played her improvisations for Eddie's beginners' class, or for the YMCA ballet classes, now somewhat poorly attended.

He had chatted before with this Sally, who was a trained classical pianist, a fresh FU graduate in mathematics which would make her about nineteen, and a chronic, gossipy complainer, with a pretty face, an occasional lovely smile – but plump. He liked the way she could operate all the Playhouse equipment, covering for the godlike Marcel whom, it seemed, she worshipped. Kenny the Lighting Manager having flu, she had volunteered to sit in. Steven told her she had a good touch.

At the first rehearsal break she whipped off her headset, rose and turned to him.

'Steven, would you mind getting the fuck out? I can't concentrate with you staring at me.'

'Sure. Sorry. I thought you hadn't noticed me here in the dark.'

'You're such a fucking dickhead,' she said, and pulling him towards her, kissed him lushly on the mouth.

He left, faintly dizzy, endorphins flooding his brain like pre-come soaking into underpants. She wasn't all that plump, not around the waist, anyway. Just nice. Warm.

He sat with Eddie who ignored him, her focus on Marcel.

'What's the next piece?' the Theatre God inquired, and Eddie explained that it was a metaphysical exploration of the quest for God in a Godless world.

He glanced up at the stage, on which a white stepladder had been set, and printed on his clipboard,

'LADDER TRICKS.'

Music Go, lights Go, and the questers began their questing.

'Hold it!' bellowed Bob, stomping out of the wings.

The swirling music cut, full stage lights came on.

'I built Eddie this ladder so some little girl could climb up to the top, maybe stand on her head, climb back down again. You want to all pile on it at once, start hanging out the sides, we're gonna have a cracking sound 'n a whole lot of bodies lying around on the stage. If that's what you want, okay. Otherwise, I gotta take it away, reinforce the steps. You go ahead rehearse without it, okay?'

With insolent strength he picked it up and stomped away into the wings.

Eddie made a high-pitched suppressed scream, Marcel gave her shoulders a squeeze and rub, and they moved on to the next piece, performed to outer-space trance music with background hammering by Bob. Odd how Eddie's neck problems seemed to have cleared up, her migraines too, though she looked pale as death and kept insisting that her own dancing was going to be atrocious.

But it wasn't. The day of Thursday, opening night she had woken with flu and no voice, but she was fine, the adrenaline having kicked in by the time Marcel's best voice came reassuringly through the changing-room speakers:

'Good evening ladies and gentlemen, this is your fifteen-minute call, fifteen minutes to curtain up; have a very, very good show.'

Steven kissed her make-up good luck, told her to break a leg and cleared out. Surprisingly, Foddertonians were filing in, chattering loudly, filling the seats. Who *were* all these people? He was too nervous himself to sit with them. He spotted Rodman, Joyce – the whole department seemed to have shown up. A little red-faced, tipsy perhaps, but here. He didn't want to see anybody: what if the evening was a total dud?

He circled through the Green Room, collected his dozen red roses from the fridge and pushed his way past the bar, where Bob was fortifying the husbands to accompany their dance-keen wives in for the show. He entered the dark lighting booth, where Kenny, with a towel round his neck, was doing the pre-sets, one cigarette glowing in his mouth, another smouldering in readiness.

Somebody grabbed him from behind.

'Sh...' she whispered in his ear, and then stuck her tongue in.

He'd never had anyone do this before, and though noisy it felt surprisingly...promising.

Her firm hand led him out a door he had not known, up a ladder, up stairs, up another ladder and out a door.

'Best view in the house,' Sally chuckled – she *was* in a cheerful mood. He followed her onto the metal catwalk that led, in darkness, over the heads of the crowd and finally to almost directly above the stage, looking down from an alarming height.

They lay together, two gods of the theatre, gazing down, as the house lights dimmed, the carefully chosen pre-show music (Steven had taped it) faded perfectly on cue, the dancers took their places, Bob hauled on the thick rope and the blood-red curtains parted to reveal...

Darkness. Eddie's show. *Undertow*. William had persuaded her to keep Jane Gotham's title.

The audience settled. Music. *Shaft* wah-wah guitar. Lights up....

The brightly-lit dancers stood stock still, resisting the beat, counting without moving their lips – and then suddenly whipped into action. It was great.

A stir in the audience revealed just how great it was. By an opening-night fluke, they all ended right on the beat, too, and applause poured in like a Manly Beach wave breaking. There were whistles and even some stamping feet. Local show makes good. Steven and Sally hugged in delight. Hugged and kissed.

It was hot above the stage lights.

By the time Bob stomped on below with his now sturdily reinforced white ladder, for the quest, they were naked and fucking steadily, greedily to a beat of their own.

So far it had been a great success, better than expected.

With plenty of time to experiment, he tried fucking a bit to one side, to the other side, a bit higher, a bit lower, as the dancers climbed and clung to the ladder below. But Sally's, 'Ah yesss, that's right! That's where!' left no doubt that her favourite was straight down the middle and as fast and hard as he could do it. Which, he found, once he had wedged a big toe on a cross beam, was quite hard and fast.

Every minute or two, while the stage music swelled unheard and the subtle lighting changes were revealed, unseen below them, she would tense towards him and hiss, in wonderment, 'You're...making me...ccc...' but she could never say the last word. Then she would relax back and in the dim light he could see the gleam of her delighted smile... Which he would remove by starting up again.

The next time she smiled, she pulled him down and announced, astonished at herself, 'I could do this *forever!*'

So could Steven, until she went just a little too far. Sally's hands were constantly down between her legs, occasionally giving her clitoris a short, surprisingly fierce rub, then with both hands rubbing her pussy lips backwards and forwards, then letting his cock slide between her fingers.

'You must have the biggest cock in the world,' was another nice thing she said. 'I've had some that were so small it was hardly worth the bother.'

One piece ended, to applause and whistles, the next one began, but up above, their sweat-wet bodies were now dancing in an eternal Now. But then Sally got carried away and undid him. Her middle finger, slipping experimentally around, slid right inside her, she added another, then another, the rest, and he felt his pelvic bone progressively hammering the back of her hand inside like a wedge, and this achievement triggered him into a noisy orgasm, his groan possibly audible on stage though probably not, as the music was rising to a crescendo.

'I...felt you...come!' she told him.

'Me too,' he panted, his head on her damp chest. Her chest, surprisingly, was completely flat. Her breasts were enormous, but they slid out to each side. She lifted her arms off them and he settled his head on one comforting pillow. An ocean of applause burst under them. Dozing, he was sure she actually *was* that centrefold model from one of his copies of *Gent*. Definitely the same face, breasts, person.

Below them the house lights came up, but they were still in darkness. It must be intermission. He decided against going down – why risk just getting in Eddie's way? Another nice thing about this warm, dozing girl: she never mentioned Eddie.

All was well and all manner of thing shall be well and the rose and the fire shall be one...

The lights dimmed, the audience rustled and coughed into quietness, and the thick red curtain swept open again. He now knew the answer to Rose Russell's impertinent question. His recovery time? About twenty minutes, the normal length of an intermission. Sally was ready for instant intromission, and hissed in his ear that, to tell the truth, she had never known what foreplay was *for*.

But then she rolled him off, clambered on top, poised, sat and started rocking determinedly backwards and forwards. Wickedly he pressed his thumb against her clitoris and held it there. She moved fast, faster than a belly dancer. But after tensing up she kept collapsing on him, back into his world, exhausted, barely breathing, and he would have to slide awkwardly in and out from underneath, slowly but determined – until she suddenly reared up and picked up the pace again.

There was no need to ask what her interval time was; he could count it in heartbeats.

They paused briefly for applause and then started up again. There seemed no reason why this should not go on forever, or at least until one or other of them died.

But as the final number began, *The Men*, with its round central light pulsing red and green on the pile of women's bodies, he rolled her off him and, staring down at her pale face and bouncing breasts he began fucking hard, hard towards...towards some mad goal that he could half-sense in the back of his skull, some distant, approaching horsemen of, of – and here they were, at his back, their hoofbeats pounding with the music.

Her pussy loosened, relaxed, and he knew she was fucked out. It was like fucking the sea. The words came into his head,

'Fucked Out,' and he came into her, the music easily loud enough to cover his groan of ecstatic agony. She had happened to touch him behind the balls just as he started coming, and he knew that this, *this* was in fact the electric secret of the universe.

Below, on earth, the bodies were now piled high, but the final escapee, long-haired Lucy was making a slow-motion break for stage right. She faltered, the new guy caught her from behind and hauled her to the centre, then turning his back, hoisted her up at arm's length, so that she hung in space, her shocked face the last thing the audience saw as the spotlight shrank and the music faded.

A moment of shock. That's it? That's it. Then thunderous, shattering applause. Whistles, even Bravos.

Curtain in. Curtain out. Curtain calls.

'Damn! My roses!' said Steven.

'Toss 'em down.'

He tossed them down.

Unfortunately they missed the stage and landed in front of it.

Tugging his pants on, Steven did not see Professor Rodman and Dean Joyce on the front row scramble for them, and then hand them up, together, beaming, for Eddie to step forward and graciously receive.

What a show!

What an opening night!

A Tough Business

The nasal blare of an American car horn signalled that the boys from Triple E were finally here. He kissed Eddie goodbye, wished her all the best for the show, her terrific show, she told him to drive safely and win, he grabbed his bag and rushed out the door – just in time to bump into Max and the two big lads coming in.

They all wanted to use the bathroom. And something to eat would be nice. Something to drink would be even nicer.

Himself, he never drank alcohol within two days of a race, but they seemed to be in a party mood.

Eddie cut them sandwiches and handed over the last of the beer, and they left, Al and Hal shaking her hand and Max sweeping her into a back-bent, sandwichy kiss. The Cortfire and gear lay roped rather agriculturally under a green tarp, and the four-wheeled trailer hardly looked up to the job, but Steven figured if they'd got this far, from Halifax, it must be okay. Max got him to drive, turned up the radio and fell asleep.

From the back seat Al (or was it Hal?) said, 'Don't go over fifty. Trailer's a bit heavy at the front.'

Steven didn't always warm to back-seat drivers, and the old station wagon felt stable enough, but he kept it down to fifty-five.

Until the bridge.

Descending towards a two-lane extension bridge over one of northern New Brunswick's black-water dams, he noticed the speedo read fifty-eight, so he lifted off and touched the brakes.

Now it was fifty something, but just as he entered the bridge the tail end began wagging lazily from side to side.

This was no problem, you just steer against it – but something odd was happening. The more he corrected the tail-wag, the worse it got. The tail was wagging the dog, and quite fiercely now.

A white van had entered the bridge from the other end and wanted its share of the road.

'Floor it!' yelled Al.

'Hit the brakes!' bellowed Hal.

'Watch it,' murmured Max, as the tail with its priceless cargo swung into his left rear view mirror and then out again, letting the horn-blaring van through, and swung out the other way towards the fence, the low fence and the hundred-foot drop to black water.

Steven steered left, braking gently, no longer correcting the berserk trailer, and it somehow missed the fence, swung back the other way – and they stopped, just clear of the bridge. But, hello? One wheel was continuing on.

'Is that one of ours?'

Halted, they all watched the wheel bowl along the Trans-Canada and then veer left, heading for the Irving gas station, homing in on the tire display rack and...

'YESS!' Scoring a direct hit. Tires flew everywhere.

'Sorry about that,' mumbled Steven.

'Great driving,' said Hal and Al. 'The way you missed that van. I thought we were going to buy it for sure.'

Max said nothing.

They piled out, picked up the scattered tires and found that the rogue trailer wheel had ripped through its wheel nuts. So Steven bought them a new wheel and tire and as they mounted it, realised two things: they were lucky. He had been helpless. Not scared then, but scared now. On the track, he had never lost a race car, never even spun (except that very first time out with the Cooper Formula Junior, and that didn't count).

He recalled Stirling Moss being asked how the Formula One Cooper handles when you lose it, and answering that he didn't know.

That weird opposite-opposite lock feeling: he had once driven a 197cc Titan kart at Oxford – in fact he'd formed The Ox-Kart Syndicate to buy the thing – and first time out the steering had failed – the wheel had just spun in his hand. Instantly his foot had stamped on the brake pedal – and snapped the brake cable, running under the tray and already worn through: he was now riding a 60 mph sled.

So he had bounced it to one side to miss their parked car and then, heading for the fence, bailed out. That had been fun. This wasn't. He was scared.

They let him, made him, keep driving. By the Quebec border they were all asleep again.

He was now in a foreign country, and when they stopped to refuel (his agreement was to pay for all gas) they ate foreign food: fries with strange cheesy stuff on them.

He tried to get a conversation going.

'What were those things that looked like upended bathtubs in all the front yards, with the Nativity scene in them?'

'Bathtubs,' said Max. 'They're Catholics.'

So's my wife, thought Steven, but went back to trying to get the cheesy stuff down past his gullet.

He paid for yet another *remplissement* and drove on. They cruised along dark roads between small farms whose fields ran narrowly down to the river. The signposts were wordy and unlighted, towns bore surreal names like St Louis de Ha-Ha, and he became deliriously, absurdly happy, at which point he stopped the car, mentioned that he was completely lost, and Al (Hal?) took over for the last leg, which he knew.

His one-finger driving technique seemed to work well and he could hold sixty.

'Al, est-ce que te parles Français?' Steven asked, on a hunch. Silence. 'You speak French?'

Al (the less fat of the two, the black guy) shook his head. 'No, but I lived here for a bit. Quebeckers don't speak *French* French. It's a sort of Franglais, like "Crossez la street, Le Pickup, Le hot dog, Le weekend."'

'What does "Triple-E" stand for?' Steven was wide awake.

'We stand for the total automotive experience —'

'No, I mean the three Es.'

Al chewed it over before replying. 'Extremely Expensive Engine Exchange?'

'That's four.'

'Extraordinary Engineering Expertise?'

Hal explained hoarsely from the back seat: 'Max's from Syria.'
'Lebanon!' growled Max. 'How many times I have to –'
'Scuse *me*! I forgot how touchy you Libyans are.'
Triple-E? Tripoli? Steven was sure there was a Tripoli in Lebanon. And Libya too? He would have to look it up. Was Max therefore a Tripolitan? A Tripolinian? Suddenly he was no longer wide awake. His neck hurt and his head felt like a bowling ball. And there was something else. He had lost...something. His phantom hand on Inge's flat belly had gone, had left him alone, as if unable to cross the Maginot line into Québec.

He felt jet-lagged. He wondered if they would expect him to drive all the way back, but he need not have worried. If he had known, had even suspected what the weekend would bring, he would have punched open the door and abandoned ship, like diving out of the rudderless Titan kart. But then, we never see our future clearly; our hopes get in the way. Nor our past, for that matter.

As they pulled into an unpromising motel Steven ached for sleep, but the others seemed to come alive under the garish, pink and green neon lights. Max, who spoke no French (where *was* he from?), even began romancing the weasel-faced beehive blonde at the bar. He was dancing with her, to a jukebox full of sad Gallic ballads of lost love, as Steven headed for his single room, clutching a key attached to a log.

The master plan was to rise at six, and when his alarm jerked him awake on this, a most significant day, he stuck his head out the door to wake the others, as instructed, and was amazed to see Max, wrapped in a white blanket, seated on the roof of the station wagon. Had he spent the whole night up there? He appeared to be contemplating the dawn, Indian-style.

Quebec breakfasts were rather good; maple syrup glistening on buttered pancakes with eggs and bacon, coffee-flavoured coffee.

The radio played jolly tunes as they headed for the circuit. Suddenly Max swerved up a farmer's red-mud driveway. He'd spotted an MGA rusting in the field, and, as Al explained while they waited for Max to complete his negotiations in sign language,

'We could use a spare rad. Ours is a bit dicky.'
  'But why an MGA?'
  'Cos it fits.'
  Max emerged shaking his head.
  'Nah. He wanted money for it.'
  'Still, we know where it is.'

Ninety dollars worth of gas. How could he have spent ninety dollars on gas? They'd filled the forty-four-gallon drum for the race, filled the Cortfire, the station wagon – but...ninety bucks already! It began to dawn on him that he was as much a wallet as a co-driver. But very soon he would show them just how fast this Cortfire thing, which he had never even sat in, could go.

Unfortunately it rained. There is nowhere in the world more miserable than the paddock of a car race in rain. It was the muddy end, the...pits. But rain doesn't stop a car race and never stopped Steven Butts. They pulled in, he hopped out, dutifully removed the tarp – and the driver's seat began filling with water; the passenger's seat being already occupied. Steven was staggered to see a complete Cortina engine sitting in it. No wonder the car was down on its springs! Then, as he and Al rolled the car down the twin planks, its exhaust system scraped agonisingly and squashed itself oval.

There goes ten horsepower, he thought despondently, noticing the high-priced local machinery emerging dry from covered trailers plastered with ads for Quebec industry – mostly cars, milk and snowmobiles.

Practice for the supporting Formula Atlantic race began, and everyone craned to watch local hero Gilles Villeneuve, in a new machine, all white like an appliance fresh from the box.

And he was quick! Diabolically quick through the chicane after the hairpin, flicking the wheel from side to side, rooster tails of spray shooting from the rear wheels.

Every lap he was faster, wilder, more desperate.

You'd have to shoot the guy to stop him, Steven thought.

But then he overshot the left-hander into the oval section, ran straight ahead into a ditch and flipped upside down.

It was not often you saw a formula car go upside-down. He wriggled out and waved to his legion of wildly cheering fans, before limping away.

The cold rain thickened now, but the Cortfire fired up instantly and Max went boldly out in the wet on the slicks, skating down the straight, and after six laps looping it onto the grass infield. Then it was Steven's turn. On the now drying track he noticed two things: it went hard, and it gripped surprisingly well.

This was a car he could toss about. But the pedals were so widely spaced that he couldn't heel-and-toe, and the rear view mirror was so low that all he could find was a close-up view of his own roll bar. He pulled in after only three laps, and switched off.

'Any chance you could mount a right-side mirror?' he asked, peeling off his helmet, '– so I can see if anyone's coming up on my right side?'

Al and Hal shook their heads. 'It just vibrates off.'

'You go hard enough, nobody's going to come up,' barked Max, who seemed less friendly than ever. Steven had been quite quick, it seemed. Or perhaps Max just needed a good night's sleep. 'Listen. You going out again or you just going to sit and chat?'

'Is the oil pressure always this low?' asked Steven, but the Triple E trio just shrugged him off. So he snapped down his helmet visor, started up, slipped it carefully into first, blipped it twice, dropped the clutch – and it stopped dead.

With a sort of clunk.

By the time they had unclipped and raised the hood, quite a crowd had gathered. The hot oil pouring out underneath had signalled a major blow-up, and the inspection hole now revealed in the side of the block was the best anyone had seen. Oohs and aahs – even a ripple of applause – greeted the sight. A rod had snapped and taken the quickest way out.

'Hmm,' said Al.

'Well,' said Hal. 'Looks like a long night. But I tell you one thing, with the good engine this baby's going to *fly*!'

Max turned to his co-driver and stood much too close.

'Try not to blow up the good engine, eh.'
'If you say so. Isn't the good one paid for yet?'
'That's the trouble. It *is* paid for. It paid for the tires and the new rear end.'
'So we *do* have to give it back,' explained Hal, already unhooking the hose clamps. Steven watched him work, holding an umbrella over him. He was good. Swore a lot, but was fast and neat.

Then Steven and Max were dispatched to the woods behind the circuit, with a small hatchet. Their mission: to return with three tree trunks strong enough to support a Cortina engine on a chain and pulley. After some wildly competitive chopping, three young birch trees fell and were transformed into a standing tripod, a key feature of the Triple-E repair facility.

Clearly no mechanic, Steven was sent to buy beer and BBQ-flavoured chips – crisps – for the work party. He chose Brador beer, having heard that New Brunswickers will make a pilgrimage all the way to Quebec just to buy the brand, and this went down well with Max and the boys. They claimed it was like Aussie beer claimed to be: bags of flavour and a kick in the head.

Came the dawn, and once again Max was to be seen squatting on top of the dewy wagon, though pointing the other way this time: Westward. Then the barmaid with the beehive hair emerged from the boys' room and clip-clicked back to the main building, smoothing her rather stylish little dress behind. Steven must have got some sleep, because he had dreamed, had dreamed that he was at the controls of an airliner, but was having to play the cello at the same time, the two sounds running together...

After a cautious breakfast of pancakes with nothing he inserted his contact lens and they headed out into a cool morning.

The sky had that clear, hyper-real look he had learned to see in some Canadian paintings, by Colville and Pratt (He gathered that there was a Mrs Pratt too, who combined her wifely duties with being an artist, by painting food.) He was very aware of sounds and smells. Three crows played about overhead, and he wondered if they understood French.

A huge crowd waited, banners advertising oil, gas and Quebec flew in the breeze. There was even a band.

Finally the hysterical announcements ended.

An eerie silence descended, as for a fallen comrade.

The starter's flag rippled down, and instantly came the sound of two dozen pairs of racing shoes pattering across the track for the Le Mans start.

Max had been practising this, and Steven's contributions had paid off. Back in the Fifties, Donald Healey had rigged his car so that when he opened the door it started, and when he slammed it the handbrake flew off, but Max did even better, despite the new handicap that seat belts had to be on.

Max sprinted hard, vaulted over the door, his thumb already on the starter button (the ignition on, the handbrake off), settled in, reached up, like a pilot ejecting, and yanked down the racing harness that had hung loosely taped to the roll bar over his head.

The left lap strap was already clipped in (Steven's contribution) so he just had to clip in the right one, snatch first gear – and he was gone.

And he was, blaring down the track past the cranking Aston Martin, the two Sprites, assorted sports and hard-top machinery, and he was up to the pricey lead bunch of BMWs and Porsche 911s before anyone else got moving. Steven and the Triple-E bunch cheered and whooped madly, augmented by a skinny girl in a yellow jump-suit with, unexpectedly, Stu's brother from Fodderton, who had together volunteered to keep the lap charts.

By the end of the straight Max was second, by the end of the lap, fourth, and flying.

Steven had to admit it: the guy was good.

The commentator, screeching hysterically above the engines' roar, could occasionally be heard saying 'Le Cor-feer d'alifax.' Ten laps later Max was still fourth, ahead of Porsches that cost a small fortune to buy and a medium-sized one to run.

'You think the...engine will hold together?' Steven shouted intermittently at Hal, as the cars circulated flat-out, as if in a ten-lap sprint.

'Sure. Bullet-proof. Built it myself. I'm just hopin' the rear suspension don't rip off the chassis. It gets these...little cracks, right where you...can't get at it to weld it. Pisses me right off.'

Hour One went by, they refuelled smoothly. Hour Two. Steven had removed his brand-new black Bell helmet but kept his earplugs in. He had resolved not to press the point about his turn at the wheel: the rules only said that two drivers must drive, not for how long each.

Hour Three. A Sprite and a Porsche blew up simultaneously, a BMW 2002 skidded and rolled, but safely off the track onto grass. No hold-ups.

Hour four. The Aston Martin was in the pits again, and both the hot Renaults were in and being torn apart. The leading phalanx of Porsche 911s bellowed around, advertising their proud sponsors, but right behind them, the clown at the parade, was the little grape-purple car from Halifax. Max was in the groove and looked unstoppable. But suddenly a blaring orange Bimmer pulled past him, and, next lap, one of the raucous Mini Coopers, cornering with its inside rear wheel hanging stationary in the air, got past.

Then Max gave him the finger, and Steven's heart thudded. His turn next lap. Max leapt out and helped buckle him in, refuelling ended – and he was racing. Redline second, redline third – the car did a nasty left-right twitch when you changed gear roughly, as if the rubber universal doughnuts were squirming in pain, so he settled into smoothness mode. The thing would last longer, too. It felt, if anything, overpowered.

He stormed up the drag-strip straight, braked early (skid marks into the grass suggested that late braking here could end badly) and set up for the right-hand hairpin, following a hard-driven white Sprite, 99. Then back and into the left-right chicane, a short straight, and the tight left-hander onto the slightly-banked stock-car oval. This track, obviously designed by a committee, used a bit of everything.

Round the oval curve, hanging on for dear life, right on the limit, and then, at the end, the track went strange. You could go straight on, under the arch, brake and turn right, back up the main straight. Or you could be brave and let the car drift out further to the left, keeping the power on for another half-second. The problem was, this approach had you heading straight at a concrete wall, symbolically protected by a row of tires and a couple of token straw bales. *Then* you dabbed the brakes, pulled right (assuming nobody else was using that bit of road) and braked very late for the right hander.

Steven tried it out. If he did this late-braking stunt, then shaved the apex on the right, and let the car drift across to almost brush the wall on the left, he could make it. Fast. Right in front of his pit, too. Certainly they were all leaning, watching for him. His exhaust blared deafeningly as it echoed off the left concrete wall each lap.

He gobbled up that irritating 99 Sprite and set off after the orange BMW, which cornered indecently fast, but not quite fast enough. Now he was tailing the 911 driven by the hot-shot woman driver, Someone Proulx. And she was good, but she was a woman. He had to find a way past.

Lap after lap he clung to the fat, macho bellowing exhaust pipe of the Porsche. The only place to pass was into the left-hander, but changing down took so long without heel-and-toeing. The outside line was risky, and inside had a low but solid-looking curb: if his tires hit it there might be damage. Oh, to hell with it. Next lap he threw the car inside, cocked it up on its right wheels so the left ones were unweighted, bounced them lightly off the curb – and was through.

Howling, flat, round the oval, grinning, kept the foot well into it as the concrete wall loomed up, pulled across to people who were yelling at him in a strange language, Lebanese? French? Shouting at him.

He couldn't seem to get his eyelids to lift, and had a moment of panic, because you can't drive far with your eyes shut without hitting something, he must have dozed off at the wheel, but nothing happened, he must have stopped, and a feeling of immense relief flooded through him: from having to concentrate

so hard, to watch every detail so carefully, he no longer had to – he was no longer driving.
He could take it easy.
A voice spoke calmly in his ear.
'Where does it hurt?'
'Both legs and my right arm,' he heard his voice say, equally calmly.
He wanted to mention his backache too, his bowling-ball head and his squeezed chest, but that was enough for them to work on.

The phone shrilled, waking Eddie, sweating, from a daymare in which she was still on stage, struggling to dance through viscous, heavy air. A feeling of immense relief flooded through her; there was no audience, nobody watching her every move.
'Hi! You Lynn?' *This has to still be some kind of nightmare.*
'Wrong name. Not me. I'm Eddie.'
'You don't know me,' said this female voice she did not know, and her heart restarted and sank.
Some nitwit wild woman from the Women's Group.
'I'm the girlfriend of one of your husband's students' brothers, Stu.'
'What can I do for you?'
'It's about your husband. I'm afraid he's had a very bad crash.'
She sat down hard on the carpet.
'He was going so well – he was going *really* well – and something happened and he went into the wall and then into the other wall, but he landed right way up, on top of the Aston –'
'HOW IS HE? TELL ME HOW HE IS!'
'– He's okay. He's in the hospital, but I saw him and he looks pretty awful, his face is all bruised, but he's going to be okay.'
'What does the doctor say?'
'Multiple Injuries, she says. It's a she. He's got broken legs, and...'
'LEGS!'
'Yes, and one arm's broken, and his back – but it's only the coccyx, you know where the coccyx is?'

'Yes.'

'But his head got banged up pretty good, and there's two basic skull fractures.'

'Basal?'

'Maybe basal, then. But they're just, like, tiny cracks. They X-rayed *everything*. He'll be fine.'

'Is he conscious?'

'No, I think they gave him something. But he *was* fine. I saw him. He said he felt really bad about the car, and he'd pay for everything. He wanted to know how his lap times were compared with Max's, and I told him he pulled a 1:13.2 and Max was only doing –'

'Can I see him? Can I come and see him?'

'I'll give you the number... All their Ones look like Sevens...'

Eddie could smell her own sweat. She gave a single, choked scream, picked up the phone and had to dial twice: her fingers kept skidding off the dial.

'Alan Burns, how may I –'

'Alan! Can you – he's gone and smashed himself up – can you help us?'

'Wasn't he racing in Quebec somewhere?'

'He's in hospital there.'

'Oh, dear. I'll be right over. Just got to feed the horses and the cats. You make some of that great coffee, a big thermos full. Pack a few things, I'll be right there – he's not dead or anything, is he?'

'No. But I may have to kill him myself.'

'We'll do it together. No! You do it, and I'll defend you in court. Absolutely. Actually, I feel like a drive, I lost all my clients today: My law partner split and took them with him. Somebody's been speaking out of turn. Second thoughts, we'll both kill him. Be there in ten.'

Out and About

Three months later when Steven was released from hospital, a couple of years older and wiser, his principal emotion was...gratitude.

He had come damnably close to dying – twice, if that's possible – within an inch of losing a leg and as Dr. Miles had told him, within a couple of thou of losing an auditory nerve, which would have meant a lifetime not of silence but of unstoppable static. He knew it. He thanked his lucky stars, wherever they were.

Clearly God did not exist, or this would not have happened in the first place, or if He did, Einstein was wrong and He *does* play dice with the universe and Steven knew that astrology was a resting-place for small minds, but still he thanked his stars, and his Nature, and...things...

Things did look astonishingly fresh and good, after so many months of examining the patterned dots in the ceiling above his bed. He had gone mad more than once, had not been a good patient and had been treated accordingly.

He swore a solemn oath to himself that he would never again sit in a racing car. This made him cry for nearly an hour, after which he felt much improved and on the mend.

He got out just in time for Eddie to win her wrongful dismissal case, to be given her job back, but to tell the Grey Ghost, her *ectoplasm grise*, to Keep it, Stuff it, Shove it up his hairy nose – or at least that her concern now was to nurse her husband back to health but more importantly to explore other career directions. That is, dance.

Her attempts to promote *Undertow* and take it on tour had led only to one offer: to stage a trimmed version of the show, half a mile up the hill, in the FU gym, for Phys. Ed students who hadn't managed to get themselves down to the Playhouse, though they'd had to write a review of the show for their Artistic credit. This she managed, to polite applause and much scribbling in notebooks, and it worked out well: the FU Arts Council agreed to support her 'further endeavours.' So all roads led back to the Playhouse stage for *Undertow II* in a year's time. Already she was full of ideas for new pieces, lighting, costumes (she would do the whole shot). Perhaps she could import top dancers from Montreal or Toronto or one of those places.

Meanwhile Steven was home from the war. He had advised his leg doctor to bear in mind that he *was* extremely fit, a fast healer, and a marathon runner. This last bit may not have been true (he once ran three miles) but it did have good results: his leg surgery was conservative, his physiotherapy brutal, and he overheard his physiotherapist whispering, 'I've never seen *anyone* recover this fast; he's unbelievable.' Against orders he did laps of his bed after lights out.

'Well, Stevie,' the leg doctor had announced with a delighted grin, clapping him on the shoulder for the last time, 'You won't be running any more marathons.'

Steven told Eddie this, so she was not surprised when, on his first day home, he went into training for the Fodderton Spring Marathon. At first it was limping laps around the house, his throttle and brake leg still in its plaster cast.

The racket brought anguished, pleading complaints from the landlord below them, but the athlete explained that it was doctor's orders, and soldiered on.

Then, finally, the much-promised, much reneged-on day came and the big cast was removed, using, improbably, a screaming power saw, and a leg was revealed that certainly wasn't Steven's. For one thing it had no muscles, and for another, it kept floating skyward like a helium balloon.

But Steven took it for walks and got to know it better. His first training circuit was down the stairs (good leg first) down to the railway crossing, where the lights flashed red at the passing cars, then return and, bathed in sweat, up the stairs (bad leg last).

Later on he went further afield, and later still began to look out, beyond his pain, and notice 'things.' Fodderton was a lovely town. In autumn, the poetry season, the Biblical Fall, riverside trees blazed like miraculous flags.

He took to writing poems about the scenery, which eased him through the dark winter and were published in a booklet by the Pink Monday Society. He also wrote darker little unpublishable poems that nearly made sense:

Sticks and stones may break your bones
But truth can really hurt you.
A well-told lie can set you free
But the truth will always hunt you.

In spring he completed the marathon in 6 hours 47 minutes, encouraged over the final, tottering miles by frisky Sam the Wonder Dog who had already run it once.

He taught up until Christmas, when his two years were up and he was fired.

'Perhaps if you went off and got your MBA or your DBA we *could* consider you again,' smiled Professor Twine, who held a bachelor's degree himself.

With his final pay cheque he bought a Fred Ross painting of a yellow-haired young man in a shabby coat and top hat.

It seemed a romantic thing to do.

And?

And so there was nothing for it: the Butts must return home.

By then, however, Eddie was determinedly creating *Undertow II*, and had no wish to be any closer to her mother, 12,000 miles being about the right distance. And with his hair now very, very long Steven began to fancy himself as a poet, working towards a book. He took to strolling about the summer campus Aussie-style, in bare feet, satisfyingly 'grounded,' feeling his soles toughen, vaguely hoping to start a trend. The library saw no evil, but within two days the cafeteria staff were refusing to let him in, on the grounds of some undefined 'health hazard.' He argued his case, showing his clean, now sweet-smelling bare feet, surely no threat to shoe wearers, but predictably lost.

Lost, he applied for a generous Canada Council Explorations grant to find himself. His feeling was that London, Oxford and the Continent would be good places to look.

But first he'd need to become a Canadian citizen, which meant giving up his Australian citizenship, and this he would not do. He was not that lost.

Eddie, on the other hand, became a full-fledged Canuck one afternoon, and soon succeeded in winning a Canada Council grant, which paid off the bills on her new credit card.

She'd truly found herself, in the mirrored dance studios of her adopted country.

Steven wrangled some part-time teaching work in something called 'Interpersonal Communication' and now for the first time began to like the idea of being an academic, an intellectual.

Of course, he would need a doctorate, a union card, and one day, standing on his lawn looking at their birch tree unaccountably full of scarlet tanagers, he felt moved to swear a solemn vow that he would get his PhD in the next five years.

Would get it or die in the attempt.

He limped in see Joe in the Psych department, but they weren't yet offering a doctorate. So he crossed the campus to the philosophy department, listened in on a shouting match between the Aussie Augustinian flat-earther and a fat linguistic metaphysician (there never seemed to be any students around), and changed his mind.

He trudged up the stairs and signed on as an English student.

They didn't like the look of his three years of English at Sydney ('It sounds like one of those British-style degrees, a bit of everything') so he 'would need to obtain another MA first, and then we would see.'

By now the MGB had rusted away to dust, so he spray-painted the rust green and sold the car to two delighted youths who had had their eye on it since the Debert race.

In his tiny, book-stuffed study carrel on the top floor of the library, he was visited by...Sally.

On and off. Off and on.

She apologised for not visiting him in the hospital, but she had heard he was 'all banged up.' What her feelings were for him he never knew, never thought, but came spring, she arrived with an entire, snapped-off branch of a white lilac tree that she had borne through the library, and thrust it at him, frowning as if she had surprised herself.

(They knew, of course. The whole town; they always know. And it was the whole town knowing that enraged Eddie more, almost, than the thing itself.)

Steven's trouble was, Sally had no sooner arrived than time sped up, and she was gone again, and there he sat, alone in his dusty, sex-scented, never-cleaned little study, wondering when she would come again.

She never said, and he never saw her outside, except once onstage at a recital energetically playing Bach. They weren't supposed to know each other, and in public she just turned away.

Days passed, weeks passed, months.

He tried not to live for her light tap-tap on his door, but it was hard. Any approaching footstep jolted his nervous system.

Through the wall he could hear the student next door singing sadly to himself in some foreign language.

He could see why she *came*: it was obvious. She came for the sex. Their silent sex was magnificent, and surely that was enough for anyone. Worse, it seemed to get better, more desperately intense, every time. Once, convinced from his agonised face that he was approaching the point of bellowing out, she had clapped her hand over his mouth – but why she stayed *away* was beyond him.

(He never imagined that she was now *trying* to stay away, was doing her level best to give him up. After all, had she not told him that she wasn't in love with him either, and why would she lie?)

He heard that she had found part-time work in Winnipeg at the Ballet School. Now she returned, complaining about the snotty ballet students, complaining in general, and mentioning his wife Eddie rather too often, to complain about her, too.

To be fair, he had early explained to Sally, face to face, that he had no intention of divorcing Eddie and marrying her, none at all. But if she wanted to be his mistress... She was excited by the word 'mistress.'

'I've never been anyone's mistress before.'

She had taken to her unpaid duties infrequently but well. The double tap at the door, his leap to let her in, into his arms, hand sliding up her dress (she said she didn't know what panties were for, and that she got all the foreplay she needed walking up the stairs). Her coat flopped to the cold floor, her dress ballooned up and overhead, she would reach behind to unclasp her bra – and her breasts would drop heavily into his burning hands.

Five seconds later they would be fucking flat out on the floor and forty minutes later still fucking, one way or another. As the blues singer declared,

She c'n look up
Long as I c'n look down

– And he adored gazing down on the crazy ripples running up her breasts, patterns of mounting complexity, the three-way rip off Newport reef with a thunderstorm coming on.

One afternoon, ten dizzy seconds after she had arrived, there was a following, authoritative rap at the door.
'Library Service. We need to clean your carrel.'
'Oh! I'm busy, would you give me ten minutes please?'
'We need to clean and inspect your carrel, Mr Butts.'
'Come back in ten minutes, is that okay? I'm really busy.'
The jingle of keys, then the sound of a key sliding into the lock! He stood, naked and erect, staring back at naked, pink Sally and holding the metal door handle firmly up with both hands.

The grunting supervisor outside departed, agreeing on, 'ten minutes, then,' and he began to dress. Sally dressed, too, and palely slipped out.

But why didn't she return in half an hour – instead of, in fact, two weeks?

Days were divided into Sally Days and Other. When she was accompanying him she was very, very good.

Afterwards they could talk, in whispers, imagining red ears pressed against the adjoining carrel walls. 'That feel good?' 'Mm hmm. I can get myself off just with my tits.'

He taught her everything he knew, which didn't take long, and she taught him some of what could have taken a lifetime. She would crane up off the floor (good stomach muscles under there) to stare down between her legs, hissing, 'That is so *horny!*' and he would slow his pace and lengthen the stroke for a better, shared look. (Eddie, by contrast, had once accused him of embarrassing her by staring down at her breasts and having 'perverted thoughts.')

Sally whispered hotly in his ear, asking, 'Do you think I'm a nympho yet?' and was delighted, excited, when he nodded, 'Yes, you're a nymphomaniac.'

She wasn't, of course; he knew the clinical definition of nymphomania as insatiable, and she *could* be sated, eventually, a Great Gatsby of sex, drawn by the distant green light for Go, the orgasmic – surely that was the word – orgasmic very near future as she beat on, hard against the tide, her breasts rippling, or, if on top, swinging like mad pale bells, brushing his chest.

Her feelings, the intensity of her plump, stretchable body fascinated him. He knew that she would die, truly die for that next orgasm. Would kill for it. He envied her her single-minded sense of purpose.

And one day she drove him mad.

Mad? Perhaps it was really an attack of sanity that drove him mad. What happened was strangely ordinary. He read her journal.

A gentleman does not read a young lady's private journal, but for once – the only time – she had let him come to her rented room, she was in the bathroom, he was lying back in her gritty bed, and there it was, bookmarked with a ripped-off slip of paper.

He read, his heart pounding.

There was a fantasy poem, how she would like 'you' to come right down her throat (which had never happened) but as he flipped the pages he saw that the diary was about him. Him.

He just keeps on going and going and then he says, calmly, 'I'm coming' and pow!

Somehow she didn't now sound quite as experienced as he had assumed she was.

She didn't seem clear, for instance, that he can't *make* himself come; it just happens. God flicks the switch and it happens.

He remembered her confusion on the summer afternoon he'd given up waiting, though he knew she was in town, and had jerked off at his desk – and then the tap-tap at the door!

He'd confessed and apologised, but she had only hissed, 'Make it hard.' She didn't know that erections, too, are involuntary. 'I've never seen it not hard,' she said, frowning.

We've been trying to do it up my ass but today he sort of spread my butt cheeks apart and it went right in!

His face was scarlet as he read on – so she had no trouble catching him red-handed, as it were.

And she was furious. She snatched it from him and pushed him down, hard.

But the damage was done.

The scrawled words, in black felt-tip, kept seeping into his brain. By nightfall his skull was pounding with the shocking truth that SHE WAS A REAL PERSON. Not a fantasy. He hadn't made her up. She was REAL.

She had feelings.

Perhaps other people were real, too. Just as real as he was.

Where had he been, all these years? *Where had they all been?*

At home, Eddie wanted to know why her husband could no longer seem to eat, sleep or stand still, but all he could do was mutter that he had some kind of a bug in his brain that would have to work itself out – and mercifully, after a dazed couple of weeks, it did, or sort of.

Sally had made him promise never, ever to call on her at home again. She'd been as nervous as a cat, and he had noticed how she worshipped her landlord (who had inherited the house), a ludicrously handsome young man, a fine actor who had been a superlative, very moving Elizabeth Taylor look-alike on the Playhouse stage.

'If he would fuck me,' she tearfully told Steven once, 'I wouldn't have to go fucking anybody else.' Later she asked him for advice. 'Tell me, what would you do about a guy who never comes?'

'What, you mean he just fucks and fucks away but never comes?'

She nodded, watching his face.

'Gee. I'd marry him,' he said, half joking, half excited.

'Oh, yes, of course I have a lovely time, but...really.'

He didn't know what to say, and the moment passed.

He always came himself, so it wasn't him.

Finally, one midwinter day when his carrel window had frozen over in the East wind, the floor was like ice, and she looked pale and not well, she broke it off, finally broke it off with Steven, tearfully saying that it was good that she had had 'The Best' but that it was over.

It was over.

... Then reappeared two months later, unhooking her bra with a beaming: 'I tried so *hard* to be good.'

... Then vanished, perhaps being good after all.

Alone in his carrel, Steven the scholar one-handedly read horny old John Donne and the Earl of Rochester, whose (usually omitted) tenth stanza of 'The Disabled Debauchee' runs:
Nor shall our love-fits, Chloris, be forgot,
When each the well-looked linkboy strove t'enjoy,
And the best kiss was the deciding lot
Whether the boy fucked you, or I the boy.

Or, weeping with homesickness and self-pity, he single-handedly struggled to translate *The Wanderer* out of its thousand-year-old pre-English:
Oft him anhaga are gebideth,
Metudes miltse, theah pe he modcearig
geond lagulade longe sceolde
hreran mid hondum hrimceale sae...
Often the lonely man lives to share in
The Lord's mild mercy, although in despair
For years, numbly rowing through rime-cold seas
He must journey the exile's waterways.
Fate is utterly relentless! Calls
The wanderer, in his wretchedness recalling
The corpses of his kinsmen, slaughtered,
His friends falling...
All joy is ended. He who must
For so long go without a word
Of counsel from his noble lord
Knows too well how sleep and sorrow
Together often wrap the solitary
Wretch.
And then somehow it seems
He embraces and kisses his lord, he
Lays hand and head upon his knee
As once he enjoyed the liberality
Of the throne... Then, lordless, he wakes again

To see pale waves, seagulls diving and
Stretching their wings, sleet and driving
Snow mingled with hail; then his
Wounded heart aches more bitterly, longing
For the beloved.

In fact, Steven's recurring dreams found him alone in empty, disintegrating houses – never the same house twice – and located neither in Sydney nor anywhere else he could recognise.

With the next 1,500-word assignment always due, he pondered such questions as what Scott Fitzgerald had meant by 'the orgastic future' at the celebrated end of *The Great Gatsby*. Orgasmic? Orgiastic? His early editor went with 'orgiastic.'

What a shame the writer couldn't spell; did he see a lonely future studded with orgasms, or a more sociable one rife with orgies?

Now he was dead, leaving behind him that green light on the end of the East Egg dock for bunnies like Steven to gaze enviously at. There had been a time when he would plunge in and swim towards it, but there's nothing like a good car crash to bring on a fearful middle age.

Thou hast committed...fornication
But that was in another country
And, besides, the wench is dead...

Now he let the dead poets speak for him, caught in the spidery past. Live ones, too: as his favourite English professor had written,

...bodies give
with no bliss or hurt
to minds that live
in rooms apart

where the noise of home
no deeper lies
than casual hum
of these two flies.

Once upon a time, in the family garage of long tall Zoë Dobson there had sat a highly-tuned, highly-polished Sprite *and* an Austin Healey, just waiting to be raced.

If, back then, Steven had only lit her cigarettes, instead of lecturing her on smoking, if only...

Chronicles of wasted chances.

When he was young, he'd assumed that everything nice that happened to him would happen again.

Now he knew it would not. This was no dress rehearsal.

He'd driven Coopers, Lotus, a savage blown Lynx, and finally the overpowered Cortfire, of which, Max had snarled at him, not a single useable part was left.

Not even the steering wheel. And the bill was past due.

He completed his MA thesis, on the Dominican feminist novelist Jean Rhys – 'All those muddles.'

He'd planned to move on to the creative writing PhD he had heard about, but he must have heard wrong: it was the *MA* that he should have submitted creative writing for.

Oh. Could he have his thesis back?

Out of the question.

The thesis was now in the hands of his supervisor, who – after an unexplained delay of nine months during which the Butts had no income – read it, finally whined that, 'this thing reads like a magazine article,' attacked Steven, his sole post-grad student, with inexplicable ferocity in the MA Oral, but then sighed, after keeping him waiting ten minutes outside the oak door.

'Oh, well, I suppose we'll have to give it to you.'

He said it with a cruel grin, as if this was just his idea of a joke.

On to the PhD, where Steven now found that no matter which graduate courses he chose, he was shunted into those with lowest enrolment, to make up the numbers.

He coughed his way through endless smoke-filled, nit-picking dissections of W. B. Yeats' prophetic tome, *The Vision*, which he suspected, but never said, had been dictated by Mrs Yeats just to get her husband to listen to her for once, instead of day-dreaming about Maud and gardens.

When he finally asked if a window could be opened to let some air into the seminar room, the worthy professor quoted Steven Leacock, "'When I have students, I like them *well smoked.*'"
Clearly, as a student he had no rights.

When he inquired how many more graduate courses he'd need to take to fulfil his PhD requirements he was told, 'We'll tell you when you've had enough.'

But already he'd had almost had too much.

As wintry darkness fell on this northern town, north of Odessa, north of the civilised world, he felt madness tapping at his door.

His terror was that he would die here and be buried here, beside the late dancer from New York, he'd forgotten her name...

In the pines, in the pines
Where the sun never shines...

He would lie forever, cold and dead, under these alien constellations – he'd had this fear in hospital but was confident then that they would ship his body back home.

But now his confidence had drained away, like blood.

Lolling in a too-hot bath he considered the razor cut, up the wrists, not across, that would resolve the awful homesickness, the sickness at heart.

Or he could run mad, manic, and wake strapped to a chair in the dark brick hospital that he'd weekly driven past at Saint John, where electroshock therapy was considered normal.

It could happen.

One of the English professors was known to be working to have his wife certified insane, on the grounds that she wanted to leave him.

All the man needed was one more signature.

Steven could define the problem: in this brutal land of ice and pine trees he could find madness, religious mania, but no place for...romance.

He did not want to tell Eddie about this, as she was busy-busy with the huge undertaking of staging a one-woman show with a large amateur cast.

Their phone rang non-stop. and her authoritative, nasal voice (which he'd never much liked) now filled the place. He heard her on the phone complaining yet again of her migraines, of being unable to walk past a cake shop without gaining weight.

Besides, if there was one thing that irritated his wife it was any hint of self-pity. So he had to watch his tone.

Her father had once attempted suicide. She'd come home from school and found him with his head in the gas oven, and her mother rushed in, dragged him out and smacked him, calling him a 'craven coward.'

His mood darkened, his assignments piled up. But he was saved by a book. No girl was ever ruined by a book, but Steven Butts was convinced afterwards that a book had saved his life. For his second-language requirement he was struggling through Alain-Fournier's *Le Grand Meaulnes*, and when the horse trotted away into the lost domain, it took Steven with it. He too crouched behind the snowbank and spied on the procession of costumed children, the make-believe bride and groom moving up the snowy road.

He heard the tinkling instruments, the children's voices piping in the freezing winter air. His spirit lifted with the possibility, at least the *possibility* of gaiety, of romance in the snow.

Fodderton's slushy streets and dark satanic mills and hills were still the same, but now there was the...possibility. Home was far away, but something could come of this place, this country.

Money was short and shrinking. With money short, the need to travel – or at least to go out to dinner, became urgent.

But he could no longer afford to take Eddie up to the Chinese place in the new mall, where the beaming owner had finally learned to make the Golden Cadillacs depicted on her place mats. This was sad, because they got on well over a bought dinner and drinks.

One snowy, hopelessly drunken night they left the car behind in a hush of snow and like kids they jacket-slid on their bellies all the way home down the Regent Street hill.

In a doomed attempt to save on rent, he bought a mobile home in the trailer park, but then sold it again at a loss when he found that there was room either for their stuff, or for them. They never moved in and Eddie never saw the place.
Their next move was real.

He accepted the vacated position of 'Resident Fellow' at Lord Beaverbrook Residence, which offered free lodging in return for his being *in loco parentis* to its (male) students, offering them moral guidance, an adult touch, a brush with culture and so on.

He brought in a top-hatted magician, followed by a python-wreathed snake enthusiast, since Oxford it wasn't.

But then the student in the rooms above them bought and installed a hi-fi system of impressive wattage, and it shook their ceiling and threw their hearts into palpitation.

The Resident Fellow climbed the stairs, tapped, knocked, then thundered on the door to find the beefy young man not listening so much as studying with the music as background. Asked to turn it down a bit he was stunned, pointing out he'd just paid 'big bucks' for the thing.

This was a new concept for Steven, who explained that, in all his studies of moral and political philosophy and of ethics, he had never heard that Rights could be bought in a mall.

He complained to the Resident Don, whose ground-floor rooms were deliciously quiet, but was told that boys will be boys and that we try not to be too strict on the lads – though he'd have a word with him.

That same night all the fire extinguishers went off, the fire water buckets were emptied down the stairs and a scholarship-winning student, who'ad unwisely asked his room-mate if he might like a blow job, was dragged from his bed and beaten to a screeching pulp. But boys will be boys, and Steven slept through it – on a foam mattress down in the basement equipment room.

Eddie, however, was distraught, and Steven, returning to their room in the morning, heard why: rhythmic jack-boot stamping, and then unison jumping of students, a dozen at least in Mr Hi-Fi's room. Plaster snowed from the ceiling, and Eddie sobbed that she'd spent the whole night crouched on the bed with the carving knife. 'The first leg that came through the roof, I was going to cut it off!' she snarled, white-lipped.

Steven took his complaint further, and that evening a knock at his door signalled the arrival of justice in the tripartite form of the residence head, a student named, ominously, 'Boomer,' and two side-kicks.

'I have had a number of complaints about your attitude,' Boomer told him. 'Accordingly I have called a meeting of the whole college body after dinner tonight. We want you to explain your side to the students.'

'Not a chance. Forget it,' said Steven, his heart thudding. 'I don't like *your* attitude. Get the fuck out of my room.'

'It's not *your* room! It's our fees pay for it!'

'That Rights thing again, is it?'

Alan Burns rescued them, driving them to his big house, for which they owed him, Eddie explained in the car, their lives.

If Steven had money – magic millions – he would of course fly home, champagne and cashews all the way, mail out cheques, small but equal, to his family members, and loll on Palm Beach while mechanics toiled, preparing a new, skunk white-and-black racing car for his private use.

Oh, yes, he would race again. Some miracle operation could fix his eye. He would buy Eddie whatever she wanted but...what would he give to Fodderton? Anything? Beaverbrook had.

Dean Michael Joyce had once explained that the great man had, 'decided to give something back to Fodderton.'

'What did he *take* from it?'

'What?'

'You said give *back*.'

'Nothing.'

Steven liked the idea of paying back, but...giving back?

He began to suspect that to be successful one has to actually do some work, and resolved to put his head down and get that doctorate, to become employable at a university.

He kept up his 'A' average, despite irritating one professor by suggesting, in an essay on E. M. Forster's *Passage to India* as a gay novel, that the great man (quite a fancier of London Bobbies) hardly deserved his reputation as England's premier humanist, not after he had declined to attend his old pal Oscar Wilde's trial, let alone put in a good word for Wilde's character.

Looming, once the course work was done, was the PhD Comprehensive Exam, whose compass was limited to English Literature since and including *Beowulf*.

In a recurring nightmare Steven opened the question paper to read, simply, 'Name fifteen characters from *Coriolanus*.' Waking in a sweat he would grope for his copy of *The First Folio* and fumble among its oversized, misprint-studded pages.

The world of motor racing receded, leaving him standing painfully reading about the latest deaths, in too-costly car magazines in cheap stores.

His latest hero Jochen Rindt, so arrogantly fast on airfield circuits, hit the brakes in the new Lotus, something snapped, and his body slid under his four-point harness and broke, bringing in the era of the six-point harness. Each technical advancement arrived one step too late.

Jim Clark, surely the quickest of the quick, felt a tire go flat, hit a tree, and joined the dead. Pedro Rodrigues, dead. Ricardo Rodrigues, dead. The insanely quick Quebecer Gilles Villeneuve, deep in a do-or-die hot practice lap to beat his hated team-mate's time, clipped a slow car's rear tire and cartwheeled into legend.

The randomness was the message. Only the good who were lucky did well. The celestial dice rolled themselves. Steven was certain now that the Uncertainty Principle held sway. Why else would two stones whiz past his face and the third hit him in the eye? – bringing in the era of the polycarbonate goggle lens.

It could have been worse. Everything could. The promising Ferrari driver Clay Regazzoni had been hit in the face by a low-flying bird, bringing in the era of the racing school for paraplegics – nobody was going to renew *his* racing licence. Steven had been at Goodwood on the day Stirling Moss, the last of the late, light brakers, tried to drive around the outside of Graham Hill's BRM the moment he caught him, instead of waiting a few seconds...and slid wide, bringing in the era of properly-designed crash helmets.

Months later, the Moss vision had returned to normal, which of course was nowhere near good enough, so after a few near-lap-record laps in a Lotus 19 he'd called it a day.

There are no accidents, as Freud had quotably pronounced.

Every odd event is determined – overdetermined – by the Unconscious. But for Steven the problem was, the unconscious mind is, as John Maze pointed out back at Sydney Uni, *unconscious*. If it were conscious it wouldn't *be* the unconscious mind. Duh!

So you had no more control over it than, say, Freud had over his current cigar. Cigar, God, Chance – what's the difference? So forget it. Therefore nothing.

Therefore chance explained everything (and nothing), in a meaning-free world of probabilities.

At Oxford he'd been struck by one afternoon's discussion in the School of Experimental Psychology, of Extra-Sensory Perception. It didn't exist, of course, any more than subliminal advertising did, or extra-terrestrial intelligence. But the fully-funded research industry, centred at Duke U., was booming.

By testing thousands of hopefuls, and throwing out everyone whose card- or number-guessing scored *below* par, the eager researchers had assembled a few subjects who could consistently guess better than chance. Most of the time, anyway.

What had struck Steven was the improbability that there would *not* be people who guessed better than average. He agreed with the brilliant Dr Truman that really, all these ESP results showed only the need to re-examine the statistics of Probability.

And what clinched it was Steven's learning that, in preparing the experimenters' Tables of Random Numbers for publication, a sharp-eyed editor read through them first and removed all the obvious patterns, the series of 1234567 and so on.

Why? Because otherwise nobody would buy the book: the numbers wouldn't look *random*. Random numbers, he saw, just like random events, *do* form into patterns.

The world appeared – for a moment – to make sense.
But it didn't. It was a cluster of random, purposeless probabilities, clearly indicating the absence of a Creator – unless one overtook Einstein's church-limited view and postulated a Creator who *did* play dice with the universe.
But why would He/She bother?
These formulations of despair entered his body.
Eddie commented on his newly bulging 'love handles' – not that any lover handled them any more – and kept telling him, 'Relax your jaw,' which he found he could not do.
One night, gazing at the upside-down full moon of Fodderton, he recalled one night in Oxford, all those years ago, well past midnight, the traffic stilled, a full moon stuck on the spire of St Mary's church. Behind him, the cylinder of the Radcliffe Camera, behind that the cube of the Bodleian, and ahead, the flat plate on the triangle of St Mary's. (It was Mary, wasn't it?) And his young heart so full of beauty he thought he would cry out, like a wolf.

Then from Sydney came an aerogramme, a bluebird of unhappiness in his mother's wobbly hand, containing a local newspaper clipping, *Local Girl Weds Overseas*.
The photo showed a bride in white, the groom – yes, it was that same bastard – emerging from the stone archway of a church he knew. In Oxford! Lynn had married in Oxford! How *could* she?
Oxford now was forever ruined for him, lost...
After yet another unsleeping week he felt calmer, but there was treachery in the air. Then from somewhere in England a mystery snapshot arrived for him. It showed a small child playing with pots and pans. On the back was printed, mock-untidily: HELLO MY NAME IS TRACY AND I LIKE TO DRIVE MUM MAD BY GETTING EVERYTHING OUT OF THE CUPBOARD
No address, nothing. He was touched, pleased that at least Linda Austen was now happily married. *Could* – ? *Was*...? No.
The kid was years too young; he'd forgotten how many years had gone by. He choked down an unfamiliar emotion.
But somewhere, in the far, far distance, pots were banging.

A New Soul Mate

Meanwhile Eddie's baby, her annual show – forty weeks of panic for one week of terror – kept packing them in, at least in Fodderton.

One tour was made to Moncton, where the audience numbered three, of whom two left arm-in-arm after the opening number. The company travelled on to Saint John, where the audience was nine, but not exactly a cheering, clapping, foot-stamping nine. More a puzzled nine. Afterwards tea and sandwiches were served, and Eddie stepped graciously forward and invited questions, but there were no questions, only the standard, polite, 'So tell me, what's your real job?'

Her annual income remained $100.00, wired from Australia every birthday, plus a little more each Christmas.

Funded by the FU Arts Council (expenses only, never anything for her efforts) Eddie invited in a hotshot dancer-choreographer from Toronto to teach master classes, leading up to her show. An expert is well defined as someone from out of town, but Angelo Decree *was* an expert. Eddie fell for him in the dressing room the moment he peeled off his shirt; winking at her was an unnecessary frill. By the time he finished doing his little solo for them, *Afternoon of a Man* to Dizzy Gillespie blues, Eddie and her whole company were his for the asking.

There was still time for his Toronto company to mount one of their works on Eddie's coming program, and she leapt at the chance. A week later the company truck hauled into the Playhouse dock and began unloading. Bob hunted Eddie down, red-faced. Trouble.

'No way they're drilling holes in my stage for that thing!'

William LeBlanc calmed him down and backed him up.

'Eddie, you *did* know they want to build a scaffold centre stage, with four guy wires?'

'Of course. Sounds wonderful! Go ahead and drill the holes, Bob. I'll pay for any damage. It's going to be fabulous.'

'Just so's you know,' the Playhouse pair muttered, turning away.

And it was fabulous. As the final light faded on Angelo's corpse, turning, slowly turning above the darkling stage, a shocked silence led first to a patter of applause – and then the thunderclap.

Sitting in the packed house, Steven had loved the show, but he had a problem, a small problem, but a problem. Angelo's neck. Hanging had not helped any, he noted at the curtain calls. Good feet and legs, good arms, great chest, but...a slight buffalo hump on the shoulders and a forward-placed head, James Dean/hoodlum style. Just like Eddie, in fact. Why didn't he just straighten up? Why didn't she? Steven's own posture, as Angelo had spotted at once, was perfect. Then he heard another of Eddie's stories.

She had come home from school to find her mother hanging herself. Not for good, just to ease her permanently sore neck: Ernie had done a panic stop in the Holden and been rear-ended by a truck, which had given his wife what they both called 'witlash.' In those days nobody got paid, or paid out, for a little thing like whiplash, and she had suffered in silence, wearing a surgical collar she had bought, until one midsummer day she'd thrown the sweaty thing away and taken to hanging herself, which worked rather better.

Steven tried to make sense of this but as usual, all his psychological training led only towards the conclusion that his wife, like most people he met, including Angelo, was crazy.

The hell with them. He had a Comprehensive Exam to study for.

The Closing Night party of *Undertow/Overtake* was a smash, Inge Fox jitterbugging onstage with a Toronto dancer who was as tall as Zoë Dobson had ever been; little Dianne performing the Tango with the handsome Premier of the Province; Merlin Fox in a cautiously professional fox-trot with the lovely long-haired Lucy;

Rose Russell (who had a nasty, childlike cough these days) somehow making Angelo Decree repeatedly hoot with laughter; Bob, his overalls hotly unzipped, persistently trying to get Carol to open up and at least Polka around the stage with him; no sign of Sally or of Marcel – Steven kept finding himself glancing up into the dark region above the stage; Alan Burns (back from his new job in Toronto for the occasion) tipsily reeling a solo polka or possibly a hornpipe – and Steven, for a delightful change once William LeBlanc had bowed out, dancing with his own wife.

Over breakfast the Butts were two heads with a single headache. His wife announced that she was off to Toronto to study with Angelo and his company. Fine, her mother had sent them both very generous Christmas cheques. (He'd squandered his on rent.)

'But I do have to say one thing.'

'Don't say it,' she said, pale.

'I have to. Angelo's great – we both know that. But he's a man's man. I just want to make sure you knew.'

'You mean what? He's gay?'

'I mean he pinched both my nipples through my shirt with uncanny accuracy. It felt surprisingly good, too.'

'Maybe you're the one who's gay.'

'Sure, who cares, but I'd hate you to think that just because *I'm* weird, *every* man who's gay still likes women. Or that Angelo's secretly just waiting for the right woman, to come out of the –'

'Okay, *okay!* So he's gay. I got it. I'm not dumb. I'm going to study with him and be his personal secretary. I'm going.'

'How much is he going to pay you?'

She did not reply, so he got the last word. This was unusual, from the garrulous, increasingly argumentative Eddie these days, but he knew that – for her – to say was to do.

So she was off.

He had two months to read and memorise *The Norton Anthology of English Literature*, Vols 1 and 2, and a dissertation topic to find, so a quiet house would be an advantage.

Landing in Toronto

To obtain free, though brief, long-distance phone calls, they used the Butts person-to-person system. When his phone rang and the operator asked to speak to Joe Blow, Mr Blow was not in but it meant that Eddie was fine, no problems, and she missed him. If she asked for Ned Kelly he, too, was sadly unavailable, but she was in difficulty so he should call her back. If she asked for John Doe she was *really* missing him and was thinking seriously of coming home.

By the hot nights of August he was snatching up the phone hoping, hoping to be her dear John Doe, but Joe Blow, always the uncommunicative absentee Joe Blow, was all she needed.

Thinking it through between his final burst of English assignments, he saw that she was in love with a dance style; that masculine, gravity-centred, Gene Kelly-style dancing that Angelo taught there. Angelo danced the way her father Ernie had skated. As a girl, once she had stopped looking for the Red Shoes under her bed, Eddie had wanted not just to dance like Gene Kelly but to *be* Gene Kelly.

So had Steven. It was an oddity they shared.

Steven hitched a ride on the twin-engined provincial government plane to visit her for the weekend. What a strange, surreal city Toronto was! There was a dead lake you could smell America's bad breath across, and an absurdly high tower, its spike lost in the polluted air. His wife turned out to be happy, confident, and well, the sole woman in a rooming house on Windsor Street whose welfare drunks tapped nightly, endlessly, hopelessly on the door of her room. She boasted that she rose at six to do her warm-ups for the challenging classes in Graham technique.

Her sad, garlic-sour little room with the high-risk hotplate in the corner looked out on a wall of the unwelcoming Windsor Arms.

She cooked two T-bone steaks with onions and they ate together off their knees. Afterwards she opened her window and together they leaned out and looked up at – five bandit-masked faces peering hopefully down at them from the roof. The biggest raccoon, 'Papa Bear' had no trouble catching the bones she skilfully tossed up.

When he marvelled aloud at Eddie's slimness, she explained that Eaton's had mailed her a credit card, which she could use only to buy meat, so she was on an all-steak diet. Instead of demanding payment, they kept raising her credit limit each month; she'd listed her husband as a professor (though in fact he was now a student on a tiny PhD assistantship, his course work finally behind him, a suitable Dissertation Topic his grail).

'Mainly Because of the Meat,' (the Dominion store motto) he quipped, but she told him, seriously, as a matter of interest, that that very phrase was now printed on the back of all the National Ballet tickets. She seemed to have pushed Fodderton, life with Steven, out of her mind. She was a woman possessed. To dance; not to choreograph or run her dance company, but to *dance*. Her ACDC (Atlantic Contemporary Dance Company back there) would just have to get along without her.

In bed they did their best to make love but she felt so, so *different* from the Eddie he'd known in Sydney – in Fodderton, even. Her long hair was cut and she had funny breath (ketosis?). Lying awake beside her he knew he had a decision to make. She was going nowhere, she was crazy, she was already deeply in debt. His own motor racing madness was behind him now, and there was work to be done, to support her.

He would do The Right Thing. He would even give up Sally (wherever she was) – all Sallys, even Inge – if that was going to be the difference that really made the difference. Eddie had said it was, and women seem to know that sort of thing. He would make a vow and, this time, he would keep it. With tears prickling, he made his marriage vow and meant it.

Next morning, when the government plane took off and banked towards the mysterious East, he was not on it.

After all that, here's my email address:

simon@mycybernet.net

Send your deductions in before 25th December, 2007.

Don't forget, there are six made-up incidents.

Here's the confusing hint again, to get you started:
One's just a date – check the record – and one is his/my meeting with a pair of brilliant creatures (whom I met, but not there) which leaves four events that couldn't possibly have happened to me/Steven (but maybe just did).